MAFIA & MAID

ISA OLIVER

Contents

DEDICATION

For all the girlies who want a man to fall to his knees for her...
And I'll let you imagine what he does next...

Acknowledgements: Thank you so much to Miha, Zui, the Angels, Hope, Amy and Amanda and their awesome team, and the amazing Jo for all your help and support. I love you guys! And thank you to the very special S7 girls and guys. You are the kindest, funniest, most supportive group a girl could ask for, and I truly appreciate you, your friendship, and all the giggles xxx

AUTHOR'S NOTE

Dear Reader, please note that while not dark, this book contains some sensitive topics. More details are on the next page. Please note that any beliefs, views, opinions, and statements in this novel are the views of specific characters as part of the storyline, and they are not the views of the author. Love Isa xxx

Marchiano Mafia Series
(all are standalones):
*

Mafia And Captive
(age gap dark romance)
*

Mafia And Protector
(arranged marriage)
*

Mafia And Taken
(captive romance)
*

Mafia And Maid
(forced proximity)

*

Mafia And Angel
(single dad arranged marriage)

SPOILERS - CONTENT NOTE

Topics referred to include:

...

...

...

Mafia violence and murder

Domestic violence (not from the hero)

Emotional ab*se (not from the hero)

Eating disorder

Cheating by a side character

No cheating by main characters (FMC has left her ex before she meets the MMC)

A full content note can be found here:

https://docs.google.com/document/d/1UMuRf1Ur9-1wc0zG5kujiW oIXf2ZID5VIQNuWJPRbjI/

Please reach out if you need help. Your mental and physical health matter very much xxx

FAMILIES

Marchiano Family (Fratellanza Mafia)
Marco Marchiano - Capo
Alessio - brother
Camillo - brother
Danio - brother
Debi - sister
Lorenzo - cousin
Juliana - Marco's wife
Cate - Alessio's wife
Anni - Lorenzo's wife

Davis Family, Chicago
Conor Davis - businessman
Cyndie - wife
Rosa - daughter
Reagan - daughter

Devlin Family, Chicago
Grayden Devlin - businessman

Rosa - wife
Ethan - son

FACEBOOK GROUP AND ARCS

Facebook Group: 'Isa's Angels & Mafia Books'
https://www.facebook.com/groups/1409806332760996

Would you like to receive a free 'Advance Reader Copy' of Isa's next release before anyone else? Please see here:
https://isaoliverauthor.com/free-arcs/

PROLOGUE

CAMILLO

Arriving at the high society wedding, I take in the display of fragrant pink flowers and floaty pretty fabric draped over every single surface. It's traditional and opulent—and it's like a bridal magazine that's thrown up all over the place.

I follow my brothers up the pristine stone steps into St. Hyacinth's Basilica, tugging once more at the sleeve of my black Brioni suit. The surrounding air is indifferent and undisturbed despite the glances and hushed whispers they don't think we can hear.

Bodies dressed in the best their money can buy blend in with the extravagant decorations that scream wealth and privilege, because Chicago's finest are all gathered here today for an over-the-top display of pomp and circumstance veiled as happy nuptials.

It's tiresome as it's nauseating.

Because I don't belong here.

If the tattoos that crawl up my arms and body don't give me away, the cold set of my face usually does. But here I am, filing in after my older brothers to extend half-hearted pleasantries and niceties to one of Chicago's most powerful financial families. As archaic aristocracy, the Davis family is used to getting its own way. And they've been a sharp thorn in our side for too many months now.

My brothers and I run the Fratellanza mafia, masterminding the shadowy underworld in this city and making our sins pay—and we don't stand for people who won't go along with our proposals. Because although the Davis family sneer down their noses at made men like us, underneath their polish and cut-glass accents, they're just as tainted as we are.

Clocking the exits and entrances as we move further in, I make a note of the sorry excuse for security that wanders through the crowd. It's not much for a wedding of this size and attention. But given the people in attendance, no one here expects a bloodbath—no one except for us. Ruthless, mindless brutes of made men. That's the world I live in. A world where the monsters wear luxurious designer suits and brilliant smiles to hide their sharp teeth and claws like wolves in sheep's clothing. Where villains and murderers run the city with pretty promises built on shadowy backroom deals.

"Stop fidgeting," my oldest brother, Marco, grits out. "It's getting on my fucking nerves."

My hand drops from my sleeve. I hate weddings, but even more, I hate dressing like some monkey on display, ready to perform while they ogle and judge. My skin crawls at the thought, making the collar of my dress shirt that much tighter.

The smell of old money stinks up the room, and if this wasn't such a necessary power play, I'd have stayed the fuck at home today. But we need to ensure that Conor Davis, one of the wealthiest businessmen in the city, understands there's no option to say no to our proposal.

Their ostentatious need to showboat and flaunt their extravagance makes my skin itch. I don't want to be here today, but this is the job. I'm the enforcer for the Fratellanza—this is the role I play.

"We need to say hello to Davis and give him and the lucky groom our congratulations," Marco says.

I fight an eye roll and nod, making another mental note of two more barely strapped bodyguards who lean much too casually against the wall.

"Let's get this over with," I mutter, hating how constricted and suffocated I feel in this suit. It's expensive and tailored to my body, but the fabric feels taut and unbreathable. The dress shirt beneath it is already plastered to my chest with dew from the humidity. This isn't how I normally choose to dress, much preferring more relaxed and casual clothing. "For fuck's sake, I feel like a goddamn circus clown."

I look at my other brother, Alessio, as his lips twitch, but he has enough sense to hold his tongue. If people weren't watching our every move, I'd have flipped him the bird already. But appearances are everything at an event like this, so I make do with a fierce scowl at him instead.

Marco shakes his head in exasperation at me as he walks on. Dutifully, we follow him to the corner of the church, where the man we've come to see stands talking in hushed tones.

He turns to us, his lip pulled up in a sneer before the carefully plastered smile falls into place. He graciously shakes Marco's hand and then Alessio's. I don't bother offering mine; my hands are shoved in my pockets.

"I didn't think you'd make it."

This time, I can't stop the eye roll. There's no chance in hell we'd have missed this. For months, we've been trying to cut a deal with him, to bring him into the fold, but the bastard has been obstinately resistant. Today is to show him that the Fratellanza doesn't take no for an answer.

"We wouldn't have missed it," Marco says in a smooth tone, though I can see the calculating gleam in his eyes.

"Wonderful, wonderful." The tone of his voice says our presence here is anything but. "We were just about to start if you'd like to find a seat."

"We need to talk," Marco drawls, leaving no room for debate.

Conor Davis has enough good sense to look scared for a brief second before his face reddens. "If you insist."

"I do."

"Very well. This way, gentlemen."

"I'm going to find a seat," I say. I'm not needed to sit in on this meeting—that isn't why I've been brought along today. I'm the muscle. The action man who stands between us and problems. Alessio and Marco can handle one sweaty balding man. "Congrats," I add.

From the corner of my eye, I catch the sneers from the crowd as I pass. A mask of cool indifference shutters over my face as I give a tight smile, slipping into the pew strategically chosen on the off-chance things go sideways. Because they often do when my brothers and I are around. One might have a little faith in the house of God, but not me, that's for fucking sure.

These people and I are from different worlds, and the mocking whispers at my back are all the indication I need to know that they realize it too. As I lean back against the polished wood, my gut churns with how badly I want to be far away from here. I tug again on my sleeve, hoping to conceal the edges of black ink that peek out. It's pointless, but I don't feel like giving them any more ammunition.

A body slides in beside me, and my back goes rigid. "Mind if I sit?" a weathered voice croons, and I shake my head. "Isn't it just lovely?" she carries on.

I turn my focus onto the woman. Older, dressed in her Sunday's finest, including a stupid hat with lace and mesh. "Yeah," I growl as politely as possible, once more taking in the ridiculous decorations and fanfare. I wonder if I should tell her that I've just been thinking how it looks like a bridal magazine barfed all over the place, but something tells me she wouldn't quite agree.

"It's so wonderful to see how traditional everything is. It just warms my heart. Do you know the bride or the groom?"

"Bride's father."

"How wonderful." I listen with half an ear as she continues to blabber on and on about the decorations. "What was it you said you did?" she asks in her singsong voice.

"My brothers and I are in the pharmaceutical trade."

"Oh, you're a doctor?" she exclaims, obviously impressed.

"Er, not quite. I'm more on the import-export side." That's easier than explaining that we distribute drugs while running clubs and casinos to launder the money through.

I see her gaze catch the tattoos running up the back of my thick neck. "*Oh*."

Her one syllable holds more contempt than a whole sentence could, and the curl of her lip causes my fist to automatically tighten, making the scars more prominent. The judgment pours off her in waves, and it takes every ounce of my strength not to move or say something I'll come to regret later.

I don't need to impress these people, not that it's even possible. Instead of furthering the conversation, I relax into the pew, one arm stretched over the lacquered back.

The woman doesn't say more, and I send up a silent prayer in fucking thanks. Perhaps miracles do happen just once in a blue moon.

Marco and Alessio slide in beside me, and from their faces, I can tell that their little chat didn't go well because Marco's usual expression is darker and harder. I raise a brow to my brothers. But Alessio shakes his head at me as he gets comfortable in the pew. We'll discuss it at home, it seems. I turn back toward the altar as the music begins, and a hush falls over the crowd while everyone shuffles to find their seat.

The priest stands tall beside a groom who looks disgustingly too old for Davis's daughter. He must be at least twenty years older than her.

The groom straightens his suit and smooths his hair back. Something about him makes him look exactly like the sort of person Conor Davis would put on a pedestal because everything about the groom screams educated, cultured, and refined—thus making him a perfect match for his precious eldest daughter.

We stand as the procession music starts, and sniffs and gasps sound as the happy bride, Rosa Davis, proceeds down the aisle, nodding greetings to her guests.

As she comes closer to me, I can see her features more clearly. And time stops ticking for a few seconds...

Because everything about this woman is absolutely perfect—beautiful. *She's like an angel.*

Her face is behind a sheer veil, her blond hair in an intricate updo, and her conservative wedding dress trails behind her with a train so long it seems like a fire hazard. But not even the dress can draw my attention away from her stunning looks, my gaze lingering on her body with its curves in all the right places.

And as she passes me, she looks directly at me. And she smiles. It's a smile that's only for me...

But before I can react, she passes, and I'm left watching her back as she walks down the rest of the aisle. She takes her place across from her soon-to-be husband, her father placing her hand in the groom's.

Her wide hips flare beautifully, and I can't stop staring at her gorgeous, full ass... I mentally shake myself. What the hell is wrong with me? She was smiling at everyone, right? Of course that smile wasn't a special one just for me. And she's about to marry another man. Why on earth am I looking at her in this way?

Anyway, who in their right mind would want something like this? Relationships, marriage, love—all that fucking unicorns and rainbows shit isn't for men like me. And shaking my head, I let my mind wander and drift off to think about business matters—about the next person I need to deal with.

At the end of the ceremony, the happy couple walks past, but this time, the bride's face is turned away from me as she looks at the guests in the opposite pew.

All too soon, Alessio nudges me, jerking his chin forward. We're moving to the reception.

I stand, following my brothers out the other end of the pew, dragging my hand down my jaw. I can think of a hundred things I'd rather be doing than making polite conversation in a room full of people who think they're better than me.

We pile into the dark SUV, and I spread out in the back as Alessio drives us down the street toward where the reception is being held at the family's ostentatious residence—because a man like Davis takes every opportunity to flaunt what he has. Thankfully, it isn't too far from where the ceremony took place.

"I assume it went badly?" I comment.

"He's fucking stubborn," Marco grinds out. "But I'll convince him."

"And if you can't?"

Marco's head snaps around to glare at me. I casually raise my hands in surrender. He's a scary man, confident in what he does as capo and protective when it comes to our family, but even I know not to push him like this.

"How long exactly do we have to stay?" I sigh.

"As long as it takes for Davis to realize that this is his best opportunity," Marco says in a terse tone. "We were cut short before the wedding."

"Just great," I mutter, earning me another dark look from my brother.

"We're here," Alessio announces as he parks up.

I can do this for another few hours. But even as I tell myself this, my skin prickles, and I itch to feel the wrap along my knuckles. To feel the canvas bend beneath my fists. I can control that, and I need that control right now.

"Just play nice, Millo," Marco orders.

I growl a response as we step into the greeting line.

The newlyweds stand at the head, shaking hands, talking, and laughing. Or rather, he does. Because with each step forward, I can't help but notice the lack of a female voice. And when it finally hits my ears, it's soft and gentle—almost melodic.

I peer around Marco's broad shoulders, getting my first real glimpse of the bride without her veil. And she's just as stunning as I thought she'd be.

The intricate updo allows for a few of her blond waves to fall around her temples, bringing my focus to her full, apple cheeks and gorgeous eyes which are light brown like milk chocolate. Framed by thick lashes and subtle makeup, her gaze sparkles with life and happiness, as does everything else about her.

Alessio shoves me forward, and I snap back to reality.

We move another few inches closer. Closer still. Finally, we reach their side. "Congrats," I rumble, extending my hand toward the groom first.

His lip curls before he limply shakes my hand, letting go as soon as he can. "Thank you," he responds.

But I ignore his refined voice and turn my attention to the bride, my hand reaching toward her.

Her soft, pink-painted lips part just slightly as her fingers stretch out to me. But then her eyes widen as she sees my bruised and scarred knuckles, and her hand quickly retracts as her gaze darts downward.

I shouldn't be surprised after her husband barely tolerated my handshake. I shove my hand back into my pocket as my tongue runs over my teeth in irritation. "Congrats," I mumble in a flat voice.

Another guest's cut-glass voice sounds behind me, and I look over my shoulder to see her shaking his hand as a soft thank you escapes her lips.

I see red. Why did he get to touch her? And why the fuck was he worthy of a response from her when I wasn't? But I already know the answer...

I push through the crowd of guests, ignoring the protests, toward the outdoor area. The Davis family has spared no expense, and just like the church, the reception is gaudy and an eyesore of too many pink flowers. A string quartet plays some boring melody that is more likely to put me to sleep than make me want to celebrate.

I make a beeline for the bar. My hand curves around the beer bottle that the bartender passes to me, and the scars across my knuckles catch my eye.

Of course, she wouldn't sully herself with someone like me.

I take a swig, watching my brothers corner Conor Davis. It's the reminder I need as I lean against the bar.

This world on display today, the one of love and happily ever after, isn't where I belong—because a monster like me always belongs in the shadows...

CHAPTER 1

ROSA

FIVE YEARS LATER

Chopping the vegetables, I watch Ethan from the corner of my eye where he silently colors. And my heart aches.

He should be out there running around, playing like all the other four-year-old boys. Instead, he makes himself small and quiet every chance he gets—even when Grayden isn't at home.

Once dinner is in the oven, I wipe down the counters and the table, laying a gentle kiss on Ethan's head. The only good thing to come from this hell has been him. He's a gentle boy who deserves the world.

"I'll be back in a bit, honey. I'm going to tackle the hallway and foyer before dinner."

Ethan nods slowly, holding my gaze.

"I'll only be just outside the kitchen door."

Grabbing the rag and duster, I set to work. In no time, sweat trickles down my spine as the cotton shirt plasters to my back. My hair is tied from my face in a ponytail, but I have to push away stray strands that keep falling into my line of vision.

I lift my head to glimpse at the enormous grandfather clock down the hall. And I wince. I have an hour, if that, to finish all this. The banisters are still in need of dusting. The floor has to be polished. The stubborn juice stain on the rug has taken up far too much of my time. The rubber gloves squeak as I grip the bristled brush, doubling down on my efforts. If I can't get it out... I cringe at the thought, pushing it aside.

It wasn't supposed to be like this. My father insisted that at the age of eighteen, I marry a man over twenty years older than me in front of society's upper elite, and the day when I became Mrs. Grayden Devlin should have been a happy new chapter of my life. Some hopeful part of me, long since broken and forgotten, dreamed that marriage would set me free.

But that day, when the words and vows tumbled from my painted lips, my fate was sealed, and I was sold—in the most legal and business way possible—to a cruel man. A man who's transformed this mansion into a cage where nobody can help me.

Despair rolls through me at the thought of what my life has become. I've long since given up any hope that there's something better out there or that leaving is a possibility. The flame of hope was extinguished years ago. Where could I go where he couldn't follow me? Where he *wouldn't* follow me?

There's no help from the man who calls himself my father. And there's no support from the rest of my family and the people who paraded themselves as my friends.

Sinking back onto my heels, I study the dark spot on the rug. Better, but not good enough. It's never good enough for Grayden...

I chew my lip, squinting at the minuscule speck of purple still staining the rug. Rising to my feet, I silently send up a prayer to whoever's listening that my husband won't notice. But I know it's a fruitless prayer. He always notices. And I always pay the price for what he calls my *sloppy work*.

I dump the water down the drain and discard the yellow gloves quickly as the buzzer for the oven sounds. I have to do better than last night's debacle, and my hands tremble as I take out the chicken.

It's dinnertime, but I know I shouldn't eat.

Are you really going to eat that?

You've already had more than enough, don't you think?

Put on even more weight huh, sis...?

The words I heard so many times growing up tumble around my head before I can force them back. I see my reflection in the glass of the oven door, and quickly look away, unable to stomach the creature that stares back.

I make up a plate of food for Ethan and put it in front of him.

While he eats, I move into the bathroom. My feet ache, and my hands are blistered along the side from scrubbing so hard.

This is not the lifestyle I'd been accustomed to when I was growing up. In Grayden's mansion, there's no help—no butler or maid to tend to the large house and no help beyond the elderly gardener who shows up twice a month to maintain the grounds.

Everything else is my job. It's my responsibility to tend to the house, to the laundry, to the cooking, and to his needs at the drop of a hat.

I wouldn't mind the work if he was happy with what I did, but he always manages to find fault with every single thing I do.

The slamming of a door startles me. I fumble to keep the scrubber in my hand.

My heart roars in my chest as I strain to hear which way he'll go.

There's a crash and a curse from the kitchen.

I'm on my feet in a second, cleaning supplies forgotten. I'll regret it later.

"Fucking hell!" Grayden's voice travels through the empty house like thunder.

My stomach twists. I will my knees to stop shaking. Checking the clock, I realize he's late.

"Where the fuck are you?" he slurs as I rush toward the kitchen.

Dread makes bile rise in my throat. Dinner has been under the warmer in a foolish attempt to keep it warm for him.

"Stop hiding, you pathetic excuse for a wife!" he yells.

I'm in the kitchen in the next instance, my gaze at my feet.

"There you are, bitch." He may look on the outside like a gentleman with unlimited wealth, a refined voice, and impeccable manners, but it took only the duration of my wedding night to discover that he's really a drunken predator with a hair trigger.

I tremble but don't say anything.

Because nothing I say will do any good.

"What the fuck did I say about keeping the house clean?"

A small sound escapes my throat despite how hard I squeeze my lips together.

"And what the fuck is this? Chicken, again? I thought I told you I don't want to eat that dry shit anymore!" he roars. His yells echo around the kitchen before his large hand clamps onto my arm and drags me out of the room.

My blood roars in my ears and blocks out any other sound except the terrified thump of my heart.

"What the fuck is this?"

He shoves me forward into the banister as I frantically search for what he's talking about. It's polished just the way he likes it. The wood gleams with not a single speck of dirt on it.

"You're a useless piece of shit!" He shoves me harder into the banister.

And I see it. On the wooden stairs is the large paperweight from his study. Ethan must have been playing with it on the staircase earlier in the day.

"I-I..." I try to find my voice as his harsh grasp squeezes my jaw.

"You what?" His breath reeks of alcohol as it brushes against my face. "You're a fucking waste of space. Can't cook. Can't clean. You can't even keep yourself in shape, you fat bitch."

I whimper as his hand squeezes harder.

He grabs my hip and pulls me into him. "Who would want to fuck someone like you? It makes me sick every time I even think about your naked body."

He releases me. And for a second, I think it's over. I think the worst has passed.

Grayden bends down to pick up the glass paperweight. When I see it clutched in his fist, I brace for the impact, cursing myself for flinching.

Nothing.

I blink. And I see fury ignite his eyes as he stumbles down the hallway.

I'm rooted to the floor, trembling, before my mind can process what's happening.

A strangled sound lodges in my throat as I scramble forward. *No. No. No!*

He lumbers into the living room.

And I can just about see the paperweight raised in his hold before it sails through the air, smacking into the wall just behind Ethan and shattering.

I hear the snarl in his voice. But it's the tiny whimper that spurs me into action. He's never gone for Ethan like this before.

Desperation flings me down the hall behind Grayden. And love causes my arms to wrap around Ethan, bowing my body over his.

He picks up the paperweight again and hurls it at me.

A crack reverberates through my entire body. And the pain splinters me in half.

I curl over Ethan, shielding him as a polished loafer kicks out and beats the oxygen out of my lungs.

His fingers rip through my scalp as he drags me up by my hair.

I don't struggle. I don't fight.

I simply focus on my son cowering in a ball with tears streaming down his face.

Out. We need out.

My body is flung into the side table, toppling a vase which shatters to the ground. But I make myself grab at Grayden's trouser leg. Anything to stop him from getting closer to Ethan.

Each breath feels like I've swallowed glass. But I shove myself up, trying to find the strength to move.

Grayden shakes me from his leg and staggers toward his study—no doubt to get more alcohol. I hold my breath as I watch, hoping that his need to drink will eclipse his need to beat me.

I count to ten before I crawl to Ethan. Soothing back his hair and kissing his temple, I want to tell him that it's over, that it won't happen again. But I won't lie to him.

Sucking in a sharp breath, I gather my baby boy into my arms. His body shakes against mine, and I squeeze him all the tighter.

The pain in my ribs makes me gasp, but I bite my cheek. Softly, slowly, I make it down the hall. Every creak and groan of the house has me on edge.

My breath stutters out of me in pained puffs as we silently climb the stairs. I stop outside Ethan's room, ushering him inside quickly.

Then I sit in a guest room, hunched over on the edge of the bed, waiting for the drunken summons into our bedroom...

I wait for the cursed bellowing that he does when he's like this—demanding and insistent that I pleasure him exactly how he commands me to.

He tells me that I'm a hole for him to fill as he pleases, but he also tells me that I'm useless in bed. His constant reminders of this only add to the darkness that swallows me up when I'm alone.

The slamming of a door inside our bedroom makes me jump. I try to listen to the sounds through the wall.

One heartbeat, then another.

I creep out of the guest room and move to the master bedroom's door, cracking it open just a peep.

Relief floods through my body as I sag against the doorframe.

Asleep. The bastard is asleep.

Clumsily, his body lays across the bed. With another sharp inhale, I quietly pad over to him, pulling the loafers from his feet. He'll expect them cleaned and polished to perfection before the morning.

He'll also be furious if he wakes up to find that he's slept in his clothes, leaving the expensive fabric creased and rumpled.

I pull off his slacks and then unbutton his dress shirt before I struggle to get it off him. Thank God he's passed out—anything's preferable to when he's yelling and beating me.

I gather his clothes into a ball to place in the laundry basket. And before I leave him, I fill a glass of water and place it beside him on the nightstand—if he wakes up without water beside him, it'll be yet another reason for him to come for me.

With a soft click of the door, I make my way back downstairs to clean up the shattered vase and mess he's made in his fit.

Each step feels like someone's pressing an iron to my lungs. I try to draw a breath in but can't seem to do it enough.

The pattern of this isn't new to me. We've been through this far too many times.

But tonight is the first time he's gone for Ethan—gone for the little boy who's his son.

In a daze, I move from the kitchen to the living room. The sound of my cleaning and glass clinking into the trash doesn't quite register as I continue to replay the image of Ethan on the floor, hands thrown over his head. And the smell of the furniture polish does nothing to remove the foul smell of Grayden's alcohol-laced breath as he sneers in my face.

I drop the polish and rag into my basket. Each breath isn't bringing enough oxygen to my lungs. My chest heaves, but it's on fire with every movement.

Gently, I push against my side, ignoring the loathing that washes over me whenever I feel the plumpness of my figure.

And when I reach a particular area, I nearly scream when my fingers gently push at the rib. White hot pain blinds me, and I grasp at the counter to stay up. Something is wrong. Very wrong.

I need a doctor. One who won't ask the wrong questions. One who doesn't report back to my husband. One whose help won't mean that my husband ends my life before it ever really gets to begin.

I've been bruised and beaten so many times, but always in places that won't draw attention. My stomach, my back, my arms, my thighs. Anything to keep prying eyes from asking too many questions.

I fumble with a bottle of aspirin, watching as the bottle rattles from my grasp and tumbles to the counter. Sucking in a sharp breath, I gather the pills I can reach, trying to put them back into the bottle.

Swallowing two pills, I stumble up the stairs, praying I don't wake him up. Praying that I can make it to Ethan's room.

By some miracle, I do, slowly edging the door open and closed without a sound. Ethan is in a ball under his covers, his favorite stuffed toy, Bernie Bear, clutched to his chest as his face buries into the fur.

My heart breaks for him. And a pained sound escapes me before I can stop it.

His big brown eyes, which are so like mine, widen as he wakes.

I grit my teeth, putting on my best smile. But the image of him recoiling away from his father flashes before me.

My mind moves before my body. Instantly, a checklist forms in my head.

I hold Ethan's watery gaze before turning toward his closet and throwing it open. Frantically, I pull out the small backpack we bring to the park and hastily shove what I can fit into it. A few outfits, a spare blanket, a book or two. I grab another empty bag, put in a few more items, and sling it over my arm despite the way my body protests.

I wish I could get some of my own clothes too, but I can't risk going back into the master bedroom and waking up Grayden.

I press my finger to my lips and motion Ethan to me, unwilling to make a single sound that might lead to us being caught.

My plan is hazy and wild. It's only partially formed, but I hang on to it for dear life.

Ethan slips his arms into a light jacket and then into the straps of the backpack.

Kissing his head, I clutch his tiny hand in mine, pull the hood over his head, and move as fast as I can to the door.

Ethan stares at me, his brow puckered and confused.

I squeeze his hand in reassurance as I let the door click softly shut behind us. Moving despite the agony in my ribs, I will myself to make it down the stairs without a sound.

In the kitchen, my fingers fumble with my purse as I hastily throw it over my shoulder. Each step sends another wave of pain through me. But if we don't leave, we'll both end up dying here.

Outside, the chilly night air energizes me. I hurry down the long winding drive, through the gate, and into the luxurious neighborhood. It isn't until I'm gasping for breath that I pause for a moment, bracing myself against the wall of the nearest building.

Taking a deep breath, I clutch my side and keep walking, Ethan's hand firmly in mine.

I wish I could run back to my family. But my father will be furious when he discovers I've left Grayden—he married me off to him because he wanted an alliance with the powerful Devlin family.

Should I try to appeal to my mother? I shake my head. She will only tell me that we have to do what Father wants—and he'll order me to go back to my husband.

I have few friends. My family largely kept me sheltered at home while I was growing up, going so far as to having me homeschooled, due to their desire to keep their children out of the public eye—except for when it came to that ridiculously over-the-top wedding. And since my marriage, Grayden has made sure to keep me as isolated as possible.

After what seems like an age, we've walked to the area we need. It's here somewhere, I know it...

My eyes fill with tears as the clinic's sign comes into view. I saw a poster for this place when I took Ethan for his pediatrician check.

I jump at the sound of something tipping over in the alley beside us, but then I tell myself that Grayden will still be out cold and it's far too early for him to notice that we're missing.

This is the right choice. An ER would notify Grayden. And the family doctor is paid by Grayden. Those options won't keep us safe.

Pushing open the door with more energy than I possess, the smell of antiseptic immediately assaults my nostrils.

Carefully, I sit Ethan on a chair in the corner, away from the windows and prying eyes. He holds onto his teddy bear for dear life while I turn to the front desk where a nurse in Snoopy scrubs sits.

Her eyes raking over me makes me tuck a lock of blond hair behind my ear and avert my gaze downward.

"I..." My voice is soft and rasping. "I need to see a doctor."

Her expression melts into concern. Through the small gap in the clear glass, she slides me a clipboard. "Just fill that out as best you can, honey, and we'll get you in to see someone."

I nod and slump down beside Ethan. My handwriting is wobbly, and the sting of fresh tears clouds my eyes.

When my name is finally called, I gather our things as best I can.

The doctor, a gentle-looking redhead with Care Bears all over her scrubs and a bright smiley face pinned on her coat, examines me with care. She doesn't ask unnecessary questions or prod me for answers.

With a soft soothing voice, she moves me from the examining room to the x-ray room and back, all while a nurse follows closely with Ethan in tow.

The look on the doctor's face is all I need to see to know it's bad.

We're back in the examination room now, and wordlessly, she sets down some clean clothing.

I just stare. "I can't... I don't want—"

"You can, and you should. We get a lot of women like you here. Take the pain meds, change your clothes, and I'll be back with an ice pack." She gives me a soft smile. "If you need us to call someone, just let me know. I'll give you a few minutes."

She's right—my clothes are in a state, ripped from when Grayden grabbed me and dragged me across the floor.

I avoid looking at my body in the small mirror as I tug on the T-shirt and hoodie. I do the same with the faded pair of yoga pants, tying them at the waist despite not needing to do so. I've enough in my hips to keep them up.

I toss the torn clothing in the trash just as the doctor returns. "Do you have a place to stay?"

It hits me that I haven't made a plan beyond getting to the clinic. I don't know what I'm doing. We're out on the streets in Chicago in the middle of night. Alone. My lip trembles, and I squeeze my eyes shut. "No."

"There's a shelter on the next block. I'm not sure if they have any spaces left for tonight, but would you like me to ask?"

I nod my head.

With that, she leaves, and I rummage through my purse, counting the measly dollars in my wallet. Enough for one meal—and painkillers. But not enough for a place to stay for the night. The answer she returns with has my body shaking with exhaustion and defeat: the shelter is full.

Gnawing my lip, I thank both the doctor and nurse before I guide us both back out into the chilly air. My body is growing heavy from the pain medicine, and my vision is blurry with tears, but I manage to read the street names.

With a quick stop to make a purchase at a corner store, I orient myself. The park I take Ethan to is just on the next street. Maybe we can sit there while I try to figure something out.

And then it hits me.

Kori.

The walk is long and sluggish, with me having to stop every so often to catch my breath. But I count each small square house as we pass, hoping I've remembered it correctly.

Kori and her son, Kristopher, were a blessing we stumbled upon at the park one day. Kori, a single mother herself, wasn't involved in the world I was in. She was different—and she was stronger for it.

My hand shakes as I knock. I don't know what time it is, but the look of the vacant street tells me that it's extremely late by now.

No answer.

My mouth fills with cotton as I squeeze Ethan's hand, putting on a brave face as best I can. My darling boy doesn't deserve this life; he deserves so much more.

"Rosa?"

I blink, not realizing the door has opened. "Kori..." My voice is thick with tears before I clear it. "I'm sorry to drop by so late. Can...can I ask a favor?"

Her brow is furrowed. "Sure, come in. Is everything okay?"

I shake my head, following her in. I don't tell her the entire story as I sit on her couch, trying to take up as little space as I can; I just tell her that I had to leave.

Kori squeezes my knee and smiles, offering me her couch and a blow-up mattress for Ethan.

She helps me get set up, bringing her spare sheets and blankets, and as soon as Ethan is tucked in, he falls asleep in moments. He's just as exhausted as I am.

Kori makes us both a cup of cocoa, and then, she curls up on the couch next to me. Concern is etched all over her face.

"I don't want to be a bother..."

"You're not. And you can stay as long as you need. What else can I do to help you? I have six hundred bucks in savings that I could lend you if that would help you?"

I shake my head. She's just as strapped for cash as I am right now. "No, I can't take your money. But do you think...your mom could look after Ethan while I work?" Kori's mom helps with childcare when Kori is working. "As soon as I find a job, I can pay her something for it," I add in a rushed voice.

"Oh, Rosa, I know she'll be happy to help."

"I just need to earn enough money to be able to leave Chicago and put down a deposit on an apartment, so hopefully, it won't be for long. My marriage is finally over. I know that Grayden won't allow a divorce, but I will *never* return to that man."

The one time I mentioned a divorce to him, he beat me up badly before telling me that he'd make sure I'd never see Ethan again if I filed for divorce—that he had the money and power to ensure that he'd get sole custody forever. And I can't risk that ever happening to Ethan. I can't let that monster be the only parent to my little boy. It's better that we just disappear and get as far away from Chicago and Grayden as possible.

"I desperately wish that I'd had the courage before now to leave. That I've stayed for so long and let Ethan witness the violence makes me feel a complete failure as a parent. I'm his mom, and I should be protecting him from all the bad in this world. I've let him down, but that changes from right now. I have to stand up for us both—even though it's absolutely terrifying—because that's the only way things will get better for us."

Kori nods as she hugs me, understanding how bad things are for me.

That night, my sleep is fitful, and I wake up in pain several times, not remembering where I am.

Finally, when dim daylight starts to filter through the blinds, I decide to get up and stumble to the bathroom with my purse in my hand.

Staring at my reflection makes my throat run dry. Too round of a face; too chubby cheeks; brown eyes that are plain and drab. Every insecurity and fault in my body screams out at me.

I grab my purse which contains the box of hair dye I bought from the corner store, and I sprawl the bottles and instructions over the vanity's counter.

I squeeze my eyes shut. It's now or never. Grayden's going to find us if I don't take precautions against being recognized.

Opening my eyes, I lift the scissors from Kori's medicine cabinet and hack at my long blond strands, watching the loose waves fall to the floor in uneven slices.

When I finish, I take my reflection in. My hair dangles in a chin-length bob, a bit jagged at the ends but passable as long as no one looks too closely at it. Next comes the black dye. I do my best, but after washing it out, the color isn't as even as I'd hoped, and the brassy orange undertone makes my skin look a little sickly.

After showering, I head to the kitchen. Kori's mom has arrived, and I explain to Ethan that she'll be looking after him today. "This is Kathleen. She's Kristopher's grandma, and she's going to look after both you boys today while I go out and look for a job."

Ethan's eyes widen with worry, and my heart breaks in two. I desperately wish I didn't have to leave him for the next eight hours, but there's no other option if I'm going to find a job.

"And today, we're making cupcakes," Kathleen adds in an attempt to distract Ethan. "And I'll need someone to help with the mixing. Do you think you could help with that, Ethan?"

He gives a wobbly smile and nods.

The smell of bacon sizzling is all around me, making my stomach grumble. But I push it off, deciding to leave before breakfast is ready. Skipping a few meals won't hurt me. It'll do me good after indulging last week on too much cake.

I kiss Ethan's head, and after promising him I'll be home before dinner, I reluctantly leave the house.

***

First, I tackle the businesses and stores around Kori's neighborhood, and then, I branch out further.

By the end of the day, my feet are sore, and all I've had to eat all day is the stale roll I snagged from the shelter soup kitchen.

Nothing. Not a single prospect for a job. All I keep hearing is 'we're not hiring.'

What on earth had I been thinking when I thought that I could set up a new life for myself? I don't have any experience. I've never had a job in my life. I'd been raised to be the perfect housewife—and I couldn't even do that properly.

Tears prick my eyes, and I take a shuddering breath to push them away. I have to keep going.

Because whatever happens now, the only thing I know is that I can't let Ethan down ever again...

CHAPTER 2

CAMILLO

I grimace at the loud laughter that fills the room. My headache is slowly blooming, and as much as I love my family, I'm definitely not enjoying this bonding time with the rugrats.

And that's the problem of sharing a mansion with my brothers—they treat me like an unpaid babysitter.

I'm twenty-seven years old and their enforcer, not some fucking nanny.

And a couple of hours spent looking after their six kids, aged between two and eight, is my idea of complete hell.

The rugrats are noisy, demanding, and hyperactive—basically, a handful to keep track of as they chase each other non-stop around the couches.

I scrub a hand along the stubble on my jaw, my eyes darting to the stairs where I know their moms are busy packing their things for their trip.

"Look what I drew!" A sticky piece of paper is shoved into my face, startling me from my thoughts and making me jolt backward against the couch.

I'm given no choice but to take the paper. Some rudimentary shapes and squiggles bombard my eyes, but I'd be lying if I said I knew what I was looking at.

"It's you!" Vincenzo says forcefully. Despite the lack of any resemblance, I try to look flattered as I hand it back to him.

"No, you have to keep it," he pouts.

"For, um, how long?"

"Like, *forever*." Yeah, like I said, they're hyperactive and demanding.

"Er, thanks." I set the paper down on the coffee table as I scope the room. One of the kids is playing with some building blocks quietly, and for that, I'm thankful. But the others? The others are busy playing tag, and I wince as the eldest two collide right into each other.

I'm up before they can even start screaming their heads off. "Hey, hey." I crouch down, inspecting, assessing.

Maximo is rubbing his head, as is Xander. "You guys are good. That's what your skulls are for—to protect you from getting hurt."

But Xander's lip wobbles, and I know what's coming next.

"Nothing but a tiny bump," I reassure him, mussing his hair. Because if he starts wailing, then I'm in deep shit.

He sniffs and nods, accepting the small hand Maximo offers. They mumble apologies to each other and take off running again as if nothing ever happened.

"Don't run!" I holler after them.

"Hey! I wasn't done with that!" Fia screams from the dining table.

I pinch the bridge of my nose. What now? If it's not one thing, it's another. I glare up at the stairs. How long does it take to fucking pack for Italy? Sure, it's hard for the women to prepare when they don't know how long exactly they'll have to be away, but surely they know the safe house is going to be stocked.

"I'm still using it!" Fia snaps as she grabs the box of markers. "You can use it after."

"I want a turn with them!" Nora whines, yanking at the box.

I watch the scene in slow motion as the markers go flying into the air and scatter, sending both girls flying to the ground to retrieve them and crashing heads. For fuck's sake, am I going to get through today without any of these kids sustaining a concussion?

This. This right here is why there's no way in hell I'd ever willingly put myself in such a situation. Terrors, every single one of them, despite how angelic they look. A wife? Kids? It isn't worth the headache.

That's for someone else. Someone whose soul isn't pitch black and dark. Someone who isn't me...

My attention snaps back to the two kids wailing. Markers are laid all over the floor and papers are balled and crumpled around them. It's a fucking mess.

"Hey." I move in to kneel before them. "What's the problem?"

"Fia won't share!"

"I wasn't done with my turn!"

"I wanted a turn!"

"You hog them!"

Back and forth, they continue before I give a sharp whistle. Both cover their ears.

"What the fuck is going on down there?" The voice of my brother, Marco, booms from the top landing.

"Nothing! Everything is fine!" I holler back. "Go finish your shi... stuff." I turn back toward the little cuddle monsters, eyeing every one of them. "Alright, enough," I say in the best commanding tone I can muster. "We're going to clean up the mess. And then, everyone is going to sit down and watch the movie I'm going to put on. Okay?"

There's a chorus of "Yes, Uncle Millo" and "Yes, Uncle Millie," Millo and Millie being the nicknames my family have given me. The children's words are music to my ears. And that's that. Peace and quiet at last. I sag back onto the couch and stare up at the ceiling.

The youngest, two-year-old Iris, clambers up beside me, taking in the paper with the scribbles done by Vincenzo. "You look so handsome in the picture, Uncle Millo," she says in her sweet little voice. Then she rests her sleepy head against me, sticking her thumb in her mouth.

And I can't help but smile down at her as I wrap my arm around her in a hug. It isn't so bad looking after the rugrats.

Yeah, it isn't so bad, but it's still not for me...

***

A few weeks have passed since the women and kids left for Italy. Our two younger siblings, Debi and Danio, have also flown out there—Danio is overseeing all the security arrangements while they're there. It's not safe for them to be in the States right now—the feds are on our backs and have been picking up Fratellanza wives and family members on spurious charges and trying to get information out of them.

I've just walked into the mansion's office to talk over some business issues with my older brothers when we hear my bedroom door slamming shut, and our latest maid, Savona, thundering down the stairs.

She bursts through the door and marches up to us. "That's it! I can't take any more! I'm out!" She jabs a finger in my direction. "What I have to go through in *his* room every day has left me traumatized for life!" And then she storms out.

Alessio looks surprised, I try to look innocent, and Marco looks like he wants to kill me.

As we watch her depart, I try to avoid looking at my brothers. "For fuck's sake, Camillo," Marco snarls. "What's been going on in your bedroom? Did you proposition her?"

My brows shoot up. "Did I *what?*"

"Did. You. Ask. To. Fuck. Her?"

I exhale a sigh through my clenched teeth. "No, I did not." I grit out the words as my brother continues to glare at me. "For God's sake, Marco, she must be at least seventy."

"So, what the hell did she see in there?" he demands. "It better not have been fucking porn magazines or something like a sex doll."

"Why do you always think the worst of me?" I exclaim in a slightly injured tone. Marco and Alessio practically brought up me and our youngest two siblings after our parents were killed, and they've never entirely got out of the habit of acting like parents to us. It's fucking annoying at times like this, but I try to remind myself how much responsibility they had to take on after our father murdered our mom—before our father was himself killed. Yeah, our family is pretty fucked up.

"Maybe we should try to persuade her to come back," Alessio suggests. "We can promise her that Millo will go to confession every day for the next week."

"I'm telling you, there are no porn mags or sex toys in my room," I insist.

But neither of my brothers are listening to me. "Nah, a week won't be enough." Marco shakes his head. "He'll have to go to confession daily for at least a month. That might swing it—you know how religious Savona is—"

I slam my hand down on the desk. "I'm not fucking going to fucking confession for the next fucking month!" I growl. "I'm telling you, she didn't see any porn mags or sex toys."

Marco narrows his eyes at me. "Then why the hell has she just run out on us after looking at you like you're the devil?"

"It'll be the goddamn mess in that pigsty that he calls his bedroom," Alessio drawls as he sits back in his chair across from the desk.

"For fuck's sake," Marco snaps.

"It isn't *that* bad," I defend.

Alessio looks at me like I've grown two heads. "It's like a warzone in there. I don't know how you can even tolerate it."

"Just because it's not like your bedroom doesn't mean that it's a warzone," I huff, my arms crossed over my chest as I glare at my brothers from where I lean against the bookshelf in the office.

Marco's hands rest across his desk, and his expression tells me that I'm in for a good chewing out if I don't play my cards right.

"Dealing with your room on a daily basis warrants hazard pay," Alessio clips.

"We can't all be obsessive neat freaks like you, dickfa—"

"Enough," Marco growls. "She quit this morning because of *your* room, Millo. That makes it *your* problem to fix."

"I hardly think that's why—"

But his icy stare makes me snap my mouth shut. This is an order, not a suggestion.

"We have other things to be doing," I start cautiously, hoping he'll realize there's a better use of my time. Things I need to be doing to ensure operations run smoothly. We each have a job to do—Marco as capo, Alessio as consigliere, and me as enforcer. And me ensuring that others are kept in line means that my brothers have the time to do what they do best: lead.

"Alessio and I will handle the business side. You fix the problem you created. It's not up for discussion. You have forty-eight hours."

"You want me to find someone within two days? You've got to be kidding me..."

"That's more than enough time to vet and hire someone. I'm sick of this place looking like a complete mess."

"Yeah, it's disrupting my zen," Alessio adds, probably just to annoy me. "And as we've no maid now, that means you're cooking dinner tonight. And make sure it's got some vegetables."

Alessio's so fucking fussy. I shoot him a dark look before turning back to Marco. "Marco, come on..."

"What part did you not understand? Get the fuck out there, and fix the issue."

I bite the inside of my cheek and nod. It isn't worth it to argue. The moment he leveled that deadly stare at me, I was done. This is my job for now, whether I want it or not. "Fine," I growl. I turn and leave his office, the door banging shut with a hollow thud behind me.

Two days. I can find someone in two days...

Making a pit stop at my room, I let my gaze move around the place. It's not so bad, but maybe it might be a good idea to tidy up a bit later. Then, grabbing my gym bag, I jog down the stairs.

Between the time it's taken to stretch and run the property as a warmup, I've called countless agencies and maid services. *How can none of them have a single maid available?*

The moment I mentioned our last name, each conversation halted with profuse apologies and the offer to put us on a waitlist until someone meeting our needs comes up. It's a bunch of fucking lies.

The last agency I'd spoken with laughed at me. *Actually laughed at me.*

No, that's a fucking understatement. The woman cackled a sound of extreme hilarity, and she didn't stop for the next thirty seconds, finally catching enough breath to explain to me that none of the maids who were open for work would ever consider taking the job. The Marchianos have a reputation: hired one day and fired the next.

We're not *that bad*; we simply have requirements—and no one seems to meet them. I shake my head. Marco is going to fucking kill me.

I growl in frustration before tossing my phone back into my bag and focusing on something I can control. Something that never fails to keep me grounded.

I'm in the gym we have in our mansion. The comforting *thud, thud, thud* of my wrapped knuckles against the canvas punching bag eases the tension riding my shoulders. Again and again, I jab at the bag before pulling my shirt from my head. A brief glimpse of the ink that decorates my arms and back catches my eye: an outward expression of the demon inside me.

Unlovable.

The word whispers through my head, and I swallow the bile that burns my throat. Monster. Thug. Beast. That's what the world sees when it faces me. A creature capable of only bloody and brutish things. A savage. I was more than glad to fill the role they chose for me before I knew what was happening or what it meant. I'm their villain.

My hands squeeze tighter, and I hit the bag harder, feeling my wrapping stretch and snap. I don't care. I need the sting to keep my mind in here, in the gym, rather than where it has no fucking business going.

Thud, thud, thud.

Even the metallic scent of blood doesn't make me stop.

Finally, putting my hands on my knees, I gulp air like a drowning man. Each inhalation through my nose feels like torture and heaven all at once. I suck down more oxygen before I stand up. Reaching for my water bottle, I squeeze my eyes shut and let the cold water pour over my hair and neck.

The knot holding the long, thick strands of my hair back from my face unravels, my strands swishing back and forth against my skull as I shake them out like the animal the world thinks I am.

The irony of it isn't lost on me, but I have better things to fucking deal with than how acceptable my hair is to society.

I scrub my battered hand down my face. Our mansion is a complete mess right now, and dealing with my furious brothers is a pain in the ass. I know I need to fix this fucking mess—but how the hell am I going to do it in only two days?

CHAPTER 3

ROSA

My clothes are the same ones given to me two days ago at the shelter. I have no spare money to buy new ones, and I'm far too big to fit into anything of Kori's. I look and feel miserable.

My hands shake as I take in my shabby appearance in the window I pass. The hair dye is patchy at best, brown in some places and an orangey color in others. It's definitely not the solid black it's meant to be. The jagged ends of my bob aren't as noticeable if I keep my hair tucked behind my ears, but I still know they're there.

My stomach protests with hunger, and I feel a little dizzy, but I ball my hand. A little less to eat won't hurt me. There's plenty of fat to spare. The words sound distinctly like my mother's as they ring through my head.

All day, I've been walking the streets again and trying anywhere and everywhere in the hope of finding a job. I need to find something, anything, to just get back on my feet. To simply provide for my son and prove to the world I'm not as worthless as Grayden or my family think.

Except as I sit on the bench, looking at my trembling hands, I think they're right. What do I know about working—about anything? My entire life, I've been reaching out for unobtainable goals and failing every time. Tears sting my eyes, and I push out a breath, willing them away.

Ethan's wide brown eyes and trembling mouth flash into my mind, giving me the energy to push off the bench and march into the sleek casino across the street from me. I smooth a hand down my side, over the curve of my hip, pulling out the wrinkles as best I can.

I keep my eyes downcast as I move into the building, hoping not to draw the wrong kind of attention.

Catching my lip between my teeth, I do a quick scan of the lobby, searching for the front desk.

Around me, women in their skin-tight clothing and designer fashion labels drape themselves over men whose high-end suits and polished shoes scream money. I freeze in the doorway. They might know Grayden or my father. My blood runs cold as I quickly look for an escape.

But the casino might be hiring. I can't leave, not without even asking if they have any job openings. But if someone sees me, they might tell Grayden.

I can't move. I can't breathe.

A body jostles into me, and I hear the indignant huff of a woman behind me. It's the push I need to take a step, and then another. The front desk comes into view. I practically fling myself to the side of it, trying to be as inconspicuous as possible as I clutch onto the edge.

"Can I help you?"

My gaze lifts to a sharply dressed woman. Her name badge tells me that she's called Stella. Her lips form a smile that definitely doesn't reach her eyes—like she knows I don't belong in a place like this.

I need to say something. I need to open my mouth.

"Hello?" she grits out.

I blink, feeling my nails bite into my palm hard enough to leave little crescents behind. "Yes. I just...wanted to ask if you have any openings? The woman at the pharmacy down the street said that she thought you're hiring."

Her brow arches as her gaze drifts lower, taking in my shabby clothing—and probably also my weight.

"We're not really looking to hire anyone."

"Please," I plead, clearing my throat when it cracks around the word. "You have to have something. *Anything*."

"There are no jobs available here. *Not for someone like you*."

It takes all my effort to keep my lips from wobbling. "Please, I'm a hard worker. I can clean the rooms. I can take the trash out. I'll do anything."

Stella gives a brief wave to someone behind me before she turns her attention back to me and her face hardens again. "We don't have any openings at this time." Her tone is terse and hostile.

"I..." But my voice fades as a man steps into my peripheral vision. I flinch and cower into the front desk, waiting to be grabbed. I can just feel Grayden's hand wrapping around my arm and squeezing, bruises in the shape of his fingers blooming in its wake. Terror paralyzes me.

"Hey," a male voice barks into my ear, pulling me back to the present. He gestures toward the door with a sharp jerk of his hand. The wired earpiece in his ear and the straight buzz cut complement the serious downturn of his lips. My eyes catch on the golden embroidery on his blazer: *Security*.

"You're making a scene," he snaps. "Do us both a favor and leave quietly. Follow me—"

"Wait! *Please*." I clutch at the front desk for dear life. "I need a job. *Any* job."

Tears blur my vision. I've failed yet again. And I slump my shoulders in defeat. What's the use? There's nothing for me here.

Stupid. Useless. The words Grayden has said to me so often echo in my ears.

"What's going on?"

I startle as a deep rumble sounds from behind me, sending a shiver skittering down my spine.

The way the security guard halts and makes his tone suddenly respectful makes me think that the new man is important. "Mr. Marchiano, it's nothing. We're just escorting someone out."

"Leave her."

"Boss?"

"I said *leave her*. Do I need to repeat myself a third time?"

"N-no, boss." His hand drops, and he steps away from this man who is now standing next to me.

He's imposing with wide shoulders and a broad chest that strain against his black shirt. I can't keep my eyes off his rolled-up sleeves which showcase his strong forearms—they're breathtaking: muscled and with magnificent dark ink scrawled across the tan skin. Everything about him is as beautiful as it is terrorizing.

My heart labors in my chest as my eyes lift to his face. A powerful jaw covered with dark stubble. Luxurious, black locks are pulled back from his face in a half knot at the back of his head, allowing the thick strands to just brush the back of his neck and curl gently around his ears.

His rich brown eyes scan me from head to toe, and I fight the urge to curl inward and make myself smaller—a worthless endeavor if there ever was one. I take an involuntary step back. I'm only five foot two, and the way he towers over me makes it clear that he's definitely well over six feet tall.

"What are you here for?"

I flinch at his voice. And I can't even form an answer as my mouth feels like it's full of thick cotton.

"She's looking for a job, Mr. Marchiano," the woman at the front desk sneers, leaning over the desk so her chest is more pronounced.

But the man doesn't spare her a glance. His eyes are solely fixed on me.

"I told her we don't have any positions open. At least none *she's* suitable for."

Stella's words make me want to curl up into a ball. Again, his eyes flicker over me, and my fingers can't help but tug at my baggy hoodie. I should leave, but for some reason, my feet are rooted to the spot.

He tucks his large hands into his pockets. "We're looking for a maid," he says carefully. "Well, the family is, not the casino."

"C-can I apply?" I stutter out the words, lifting my gaze to his for just a second before my eyes drop.

"Follow me," he commands.

"But Mr. Marchiano—" Stella starts to say something in an appalled tone.

But all he does is shoot a look at her to make it clear that she should stop talking.

Stella narrows her eyes at me, and the security guard quietly moves back into place.

I watch as he sets off at a stride, stunned that someone is finally offering me an interview. Then, I remind myself that it's only an interview, and I still have to convince him to actually give me the job.

I stare at him. Even from the back, he's built full of muscle and is intimidating as hell. My knees shake for a second.

"Well, don't keep him waiting," Stella snaps, her words making me jolt forward and take off after him.

His large body slides gracefully into a booth, sleek and powerful like a panther waiting to pounce. I swallow. *This is for Ethan. That's all that matters.*

The plush dark of the seating blends in with his black attire. "Sit."

I don't belong here, and I know it. "Okay," I mumble, mortified by how awkward and ungraceful I am as I squeeze into the booth.

"What's your name?"

"Rosa Dev—" I stop myself. "Um, just Rosa." I curl my hand tightly under the table, unable to keep the trembling at bay. My gaze lands on the immaculate table of the booth, a beautifully polished and lacquered oak wood that blends seamlessly in with the rest of the surroundings. Elegant and modern.

"Camillo Marchiano." He extends his hand toward me, but I refuse to shake it. My hands are clammy and shaky, and I can't let him notice this.

The sound of a tray dropping from somewhere nearby makes me jump and yelp. *Get yourself together.* "Sorry. You, er, said you were looking for a maid?"

He leans back into the booth, his massive arm spread across the back. I don't stare for too long and quickly avert my gaze again. But my mind continues to roll over his name. Camillo Marchiano. It tickles the back of my mind, but I can't seem to place it, especially not with the thundering of my pulse in my ears and the roiling of my stomach.

"I am. My brothers and I have found ourselves in a bit of a...jam." He hisses the last word, aggression rolling off him in waves, making me push back against the booth.

I give the tiniest nod.

"How many years' experience have you got? We're only looking for someone with excellent skills and references."

My heart plummets as he says this, knowing that I have exactly zero work experience in this or any other job. My eyes look at the table instead of his eyes as my mind scrambles to find a way to fix this situation that's already falling apart at the seams. I need to have confidence, and I need to make eye contact and smile—neither of which my body wants to do right now.

"Well?"

"I don't have any professional experience," I whisper.

He clenches his jaw, and I can tell that he's annoyed at me. He must think that I've got a cheek asking for this job and that I'm wasting his time. "We don't just hand out jobs to anyone," he clips.

"I understand." I pray that I don't have tears in my eyes even though I can feel the sting. I lift my chin and stare at his face—a face that's rugged and rough in a way that makes my insides flutter.

But his posture and the way his mouth curls in the corners into an unimpressed scowl terrify me.

He's the type of man that you hear stories about. The ones even Grayden and my father seem to tremble near and avoid. My chest tightens at the thought. *Why would someone like him want to give me a chance?*

My eyes dart around the place once more, and my foot bounces beneath the table. This has to work. Short of getting on my hands and knees for this man and begging, I'll do anything I can. "But I'm a hard worker." The words blurt from my mouth before I can stop them.

I take a breath, trying to make myself sound far less desperate than I am. For Ethan's sake, I have to get this job. He can't say no. I won't let him. "I...I can clean and do laundry and know how to stock a pantry. I'm used to doing housework—I've had lots of practice. I can do whatever you need me to do as a maid."

"Can you cook?"

"Um, perhaps. Yes, a bit, I think."

His brow arches. "You don't sound sure."

I know I'm not a very good cook. Grayden's told me this so many times over the last five years. I've tormented him with dry chicken, tough steaks, and overcooked pasta. But if I have to cook to get this job, then I'll try my hardest to improve my cookery skills—I'm willing to do whatever it takes.

He drags his hand down his jaw and looks past me. "Hard work is great and all, but my brothers are demanding. It's not a job for the faint of heart. They're *particular* in what they like."

He's looking everywhere but at me now. He's avoiding eye contact. I've made him uncomfortable. Shit. Shit. *Shit*. How did I mess this up in such a short time?

"I can deal with demanding." Again, I blurt it out, desperation clinging to each word as it leaves my mouth. "I'm not scared of hard work. I can handle whatever you throw at me. I just need a chance. Please."

Now I'm begging. There's no dignity. She's left the building, alongside my sanity and self-worth. But I'll beg and beg until I can find something.

He mutters something under his breath. *"Nulla è difficile...per chi..."* I can't quite catch all the words, but it's something in what must be a foreign language, and I'm not sure what it means. His massive body doesn't move, but the muscle in his jaw ticks.

Please don't say what everyone else has been saying to me: *No. No, thank you. Sorry, but no. You're not the sort of person we're looking for. Good luck with life, but you've failed.*

He gives me a soft smile as he looks at me.

My heart hitches with hope...

And his smile is genuine—not one of those fake polite smiles you're given just before you're turned down.

I hold my breath as he gives his answer...

"I don't think you're right for the job."

Wait, what? He didn't really just say that, did he?

"I'm sorry, Rosa."

I close my eyes, my head dropping.

I really thought I had a chance, and the only thing I can do now is will my tears to stay back until I'm at least out of the building. My body is sagging, and I start to slide from the booth.

"My brothers are difficult to work for," he says in a rush, his body softening and his brown eyes swirling with a different kind of emotion. "It wouldn't be fair to you..."

"I understand. Thank you for your time."

"But why don't you fill in one of our casino application forms? Then, if something comes up, they can contact you."

"Okay." The word puffs out on a breath of air. Because it's worth a chance. All I've got to lose is another few minutes of my time.

"Follow me." He stands, giving me the once over again, slower this time, before curling his fist by his side and marching away. Each step forward is purposeful and powerful.

He's leading me back toward Stella. My insides clench at the thought of her looking down at me again. But I know I have to leave my details with the casino. Because maybe, just maybe, it'll lead to a job for me. And I remind myself that I'm doing this for Ethan. This is all for the boy who's my whole world.

I start to fill out the form that he takes from behind the front desk and hands to me.

I sit a few tables away from him, but I can feel his gaze lasering into me.

And it makes me shudder.

Because he's dangerous—and I don't understand him. And it's almost as if he's feeling guilty for not giving me the job...

CHAPTER 4

CAMILLO

Why do I wish I could give her the job?

I don't know the answer to this. What I do know, however, is that she wouldn't last five fucking minutes around Marco. He'd be pissed off in no time with her constant flinching and stuttering.

He's not one to mince his words. I can tell that this woman—Rosa—is fragile. And I can't put her through that.

The thought continues to tumble through my mind as I move about the casino, leaving Rosa so that I can finish doing what I came here to do in the first place.

It's taken me most of the interview to place her face. To put a name to the pretty cheeks that flushed pink and the full lips that trembled as we spoke. She's Conor Davis's daughter.

It looks like she's no longer with that stuck-up stiff she married—I noticed she wasn't wearing a wedding ring. But it's none of my business. I don't give a fuck about what's going on in Davis's family—although by the look of her, she clearly no longer has the benefit of the Davis money. She's just a woman in need of work, and the only thing I care about is her doing a good job for us.

Two of our soldiers across from where I sit are going on and on about yet another problem with distribution. I haven't been able to focus on any of it. Instead, my attention keeps flitting to the woman a few tables down who is writing her details on an application form.

"Boss?"

My gaze snaps back to them. "I'm listening."

"Who is she?"

"No one you need to know," I growl.

Both men nod and don't dare to even look in her direction again.

My eyes wander back over to Rosa and her beautiful curves. I catch her flinch as a customer shouts at their win. She's a timid thing and jittery with it.

I take the last swig of what's left in my glass, allowing the burn of alcohol to clear the thoughts away.

But a small yelp sounds. And my head whips toward Rosa, a low grumble of annoyance reverberating through my chest as the same customer shouts out yet again as the roulette wheel gives him another win.

I call another soldier over to my table with a flick of my hand. "He's drunk." I jerk my chin toward the customer. "Throw him the fuck out."

"Boss, he's teetotal. I've never seen a drop of alcohol pass his lips. And he's one of the casino's biggest spenders every month—"

"Do it," I snap.

"But..."

"Now!" I roar.

"Got it, boss." He strides off, and I watch while he carries out my order. The customer isn't happy and is threatening never to grace our casino again. Like I give a fuck.

And as I look over at Rosa again, I realize that I have no idea why I just acted like this...

On my way back to my car, I keep thinking about this woman. I shake my head. Why am I even still thinking about her? I must just feel sorry for her.

That has to be it. Because she said it herself—she has zero experience. And with her complete lack of confidence, I can't see any job with us working out for her.

***

Last night, I managed to get out of cooking dinner by ordering takeout. But Alessio was less than impressed and told me that tonight he expects a home-cooked meal—or he's going to whip my ass.

I decide to make pizza. That can't be too hard, right? It's just dough, you sling toppings onto it, and you shove it into the oven. *Even I can manage that.*

I'll also have to break the news to my brothers that I haven't found a maid, but I'll cross that bridge when I come to it.

On the way home, I drop by the deli and pick up some readymade pizza crusts. It's sort of cheating, but my brothers won't ever find out. Ever since Alessio's been on his latest health kick, he's become obsessive about only eating stuff that's fresh and homecooked. I don't see what's wrong with takeout, but the way he looked at the food I ordered last night would make anyone think that it was food that I'd scavenged from the trash.

While I'm at the deli, I also pick up some corn on the cob. With that shoved in Alessio's mouth, hopefully, I won't have to hear any more fucking whining from him.

Getting home, I look up how to cook pizza on my phone. Scratching the back of my head, I read through it twice and then get to work.

Right on time, I hear my brothers arrive home. Shit, I forgot all about the corn. An acrid smell is coming from the oven, and I snatch the pizzas out, burning the tip of one of my fingers. "Fuck," I growl.

"That burning smell better not be our dinner," Alessio drawls as he and Marco take a seat at the kitchen counter.

I put the pizza in the center, and throwing the corn onto a platter, I add that too. Marco grabs some beers, and we're all set.

Even Mr. F, a large rust-colored Chow Chow dog, has woken up from his lazy slumber—the animal is sitting next to the counter, panting loudly as he waits expectantly for us to share the food. The dog's full name is 'Mr. Fluffy,' but we usually call him 'Mr. F'.

Marco frowns as he takes a pizza slice which looks floppier than it should be. He pokes at it. "The crust is soggy."

I shrug. "That's not my fault. The deli must have got something wrong with their dough."

Alessio slams his fist onto the counter. "For God's sake, I told you that I wanted proper *homecooked* food tonight."

Oh fuck, I wasn't supposed to mention the deli's contribution. "I made sure that it's organic and all that shit," I say in defense of myself. "It's not my fault that they don't know how to make proper pizza crust."

"Why are all the toppings burned?" Marco complains.

Jeez, not him as well. "There must be a problem with the oven," I reply.

"There's no problem with the oven," he growls.

"Yeah, there is. I mean, your wife's managed to burn every single thing she's ever tried to cook in it..."

His dark eyes flash at me—he doesn't take it well when we criticize his wife's cooking even though he knows everything we say is true. But before he can say anything else, Alessio takes a large bite out of a piece of corn. "Fuck! This corn is raw!"

I clear my throat. "Yeah, er, I know. Isn't it great? You can really taste all the vitamin C and all the, um, sunshine, that went into growing it..."

"For Christ's sake, Camillo," Alessio snaps. "There's no way this can be described as an adequate dinner."

I drop a bit of pizza on the floor for Mr. F. But taking one sniff at it, he gives a whine and then wanders off without a single bite. "*Traitor,*" I mutter after him.

"Maybe we should try again to get Savona back?" Alessio suggests in a desperate voice. "We could promise that Millo will go daily to confession for two whole months."

"No way." I fold my arms across my chest, but a slight panicky feeling comes over me. There's no way in hell that I could endure two months of going to confession daily. "You know how hard it is to find anything to confess about. As we can't mention any of the killings or other stuff, I always have to resort to confessing inane shit—and the priest always knows I'm lying by not confessing the really bad stuff we do. I mean, last time I went, I even had to pretend to feel repentant that I was having dark thoughts about Maximo being the reincarnation of the devil."

Marco narrows his eyes at me as soon as I mention his eldest son. "You said *what* about my son?"

"Come on, you can't be surprised about that. I mean, the little shit did put superglue in my shampoo bottle just a few weeks ago..."

Marco's obviously in one of his volatile moods—as always—and he looks like he wants to grab me by the throat and choke me.

"Don't worry, we're gonna have a proper homecooked meal tomorrow night," I say quickly.

"And how do you think you'll manage that, numbnuts?" Alessio clips.

"Because I've found a maid."

"You did?" Marco looks impressed, his attention instantly diverted from me insulting his son.

"Of course, I did..."

My brothers look relieved. But all I can think is... *why the hell did I just say that?*

***

As soon as dinner is over, I hole myself up in the office and dial the casino, telling them to give me the number for the woman from today. Then I call her.

"Um, hello?" she answers.

"Do you still need a job?"

"Who is this?" she says softly.

"Camillo Marchiano. Are you still looking for a job?"

"Yes..."

"You're hired. You start tomorrow morning. It's a live-in position, so bring your stuff with you."

I hear her suck in a breath. "I wasn't expecting to have to live in."

I sigh. Does she want a job or not? "Look, that's the deal. Take it or leave it."

"I'll take it," she says quickly.

"Okay. Meet me at the casino tomorrow at 10 a.m. I'll drive you to our estate and show you what you'll need to do."

Hanging up and sitting back, I tell myself that I only gave her the job to get myself out of a hole with my brothers. *Because there can't be any other reason, right?*

As I mull over my thoughts, my immediate relief at finding a job for Rosa and getting my brothers off my back starts to sway toward second thoughts. I scrub my hand across my jaw. What the hell am I thinking of, hiring a maid with zero experience? One who's as jumpy as a jack-in-the-box, no less.

All the things she'll break in our house if she's startled flash through my mind. Alessio's going to be whining like a bitch if she disturbs his fucking zen by dropping things left, right, and center.

She was beyond nervous during the interview. Her gaze kept darting away, unable to quite meet my eyes, and she kept startling at all the loud noises in the casino.

I wonder how good her housekeeping skills actually are. Because she definitely won't hang onto the job if she can't clean properly or, more importantly, cook. I groan as I remember her answers about her cooking skills. *Jesus fucking Christ, we're in for the worst week ever of meals.* My stomach clenches at the thought.

Oh God, Marco is going to chew her up and spit her out.

CHAPTER 5

ROSA

"You're hired."

Disbelief and elation rocket through me at the same time. I can't believe that he's called me back about the maid job. I thought he'd decided I wasn't worth taking a risk on.

"It's only for a month. Consider it a trial."

The relief that I just felt fizzles out at his words. Of course, it isn't permanent. I haven't got any experience—or any confidence.

I try to make my voice strong. I don't want him to hear my self-doubt, or he might just change his mind about even giving me the one month of work. "I understand."

"You start tomorrow morning. It's a live-in position, so bring your stuff with you."

Oh God, I never realized that he'd expect me to live in. But I can't turn down this job—because who knows if and when another offer will come along. And one thing's for sure: the sooner I can get enough money together, the sooner Ethan and I can leave Chicago and move somewhere where we'll be safer.

But the thought of what I need to do has my heart breaking.

Kathleen has stayed for dinner with us tonight, so I explain the situation to both her and Kori. "Please can you keep Ethan here and safe for me? I'll be back as soon as I've earned enough money to get away from Chicago. I wouldn't ask if I had any other option…"

And they both agree immediately, and their kindness makes my eyes fill with tears.

But the hardest part is when I have to explain to Ethan that I'll be away for a little while. "I'll visit as often as I can, I promise, and it's just while I earn some money so that we can make a new start."

He looks at me with his huge brown eyes, and my chest tightens. I can tell he's confused, and by the time morning comes, I've almost changed my mind. But then I tell myself that he'll be safe with Kori and Kathleen and that this is what I need to do if we are ever going to get enough money to start a new life for ourselves—somewhere far away from Chicago where we'll be safe from Grayden.

***

I make sure I arrive at the casino with plenty of time to spare. I instantly regret this, however, when I find myself having to hover in the foyer with Stella and the same security guard from yesterday looking down their noses at me.

I slept naked with just a sheet wrapped around me last night so that I could wash my clothing and leave it to dry until morning, but I can tell by their sneers that they've noticed I'm still wearing the same clothes as yesterday.

I try to tell myself that I showered this morning as always, including shampooing my hair, and my clothes are freshly washed and ironed, but I still can't help the flush from rushing up my cheeks.

I have a small bag that Kori lent me. Inside is a precious photo album of Ethan that I took with me when I fled from Grayden, plus an oversized sweater of Kori's that I can just about fit into.

Kori also insisted that she lend me a couple of books in case I have any spare time and want to try and keep my mind off things—as if I'm going to be able to do anything except think about Ethan—but I appreciate her trying to help me. Kori knows how hard it is for me to leave my son, especially after what we've just been through, but I know for certain that he'll be safe with her and taken care of.

Just after 10 a.m., I breathe a huge sigh of relief when Camillo—Mr. Marchiano, I correct myself in my mind—arrives. With each minute that ticked by past the allocated time, a hundred doubts rushed through my mind, worrying that he'd changed his mind.

He frowns when he sees my small bag. "Is that all your stuff?"

"I don't need much," I say quickly.

He reaches out a large hand. "I'll carry it out to the car."

"Oh no, please don't trouble yourself. I can manage..."

"Give it to me," he growls in a low voice, and I immediately hand it over, trying not to let my hand shake.

We get into his sleek black SUV, and I sit huddled in the passenger seat, trying to make myself as small as possible.

He drives through the streets with ease. His phone vibrates with messages in the holder on the dashboard, but otherwise, it's silent. His right hand wraps around the steering wheel, bulging the veins and drawing my attention to the pattern of lines that lead up his arms under the rolled-up sleeves of his dark shirt.

The open-mouth skull swallows a rose as it fades into the crackly branches of a tree, surrounded by more roses in some seamless blend of dark shadows and highlights like smoke. There's a story behind them, but I know it's not one I should be interested in. I swallow hard, turning my attention back to the front and not to the man beside me. Ruthless and bloody to the very core, he's dangerous—especially with those thick scars along his knuckles.

"Do you have questions?"

"No," I whisper.

"None?"

"No, sir."

He exhales before his hand flexes against the steering wheel, straining those inky lines. "Okay. I have a question."

I nod.

"Why did you agree?"

"Like I said, I need the job."

"Why?"

I open my mouth and snap it shut again.

"Never mind," he says when he sees I'm not going to explain further.

I fiddle with my hands in my lap, and I'm thankful when he changes the subject.

"Now, I know we addressed this in the interview, but you need to know a little more about what you're getting into with my brothers. You'll be in charge of the cooking, cleaning, maintaining the house, and ensuring that all our domestic needs are met in full. Okay?"

"I understand," I whisper.

The hand with the open-mouth skull rubs at his jaw, and he mutters another one of those Italian curses I don't understand. *"Nulla...difficile per chi..."* I want to ask him what he means, but I know my place. I'm an employee now. Seen and not heard. Spoken to and not with. I'm not here to get to know him or his brothers. I'm here for a job. Not to learn what makes a man like him tick, or why he'd chosen those specific ink designs. Ethan's counting on me.

"Why have the previous maids not lasted?" I ask carefully, wanting to know exactly what I should avoid doing.

He rubs the back of his neck. "From the maids we've had over the last month, I would say that there were four main issues. Maids 1 and 5 couldn't clean to my brothers' exacting standards. Maids 2, 3, and 6 couldn't cook for shit. Maid 7 lied to us by not telling us that her brother was a cop. Maid 8 stole from us and hoped we wouldn't notice. And Maid 9 just didn't last."

I take a deep gulp. Now I know what I have to do to keep this job...

I'll have to impress with my cooking and cleaning—but as Grayden has always found fault, I know I'll have to try much, much harder.

I can't lie to them in any way. Which is okay because I never lie—except when I forgot to tell Camillo that I'm on the run from my husband and that I have a son.

And I can't steal. Which is fine because I never steal. Although Grayden would definitely disagree with this—because he'd say that I'd just stolen our son.

Oh Jesus, I haven't got a hope in hell of keeping this job.

"We're here," Camillo says as he guides us smoothly through the gates, past scary-looking armed men, and up the drive.

His house—his mansion—is stunning, but the only real detail I can take in is the huge statue of the Virgin Mary which stands on the front lawn.

Then my eyes drop from Mr. Marchiano and hit my lap as finally I place his name and face... He and his brothers are business associates of my father—they're bloodthirsty made men. *Oh God, what have I got myself into?* Men like the Marchianos, Grayden, and my father take what they want and snuff the life out of things that stand in their way...

Grayden's criticism is one thing, but who knows how men like the Marchianos deal with failure and mistakes? I'm their employee now, and every single detail of my work and performance will be put under the microscope by them. The SUV parks up, and I stumble out. But my feet are rooted to the floor of the garage. And I feel panic rise.

My chest tightens.

This is a mistake.

I've been so desperate that I haven't thought it through.

I've traded one house of horrors for another.

"Rosa?"

My fists clench at my side. That faint little voice, the one that told me to run from Grayden, whispers it'll be alright. And I desperately want to listen to it now. Even if it's just for a week, I'll earn enough money to buy me some time to try again.

I can hear the breaths coming in and out of my mouth, faster and faster. The world swims, and dots dance across my visions.

"Rosa?" The urgent snap of his voice jerks me back to the present.

Ducking my head, I start walking toward the newest devil in charge of my life. I clench my teeth together and will my mind to quiet—to stop the string of thoughts that bombard me like bullets, each one shattering more of what remaining confidence I have after it's been battered again and again over the years. And now, there's nothing but a husk left behind—a husk of a woman I should have been but will never be.

With a feigned confidence and some semblance of dignity I don't feel or have, I lift my chin and meet Camillo's arched brow. He stands by the door, his head tilted as he regards me.

This is rock bottom, a pit of hell I'm willingly walking into, and I'm not going to give up. I can't give up.

My jaw nearly unhinges as I take in the interior of the mansion. From the outside, it seemed massive, but inside it hits me that this is now all my responsibility. Dread wells inside of me, threatening to cement me to the ground as he gives me a brief tour of the first level.

First, he shows me into a sprawling open plan reception room that's home to a spacious living room, a dining area, and a kitchen that is piled with dirty dishes everywhere.

He opens the refrigerator. "You'll probably have to stock up on food, but see what you can find for dinner."

I catch sight of some readymade pizza crusts and tons of various toppings—pepperoni, sausage, ham, mozzarella. They must like pizza—and that's definitely something that I can't get too wrong. "Shall I make pizza for tonight? There's plenty of ingredients—"

"No," Camillo snaps, making me jump. "Those ingredients are leftovers. I bought too many."

"What, er, would you like me to cook?"

"I'll leave that to you to figure out. Just make sure that it's not pizza."

I give a quick nod.

"And make sure that it's cooked through and not left soggy at the bottom," he blurts out.

My eyes widen as I nod again.

"And it can't be burned on top..."

I gulp. He's obviously remembering my feeble answers when he asked about my cooking skills.

"And make sure you include some vegetables."

"I can do that," I squeak.

"But make sure they're not raw."

Oh God, he's convinced that dinner's going to be a disaster—and after all the feedback I've got from Grayden over the last few years, I know that he's right.

He leads me into a small room a little way from the main reception room. "The previous maid used this as her bedroom." The room is tiny, almost like a broom closet, and it has a small attached bathroom. "We gave her the choice of our guest rooms, but she insisted she wanted to be on the first floor." He shrugs. "I think she might have heard Marco having sex. I mean, he *is* pretty loud—"

"This will do me fine for a bedroom," I say as quickly as I can.

He shows me the rest of the rooms on this level, including an office, plus so many other rooms that I find it hard to keep count of them all.

I climb the stairs slowly after him, holding onto the dusty banister as I follow his broad back up the stairs. A running list starts in my head as soon as I see each room and make a mental note of all the things that need to be cleaned if I'm to do a good enough job.

"This is my brother Alessio's room." He pauses, rubbing at his neck. "He's, um, particular about how things are put away."

I nod quickly. The heavy door opens, and I peer inside. It's relatively clean.

The next few rooms aren't too terribly kept either, but with each new room, the list in my head grows longer and longer. It'll be a tough job, but doable—I hope. Already, I'm mapping out the path to get it done in the most efficient way possible, plus what products I'll need and what equipment.

Camillo stops before another door, and he heaves a sigh. "You'll be starting here."

"Yes, Mr. Marchiano," I murmur.

"It's just... You can just call me Camillo."

I merely nod. Because calling him that would be far too familiar for someone I'm supposed to be working for. Even Grayden hadn't wanted me to call him by his first name. I shudder as I remember what he would say: "*Keep my name out of your filthy, worthless mouth, you stupid bitch.*"

Perhaps Camillo doesn't mind if I call him by his first name, but his brothers definitely might. I make another mental note not to call them anything other than 'Mr. Marchiano' or 'sir'—else I'll probably find myself out on the street once more.

"This is my room," he says as he gestures at the closed door in front of us. "I have to go and deal with some work stuff, so I'll leave you to sort out what you need. There are supplies down in the hall closet, some under the basin in the bathroom, and more in the cupboard next to the pantry."

So, spread out and far from each other. I nod, not wanting to cause problems already. Grayden always hated how I'd make sure all my supplies were on hand in a small rolling caddy unless it was specific to a room. He said it made me look like a cheap motel maid and not the wife of a prominent businessman like himself.

The sound of Camillo's thundering feet on the stairs makes me flinch, and I take a deep inhalation through my mouth, trying to settle myself. My hands shake as I turn the doorknob.

I immediately regret it.

The piles of dishes in the kitchen were bad enough, but this room looks like a bomb's gone off in it.

The same wood flooring from the hallway is buried beneath the piles—no, make that mountains—of clutter. Discarded clothing is tossed in heaps all over the place—it's hard to know what's clean and what isn't—and a multitude of empty drinks, car magazines, electronics chargers, and other various items lie discarded wherever they were finished with.

Oh God, what did I sign up for?

I take a few steps back into the hallway. Surely, he doesn't really live like this, does he? This is a test. It *has* to be a test. Right? And if I fail, I'll be out...

Okay, Rosa. One step at a time.

The mental pep talk does nothing for the way my body quivers. I ball my hands and make a quick beeline downstairs to what is now my bedroom.

There I find a closetful of clothes that the last maid must have left behind. She looks like she might have been a similar size to me. I run my hands over a pretty jade green velvet dress. Why on earth would she leave this all behind? I can only think that she must have left in a hurry.

I pick out a pair of black sweatpants and a simple white T-shirt. They're freshly laundered and ironed, and I decide that these will do as a makeshift uniform for now. Even though the top is a little too tight around my breasts and middle, at least it's clean and presentable.

From a simple glance, it's clear these men are almost as desperate as I am. The thought should make me feel better, should give me some semblance of power, but all it does is make me anxious. Because what it actually means is that there are even more things that they'll expect me to do perfectly, with every remaining speck of dust or smudge being stacked against me, just like Grayden used to do.

I go to the places Camillo mentioned and gather everything I can find to tackle the problems I've seen. The familiar feel of the bright yellow rubber on my hands and forearms is oddly soothing and enough to keep the panic from dragging me under its waves. And with the quick snap of a trash bag, I set to work in Camillo's room.

I start with the empty drink containers, mostly energy drinks, which look like they haven't been here for that long, thank goodness. Then, I decide to tackle the endless piles of clothes. On closer inspection, most of the clothes appear to be clean, but I don't want to risk putting a used item back into the closet, so instead, I bundle them to take down to the laundry room later.

Beneath the mass of clutter lies a luxurious dark room that might just suit the man I've met. The black wood paneling behind the enormous bed with rumpled black bedding is accented by a large ornate mirror that is too high to be anything but decorative. It's beautiful, even covered with dust.

I stirp the bed sheets and put them on to wash in the laundry room. And by the time I've cleared half of the room out, it starts to look hospitable again, and it's enough for me to see the finish line. Hauling another basket of laundry down, I notice the minuscule number of suits Camillo possesses. Instead, he appears to prefer plain black shirts, T-shirts, and tank tops, together with combat pants, jeans, chinos, sweats, and dark leather jackets.

I thought mafia men all prefer to flaunt their wealth with obvious designer suits that tell the world that money's no object?

Grayden certainly had loved to show off his money, opting for the most expensive and well-tailored suits he could afford, together with polished Italian leather loafers, expensive wristwatches, Cuban cigars for celebration, and anything and everything to prove to the world that he's someone of importance.

I step inside his closet and run my fingers over the clothes hung in there. I wonder why he dresses in the way that he does. But then, I dismiss the thoughts about Camillo's clothing choices from my head with a decisive shake. I'm snooping on day one. *What the hell is wrong with me?*

Getting back to work, sweat drips down the crevice between my breasts and down my spine by the time the floor is immaculate. The dark wood dresser that matches the bedframe is clear of clutter, dusted, and polished to perfection. Its sleek black surface shines back so brightly that I can see myself in the glimmer of the refection. But I wince away from looking at myself before I get trapped.

Going back to the task in hand, I notice that there's hardly anything personal in the room but work out equipment and wrapping for hands. Does he box, perhaps? With a body like his, that wouldn't surprise me.

I tell myself to focus as I move onto making the bed with the freshly washed bedding. The silken fabric is soft and warm against my hands as I struggle across the massive bed to get the sheet in place. My hands only tremble slightly with each crease of the corners. Perfect. It has to be perfect—the corners have to be tight enough to bounce a quarter off.

I swipe at my brow, dabbing the glow of perspiration away as I take in the now spotless room. It's massive, dark, and brooding, just like Camillo. It suits him.

The attached bathroom is actually quite clean, although again, it's beyond messy. I'm beginning to think that Camillo's real issue is a lack of putting things away rather than being dirty per se.

Next, I set to work on Marco's and Alessio's bedrooms, fighting the wince at the sting from the residual pain in my ribs flaring to life. But I charge on with cleaning, laundry, and ironing until a text from Camillo tells me that they'll be home in two hours. With most of the lower level now also clean, I decide I'll have to leave the remaining areas until after dinner.

Setting my sights on the pantry, I step inside, but my mind ignores all the ingredients that I could potentially use for tonight's dinner. Because my senses are overwhelmed by the far wall...

My eyes widen in wonder, taking in the sheer abundance of cakes and candy. The shelves there are stacked with colorful packages, each one a promise of sugary bliss. I remember now that Camillo said his brothers have six kids between them. That explains it. Although I should get back to planning dinner, I can't help but linger.

Because cakes are my weakness. My difficulty. *My Achilles' heel.*

Cakes are what lies between me and a thin, beautiful body.

I know I should turn around and vow to never look at these shelves again, but my feet stay rooted to the spot.

Brightly colored boxes of Twinkies catch my eye first. The golden sponges with creamy filling practically call out my name. I reach out, almost on instinct, my fingers grazing the cool wrapping. I can almost taste the spongy sweetness and the burst of vanilla cream as it melts in my mouth.

Next to them are Ding Dongs, and I imagine biting into the sumptuous chocolate cakes filled with fluffy white cream. And to the right, the shelf groans under the weight of a variety of Hostess cupcakes, their chocolate frosting glistening under the pantry's soft light. Each one is a work of art, topped with that iconic swirl of white icing.

Rows of Little Debbie snacks are neatly arranged, and Zebra Cakes, with their white icing and chocolate stripes, jump out at me. I pick up a box, feeling the familiar crinkle of the wrapper, as I imagine the first bite—the soft cake giving way to the sweet cream center, the chocolate drizzle adding just the right amount of richness.

It's a treasure trove of indulgence, and I can practically smell the sweet, tantalizing aroma—and the hundreds of calories packed into every little package.

And that one word—*calories*—wakes me up from my dream. It curls around me like an insidious whisper. Because all these tempting treats are off limits. I'm on a diet. I'm always on a diet. I can't remember a time since my teenage years when I haven't been counting every single calorie whether it's been a day of bingeing or fasting.

But the cakes look so good. My stomach growls, a traitorous sound that echoes my thoughts. I've been down this road before, and it never leads anywhere good.

I wrap my arms around myself, as if holding on tight will keep me from reaching out. The memory of the promise I make to myself every night before I fall asleep flickers through my mind.

It's not just about the cakes. It's about the feeling that comes with eating them. The momentary bliss that floods my senses with every bite—and the sweet escape from my troubles.

But that bliss is always short-lived, giving way to guilt and self-loathing that stick around much longer than the taste of frosting on my tongue. I know this cycle all too well.

I close my eyes and take a deep breath, trying to center myself. I picture the version of me that I want to be—thin, confident, healthy, and beautiful. She wouldn't be staring longingly at a table full of cakes; she would walk away without a second thought.

But that idealized version of myself seems so distant, almost like a stranger.

It's only when I check the time that I force myself to turn away. Because I have to keep this job. I have to get enough money for Ethan and me to get away for good.

Dinner. It still needs to be tackled. It has to be something simple that I can't mess up. With another glance at what's available, I settle on steak and homemade fries alongside a fresh salad.

As I peel and cut the potatoes, my gaze drifts to the kitchen counter, and a pang of longing shoots through me. Ethan should be sitting there doing his coloring while I prepare the meal. My heart seizes, and I nearly slice my finger before I banish the feeling and focus on what I'm doing.

The smell fills the kitchen and my mouth waters. I survey the spread. Freshly chopped salad with a homemade dressing and the steak and fries sizzling away as they cook. An angry growl erupts from my stomach. I've gone days without eating much, and this meal isn't for me.

I pull out the dishes and set the table. The last plate and the napkin leave my hands just as the front door opens.

I tug at the white T-shirt that's rising over the slope of my hips. My hands are clammy and shaking as I move back around the counter to clean up the small stack of dishes.

I hear someone go into the office while someone else goes up the staircase.

Dessert. Oh God, I've forgotten about dessert. "Shit," I mutter, wincing at the way the sound travels around the quiet space. The flannel slips from my hand and splashes into the hot soapy water, flinging the suds onto my T-shirt and chin. Hastily, I mop at them with one hand while the other hand fumbles around in the water to find the sponge.

Terror seizes my legs, and I lock them in place to keep them from wobbling over. The last thing I need to do is faint on my first day. But I know I've already messed up.

After a few minutes, I hear a couple of people coming into the kitchen, so I start to dish up. Their voices carry toward me until there's an abrupt halt in their conversation.

A low snarl sounds.

I whirl around.

"Who the fuck are you?"

And the blood drains from my face.

Two men dressed in black tailored suits and dress shirts glare at me. The slightly older looking one must be Marco. I can't find my voice as his pitch-dark eyes narrow onto me.

The other man, who must be Alessio, tilts his head and crosses his arms over his chest. "He asked you a question," he growls.

The walls close in, inch by inch. And Marco's eyes scan me like a predator about to pounce.

"I-I..." I swallow thickly. My mouth gapes open like a fish.

Marco's large hand slams against the counter.

Flinching, my back pushes up against the sink.

"Who. The. Fuck. Are. You?"

"Rosa," I squeak out.

"Rosa who?"

I try to speak again, but only a croak comes out. I grasp the counter with a tight grip to keep myself up. "I'm the...new maid."

"What's for dinner?" A familiar voice sounds as I watch Camillo shoulder past his brothers and slide into a chair at the table. "I'm hungry," he complains. "Can't you wait to chew her out until after we've eaten?"

"The new maid will tell you what's for dinner," Marco taunts without taking his eyes off me.

"I told you I hired someone." Camillo's voice rumbles in defense.

Marco looks me up and down. "Are you actually qualified to do this sort of job?" he demands in a terse, terrifying voice.

I can't breathe around the lump in my throat. It's like he can sense that I'm weak, worthless, and totally wrong for this job. He's like a shark in the waters scenting blood.

Everything is swaying.

I can hear the thunder of my pulse in my ears drowning out everything around me.

"Mr. Camillo hired...me today. One...month's trial."

Marco leans closer and looms over me, looking me up and down, pinning me with his terrifying stare. "I've got three rules for new maids," he says in a low, dangerous voice. "One. If you break it, you pay for it."

I nod my understanding.

"Two. If you fuck up, you're out."

I give a small squeak in response.

"Three. If you steal from us, you're fucking dead," he snarls.

And the only thing I can manage is a large gulp—as I wonder if the clothes left behind in the maid's room belong to a woman they killed...

I rapidly blink back the tears that are burning the back of my eyelids.

"Oh, and rule four," Marco clips.

"Come on, Marco," Camillo interrupts in a low tone that I can't quite identify. "You said there were only three rules."

Marco glares at him before turning back to me. "Four. If you're going to cry, go the fuck outside. I can't stand fucking criers."

I don't trust my voice, so I just give the tiniest nod while praying that the threatening tears don't fall.

Alessio narrows his gaze. I can see his mind whirling behind his eyes. But I can't work out what he's thinking.

"Smells good," Camillo says into the awkward silence as his brothers take their seats.

Marco grunts and sips at the glass of water. "We'll see." He's big and not as muscled as Camillo but nearly. The dress shirt pulls tightly across his chest, and his jaw is set tight. A perma-scowl wrinkles his forehead as he doesn't take his glare off me.

My legs feel wobbly as I place the serving dishes on the table before backing away slowly and tiptoeing into the hall.

My legs give way halfway to my room. I cover my mouth to muffle the sob as I press my head to the cool wall.

I shove myself up and make it the last few feet to my bedroom, closing the door.

Useless.

Waste of space.

You call this clean?

Do you really want to eat that now?

You don't have to take another serving. You can say no, it won't kill you.
You think this shit is something I'd eat?
You're just a worthless hole for me to fill tonight...

The words whispering in my head sound just like my father, mother, sister, and Grayden. They roar into a crescendo of noise, leaving me unable to hear anything but these words, each of them feeling like a knife in my gut.

I manage to make it to the bowl just in time before I lose what little's in my stomach, before sinking to the floor and letting my tears rush out.

But I know I can't stay here. I have to go back out and face them...

CHAPTER 6

CAMILLO

My fist tightens around my glass of water as I glower at Marco. "What the fuck was that?"

Alessio gives us each a glance before looking back down at his plate. Smart guy.

"What was what?" he snaps with his trademark impatience.

"That." I point to the kitchen where Rosa no longer stands. She'd quietly mumbled an excuse and moved into the hallway. "It's her first fucking day!"

"Why should I pretend to be nice now when I won't be later?" he clips. "There's no point in sugarcoating shit."

Walking in on Marco hovering over Rosa like that sent red across my vision. I only stopped myself because Rosa was almost in front of me, and there was no way in hell I was knocking her aside just to pummel Marco.

What the hell has gotten into me?

She's the maid. She works here, and I warned her what they were like. It's not my problem how Marco and Alessio talk to her. But it sure as shit feels like I need to stand between them and Rosa. She'd gone pale, and her eyes glistened with tears—but she'd nodded mutely, just taking it.

"You," I start, leaning forward in my seat, "told me to find a fucking maid. I found one."

"She needs to learn, Millo," Alessio says in a serious tone, swallowing a bite of his salad with a grimace.

I eyeball Marco. "You don't have to be so pissed off with her, Marco," I say as I eyeball him.

"I'm always pissed off in case you haven't noticed."

"Look, I know you're missing Juliana and the kids, but don't take it out on Rosa."

"Why do you care? And did she tell you that she can cook?"

"Yeah, she said that she could kind of cook," I say slowly. "Why?"

"Judging by the look and taste of this food, it's obvious she was lying just to get the job. And there's no way you, AKA Mr. Greedy Guts, is going to put up with a maid who can't cook. I should just give her the flick now. It looks like she's gonna be a crier as well, and you goddamn know that I can't fucking stand that."

"Look, Marco," I begin, but my words come to a halt as Rosa tiptoes back into the kitchen, her face a beautiful cold mask as she looks past us and stands by the stove. Her hand trembles as she starts to clear up.

"You," Alessio clips at Rosa, "and I need to talk."

Rosa lifts her head before dropping her eyes, and as I watch my brother glare at her, every muscle in my body constricts.

"You messed up my closet. I have a system for a reason," he growls as his knuckles whiten around his fork.

"Everything is sorted into color-coded order," Alessio continues. "If you can't do it right, don't goddamn do it."

"For God's sake, Alessio," I say. "Just about every item of clothing you own is black, so how can it have an order?"

"Even black has different shades, numbnuts, and my black clothes are all organized into a graduated order."

"Cry me a fucking river," I snap, taking another long gulp of my water. "Give her half a chance, and she'll learn your anally retentive ways." *Why the hell am I defending her?*

Rosa just nods and turns back to the sink, and we get on with the meal. And although it smells okay, the food is far from good—and I can tell that my brothers are thinking exactly the same thing. The steak is overcooked and dry, the fries are still raw and hard in the middle, and the salad dressing is too sharp with way too much vinegar. Thank God Marco doesn't point this all out to her—*it would probably* finish her *off*.

Conversation between my brothers fills the room, but I don't join in unless addressed. I spend most of dinner watching her.

From the outside, the woman is a skittish, meek, little kitten who a big bad wolf like me could play with and ruin until nothing's left. But there's something else there as well.

Secrets.

And secrets are a dangerous thing.

Because the more I watch her, busying herself with meaningless crumbs and specks of dust none of us would have ever even noticed, the more I sense there's something else which she's not telling us.

I'm not like Alessio who considers every angle before the attack. And I'm not like Marco who's like a finely honed knife. I'm blunt and to the fucking point. A bludgeon we use against anyone we deem unworthy. It's my job to tear down anyone and everything in order to protect our family and the Fratellanza. And as much as I'd like to think Rosa isn't a threat, she's a puzzle I can't figure out. And that's worse.

I need to figure it out. Then maybe I can explain this feeling in my chest and the way she draws my attention unlike anyone else has ever done. Because once I know what makes her tick, I can protect my family if things go sideways...

"Let's get ready to head back out." Alessio's words interrupt my thoughts.

"What?" I blurt out

He raises a brow. "The casino. We have *things* to do, Millo." His eyes lift toward Rosa, making sure that she's not paying too much attention to what he's saying. "We had a meeting about it, remember?"

"Right," I say after a moment's hesitation, pushing back my chair and standing.

And we waste no more words as we move from the table and down toward the front door. Like my brothers in front of me, I tuck the gun into the back of my belt. We pile into the SUV and clear out all thoughts except for what we need to do next.

"Alright, let's get this shit over with," I murmur.

***

I drag a hand down my face as I sag against the seat of the SUV. It's dark outside, and inside the vehicle, it feels like a lifetime since we had dinner.

I rub my jaw as I jump down from the SUV. Exhaustion pumps through me as I jog up the steps to the front door. On instinct, my gaze darts around the property, watching and waiting.

The electric perimeter around us is fully functional, and there are guards strategically placed in all key locations, but that doesn't stop me from checking every time I enter or exit the property. It's a habit. The thought of something happening to my family bothers me more than they'll ever know.

Alessio pushes me forward. "Move. I'm tired. I need to shower and sleep."

"Knock it off," I growl as I move into the foyer, shaking my head. The estate itself is quiet, and I strain to listen to anything out of place. Nothing.

The first thing I notice is that the place is clean—a spotless kind of clean. The kind it hasn't been since the day the women and kids hightailed it to Italy and the maid quit.

The second thing is the smell. The smell of something sweet takes its place. It's distracting and aggravating all at once. It smells good, but it also reminds me of Rosa sitting in the SUV. *Goddammit.* I shouldn't be entertaining thoughts of her at all.

Alessio brushes past me with a rough shoulder check before stomping up the stairs, leaving me at the bottom. Marco jerks his chin to the corner of the office where a drinks cabinet stands. God, yes, please.

Pouring two tumblers of whiskey, he hands one to me with a scowl.

I know what he's going to say, so I try to preempt it. "Marco, there wasn't anyone else."

But he continues to glower at me.

"You know, we've got a terrible reputation with the agencies..."

He narrows his dark eyes at me. "Quit making excuses for your shit choice of maid, Camillo."

"Aw, Marco, you don't know what I had to go through. One woman at an agency *actually laughed at me.*"

The scowl on his face eases a little, replaced by a murderous intent that's directed at the old bat who had the audacity to laugh. *I wouldn't like to be in her shoes tomorrow.*

We walk side by side into the lounge, but he comes to an abrupt halt in front of me just as he crosses the threshold.

"What?" I murmur.

Marco stalks forward, and I file in after him, my muscles tensed and my fists bunched, ready to defend us all if need be.

"For fuck's sake. What are you doing in here?" he roars at someone I can't see until I take another few hasty steps forward.

Rosa seems to have been sleeping on the couch. She leaps up and jumps out of her skin, nearly tripping over her feet. She blinks once, twice. "I-I'm sorry. I was..." Her gaze darts around the room with a wide-eyed look of alarm as if the walls might hold the answer.

Marco's arms cross over his chest. "I asked you a fucking question."

Jesus, the smell in here is even better than in the foyer—it smells sweet and delicious.

"I know, sir." Her gaze drops. "I was just finishing the dusting, sir. I just closed my eyes for only a second, I promise..."

I try to school my face into a neutral expression, but I can't help my brows from shooting up. We've been gone around four hours, and it's midnight now—has she been working that whole entire time?

Marco's glare at her doesn't change. In fact, it seems to only worsen. "That's not what I meant." His face is contorted into an expression I know only too well.

Rosa blinks, sucking her trembling lip between her teeth. Her brow crinkles. "I'm sorry, I don't understand," she whispers.

He walks forward, and I stride to slip in between them, giving my brother my shoulder as I turn to Rosa. "What he means is why are you still up?"

Again, her face morphs into confusion. "I'm, um, working."

"That eager to lose your job?" he snarls.

"Marco," I say in a warning tone as I turn to face him. I can see the flicker in his eyes before he settles them back on Rosa. The expression he wears used to make me flinch, but that was before I learned to read between the lines. Rosa doesn't have that experience.

"I'm not fucking paying you to work late hours and through the night," Marco growls.

"I understand, of course, sir." Her hands twist in front of her. "I don't expect you to pay me extra..."

She thinks he's concerned about how many hours she's doing because of what it will cost us? "I don't think he's worried about you charging us more," I say dryly. "He just doesn't understand why you're still up and doing more work after you've already spent the whole day working."

Her brow furrows in puzzlement. But before I can try to explain it any further, she mumbles out another apology and dashes down the hall into her tiny bedroom.

I shake my head. *Why the hell did she think just now that she had to apologize?* It's us who are taking advantage of her if she thinks we expect her to work fourteen-hour days.

Marco storms his way to the kitchen, downing his drink, and heading straight to the whiskey kept in there for a second shot of liquor.

"You could be a little nicer to her."

"Should I? You think you get to tell me how to treat my employees now because you what? Hired her?"

"No. I just—" I pause and look around the kitchen. "She's been here less than a day and already cleaned most of the place. The kitchen is fucking spotless." I gesture to the sink, no longer filled with dishes, gleaming under the glow of the lights. There's even a stand of cupcakes that look heavenly. That's what the delicious smell is.

I make a beeline for them. I take a sniff—lemon sponge with buttercream. My mouth waters. Sign me the fuck up for this. I'm starving now. I unwrap the cake from its paper cup and take a bite, holding back a moan of pleasure as the flavors explode on my tongue.

"I'm just saying, you weren't this harsh with the others on their first fucking day." I swipe a stray crumb from my lips as I talk around another bite of moist cake. "You told me to fix the problem, and she's the fix. You need to lay off a little."

Marco raises a brow, impatience flickering across his face. "Don't talk with your mouth full," he grits out. *Now he wants to talk about fucking table manners?* Sometimes, he still acts like the parent that he had to be to me and our youngest siblings when our parents died—it's like he can't ever shake that role off entirely.

I swallow, trying not to roll my eyes. He crosses his arms and studies me for a second as I polish off the last bit of cupcake before grabbing another. I'll work it off in the gym tomorrow. "I'm just saying that you snapping at her like that is the reason it was so fucking hard in the first place to find someone."

"You finished?"

"Yeah, maybe."

"Why do you care, anyway?" Alessio's voice sounds from the doorway where he leans with his arms crossed. He's freshly showered and has come back down to get some water.

"I don't care," I say over another mouthful of cupcake. God, if she bakes like this all the time, I'll have to up my gym reps. "She's already as scared as a baby kitten. Marco's just going to make it worse. That's all I'm saying. Look, not a fucking single agency wants to give us a maid. We're too terrifying. So, if she leaves or you fire her, then we're back at fucking square one."

But even as I say this, Alessio's words keep echoing in my mind. *Do I care? And why...?*

CHAPTER 7

ROSA

I purposefully got up at the crack of dawn this morning despite the late night, determined to do better than yesterday. Because I know that it will take just one small thing to make them send me back onto the street.

Things didn't start off well this morning after I knocked over Marco's glass of water at breakfast and burned the pancakes.

However, by the time it's late afternoon, with most of the heavy lifting taken care of, the mansion seems a little less large and overwhelming.

Sure, a couple of rooms have taken me a few hours longer to clean than I hoped, but I managed. It's nearly three now, and I'm finding that there is less and less to do except wait for laundry to be done.

I carefully place one of Alessio's shirts on a hanger and set it into his closet with care. Then I snatch it back out again, worrying that I haven't put it in the right place.

After he said that I'd messed up his system, I'm determined to prove to them all that I can learn and adapt. At first, I have no idea how I'm ever going to arrange Alessio's clothes to his satisfaction. The vast majority of his clothing is black, and although I understand there are subtle differences between the shades, how on earth am I supposed to grade those shades so that his clothes are arranged in a row of perfectly graduated black color?

I sink onto the side of the bed and put my head into my hands. I have to get this right—because it was clear as day that he was far from pleased with me last night.

An idea comes to me. I grab my cell from the kitchen and use it to take photos, one by one, of the clothes in his closet, also taking a picture of each label so that I know exactly what order he likes them hung in. Then, I do the same with the items in his dresser.

This should help me when I need to put away his laundry in future. Because this job needs to work out. There's no backup plan, and with the fear of facing the streets again, my fingers fumble as I take the last of the photos I need. Nausea sweeps through me at the prospect of failure—what will Ethan and I do when I fail?

When I fail. The words feel like a slap to the face, and I fight back a wince.

I told Kori I'd call tonight, but what will I tell Ethan? I can't get his hopes up yet. The ground under my feet is anything but solid. But if I can last the month's trial and get taken on permanently, then I might have enough money after three months for us to leave Chicago altogether. I just need enough for bus tickets, a deposit, the first month's rent, and something to keep us going until I find myself another job.

I bounce from room to room, my head a spiral of dark clouds. Each item I go to pick up comes with a second guess or a hesitation. Do they prefer it there? Have I messed up yet again? Will I be cornered in the kitchen again tonight when Marco and Alessio inevitably critique my work?

The clock down the hall chimes, and I make my way to the kitchen in a fog. Last night's meal wasn't great. And the unhappy expression on Marco's face told me that I need to do better. Be better. He's the one who'll ultimately tell me to go packing or not. He's the one who holds my future in his hands, though I'm sure the others will have a say as well.

Fear and doubt bubble in my chest as I wash my hands and set to work. I'll do a nice, easy chicken parmesan. I can manage that. I carefully slice the chicken, forcing myself to just focus on the knife and the cutting board—and not the words that utter in the back of my head, the ones that make my hand shake unevenly.

Grayden hated this for dinner, but it's the best option until I can get to the store tomorrow given what's in the fridge and pantry. Grayden always said my chicken was too dry, the sauce too salty, and the pasta too overcooked.

Setting the knife down, I close my eyes and take a calming breath. If this is the last night I get to work here, I'll have experience then. Someone else would hire me after that, right?

But the reality of it is that two days are not any better than no experience at all.

My mother and father are right. I'm useless. I'm just here. Taking up too much space. Far more space than I want to. I wish I could have returned to my family when I left Grayden—I'd wished for that so many times during my marriage. But marrying him is the only thing I've ever done that's made them happy and proud of me. Grayden's bound to go there, looking for me, and I shudder to think what they'll say when Grayden tells them that I've run away—and I know that my father would force me to return to my husband.

The time passes quickly, and as I'm checking the clock, there's a commotion at the front door before it opens and then slams shut, making me yelp.

I carefully set down the plate I'm holding and try to calm myself. It takes nothing at all for my heart to begin its frantic beating and my muscles to lock up tight in anticipation. I know that any one of them could come marching in here with fire in their eyes and a raised hand—and the smallest thing will cause them to ask me to leave right away.

"Try to stay the fuck still!" Camillo's deep voice hits my ears first.

"Next time you can get shot," Alessio says in a hoarse voice.

Shot? Did he say shot? Like bullets and actual blood? Oh my God...

"I told you both to fucking wait for me, but you had it all figured the fuck out," Camillo snarls before his broad body fills the doorway.

Alessio's arm is draped over his shoulder, and he's clutching his red-stained shirt. With a hiss, Camillo lowers him to the chair without so much as a glance at me.

I'm frozen on the spot, my breaths coming in and out, faster and faster.

"I don't need your fucking help." Marco's deep growl makes me want to hide. I swallow thickly before my body moves to the stove where the sauce sits in wait. None of them have addressed me yet, and I know better than to speak before being spoken to.

"Bullshit. You were nearly Swiss cheese. Now sit the fuck down."

Camillo flicks a long, glossy strand out of his eyes from where it's fallen out of the half knot at the back of his head. Crimson smudges against his forehead. His blood or his brothers' blood? I can't tell. "I need the first aid kit in the hall bathroom," Camillo says, peeling off Marco's ruined suit jacket.

Dark splotches of blood make bile run up the back of my throat.

"Rosa!"

I can hear the stuttered breathing from my lips, the clammy feeling of my body.

"Get the first aid kit. Now!"

Somehow, I manage to nod and turn on shaky knees. In the bathroom, my hands flounder with the box under the sink as I grab it. My feet tangle together, and I nearly trip as I move back into the kitchen to the injured men. Blood is seeping from their arms, and Alessio's side is leaking crimson.

I'm going to be sick. I can feel it rising higher and higher.

"H-her-" The words won't come out of my mouth, but I shove the kit into Camillo's outstretched hand.

"Fuck!" Alessio snarls.

"Don't be such a wimp." He laughs, though it's strained, forced. The tightness of his muscles beneath his black shirt tells me he's worried. "And don't move an inch until I get back."

I stand there in the middle of the kitchen dumbly. My gaze bounces between the two bleeding men and then to the floor. Drops and smears of deep crimson make a path to where they sit. My knees wobble as I clutch the counter before looking down at the unfinished dinner.

Camillo charges back in and shoves a bottle of whiskey into Alessio's face, earning him a grunt of what I can only assume to be satisfaction or gratitude.

As he gets to work, Alessio hisses again, a string of curses leaving him.

"Stop moving, and it won't be so bad."

"You're goddamn prodding me like cattle."

"Do you want the bullet to come out or not? I told you it was going to fucking hurt."

Numbly, I listen to the exchange. This is their normal life. *My* normal life now. The thought is terrifying.

"Stop! Christ, I swear to God and all the goddamn saints if you don't stop—" Alessio's words fade into foreign curses and grunts as Camillo continues to poke his side.

"Fine! Fine." Camillo looks around the room, distraught. His hands rake through his hair, dragging his brother's blood through the disheveled strands. "Fuck. Okay."

He meets my gaze, begging for an answer. There's something there in his eyes, something that breaks my heart and makes me want to move closer. It's just under the surface of his usual mask—but it's gone in an instant.

"Come here, Rosa."

He wants me to do something?

"I need your help."

"Me?" I squeak.

"Yes. Come here."

Slowly, I move forward. What's he going to ask me to do?

"I need you to get the bullets out. I can't get a good grip."

I look at the wound oozing, then back to Camillo. My breathing is rushed and harsh, coming in small pants.

"*Now, Rosa!*" Marco yells as Alessio's head sways and tips forward. "*Before he bleeds out!*"

My body snaps forward like my brain isn't sure what's going on. I carefully take the forceps from Camillo's hand. I ignore the way his fingers brush mine and the feeling in my stomach before I grab the pitcher of water.

"I'm sorry," I mumble repeatedly as I flush the wound with water. My hands wobble and shake as I approach the first of several bullet holes. My fist clenches on my thigh as I try to steady my outstretched hand.

"Here, put them in here," Camillo orders, tipping the salad out of the bowl I prepared for dinner.

The ping of metal against ceramic echoes, and it takes every ounce of my strength to keep from keeling over and puking right then and there.

Once Alessio is done, I turn toward Marco. I don't meet his gaze as I gently poke the wounds, unable to keep my hand steady. I don't want to see what kind of monster is lurking there tonight or what kind of brutal villain I'll see if I lift my eyes.

"*Hurry up*," Marco snarls, his jaw clenched.

I bite back a whimper and tell myself that it's no different from patching myself up or helping Ethan when he's scraped his knee. I've seen blood. And I've had it on my fingers... But this time, it's very different.

I take one inhale, then another, and set to work.

Once the bullets are out, Camillo hands me a needle. "You stitch Marco. I'll do Alessio."

Avoiding Marco's dark gaze lasering into me, I work the needle through his skin, watching each insertion and extraction as if I were in someone else's body.

When I finish the last pull, Camillo is wrapping Alessio's wounds and muttering to him about something I can't quite catch over the frantic beat of my heart.

The buzzer for the garlic bread in the oven sounds. I yelp and jump nearly a mile high, almost knocking over the bowl filled with bloody bullets and a few stray lettuce leaves.

My fingers pinch at my thigh in an attempt to distract me from the agitated beating in my chest.

I need to move. To do *something*. But I'm rooted to the spot. A shaky breath leaves me.

I tell myself I can't burn dinner. I take one step, then another, and feel how unsteady each movement is. My fingers are stained with red, and each finger has a tremor that won't stop.

My hands leave small prints on the counter until I make it to the sink. And then reality crashes into me.

These men behind me are far worse than my father or Grayden. They're the true terrors of the world. Every single one of them. Unphased by the blood that mars their pristine kitchen or the metallic smell of it in the air, they live within it, unbothered by the wounds that are now being wrapped up as if it's simply another day of the week.

And it is. *For them.*

My father was right when he spoke about them. His words come flooding back to me. He said that they're ruthless, brutal, bloodthirsty. Deadly in a way that sucks the air from the room and suffocates you. I'm nothing to these people. Expendable and replaceable. And that's never been more apparent than right now. They have enemies, and those people are just as dangerous when they retaliate against them. This is nothing like Grayden or the world I ran from. I've jumped from the frying pan into the fire. I'm trying to make my life safe—but it can never be this while I'm around men who are criminals for a living.

This is an entirely different world.

And I can't stay here for too long...

I willingly walked into the lair of a monster and thought if I worked hard enough, if I just did as I was told, I'd be okay. That I'd make it out of this. That I'd turn a blind eye and ignore whatever happened.

Stupid, stupid, stupid. I can hear Grayden's taunting laughter in my head, echoing the thoughts that continue to beat into me like punches.

Washing my hands, I watch as the red circles the drain, my fingers turning pink from the heat of the water. Tonight, after my call with Ethan, I'll have to figure out my next step.

Mutely, I turn toward the counter and begin to scrub the evidence away. It's not my blood, but it might as well be.

The soft murmurs of the brothers talking hit my ears before Camillo hauls Alessio out of the room and upstairs to his room.

And I'm left all alone with Marco...

CHAPTER 8

CAMILLO

After getting Alessio into his bed, I quickly shower, and then head down for dinner. Not much puts me off my food, and a delicious smell is wafting from the kitchen.

Getting back downstairs, I see that dinner is chicken parmesan—one of my favorites.

Rosa is creeping around Marco as she dishes up dinner at the table.

"For God's sake," Marco growls, "stop tiptoeing around. Just put the food on the fucking table."

"*Marco*," I say in a warning tone.

We start to eat while Rosa washes the pans. I try not to wince, not wanting to draw Marco's attention to how bad the food is. As if there's any chance of him not noticing...

"This chicken is raw in the middle!" he yells, clearly forgetting everything I said to him last night about being nicer to her. "Are you trying to fucking kill us?"

"N-no..." I see the moisture in her eyes before she ducks her head down and rushes to her room.

"Cut it out," I snap. "She's had a shock. We should be grateful that she helped and didn't faint."

"If she'd fainted, she would have definitely been out," he growls. "Next to criers, the next worse thing I can't stand is fucking fainters."

I can't help but roll my eyes at my brother.

"She did okay tonight," he grudgingly concedes after a few moments.

I wrinkle my nose at the meal in front of me. The chicken is bad, and the vegetables are soggy from being cooked for far too long. Maybe the salad would have been okay had I not slung it out of the bowl for the bullets.

The whole thing is a disaster. Except for the garlic bread—that is absolutely heavenly. Crispy perfection on the outside, melt in your mouth deliciousness on the inside, and the perfect amount of garlic. I'll definitely be filling up on this.

After eating what I can, I clear the dishes, not wanting to leave it for Rosa to do. I hide the uneaten food under some cartons in the trash—no need to hurt her feelings any more than Marco already has.

By the time I've finished, she still hasn't come out of her room. I walk to the door and listen.

I can't hear anything.

I knock softly.

There's no response.

"Rosa?"

But still no answer.

Some emotion bubbles up in my throat—I'm not sure what—and it makes me open the door a crack.

From there I can see her in the attached bathroom, scrubbing furiously at her hands.

And as I take a few steps closer, I see the expression on her face.

"Is everything alright?" I say, trying to sound casual, but there's a jolt through my chest. Ever since she arrived, she's been reserved and quiet, almost physically shrinking into herself to make herself as inconspicuous as possible.

Her gaze darts up and meets mine in the reflection of the mirror over the basin. There's no response to my question, just a shuffling of her feet as she reaches for the towel that is already stained with vivid red.

Her eyes are wide, unfocused, and she looks lost, like she's somewhere far away from this room. I glance quickly at her hands, at the crimson stains still smeared across her pale skin.

"Rosa." I keep my voice low, not wanting to scare her any further with the state she's already in.

Her eyes meet mine briefly, and she sucks in a sharp breath, but she still doesn't say anything. She can't stop looking at her hands, and it's like the blood on them is finally bringing home the reality to her of what's just happened.

As I watch her, it's obvious to me that I'm seeing only one thing in her right now: terror.

Without thinking, I step closer, my own heartbeat quickening. "Let me help you." My voice is gentle yet firm.

She doesn't resist when I reach for the towel, slowly loosening it from her grip.

I set it aside and let my arms guide her toward the basin. "Let's get you cleaned up," I murmur.

She follows my lead, her movements stiff. I turn on the tap, adjusting the water until it's hot, and then, very carefully, I take her hands in mine. Her skin is clammy and ice cold. Holding them under the water, I start to rub at them with gentle caresses, watching as the blood begins to wash away and swirl down the drain like thin red ribbons. This is nothing to me, but as Rosa sees the crimson in the water, a whimper escapes her lips.

My fingers whisper over her skin, and I can feel her eyes on me, confused and uncertain. She watches me with a sort of disbelief, like no one's ever shown her this kind of care before. The thought makes something twist inside my chest.

I rub my thumb over the back of her hand. "It's alright," I say softly. "The blood is coming away now. Hot water is better when it's started to dry."

When her hands are finally clean, I turn off the water and reach for a fresh towel. I pat her hands dry, taking my time, being as gentle as possible. I find myself thinking about what kind of life she had before coming here—what's left her so fragile and withdrawn.

I finish drying her hands and meet her gaze. Her expression is a mixture of confusion and something else—something softer, almost like gratitude, but hesitant.

"Why are you doing this?" she whispers.

"Because you needed help."

Her eyes widen slightly, and for a moment, I think she might cry. But she doesn't. Instead, she just looks at me, searching as if she's checking for a sign that this isn't a trick or a test.

I find myself hoping that she can see I really mean what I'm saying to her. "You don't have to be afraid," I say in a low voice. "Not here."

She blinks rapidly, as if trying to process my words, and then, almost imperceptibly, nods. "Thank you." Her voice is so quiet that I almost don't hear it.

And without another word, she turns and leaves the bathroom, leaving me standing there and holding the towel as I watch her go.

***

I come home mid-afternoon, and straightway, I'm drawn to the mouthwatering smell coming from the kitchen. I follow my nose and find Rosa putting freshly baked muffins on a cooling rack. "What flavor?" I ask as I grab one, not caring that they're still piping hot.

"Blueberry," she says shyly.

"Great." I take a bite, and closing my eyes, I give a sigh of ecstasy. "Absolute perfection."

But it's not just the food that's making me happy. I'm just glad that Rosa is still here and hasn't decided to hightail it out of here after what she saw last night.

Before she can turn back to the dishes in the sink, I know there's something I want to say to her. "Rosa?"

"Yes?"

"I...I'm, er, going to the hair salon this afternoon." I rub the back of my neck. "I wondered if, um, you'd like to come with me?"

She lifts her hand to her hair, a flush rushing up her cheeks. "Are you saying that my hair looks a mess?"

"Oh no, it looks nice. It's just I thought..."

How the hell do I explain this?

I clear my throat. "I thought that you might not know any hair salons around here," I finish lamely. "I thought I could show you where I go. They do both men and women's hair…"

"Your hair does always look good."

I feel my chest swell with uncertainty—but also with hope. Does she like what she sees of me?

"Is it expensive?" she whispers.

"No." Actually, it is. "They don't charge me—and they wouldn't charge you either as my friend. The salon is owned by one of my business associates." That's not strictly true, but I don't want her worrying about the cost and that being a reason for her to say no.

But she's still hesitating.

"And I can have you back in plenty of time to cook dinner," I rush on. *Jesus fucking Christ, that just makes me sound like a greedy guts who only thinks about his stomach and thinks her sole importance is as our maid and cook.*

"Okay," she says softly after a few moments.

And I let go of my breath, not realizing that I've been holding it while I waited for an answer.

***

I drive us to the salon, the radio on to fill the silence between us. I look across at her, hoping she's not regretting that she agreed to come with me. I wish I could think of something to talk about, but words escape me. I'm not the biggest talker at the best of times, but today I'm really struggling for some reason I can't explain.

When we arrive, I tell Rosa to take a seat. Then, I take the manager to one side. "Don't mention a single fucking price in front of her," I snarl.

His eyes widen as he nods quickly.

"And make sure you give the bill straight to me, and don't let her see it, or you'll regret the fucking day you were born, got it?"

He takes a huge gulp of air and nods frantically.

With that settled, I sit down in front of my usual stylist, Derek.

Derek is what can only be described as flamboyant. He has big hair and bright clothes, but he's one of the best stylists in the city.

Rosa sits in the chair next to me, and another stylist walks up behind her and gives her a warm smile through the reflection of the mirror. "Hey, I'm Helen. What can I do for you today?"

Rosa lifts her hand to her hair and flushes. "My hair's a bit of a mess. I cut it myself last time, but the scissors weren't sharp enough. And the color is fading."

She runs her fingers through the unbecoming faded black and brown-orange. "I think this color is a little wrong on you. I could take it back to your natural blond. It's really pretty, and most women would kill to have hair this color, you know—"

"I want to keep it black," Rosa blurts out in the loudest voice I've heard her use since I've met her. "I...I, er, like it this color."

"I guess it's nice to have a change if you've been blond all your life, right?" Helen says with a relaxed smile.

"Right," Rosa says quickly.

"I'll just freshen up the color and take out the brassy orange tones, if you'd like?"

"That sounds great, thank you," she replies softly.

"I take it I'm doing the usual for you, Camillo?" Derek asks.

"Yep," I nod. I catch Rosa's eye in the mirror. "I mean, why mess with perfection?"

And that makes her giggle, and it's a sound that lifts my soul. When she laughs, it's almost magical. Gone is the careworn woman, and in her place is a lighter, freer girl.

Helen is running an eye critically over Rosa's hair. "To get all the uneven ends level, I'll need to take it up into a shorter bob. The new length will be around the bottom of your ears—"

"No!" Rosa blurts out, her eyes widening. "It needs to reach my chin at least!"

Helen looks surprised, but she gives Rosa a reassuring smile. "Of course, we can keep it that long for sure. You have the sort of face that would look great with either length, but I'll keep your hair chin-length."

A look of relief washes over Rosa. I guess she doesn't like her hair too short, although it's a little strange that she doesn't want to get all the uneven ends off.

"We should get the head massages," I say to her. "They're, um, divine." I don't know why I just said that, but I once heard a customer in the salon say this to her friend.

"Okay." She smiles. And I can't help smiling back at her.

We sit side by side in the reclining chairs as we get our hair washed and our heads massaged. And to my surprise, the massage feels heavenly—or maybe it's because of the woman who's sitting beside me.

I sneak a peek at her, her eyes closed in bliss and a smile settled on her beautiful lips.

And I realize this is the most relaxed I've seen her since the day I met her. I don't know why, but she always seems as if she's carrying the weight of the world on her shoulders.

I know she's probably just naturally timid and nervous, but sometimes, it seems like there's something else going on with her.

My thoughts are interrupted when the massage comes to an end and we're ushered to sit in front of the stylists.

Derek and Helen chat away as they see to our hair, and Rosa even appears to let her guard down as she talks with them.

Helen is talking away as she lifts another section of Rosa's hair to cut. But then, Helen suddenly stills, and her unfinished sentence hangs in the air.

I look across at them. And I see that Rosa's face is frozen in horror.

"Oh, honey..." Helen says softly. "Is this why you didn't want your hair too short?"

Rosa nods slowly, her eyes shining.

And I look down to see what Helen is staring at.

It's at the base of Rosa's scalp—it's a large bald patch.

"Have you suffered some hair loss?" Derek asks after a quick glance. He's concentrating on my hair and isn't really paying attention to Rosa and Helen, and he hasn't noticed Rosa's expression.

When Rosa doesn't say anything, Helen reaches forward and grasps her hand tightly. "I've seen patches due to hair loss," she says quietly, "but I've also seen patches like this—I can tell that someone ripped your hair out... I'm so sorry, honey."

Derek's eyes instantly gleam with sympathy, and he pats her arm. "Don't worry, sweetie," he says in a kind tone, "no one can even see it, and it looks like it's already growing back. You'll be back to your old self in no time."

While they comfort her, I give her a small smile, hoping that this won't make her feel too awkward in front of me. "I'm sorry you had to go through that," I murmur in a low voice, and she shoots me a grateful smile.

The rest of the appointment passes with some casual conversation, and when we're back in the SUV and driving home, I look across at Rosa. But the only thing I can see is red.

And I know that when I find out who the fuck did this to her, he's going to be really fucking sorry...

***

As I dig into my stack of pancakes, I hear the heavy footsteps of my brothers echoing down the hallway. The scent of sweat and the faint metallic tinge of blood hits me even before they step into the room, telling me that they've just done their morning boxing training in our gym.

I barely spare them a glance as they stride to the kitchen counter, both bare-chested, wearing only their gym shorts.

Rosa looks up as they sit down, and her eyes widen as she takes in the sight of them. Her face pales as she stares at the blood on them, and I can see the fear in her eyes, the kind that's raw and instinctual. *She's scared.*

My eyes watch the way she's shrinking into herself and trying to make herself inconspicuous.

I glance back over at my brothers. Their muscles are gleaming perspiration, and the tattoos stretching across their broad chests each tell a story of the countless fights they've been through, the battles they've won, and the enemies they've made along the way. Them turning up to breakfast like this is nothing new to me, but it's crystal clear that it's making Rosa uncomfortable—more than that, it's outright terrifying her.

"Rosa," Marco barks.

"Y-yes, sir?"

"Maple syrup," he demands.

She grabs the bottle from the shelf, almost tripping over her feet as she rushes to bring it over to Marco. As she sets it down with a shaking hand, she knocks over the glass of juice he's just poured.

"Oh God, I'm s-sorry," she stutters.

Marco just looks at her with his trademark glare, doing nothing to help matters.

"Don't worry about it, Rosa," I say quietly.

Her gaze darts downward, and she dashes back to deal with the dirty dishes in the sink.

Marco pokes at his pancakes, scowling as he notices all the burned bits, but thankfully, he keeps his mouth shut for once.

We talk about casino business as we eat, but I find it hard to ignore the tension in her shoulders.

She mumbles something about seeing to the laundry and hurries off.

Marco frowns at her departing back. "I wanted her to make some more coffee," he complains.

I set my cup down with more force than necessary, the sharp sound making my brothers pause. "Make your own fucking coffee," I growl.

"What the hell's gotten into you this morning, Millo?"

"*You.*"

"Huh?" Confusion flickers across his face.

I eyeball my brothers. "Let's get a few fucking things clear," I snarl. "One, breakfast isn't the time to be parading around half-naked like a bunch of savages, so you wear a fucking shirt from now on. We're having breakfast, not going to a fucking brawl. Two, you say '*please*' to Rosa whenever you need her to do something. And three, I don't care if Rosa's food is fucking burned or if she's given you salmonella poisoning or if it's making you puke your guts out, you say '*thank you, that was delicious,*' after every fucking meal. Got it?"

My brothers just stare at me.

"*You were both scaring her.*"

"Are you talking about the maid?" Alessio asks with a puzzled look.

"Of course I'm fucking talking about the maid," I practically roar. And I see the realization dawn on their faces, but they still don't understand the gravity of it. They never do. To them, this is normal. To them, this is their home. But I see what they don't.

Marco raises an eyebrow. "Come on, Millo. We just finished training. It's not like she hasn't seen a man without a shirt before." Alessio shakes his head as he chuckles under his breath.

"I'm not fucking joking," I snap. But they still don't say anything else. "So help me God, tell me that you both fucking understand me before I punch you both in your fucking faces."

They hesitate for a moment, the stubbornness that runs through our blood making them want to push back. But they know better than to cross me when I'm like this. Slowly, grudgingly, they both nod. "Sure, if it stops you acting like a bad-tempered bear at breakfast time," Marco grits out. "But tell me, Millo, why the hell do you care so much?"

I pause for a moment. "She's new. Be nice to her." And that's all I say—because I don't know how else to explain it.

"She's caught your eye, hasn't she?" Alessio clips.

I choke on my mouthful of food and shake my head. "What?"

"I *said* she's not terrible to look at. That's why you want to keep her around, right? It's been a while since you've gotten any ass," Alessio clarifies.

Marco shakes his head. "Bad fucking idea, Millo."

"First off, fuck you both." I take a gulp of my coffee. "Second, she made the best cupcakes I've had in fucking months. I'm not letting Mr. Moody Muppet here ruin this for me. That's all."

Alessio and Marco exchange a look as I slam my cup back onto the counter. My fucking brothers think they know everything there is to know about anything now that they've gotten families of their own. But one thing's for sure—they couldn't be more fucking wrong.

As we finish up and are pushing back our stools to stand up, Rosa comes back. She's still shaking a little, but I can see that she's trying to compose herself.

Marco and Alessio start to walk away, but I block them, bunching up my muscles and shooting them a glacial glare.

"Uh, thanks for breakfast, Rosa," Marco says slowly.

"Yeah, it...was delicious," Alessio adds with reluctance.

And I give them a satisfied nod before letting them pass.

They turn and leave the room, their footsteps heavy with irritation. I don't care. They need to learn that this isn't just their home; it's mine too. And I need Rosa to feel safe here...

CHAPTER 9

ROSA

After the men leave for the casino and I finally calm myself down, I tidy up the rest of the breakfast dishes. The sight of Marco and Alessio bare-chested, bloody, and scarred was utterly terrifying, reminding me too much of when Grayden used to stalk toward me with that crazed look in his eyes and his fists bunched, ready to take out his anger on me.

I'm puzzled why they said breakfast was delicious though—I tried really hard, but the pancakes were all burned, and I know they must have noticed.

As I start on the cleaning, I can't help my mind drifting back to yesterday at the hair salon. I thought I'd feel embarrassed when Camillo, Helen, and Derek saw that some of my hair had been ripped out. But their reaction—it was unexpected...

They didn't blame me or say that it was my fault. *They didn't make me feel any less for it.*

I twice confided in my mother about what was happening with Grayden—how he treated me badly and hit me.

I still remember her words: *"You must have done something to upset him. Can't you even do this one thing right? Don't ruin things for your father—he married you off to Grayden to help their business relationship, not to wreck it."*

And the second time, her reaction was even worse when I told her that Grayden had beaten me after I refused to have sex with him when he was drunk: *"Did you think that your marriage was just going to be about wearing pretty dresses and spending all of Grayden's money? Of course, he expects to have marital relations with you. Don't ever bring such a vulgar topic up again."*

I still shudder when I remember her sneers at me. Her blame. Her disgust that I was her daughter.

But after what happened at the salon, another thought skitters through my mind: maybe, just maybe, I'm not to blame for everything that's happened...

***

I'm holding a notepad and paper to make a shopping list as I stand in the pantry. I should be writing, but instead, my senses are drawn to the far shelf, looking for just a little snack to keep me going until dinner. I'll just get something like a rice cake—that'll be fine because it's something that won't upset my perpetual diet.

But then I see them, sitting there innocently on the shelf. *Lemon sponge cupcakes.*

Automatically, my mouth waters just thinking about them, especially imagining the soft spongy cake melting on my tongue.

I tell myself to walk away, firmly shut the pantry door behind me, and find something else to do.

But my feet stay rooted to the ground. My hand reaches out as if it has a mind of its own. I pick up the box and crack open the lid. Just a sniff of their delicious scent will be enough to tide me over...

As soon as the lemon and sweetness waft up, my resolve crumbles. I'll just have one. It's just so I can satisfy my sudden craving for something sweet, and it'll mean that I stop obsessing about food for the rest of the day.

I take the first bite of deliciousness, and that's when I know I'm in trouble. The cake is soft, moist, and has the perfect balance of tart and sweet. The frosting is perfect with its creamy texture, and before I know it, the first cupcake is gone. I stare at the empty rippled paper in my hand, feeling the guilt start to creep in. I should stop now.

But I don't.

I reach for another cupcake, my hand trembling slightly as I peel it from the paper. The second one disappears even faster than the first. I know I should stop. I know I'll regret this later. The pull is too strong, the need too intense.

My heart is racing with the third cupcake, my body going into a sugar high. And the addictive taste makes me snatch a fourth cupcake, barely tasting it as I shove it into my mouth.

When I've finished all four cupcakes, I'm left staring at the empty paper scattered on the shelf in front of me and feel a tsunami wave of self-loathing come crashing down, taking with it some of the pleasure I've just felt.

How could I let this happen again? How could I be so weak and so greedy? My stomach churns, and it's not just from the cupcakes but also from the sickening realization that I've failed myself once more. This week, I'd been doing so well, counting every calorie, sticking to my plan, and being strong. But all that hard work is undone in the space of a couple of minutes.

I'm left wanting to cry and scream at the same time. But instead, I just stand there and look at the crumpled paper cups in front of me as I feel utterly disgusted with myself. I've always been the fat one, the girl who couldn't say no, and I've proven it once again.

I wish I could turn back time, just go back a few minutes so that I could choose the right path and undo the damage I've done, but I can't.

Tomorrow, I'll start over. I'll be good again, I tell myself. But today, the bitter taste of regret lingers, and I can't escape it.

***

Marco comes into the kitchen about an hour before I expect the brothers home.

"You're early," I blurt out in panic. "I was just about to start on dinner, but I thought it didn't have to be ready until 8 p.m."

"I'm not early," he growls.

I swallow the knot in my throat. "But—"

"Rosa, explain to me why your cooking is so shit."

My stomach drops.

And I can't catch my breath as his gaze lasers into me.

Deep down, I should have known this moment was coming.

I'm standing in his grand kitchen and trying to find the right words to get me out of this. But my mind is racing. Even the pots and pans seem to glare at me—as if they, too, are disappointed.

His stare at me is ruthless. Calculating. He's waiting for an explanation. I know he's not the kind of man who tolerates incompetence.

I have to keep this job. Oh God, what will I do once he fires me?

"I... I'm sorry," I finally manage in a voice barely above a whisper.

I hate how small and shaky I sound. I'm trying to inhale through my nose to steady my racing pulse. My hands are trembling. I clasp them together in front of me in a futile attempt to hide the state I'm in.

He's still glaring at me with those piercing dark eyes. But I can't quite work out what he's thinking as he stares. His expression is unreadable. And that only makes things worse.

I wish he would say something, anything, to break the tension. But he doesn't.

He's waiting for me to continue. And I know I have to explain myself.

"I'm just not used to...this kitchen." I gesture vaguely around the room.

"Bullshit," he snaps.

I'm taking shallow breaths. But my lungs can't get enough oxygen.

He takes a deliberate step toward me.

My heart is thudding louder and louder as he gets closer.

He's going to tell me to pack up my things and leave.

"You make these." His fingers jab at the cupcakes I've made on the cake stand. "Which means that you are used to our kitchen."

My cheeks burn with embarrassment. How do I explain that I know that I'm useless? How do I tell him that he doesn't need to say anything more because I get the message?

"If you can bake cupcakes, muffins, and all that other sweet stuff, you clearly know how to use kitchen appliances, read a recipe, and tell the time. So, why the fuck can't you make a single meal that isn't burned, undercooked, or soggy?"

"I...uh...I...uh..."

My thoughts are in freefall, and I don't know what to say. How to explain. But I know I have to try if I've got any hope of keeping this job.

I swallow down the lump lodged in my throat. "It's not that I can't cook, sir. I can, really. I just...get nervous."

"Why?" he demands.

I close my eyes for a second. "When I've cooked in the past, no one...else ate the sweet things." What I really mean is that Grayden never ate the cakes I made because he hated desserts. "I was baking the sweet treats for myself." And for Ethan, who loved my cakes—but I can't mention my son. "I got confident at baking because I had plenty of practice and no one to judge me." Because I didn't have Grayden criticizing every single aspect of it. "But I never gained confidence at cooking dinners and meals—I always knew other people would eat them and judge my cooking skills." Because Grayden made sure to knock me down every chance he got.

Marco continues staring at me. "What makes you relax when you're in the kitchen?"

"Relax?"

"Yes," he grits out with impatience. "Relax."

"I, um, like music. And dancing to it." I can't believe I'm admitting this to anyone, let alone to the fierce man who employs me.

"Dance then."

"What?"

"I said dance. Listen to music, dance, and pretend you're the only one who's going to eat the dinner you're cooking."

"But I can't do that—"

"Yes, you can. And I'm going to stay here and make sure you cook our dinner properly for once."

I shake my head. "I can't dance and cook while you watch me," I exclaim in horror.

He narrows his eyes at me and gives a small sigh. "I'll sit in the breakfast nook, facing away from you. I'll do some work on my phone.

But I'll be able to smell if anything's burning." He glares at me. "Because you've managed to burn something in every single meal you've made so far. And as you're staying, you need to stop ruining every fucking meal."

I take a big gulp. "I'm staying?" I murmur. I can't have heard that right.

He gives a sharp nod but still doesn't smile. "You helped us the other night—getting the bullets out and stitching the wounds. You proved your loyalty."

"I really wasn't trying to kill you with the raw chicken," I blurt out. Shit, why did I bring up the disastrous chicken?

"I know."

"You do?" I'm holding my breath. He could still change his mind.

"Yeah. If you really wanted to kill one of us, you would have let Alessio bleed out...or at the very least, put poison in one of our meals by now."

It's my turn to narrow my eyes at him. *Is he mocking me*? Does Mr. Marco Marchiano have a sliver of a sense of humor lurking beneath his steely exterior?

"You better get started," he drawls. "My brothers will be home in fifty minutes."

I watch him walk to the breakfast nook, and as promised, he sits with his back to me, taking out his phone and dealing with what looks like emails.

I collect the ingredients I'll need and stand in front of the kitchen counter while my fingers grip the edge as I stare at the things laid out in front of me. Beef, mushrooms, onions, garlic, sour cream, plus a few other things I'll need.

Despite what Marco's just said to me, my nerves are winning by a landslide.

My hands tremble as I tie the apron over me, delaying starting by smoothing down the crisp fabric to steady myself. I have to keep reminding myself to breathe, in and out, deep and slow. But whatever I do, my stomach's still in knots.

"Forty-five minutes, Rosa," Marco says in a terse tone, unhelpfully reminding me that the time is ticking by. "Imagine that you're the only one this meal's for. And for God's sake, get some music on."

I clear my throat and grab my phone. Scrolling through the screen, I choose an upbeat playlist—something that will keep my mind off my anxiety.

As the music fills the kitchen, I chop the onions. I keep peeking up at Marco, but true to his word, he's staying faced away from me.

Biting my lip, I start to move a little, just a sway of my hips and a tap of my foot here and there, all the time making sure that Marco doesn't go back on his word. As each song finishes, the next one on the playlist starts automatically.

After a while, I'm confident that he meant what he said, and I let the rhythm take over. My feet shuffle across the tiled floor, my body swaying, turning, twisting to the beat. The tension in my shoulders melts away, and my hands become steadier, more confident.

The sizzle of the beef hitting the hot pan blends with the music, and I stir the pieces around, browning them to perfection. I can feel myself smiling, my earlier nerves starting to fade as I focus on the task at hand. The music is like a shield, something that can block out my worries and my fears of making a mistake.

The scent of garlic and onions fill the air around me as they sauté. I put on the rice to cook and make a salad. I move to the fridge, still dancing after grabbing another quick peek at Marco, and select the mustard. Twirling around, I return to the stove, and I'm in my own little world. I don't even think about who's going to eat this meal. It feels like it's just me in the kitchen, cooking, dancing, and feeling free.

The stroganoff is coming together beautifully, the sauce thick and creamy as it should be, while the meat is tender and flavorful. I add a few finishing touches with a sprinkle of parsley and a dash of pepper, all while moving and spinning in time with the music. The kitchen feels alive, full of warmth and energy, and for a moment, I forget about everything else.

As the current song reaches its final notes, I glance up, and my heart nearly stops. He's looking at me, a slight smile playing on his lips.

I put my hands on my hips. "You said you wouldn't watch." My tone is indignant, forgetting for a moment that he's my employer.

He walks over to the counter and chuckles softly. "I only looked up at the end to make sure you had everything under control."

I relax ever so slightly. "And?"

He takes a plate and puts a small taste of stroganoff, rice, and salad on it.

I'm holding my breath as he eats it, my eyes glued to his face for any signs of a grimace or wince.

But he smiles. "Delicious. I knew you could do it."

My brow crinkles. "*You did?*"

He looks up. "Look, Rosa, I don't know what happened to you before you got here—"

"I-I…" My words stutter out in horror.

He puts his hand up to stop me. "I don't care about your past." He looks at me carefully. "But you can't let fear take you over. You're more than capable—you proved it the night we were shot. Sure, you were a little shaky, but you managed to hold your own. Your confidence is in there somewhere, buried under all the doubt and anxiety. You just have to let it out."

We hear the front door open, and Alessio and Camillo's voices drift toward us. And with that, Marco turns and walks away.

***

Later that week, I'm in the kitchen and hum softly as I finish putting the oat and honey flapjacks on the cooling rack. The house is quiet. The Marchiano brothers have gone to do whatever it is they do. I try my hardest to keep my mind off that very topic.

I don't have a plan to get away from here yet. I should, but it's moments like this when the estate is at ease that I feel oddly safe.

It's wrong to feel this way. But my brain doesn't seem to realize that this house of vipers is just as bad, if not worse, than Grayden's mansion.

But that's not exactly true, is it? I've adjusted to the harsh commands and tones of the Marchiano men—their barked orders and eccentric way of doing things. They have a ferocious bark, but I've yet to see any of them bite. They're harsh but not insulting.

Maybe that makes me naïve. Grayden didn't have nearly as bad a bark, but his bite was deadly. I should have learned this lesson already.

But watching how the brothers interact with each other at meals or in daily life, I've seen brief glimpses of something different lurking past the hard veneer of these made men. It's not tender by any means, but it's there. They fiercely protect and love each other.

Envy crawls through my chest. I want that, but I don't deserve it. That's reserved for someone who's better than me. Someone who's worthy and not unlovable. Grayden never said he loved me, but he didn't hesitate to tell me how much he hated me.

I shake my head of these thoughts, turning back to my next task.

I've come up with a system for dealing with the estate. I tackle the ground level before anyone wakes up, see to breakfast, and then, turn my attention to the first-floor rooms and laundry. From there, the day blurs until I'm setting out the food for dinner.

My stomach churns and clenches every time my gaze lands on the polished wood floor. Phantom splotches of blood linger there, despite having scoured them away.

It should scare me, and it does, but not enough to give up this job.

Pushing the thoughts away, I focus on setting the table. My stomach rumbles, but I ignore it. I don't take breaks unless dizziness sets in, and even then, it's only for a quick nibble of a cracker before I go back to work. I don't want anyone to think I'm slacking. *And skipping another meal won't kill me.*

The heavy thud of a discarded gym bag hitting the floor echoes through the house. It's early for anyone to be back, but it's not my place to say it.

Camillo strides into the room, his face glistening with sweat, and a few loose strands that have fallen from his usual knot are plastered to his face.

Surprisingly, my small bubble of serenity doesn't shatter even with the intrusion from him.

He's wearing black sweats that hug his muscular thighs and one of those work out tanks with large armholes that show off the ropes of muscles beneath. The black ink that crawls over both his arms is exposed, and I swear the smokey effect moves with every flex of his body.

He makes a beeline to the fridge without a word. And I watch as he guzzles down water from a large bottle. The way his throat works and the trickle of a single drop from the corner of his lips to his chest... My eyes drop to the counter as I feel heat crawl up my neck.

The crinkle of plastic makes me jump. It's too loud and too sudden. And seeing his massive hands curling around the plastic and crushing it makes my heart rate triple.

I try not to look at him, but I can't help a glance as he grabs another bottle. His knuckles are battered and freshly bruised.

Alessio said he needed Camillo to take care of a problem. I'm not stupid enough to forget that Camillo is the muscle and deals with the messier side of things. That much I've been able to figure out.

I can't tear my eyes away from his hands as he crushes the empty bottle again. I'm enraptured by it.

"What's for dinner?"

My eyes snap up to his, holding them for a quick moment. I glance away and clear my throat to keep the words from shaking. "I was planning on making beef ravioli with a pumpkin sauce."

"Sounds great." He goes to walk off but then pauses. "Can you make some of that garlic bread again? It was delicious."

I give the tiniest nod, pleased that my cooking has improved no end since that little pep talk from Marco.

I turn back to the counter where I was chopping. Carefully, I slice the carrots and bell peppers, setting the pieces out on a platter. I realized after my second day that Camillo is a big snacker, and rather than risk accidentally messing up and being tossed out on my ass, I've made it a point to make sure there is a healthy amount of fruit and vegetable platters always available.

Wordlessly, I push the platter toward him and start to wash the board and knife.

"Thanks," he murmurs as he flops onto a barstool. "Can I do anything to help?"

Alarm flares to life inside me. "No!" I blurt out before mustering a weak smile. It's the same one I mastered living with Grayden, the one that doesn't quite reach my eyes. "No, no, it's okay. I've got it under control."

Does he think I'm slacking off? That I can't do all the work they've given me? My breathing picks up, but I struggle to take a full breath. If he thinks that, then maybe so do his brothers. Maybe Marco has changed his mind about giving me the job, and this is their way of telling me to pack up and hit the road...

The screech of his barstool against the wood flooring makes me wince. I can't quite find the courage to look back up at him. "Rosa?"

I hesitate. "Yes?"

There's a long pregnant pause, and I distinctly hear him curse under his breath. "I'll leave you to it. Thanks."

I nod slowly, lifting my eyes back up to his retreating form, the muscles of his back bunching and pulling tight.

It takes me another heartbeat to realize I'm not moving. Instead, I'm rooted to the place, trying to identify the feeling rumbling to life inside me.

But I come up empty-handed.

***

The rest of the afternoon passes in a blur, and the next thing I know, everyone is arriving home for the evening meal. I'm standing at the counter slicing the garlic bread I've just baked.

"God, it smells like heaven in here." Camillo's low voice rumbles as the men slide into their usual seats around the table.

He's changed from the work out gear he was wearing earlier into what I've realized is his usual attire—an expensive black shirt pulled taut against his giant frame and designer jeans. It's different than the suits his brothers wear, but it suits him. His thick, glossy hair is in a messy knot, a change from the half-up style he usually sports.

I want to brush the compliment away to the side. I want to tell him it's not that fancy or worthy of praise. I want to tell him that he doesn't need to lie to save my feelings. My head dips, and I set the plate with the bread down on the table.

Camillo's large hand catches my wrist.

I freeze. My cheeks heat at the realization that he's so near that he can probably hear the frantic beating of my heart.

Tingles race up my arm. And my hand trembles within his grasp. It's a loose hold, and if I wanted, I could pull my wrist back.

But I can't move.

His sandalwood and sage scent fills my nose, and I fight the urge to inhale deeply. It's warm and inviting—and nothing like the man who wears it.

"Thank you for the bread...and well, dinner."

His voice is soft yet gravelly at the same time. I want to think that there's something more to what he's saying.

But that's simply wishful thinking in some fantasy land I've been dropped into. I bite the inside of my cheek to snap myself out of it. I'm reading into something that isn't there.

My mouth opens to brush it off, but the words are lodged into my throat.

Camillo releases my hand as if it's burned him and clears his throat. I hear him gulp at his glass of water. His brothers don't seem to have noticed a thing.

But I can't bring myself to look at him. To see if there's something in those deep brown eyes that'll explain what's just happened.

I hurry back to the counter for the rest of the meal. Someone moves behind me, but I don't turn. I don't dare look back—because I know I'm seeing things that aren't there. My stomach is in knots as I quickly finish putting the dishes out.

Afterward, on shaky legs, I manage to make it back to the island and begin cleaning up. It's not quite the distraction I need it to be as my traitorous brain keeps replaying the feeling of his calloused fingers wrapped around my wrist, the heat from his hand permanently seared into mine.

What on earth is going on with me? Maybe I'm coming down with a fever or something. Is that why I'm reading too much into a simple friendly gesture?

Of course, that's it. It has to be. One nice thing was said to me, and I got a fuzzy feeling inside my chest.

He's just being polite. Thanking me and complimenting the cooking. He doesn't mean it in the way I'm taking it.

What can I expect, though, when I learned to lick scraps of love off knives instead of being fed it on a silver spoon?

I shake my head. I need to get a grip and remember why I'm here.

Remember just how important this job is.

I can't mess it up.

And ogling one of my employers or letting myself develop any sort of attachment to him is definitely a step in the wrong direction.

But each time he speaks, his gravelly rumble sends a shiver of something down my spine.

It's messed up and wrong to want a man like him—to hope that he might see me in some way that isn't fat, repulsive, and broken. The words of everyone in my life haunt me like ghosts, reinforcing what I already know. I am nothing. Not to Grayden. Not to my family. Not to these men. And especially not to *him*.

Yet the little pitter-patter of my heart tries to stoke that crushed and crumbling spark inside me back to life.

And it whispers faintly, *but what if...?*

CHAPTER 10

CAMILLO

Rosa's cooking has improved by leaps and bounds lately. I don't know what's changed, but she's less nervous when she's in the kitchen.

It's still early as I sit at the island with my coffee while Alessio is flipping through the newspaper. Not much goes on at breakfast except for some business talk usually. But today is different because the tension in the air is thick. And it's all about...

Cupcakes.

Yesterday, Rosa made chocolate brownies, all rich, soft, and gooey. The day before, it was a peach pie that nearly made me weep. But today is cupcake day. And cupcakes are my absolute favorite.

"Rosa, I think you should make banana chocolate chip cupcakes," Alessio says, trying to sound casual, but I can hear the underlying edge in his voice. As his arms lean on top of the kitchen island, he stares at Rosa with that intense look he gets when he really wants something. And things with banana or chocolate chips are his favorites, but when they're both together, he feels like he's won the lottery.

Rosa, standing by the oven, nods politely. "Banana chocolate chip, okay."

"Wait," I grit out as I slam my coffee cup down, the liquid sloshing out onto the counter. "Rosa, if you're making cupcakes, I think your peanut butter cupcakes with the special frosting are the way to go." I can already taste the decadent frosting with the special drizzle of honey that Rosa adds at the end. "You know, a little something rich and satisfying, not just predictable banana chocolate chip."

Alessio rolls his eyes. "Banana isn't predictable, and chocolate chips are a classic and the foundation of all good desserts."

"Foundation, maybe," I shoot back, "but it's boring. Peanut butter has depth, it's—"

"Boring," Alessio cuts in. "Everyone's doing peanut butter cupcakes right now."

Food is an important part of my life; when it's something made by Rosa, however, I just turn into a crazy person. I don't know why but I want her to cook and bake only for me, and I don't want to have to share her with anyone else. I want to be the one showering her with compliments, I want to be the one building up her confidence—and I want to be the one making her smile.

"I could make a small batch of both?" Rosa suggests carefully. "That way, you can both have your favorite."

My head automatically shakes, my freshly washed locks swinging from side to side. "No, no, no. Nuh uh. That won't work. If you're making banana chocolate chip *for him*, that means less peanut butter cupcakes *for me*."

Rosa raises an eyebrow at us both.

"A small batch of both flavors sounds a good compromise," Alessio says with a scowl.

"Although, if you don't have enough chocolate chips, then you can make all of them in peanut butter flavor," I add.

"And why exactly would she not have enough chocolate chips?" Alessio growls.

But I keep my mouth zipped. I'm not about to tell him that I hid all the chocolate chips last night, knowing that he would probably ask for banana chocolate chip cupcakes today. Like I said, he's *predictable*.

He opens his mouth and starts to snarl a response when his cell rings, and taking the call, he has to leave for the casino on an urgent matter.

I give Rosa a wink. And when she smiles shyly at me as she starts to pull out ingredients, I can't help it and smile back at her. And it's not just about the cupcakes...

***

The next morning, I've just come in from a run around our estate; sweat sits slick against my skin as I yank out my earbuds. I ran an extra three miles today in an attempt to compensate for the three peanut butter cupcakes I had after dinner last night. They were fucking delicious, and I would run an extra fifty miles daily if Rosa made them every single day for me.

Conversation comes from the kitchen, and the smell of something delicious moves me in that direction. Lingering in the doorway, I observe my older brothers. The very people I'd do anything for. Cross any line as long as it ensures their protection.

It's a loyalty engrained in me that only they deserve.

The reason I became the monster I am...

"This is delicious," Alessio says to Rosa.

"Best meal yet," Marco adds.

The words are complimentary enough, and I'm glad my siblings are starting to behave as they should. But it's not them who I watch now. It's her.

My eyes linger on her as she chops up fresh pineapple for breakfast. Her hair is tucked behind her ears, with a few loose strands escaping to frame her face. Her full body fills out the dress she's wearing, the curves of her breasts and hips flaring out like a tantalizing tease.

I drop into the chair and pour myself a cup of coffee.

"Nice of you to join us," Alessio drawls.

"If you want to spend more time with me, you should try getting up earlier."

He glares at me, although he knows I'm right—I've been up two hours already, getting in my gym workout and run. "Did you handle it?" He changes the subject, referring to the situation with the runner trying to double dip into our profits.

The cup pauses halfway to my lips. I sigh, thumping my cup back down. "This conversation can't wait until I've at least had some fucking coffee?"

And until we're not in front of Rosa. Because even though she knows exactly what I do, I find myself not wanting to talk about it in her presence—and not wanting her to see me as just a monster.

"Look, it's handled," I tell Alessio. "He won't be a problem for us anymore."

"Better be."

The fresh bruises and split skin of my knuckles are enough to signify what's happened to the runner. He's dealt with. But then, my brothers already know that. It's why I was sent.

"We have a few more people who you need to make a house call to," Marco says, not bothering to look up from the email he's reading on his phone.

"Why me?" It's a stupid question. It's my role in the entire operation. My brothers are scary fuckers, but I'm the boogie man the soldiers and runners whisper about.

"Have other plans?"

My eyes flicker to Rosa, but I shake my head. "No."

Rosa sets a plate down in front of me, a large omelet filled with cheese and mushrooms, with a stack of bacon at the side—crispy on the edges which is exactly how I like it.

"Thank you," I say with a small smile at her.

She stares down at me, that beautiful flush on her cheeks spreading before she drops her gaze and nods. She turns and heads out of the kitchen. With her back to me, I follow the bounce of her ass with each step she takes until she's out of view.

"Did she eat already?" The words are out even before I can stop them. In the time she's been here, I've yet to see her eat anything that she's cooked. Maybe she eats in her room when we're all gone. But that thought doesn't sit well with me.

I'm met with a shrug from my siblings. I make a sound in the back of my throat before taking a large bite of the omelet. It's delicious, just like I knew it would be.

Ten minutes later, looking up, I meet Alessio's arched brow. His arms are crossed over his chest, and he leans back against his chair. We're the only two left at the table now.

"What?"

"First, where the hell do you put all that food? Second, really?"

"Really...what?"

"How long has that been a thing?"

Oh shit, he's on about that again. Deflect, just deflect. "Has what been a thing?"

He shakes his head. "I'm not blind. I saw the way you were looking at her and then at her ass. You got a thing for Rosa?"

I force a laugh. "Of course not."

"Uh huh, so that look was just what?"

"I don't know what look you're talking about. I was just being polite—you know, since neither you nor Marco can seem to muster it."

His eyes narrow, and he leans forward. "Uh huh."

Fuck, fuck, fuck. "Look, I'm just being nice. She looks like she could use a little kindness. Plus, she's a skilled cook and baker. Even you have to admit she's the best one we've had for a while." But I don't sound as confident as I intend.

She's a mystery I still can't figure out.

"That's it? You just *like her cooking*?"

"Yeah." I won't admit to him that Rosa interests me—and beyond just her gorgeous body. She's quiet and keeps to herself. She's submissive and obedient and doesn't talk much in our company. Occasionally, I hear her on the phone in her room late at night. But we don't know who Rosa is as a person. Maybe it's her keeping it professional. But fuck that—I want to know her.

Because if I know her, I can protect myself from her. I can better ignore what she does to my body and the frantic confusion going on in my head.

He doesn't say anything, just tilts his head like he can unweave the lies that are coming from my lips.

"What else would it be? She's not my type. I'm not into the innocent type." I'm not a gentle kind of lover. I rarely bring women back to the estate. I take care of my needs in other ways—quick fucks in the casino. Rough and fast to satiate my needs, and when it's over, I walk away. It's that simple. Rosa deserves better. She deserves to be worshipped, and I'm not the man to do that. I'll bend and break her into a million pieces.

"Good. Keep it that way."

"Yes, sir," I grit out sarcastically with a mock salute as I push my chair back from the table with more force than is necessary.

He adjusts his suit jacket as he stands. "You have a job to do for us. For the family. Don't let some doe-eyed maid complicate things."

My jaw ticks as I grind my teeth together. "I heard you the first time."

"Just making sure it gets through your thick skull."

I flip him the bird before letting a breath whoosh from my lungs. My hand drags down my face. My body is so wound up now that the work out I did this morning feels meaningless.

This is the second time since Rosa started that Alessio has brought this up. I need to fucking get my shit together, and fast.

***

I rub at my jaw where I know a fresh bruise is blooming. It's late and dark, and once I've updated Marco, all I want to do is to sink into the sheets of my bed.

The estate itself is quiet. Which is what I need after a shitty day of playing bad guy. It never used to bother me before—doing these things and watching these so-called men weep and cry in my presence. But now I don't want to come home and accidentally stumble upon Rosa while looking like I went a few rounds with a rottweiler. I don't want her to see this side of me yet...

I yank open the freezer and rummage around for something, anything, to press to my face. My hand fits against a bag of frozen peas, and I press it to my tender jaw before snagging a water bottle as well.

A soft laugh trickles down the hall, stopping me in my tracks.

It's a beautiful sound.

Every muscle in my body tightens. I tread softly through the hall and toward the sound. Toward Rosa's room.

A soft yellow glow spills out into the hall from a crack in her door where it's not fully closed. Again, her soft laugh sounds, making my heart drum against my chest. God, nothing has ever sounded so fucking perfect. And it reminds me of when I first heard her laugh when I took her to the hair salon—just before I found out a little bit of what she's been through before she became our maid.

"I miss you too," I hear her say.

My blood freezes.

I shouldn't be listening to this.

I should turn around and give her privacy and respect. But I can't move. I'm rooted to the spot.

Who the hell is she talking to at this late hour?

"No. Soon, I promise." Her voice is tinged with some emotion I don't like hearing her use toward someone else... It strangles my chest, and an uncomfortable feeling settles in its place.

I lean forward to peer between the crack in the door and the jam. She's sitting cross-legged on her bed. A phone is settled onto the pillows in front of her. She's in a baggy T-shirt that hides most of her full body, but it's the bare creamy skin of her thick thighs that takes my attention.

Fuck, is that what she wears to sleep? She's fucking perfect.

My hand tightens on the bag pressed against my cheek when she swipes at her eyes as if she's crying.

What the hell is going on?

"I know. I love you too."

The world stops. My nostrils flare, and my blood pumps loudly in my ears. Who the hell is she saying that to? And why the hell do I even care?

She's obviously left her husband, but does she have a boyfriend now?

As the information trickles through my brain, the anger boiling up in my chest is nothing compared to the feeling twisting in my gut.

Maybe Alessio is right; maybe I'm getting too distracted by her—and maybe that means I'm not doing my job as well as I should be.

"Goodnight. I love you."

I love you. The words repeat over and over in my head. My body kicks into motion before she can spot me.

I'm down the hall and up the stairs, fuming. What did I think was going to happen? That she'd get to know me and not run the other way? That a woman like her, used to the finest the world has to offer, would give a man like me the time of day?

I need to clear my head and head to the gym before I lose my shit.

And as I try to work the anger out of my system, I tell myself that I'm not jealous—because that would mean that I care more than I should.

CHAPTER 11

ROSA

It's time for my weekly weigh-in. I strip off every single ounce of clothing. I'm not leaving anything to chance.

Taking a deep breath, I make myself take a step forward onto the scales.

And keeping my eyes closed, I psych myself up to face the number.

Cracking one eyelid open, I peek at the digital display.

That can't be right.

I step off and on again, this time with my gaze wide open.

And my heart dives with despair.

Because despite my best efforts, I've gained three pounds. *Three whole pounds.* All my efforts for the last few days have been totally futile and amounted to nothing. And even worse, I'm heavier than when I started.

But then, I tell myself to stop pretending that I made a real effort. Because I know the real reason for this weight gain. It's all those cakes that I ate. Not just that day with the lemon cupcakes, but also all those other days when I've been stuffing myself with cakes and muffins, each time thinking that I'd get back on track tomorrow.

I'm so stupid. And weak-willed. And greedy. No wonder I'm so fat—*no wonder nobody wants me.*

I try to shake the memory of the cakes out of my mind. Those small bites of heaven might look like innocent treats, but their sugar-crammed calories are always enough to make me completely lose my way because I can never stop at just one cake.

A rational person might try to put the weight gain down to their time of the month or water retention. But I've used all those excuses so many times already in the past—and I know that it's what I'm eating that's responsible for my weight issues.

Why is it always so hard? It's just food, just a momentary pleasure. But I know it's more than that. It's a symbol of everything I struggle with—self-control and body image. I've read countless articles and joined online support groups. I even tried therapy once. But in moments like this, all that knowledge and all those strategies feel useless and just fly out of the window, leaving me alone, naked, fat, and ashamed of my body.

***

A little while later, I decide there's only one thing for it.

The gym. I have to work off the extra weight. And given that the Marchianos have their own fully equipped gym right here in their mansion, there's absolutely no excuse for me not to start straightaway—especially as they're all out, so I know I'll have it to myself.

I hate working out. It leaves me hot, breathless, tired, and looking even more of a mess than usual. Plus, it always leaves me hungrier than normal. But I know I have to do something. My diet isn't working, so I need to start working out as well.

Getting dressed in a gray T-shirt and black leggings, I go down to the gym, clutching my water bottle like it's a lifeline. My heart races, not only from the thought of exercise, but also from the anxiety that courses through me every time I think about the mountain I have to climb to get to where I need to be—thin and skinny.

My gaze wanders around the stacks of weights and fitness equipment, trying to decide how to start. I choose the treadmill. Even I can't manage to mess that up.

Switching on the radio so that it filters through the speakers, I get to work. Flicking a switch, the treadmill hums to life, and I start with a slow walk, gradually increasing the speed. I try to lose myself in the rhythm of my steps and the music around me.

In no time, I'm working up a sweat, trying to kickstart the process to shed the pounds that have crept on over the last week and the pounds that have stubbornly clung to me for far too long. My cheeks are flushed, and sweat trickles down my back, but I keep pushing myself. *I need to do this.*

I'm out of breath and struggle to keep going at anywhere near a decent pace. Thank God no one is here to witness my pathetic attempts.

Catching sight of my body in the opposite full-length mirror, I cringe at the blob. I shake my head and try to block out the self-conscious thoughts gnawing at my mind.

I keep thinking about how different things might be if I were thinner, more confident. Would that make me feel less out of place, less exposed? Would it make someone actually want me and love me?

Suddenly, a familiar voice startles me, and my heart races as my head whips over my shoulder.

Oh shit. It's Camillo.

I want to hide behind the nearest weight rack, but it's too late. But who am I kidding? Even that wouldn't be big enough to hide my huge, hideous body.

My heart is thudding out of control as he strides over to me.

I thought I was out of breath before, but now I'm practically suffocating as I struggle to drag a single ounce of air into my lungs.

"Hey," he calls out over the music.

I try to muster a smile, but I think it comes out more like a grimace. "Hi," I manage to squeak, my voice barely audible over the pounding in my chest.

He approaches, looking effortlessly calm and collected in his work out gear. Is he here to use the gym as well? He never normally works out at this time. I feel a flush creeping up my neck. Of all the days for him to change his workout time, why did it have to be today?

His smile at me is tinged with warmth, and for a moment, I forget about my embarrassment.

But then I catch a glimpse of myself in the mirror—my face is red, my hair is a mess, and my T-shirt clings to my body like an unflattering shrink-wrapped package. My face burns, and I just want the ground to swallow me whole.

"Didn't know you used the gym here," he says.

I tug at the bottom of my tee, wishing desperately that I'd picked a longer top that would have at least hidden some of my thick thunder thighs.

"What do you think of the set up? I designed it all myself."

"It's, um, nice," I say in a feeble voice, unable to think of anything else to say because my mind is a complete blank. All I can think about is how stupid I must look. "I thought I'd try to get in shape," I mumble, avoiding his eyes.

"You look great," he says after a moment.

My gaze drops down to my feet. "Thanks, but I've got a long way to go."

He shakes his head, his expression serious. "You really don't, Rosa. You're great just as you are."

His words hit me like a punch to the gut, and I can't help the tears that sting the back of my eyes. "You don't have to say that," I mumble, my voice barely above a whisper. "I know what I look like."

He steps closer, and I feel a jolt of panic. He reaches out to touch my arm lightly. "I'm not just saying it," he insists.

I swallow hard, trying to keep my emotions in check. "You don't understand," I say, my voice trembling. "It's not easy, being...like this. People judge. They stare. And I just always feel so out of place."

His expression softens, and he gives my arm a reassuring squeeze. "I do understand, more than you think. Everyone has insecurities, things they struggle with. You're doing something incredible by being here, by taking charge of your health. That's something to be proud of. And whether you work out or not, you always look beautiful to me."

Beautiful? Me? I've spent so long feeling invisible, trying to blend into the background, that hearing someone say that feels surreal.

His words are like a balm to my wounded spirit, and for the first time, I feel a glimmer of hope. Maybe he's right. Maybe I don't have to be perfect to be worthy of kindness, of admiration. Maybe it's enough that I'm trying, that I'm here, sweating and struggling but still moving forward.

"Thank you," I whisper. "That means a lot."

He smiles in reply, and it's like the sun breaking through the clouds.

"I have to go now—"

"Don't leave just because I'm here," he says quickly.

"I have work to get done," I say with a small nod before hurrying away.

As I head upstairs to shower, I keep thinking about Camillo's words. I'm still self-conscious, still aware of every extra pound, but maybe, just maybe, I can start to see myself through kinder eyes.

It gives me a renewed determination. Because I'm here, and I'm trying. And for now, right at this very second, that's enough.

And as I wash, there's another thought that keeps running through my mind—does he really think that I'm beautiful...?

CHAPTER 12

CAMILLO

I'm drawn to the kitchen as the scent of something delicious wafts through the house. As I come closer, I hear the clatter of pots and pans and hear the sizzle of something frying. *Bacon.*

Lingering by the door, I watch Rosa work. She's concentrating intently, like she's cooking for someone she cares about...

And then, my arms crossed, I watch as she fusses over Mr. F like he's the king of this household. Her soft voice coos as she scratches the dog behind his ears, and the sly mutt leans into her touch with a contented groan. She's completely absorbed in making sure Mr. F is comfortable, happy, and utterly spoiled.

A feeling twists in my chest. When was the last time someone fussed over me like that? Sure, I get laid often enough, but it's just not the same. And now, here Rosa is, but all her attention is focused on the dog.

"Mr. Fluffy, you're such a good boy, aren't you?" she murmurs as her fingers work magic into his fur. "And you definitely deserve a treat, don't you?"

My shoulder muscles bunch up, and I feel like yelling that *I'm* the one in this house that deserves a treat.

She crouches down onto her knees, practically now on the floor with him, as if there's nowhere else in the world she'd rather be.

I clear my throat to draw her attention. But she's too absorbed in fussing over him. And I can't help feeling annoyed at how easily she ignores me. *I'm* the one who hired her, *I'm* the one paying her salary, and yet she's lavishing all her attention on *him*. I just don't get it.

She puts some bacon on a plate and sets it down on the floor in front of him. His tail wags at a furious speed, and his snout dives in as he devours it with relish. I bet it's delicious...

Smiling down at him, she pats his head, and I'm struck by how beautiful she looks when she's happy. "Good boy, Mr. Fluffy," she praises, patting his head as he eats.

I let out a small, involuntary sigh, and her head snaps up, finally noticing my presence. Her cheeks flush a little, and she stands quickly, brushing her hands on her apron. "I didn't see you there. Is there anything I can get you?"

Is there something I need? How do I even begin to answer that? Because I know that I need a lot of things, and most of those I didn't even realize until she walked into my life. "It smells good in here," I say, gesturing vaguely toward the stove. "I'll have some bacon too. In a sandwich please." My stomach growls in anticipation.

Her eyes widen as she glances at the stove, then back at me. "Oh, that was the last of the bacon. But I can make you something else if you're hungry?"

I suppress the growl building at the back of my throat. As if *fur face* getting spoiled by her isn't bad enough, now he's eaten all the fucking bacon as well?

"Sure," I say, trying to keep my voice even, like it's no big deal. Like I'm not desperate to stay here a little longer. Why can't she give that sort of attention to me? Why can't I be the one she's fussing over? And why can't I be the one to make her smile...?

***

After Rosa moved in, I thought it'd be easy enough to ignore her and go on about my business. I thought I'd be able to do what I've always done when it comes to pretty maids in the house. Ignore them and stay the fuck away. But that's a fucking joke now.

I'm uncomfortably aware of where Rosa is in the house at all times. Of what she's doing at any given moment. I track her constantly as she slaves away, busting her gorgeous ass to meet the demanding orders of my brothers.

Even now, as I watch her stretch to reach for something that's too high, I'm honed in on her.

And it pisses me off. *I shouldn't care.*

Inserting myself into anything to do with her is a dangerous move, not to mention stupid. There's still so much I don't know about her. So much that could bite me in the ass.

But ever since she helped me stitch up Alessio and Marco, I haven't been able to stop watching her. I keep telling myself that it's because I'm just checking on how she's processing the whole thing—and watching for if she bolts.

She'd been terrified that night. And yet, she'd carried on the next morning as if nothing happened.

I'm simply looking to make sure she doesn't leave us high and dry. That's what I'm telling myself.

It has nothing to do with how my body reacts when she's around or how frustrated I am that I can't seem to escape that sweet rose fragrance that follows her around. Even in my own goddamn room or shower, it follows me. My nostrils flare, taking in a deep huff of the smell, cursing myself to the deepest parts of hell. It's quickly becoming a problem.

A flash of creamy skin catches my eye as Rosa stretches further onto her tiptoes, trying to grasp the silver mixing bowl from the shelf. The edge of her shirt rolls up just enough that I'm privy to a tease of her skin there. My body jumps into action, sending blood pumping in the wrong damn direction before I can stop it.

A good person would go over there and help. A good person would offer to get a step stool or something before she breaks her neck.

But I'm not a good person. I sit there at the counter and watch, pretending to be preoccupied with the paper and the breakfast pancakes she's made.

I sit there and take in my fill of her openly. She's all curves and softness. Just enough weight on her that she fills out her clothes and makes my mouth water. The slope of her neck is tantalizing in a way I don't understand, but I want to wrap my hand around it and feel her pulse thrum frantically beneath my fingers.

The bowl tips forward, and she catches it, settling back down to her feet with a triumphant smile.

The smile on her face sucks the air right out of my lungs. It's rare and lights up her entire face so that I'm instantly hooked. It's almost as sweet as the soft humming she does when she thinks no one is watching. It's another item on the list of things about Rosa that shouldn't interest me but does.

She puffs out a breath, blowing a few strands from her eyes. Her cheeks flush with color, a delectable hint of rose painting her skin and highlighting the soft freckles on her nose. Hastily, she readjusts her shirt and gnaws on her bottom lip.

My eyes zero in on the action.

This is wrong. Bad. And exactly what I don't want to do. But fuck it if I don't want to replace her teeth with my own and see what kind of wicked sounds she'd make for me. Would she whimper? Would she moan? Would she be submissive and let me have my way with her?

I shouldn't be having those thoughts. I shouldn't be entertaining them at all.

Never in my life have I wanted to make small talk with anyone as badly as I do with Rosa. Never in my life have I wanted to unravel someone the way I want to unfurl the layers around her to find out what makes her the way she is.

It's wrong. And yeah, I'm so fucked.

"There you are." Alessio's voice sounds from behind me.

"Here I am." I take a long sip of the orange juice Rosa squeezed fresh this morning.

"We need you to go solve a problem."

"Right now?" I motion to my food and the newspaper with its pristine pages that I've clearly been ignoring. "Or are you going to allow me to finish my breakfast first?"

"Shove it in your mouth, and let's go. Marco is waiting."

"Morning to you too," I mutter.

I swallow the last mouthful of my pancake and down the rest of my glass.

"Thanks, Rosa," I say in a low voice as I pass.

Then I try to clear my mind and focus on the task ahead. As nice as it's been having a tidy room, clean house, and amazing home-cooked meals, I need to stay the fuck away. I've never had this problem before. I've never felt so out of control. Like I'm spiraling, and I can't stop. I'm pissed. At the world. At Rosa. At the way her perfect curves fill out her clothes.

But more so I'm pissed at myself. For letting my dick run the show. For letting that little voice of hope I thought burned to a crisp years ago flicker back to life and convince me someone like Rosa would find a man like me worthy.

It's temporary, I tell myself over and over with each step away from the kitchen. The fixation will pass in a few weeks like it always does, and it'll be back to business as usual. She's new and intriguing, and my body sees it as a challenge. Something new to sink my teeth into.

My anger flares. Because I can't be responsible for someone else. I can't have something as heavy as that on my shoulders. But watching how she yelps, cowers, and tries to make herself small in every interaction, it makes me want to protect her in every way possible.

She's temporary. That's what I have to keep reminding myself of. She's only here until Marco sends her packing. He says she passed the trial, but we all know how volatile he is. He'll end up firing her—one way or another—just like he has everyone else.

I need to get her out of my head.

I need to hit the gym. Do something to distract me from the flood of arousal pumping through my body. And then, I'll take the longest cold shower known to man. Or I need to kill someone—in the most brutal way possible

Because I need to distract myself so that I stop thinking about doing depraved things to her that will only fuck up my carefully laid out life.

But do I? That small annoying voice in the back of my head whispers as I slide into my SUV. My hands curl around the steering wheel, and I shudder out a deep breath. That's the problem with hope. It flickers to life and refuses to fucking die.

There's no world in which I can taste the forbidden fruit and not get addicted. I wish that little voice would just go for good. Leave me in peace for once in my life.

She's off-limits. She's a reminder of everything I want but can't have. And the sooner my body fucking gets with the program, the easier this is going to be.

Because it's wrong. It's so very wrong to want something I can't have. To taunt myself with the idea of what it could be like to have her and taste her the way my body wants to.

Yeah, I'm well and truly fucked.

But I'm not even sure I care.

***

I feel like a fucking teenager. My palms are sweaty, and my heart is racing like I've just run the estate twice over. I hate this feeling, and yet, the rush of adrenaline pumping through my body is hard to ignore.

This is stupid.

Of course, it is. But I can't stop now.

I think of Rosa's nervous, scared look every time she looks at me. It's burned into my brain, and it only makes my blood boil. I don't want her to look at me like that, even though she should.

I'm the monster the devil's afraid of, but I don't want to be like that with her. I want to be something else—something I don't think I can be.

I knock at her bedroom door before I can chicken out and stop myself.

With one quick check down the hall to ensure none of my siblings are lingering to witness what I'm sure will be a dumpster fire of a disaster, I wait. It's early, and they're probably still asleep.

I inhale sharply, impatience swimming through me.

"Mr. Camillo?" She still won't drop the Mr., but maybe she will in time.

The air from my lungs seizes in my chest as Rosa's body fills the small gap in the door. She's wearing that oversized T-shirt that just brushes the top of her thighs again.

I can just make out the outline of the curves of her breasts which are bare beneath the fabric. She looks beautiful early in the morning. She looks beautiful all the time, but something about seeing her sleepy-eyed does something to me.

Something I'm ready to acknowledge.

"Is something wrong? Did I do something?"

I shake my head, "No. Uh… I…" This is so much harder than it sounded in my head twenty minutes ago when I came up with this plan.

The urge to know more about her has been clawing at my insides. It's a compulsion almost as bad as needing to feel my knuckles wrapped and bloody. "Go for dinner. With me." My words blurt out.

Her brown eyes widen, and I watch as her tongue darts over her lip. "I'm sorry?"

"I mean, er, would you like to go to dinner with me?" I take a big gulp. "Um, please?"

"*Me?*" she squeaks.

I nod. "Yeah." This is where I should tell her that I want to get to know her, spend time with her… "You've been, er, working really hard. I figured it was the least, um, we could do for you."

Christ, why do I sound so fucking feeble? I'm used to telling my soldiers every single day exactly what I want, so why can't I just tell her that I fucking want to take her on a date?

"I…" That bottom lip of hers is sucked beneath her teeth, and my gaze zeroes in on it. She's going to reject me. Of course, she is. A woman like Rosa doesn't want to be seen with a man like me. My body goes rigid in the doorway as I shove my hands into my pockets. "Okay. Sure."

I blink slowly, trying to process what she's just said. "I'll make arrangements to have takeout ordered for everyone else," I say quickly before she can change her mind. "So, you don't need to worry about anything tonight except going out and enjoying the meal. I'll meet you downstairs at seven. Okay?"

A tentative smile graces her face, and I can feel my heart stutter. She should smile more often, and the fact that she doesn't is a crime against humanity. She mumbles a thank you and closes the door.

The entire jog up the stairs to my room feels like I've won the lottery.

It's selfish. It's the wrong thing to be happy about. But I need to know her more. I need to crack into the hard shell around her and find what makes her tick.

I know it's foolish to indulge myself when nothing will come of it. When it'll only lead to a crash and burn. But I can't help it. Not with Rosa.

***

After finishing work for the day, there's still about three hours until I take her to dinner. I pass the time in the gym, allowing my nervous energy to pour out into each jab and punch against the canvas bag.

Eventually, the world around me fades, and it's just me and my demons wrestling for dominance, the darkness pulling me under.

When the alarm on my phone sounds, I snap back to reality. The nerves that I managed to ease now return tenfold. I run up the stairs, shirt yanked over my head before I even make it to my room. I kick the pile of clothing from my path as I toss my shirt onto the floor. I know I should try to be tidier after all the efforts Rosa's made with my room, but today, I can't help it as an agitated feeling skitters through me.

After showering, I jog down the stairs while buttoning the sleeves of my dress shirt. It's suffocating despite the breathable fabric. If we weren't going somewhere so public, I wouldn't have bothered.

My foot hits the last step, and I inhale deeply, checking my reflection in the mirror. The top layer of my hair is tied back, and the edges of my ink peek out from under my collar.

I hate dressing up, but it'll all be worth it. I need to put to rest whatever hold Rosa has over me. That's the only way I'll be able to think clearly with her around. Once the distraction is gone, I'll be able to focus on whatever the fuck I need to.

"You know, don't you, that you don't have to dress up to take your hand on a date?"

I whirl to face Alessio who is leaning against the archway.

"Fuck off. I thought you were still working."

"I am. The question is, Millo, what are *you* doing?"

"I'm going out. Not that it's any of your business."

His gaze drags over me in a way that makes me feel like a kid again. I hate how he and Marco can do that so easily to me. I arch a brow. Shaking his head, he disappears further into the house. And I exhale a breath.

I'm not trying to hide anything from my brothers, but they don't need to go poking around into my private life. I'm a grown ass man, for God's sake.

I glance at my watch, and the nerves choke me as I pull on my suit jacket, hiding the concealed gun in my holster. I can do this. Employers take their beautiful, curvy employees out to dinner all the time. Right?

"Hi." Rosa's soft voice hits my ears, and I whirl around. "I hope this is okay. It's all I have."

My eyes rake over her body before slowing down to enjoy the view. Wrapped in a velvety thin-strapped jade green dress that just hits her mid-thigh, she looks like sin.

The dress hugs each of her curves like a glove, accentuating the way her body tapers in at the waist before flaring over her wide hips. It doesn't hide the fact that she's got meat on her bones, and that alone makes my mouth water.

The heels she wears elongate her legs, and the urge to touch them nearly overtakes me. Her hair has pretty waves in it, and I can't help my gaze trailing over her cute, rounded cheeks and freckles. Her lips are painted a soft pink, giving them a natural and glossy look. Venus rising from the ocean has nothing on the vision in front of me.

She fiddles with the strap of her watch, her gaze dropped.

"You look beautiful," I breathe.

That delicious color spreads across her fair cheeks, and my body stiffens. She shifts from foot to foot, still not meeting my eyes, but I can't take my eyes off her.

"I know I have some weight to lose…" Her voice is a low murmur.

My eyebrows shoot up. "No, you don't," I say quickly. "I like a woman with proper curves."

A look of confusion flickers over her face. "You don't have to say that."

"I mean it." I clear my throat, pulling at my collar. "Shall we?"

Mutely, she nods when I motion to the door. I hold it open as the hint of her scent billows past me. My mouth waters for another hit. Her rose scent with a hint of lavender is better than any drug out there.

With a shake of my head, I curl my fist. I can look, but I can't touch. That's not what this is.

"I hope you're hungry," I say as I open the passenger door to my SUV.

She gives me a tight smile in return.

The car ride is filled with mostly silence while I observe her fidget slightly in her seat. I can't quite decide if it's nervousness or something else. Thankfully, the ride isn't long.

"Have you ever eaten here?" I ask as I pull us into the valet line at the best Italian restaurant in the city.

"No."

"Oh?" I figured everyone in Chicago's upper elite had dined here at least once in their life. I nod, unsure what else to say.

I notice a shiver run through Rosa. It's cool in my car, but I know from experience that this particular restaurant always has its AC on even higher.

I hand my keys off to the valet before moving around the SUV, unbuttoning my jacket as I go to open Rosa's door. I don't miss the curious eyes of those milling around the building, all too eager to see who's out on the town and hoping to catch a glimpse of the rich and famous who often frequent this establishment.

As she climbs out of the car, I quickly cover her shoulders with my jacket. I don't like seeing her shiver.

But as soon as the fabric wraps around her, her gaze snaps to mine. She takes a sharp inhale, and her eyes widen with a look of alarm. Her body goes ramrod straight with tension and something else I can't identify.

Alarm bells ring in my head. *What just happened?*

Offering her a soft reassuring smile, I gently press my hand to the small of her back, guiding her inside.

Warmth radiates from her, and the thought of her smelling like me does all kinds of bad fucked up things to my thoughts. She fits perfectly into my side, tucked away from the nosy vultures of Chicago. I like her protected like this.

Some primal part of my brain roars to life, and I clench my fist to keep from growling at the men who openly ogle her as we pass. One glare from me is enough for them to pale and turn away quickly.

I usher Rosa straight past the bodies waiting in the queue, and it isn't until we hit the hostess stand that Rosa lifts her gaze to take in the elegance.

We're immediately seated, much to the chagrin of some other well-to-do nobodies. Rosa slides into the chair across from me. The particular table I requested is tucked in a corner, private and exclusive.

"Do you want wine?" I ask.

Rosa shakes her head.

"Something else? Beer? Or a cocktail? It's my treat, Rosa. Order whatever you want."

But she shakes her head again and lifts the menu, hiding her face from me.

I swallow thickly. How is this already going so wrong?

I mimic her and let my gaze roam the list of items. The light airy feeling that bubbled through me at the start of this has slowly sunk into something else.

Though she declined the wine, I get a bottle just in case and a beer for me. Marco and Alessio would be smacking me on the back of the head for the lack of class, but I'm here to enjoy myself with her, not put on a show.

"See anything you like?"

"I'm not sure," she murmurs.

The quiet, timid response makes my stomach churn. Is it so bad to be seen with me? Did I cross some line I can't quite see? My hand tightens around the bottle as I bring it to my lips.

Without another word, Rosa and I order when the server arrives at our table. And after ordering, once more, an awkward silence fills the air.

The soft hum of chatter around us fills the space. But I don't want that. I want to ask her questions. I want to peel the layers of her back, one by one, until whatever spell she has on me breaks and I can move on.

But I can't seem to find the words. I'm not a small talk guy. I'm not suave like my siblings.

I take a long swig of my beer, letting my gaze fall to the bar on the other side of the room.

"This is...a very nice place," she says in the faintest voice.

I barely hear her words, but it's all the encouragement I need. "Although kind of loud. I prefer more relaxed and casual places usually."

She nods. "Do you come here often?"

"Not really." I sit back into my chair a little, watching as she tugs my jacket tighter around her, hiding more of her creamy skin.

"You didn't have to bring me here."

"You deserve it, Rosa. What you've done in such a short time is a miracle."

"It's nothing. It's what you pay me for." She fidgets with the rim of her glass, eyes darting around quickly before dropping back down to the tablecloth. The dismissiveness of her response bothers me. Did I say something wrong?

"And here we are." Our waitress smiles, setting out the food before us. "If you need anything else, please let me know."

"Thank you," Rosa murmurs.

The waitress looks at me, and I nod, dismissing her. I want to be left alone with Rosa.

I should try to carry on the conversation with her. Say something. Instead, I shove a forkful into my mouth. It's exactly what I remember. Rich and decadent—but overpriced for the portion size. How anyone can be full after a meal like this, I'm not sure.

I swallow my mouthful and wipe my napkin across my mouth—I can be civilized if need be. "This is nearly as good as your cooking."

"That's very kind," she hums in response.

My head tilts, and I watch as she pushes her pasta around the plate. Has she even taken a bite?

"Do you not like it? We can order something else?"

"No," she rushes, shaking her head, "It's fine. Really."

"Are you sure?"

"Yes." She lifts a single piece of pasta to her mouth as if to show me.

I nod slowly, taking another gulp of my beer.

This evening was meant to fix my problem, not make it worse. And yet, spending this time with her has made me even more intrigued and beguiled by this gorgeous woman.

"So, how are you adjusting?" I broach, hoping to find something, anything, to talk about. "At the estate. I know the first few days were rough."

"It's better. I'd like to think I'm doing well."

"More than well. You're doing fantastic, if my opinion counts."

That's all it takes for Rosa to relax a little in her chair. And from there, the conversation flows to other mundane topics. The weather and things that make no fucking sense for small talk, but I don't care because she's talking. I even manage a few soft chuckles of laughter as I start to loosen up.

With anyone else, I'd have eaten and walked away by now. But something about Rosa keeps me rooted in place. Enjoying it all, soaking up the atmosphere and the company of the person opposite me.

It doesn't feel like it does with other women—with them, it feels tedious and fake. It's like she's looking at *me*—and not the brutal man everyone believes me to be, despite the truth in the matter. The feeling is unsettling and arousing all at once.

"Would you like a box, miss?" the server asks when she comes to clear the table and notices Rosa's plate.

"No, that's okay," Rosa says, finishing her glass of water. Her plate has hardly been touched. My gaze narrows. A question burns my lips, but I've just started to break through her hard exterior. I've slowly made progress, and I can't risk her clamming up now.

The silence carried home only makes the situation worse. My hands tighten around the steering wheel.

Something is wrong, and I know it's me.

I've done something to upset her. To offend her. Rosa slides from my SUV, and my eyes are fixed on her as she makes her way toward the door that connects to the mansion.

The garage is quiet and dark, but I clock both Alessio and Marco have gone out as their cars are missing.

Quietly, I walk behind Rosa as she shrugs off my jacket and returns it to me. "Thank you. Tonight was lovely."

Her words don't match the expression on her face. The sound is hollow and fake. A platitude meant to appease me. It's not how Rosa acts.

Anger boils through me, and I can't help how my hand slams into the doorframe, cutting her from the doorway and any escape.

I toss the jacket over my shoulder and lean toward her. "What's wrong?"

"What?"

"What's wrong? Was the food bad? Did you want something else?"

"No. It was lovely. Really."

"Then what? You've been fiddling with your watch strap and hands since we sat down at that table. You hardly touched your food. Are you sick? Do you need time off?"

She's cowering beneath me. Trembling like a leaf. I should back off, give her space, but fuck that. I want answers.

"You can tell me, Rosa." I breathe, unable to stop myself from tucking the falling strand of hair behind her ear.

Her gaze jerks to mine, and a million emotions swim in them. But none that I can pick out and identify. Everything about this woman is a mystery to me.

She murmurs something I don't quite catch.

"What?"

"I didn't mean to embarrass you."

I jerk back like she's slapped me. Her? Embarrass me? Who the fuck would be embarrassed with someone like Rosa on their arm? I can feel my brows pull together. "I'm sorry?"

She looks down at her feet and murmurs something else. Gently, I lift her chin to meet my gaze. "I wasn't embarrassed to be seen with you."

"You covered me up," she says quietly.

"You were shivering in the car, and that place is notorious for being cold. I thought you'd be more comfortable." I don't understand how she'd ever think I'd be embarrassed by her. "You thought I was covering you up?"

"Why wouldn't you?"

"Because you're gorgeous?" *Isn't that obvious?*

She makes a little sound in the back of her throat but shakes her head. "I'm not."

"The fuck you aren't." I watch her like she's a wounded deer. One wrong word and she'll flee. For the first time since I've brought her to the house, I feel like I'm seeing the real Rosa. I lower my voice. "That's why you didn't eat dinner..."

A piece of the puzzle falls into place, but I'm not equipped to solve it, though I fucking want to. Badly.

Meekly, she nods, turning her head to the side to look away from me. She chews on her bottom lip. "I know I'm not...the right size."

With my thumb, I guide her face back. Tears rim the edge of her eyes, and my chest squeezes.

Something roars to life inside me. The need to defend her, but something else. Something darker. The urge to make anyone who's made her feel less pay. To watch the life drain from their faces under my hands. My hand twitches at my side, but I swallow the fury.

I need to be gentle with her. Soft. She's broken in a way some buried part of me understands.

"I don't know what that means. But you're gorgeous, Rosa. Seeing you in my jacket, smelling like me, it was something I liked."

Fuck. Even now, the thought has my body tightening. "It was damn sexy. Everyone was looking at you because you're stunning, not because of anything else. You've got curves and fill out that dress like a sin. There is *nothing* wrong with how you look."

I hold her gaze and can see that she doesn't quite believe me. Her lips are slightly parted, glistening after she licks them.

It'd be so easy to taste her, looming over her as I am, holding her chin between my fingers.

All it'd take is one bend of my head.

One taste, and I'd know for sure.

The urge pounds against my chest like a hundred men marching.

"You are stunning, Rosa. You turned several heads tonight because of it. Several women were staring, jealous of you." My thumb brushes her bottom lip on instinct.

Time freezes for a second before she nods.

"Anyone who says otherwise can go fuck themselves."

"Okay." She exhales.

She's not dismissing me outright at least. It takes every muscle in my body, every ounce of self-control to keep me from claiming her mouth. From making her see just what her body is doing to me. I want her. I want to show her just how beautiful she is.

But there's something that makes me back off...

My hand drops, and I take a step back, letting the cold air rush in between us.

She pauses in the doorway, her head tilted.

My heart's hammering in my chest, my cock pressing uncomfortably against my zipper.

Fuck.

"Good night, Rosa." I breathe out, walking back toward the garage doors.

I hear the soft click of the door behind me as she hurries into the mansion, and I swallow thickly.

***

Even though it's late, I fit in an extra workout in our gym, and then head to the kitchen, passing Marco as he arrives home and makes for the office. Rummaging through the refrigerator, I find some lime and coriander chicken drumsticks left over from the lunch Rosa cooked for me yesterday when I unexpectedly dropped back home for lunch. *Delicious.*

Getting the dish out and setting it on the island, I realize I've left my phone in the gym. I sigh as I turn to get it, needing to make a quick call to the casino before I have my snack.

I'm back in a couple of minutes. And looking forward to my first bite of that juicy dish, I hurry into the kitchen.

And I stop dead in my tracks.

Because I can see the chicken.

And I can also see Marco's stupid dog.

With a smug grin all over his dumb face.

As he eats my chicken and licks his greedy, slobbery lips.

"What the fuck! Why the hell are you eating *my food*?"

But he just ignores me, his paws all over the drumsticks while his snout digs around in the dish for his next bite.

"Marco, get in here before I commit murder!" I holler at the top of my voice as I clench and unclench my fists.

"What now?" he says as he stomps into the kitchen.

"That," I snarl, jerking my chin toward the animal. "Your dog is completely out of control."

"Technically, Mr. F is Juliana's dog," he drawls, referring to his wife. When they got married, Juliana unexpectedly brought with her Mr. Fluffy—which has to be the dumbest name for a dog I've ever heard. Most of us call him 'Mr. F' as a compromise. I mean, can you imagine a made man shouting out 'Mr. Fluffy' every time he takes his dog out to the park and needs to call him over? I'd die of embarrassment. Nah, actually, I'd shoot myself before I let myself be humiliated like that by an animal.

"I don't care who he technically belongs to," I grit out. "She's your wife, and she left him in your care. Why the hell couldn't she just take him to Italy with her? We're not her fucking dogsitters."

"You hardly lift a finger to help look after the animal," Marco points out dryly.

I just glare at him and his dog. The animal seems to have a bottomless pit for a stomach and a fondness for stealing food.

I cross my arms over my chest. "Look, *fur face* here is eating all my food," I snap. "Rosa cooked that *especially for me*. Feed your own damn dog, and leave my food the fuck alone." *I'm not fucking sharing Rosa's goodies with anyone fucking else.*

Marco just stares at me without a single word of remorse or fucking sympathy before striding off and leaving me to clean up after his dog—all on an empty stomach.

First, Alessio tries to get Rosa to make his favorite cupcakes, then Mr. F getting all the bacon and all Rosa's attention, and now this thing with the chicken. The dog, Marco, and Alessio all just need to leave Rosa the hell alone. Because Rosa is all mine—*and only mine...*

CHAPTER 13

ROSA

It's my half day off, and my hand presses to my chest as I lean against Kori's door after closing it behind me.

The sounds of the bustling Chicago neighborhood are a distant echo, and my lip wobbles as I will my feet to move down the porch steps—and away from Ethan again.

I didn't think leaving him would be so damn hard this time, but each step feels like someone carving my heart out.

Video calls and phone calls only do so much, and I really needed to see him today. I wanted to hold him in my arms and remind myself that he's safe. But all I can feel is a renewed surge of guilt as my vision blurs with tears.

Despite the money I've saved up—neatly stashed in an envelope under my mattress at the Marchiano estate—I've only squirreled half the amount I'll need for a deposit, and it's still not enough to get us out of the state and away from the horrors that haunt me around every corner.

Despair squeezes my chest at the thought, and I fight to keep the sob falling from my lips. I need to get myself together before I get to the estate. With one last parting glance over my shoulder, I fist my hand, forcing my eyes to drop back to the sidewalk.

Weaving in and out of the bodies that line the street, I walk to the bus stop. I stifle a yelp as a car backfires. As much as I want to enjoy the fresh air and freedom of being in the city, it's too risky. The longer I'm outside the estate, the easier it is for someone to see me. The easier I am to *find*. And if that happens, it's over.

I need to get off the streets and back to the estate to some semblance of safety. At least the monsters that roam there don't pretend to be anything less.

Getting to the bus stop, I jump onto the bus that is just about to depart, pulling the hood of my jacket over my head and face as the doors close behind me.

Restlessly, my knee bounces as I'm in my seat. As the movement of the bus lulls some of the tension from my body, my mind drifts back to the way Ethan's face lit up when I met Kori and the two boys at the park. I sniff quickly, pushing back the tears that threaten to fall.

I reach the stop where I have to change buses. And after taking the second bus, I finally arrive at my stop.

It's still a walk back to the estate, but I need the time to compose myself—and I also need the exercise. I wince at the thought, staring down at the curves of my body.

I shudder, knowing exactly where this line of thinking is leading. Nowhere good, but I can't help my thoughts. Like a beast prowling inside my head, the words pounce upon me.

You should think about working out more.

Don't you think that shows a little too much skin...you know, for someone with a body like yourself?

No one could love a fat pig like you...

The voices of my sister, my mother, and Grayden tumble around my mind—and they slash into me until I'm raw and bile burns the back of my throat.

I swallow it back and focus on making my way down the street and up the hill toward the Marchiano estate. I ignore the way my vision swims and the painful cramping of my stomach from lack of food and force my thoughts to something else. Anything else...

The image of Ethan at the park fills my mind. The way his clothing is worn thin but his cheeks are fuller. He's a shell of the boy he should be. He's reserved when he should be as boisterous as the other young children at the park.

He was permanently glued to my side, and yet I selfishly soaked it all up. Even now, the phantom warmth along my leg lingers. Blinking quickly, I try to keep the tears from my face.

"Everything okay, Rosa?" a guard asks as I pass through the gate.

I should know all their names by now, and I should make an effort to be friendly, yet I can't even meet their eyes when they speak to me. I nod and scurry away toward the mansion, my purse clutched to my chest and my gaze downcast.

Even though I'm supposed to also have the evening off, I'm back in time to prepare dinner. I'll squeeze in a quick stop at my room. The house is quiet when I enter, and I tiptoe my way toward my room. The less I'm seen like this, the better it is for me.

I try to distract myself with thoughts about my work. I like to think I'm doing a good job. The state of the house itself is pristine, including Camillo's bedroom. I've yet to ruin a dinner or dessert since the day of Marco's pep talk. I've nailed down Alessio's closet system. Things have gotten better, if anything. I've made their lives easier—I hope.

My mind drifts to the dinner Camillo took me to. He said it was a thank you for my work, but after everything he said that night, I realize that it was actually meant as a date.

He called me *gorgeous, sexy, stunning.* And he said he likes a woman with proper curves. And the way his thumb brushed my bottom lip...

Those definitely aren't things that an employer would say.

As I pull out a fresh T-shirt to change into, my gaze catches the photo album with Ethan's baby photos. Pulling it out, I sit on the edge of the bed and leaf through it. And the ache that is never far away rushes back into my heart.

Footsteps echo down the hall. My body automatically freezes in response, my breath lodging into my throat.

It takes me a moment to remind my body that Grayden isn't here. It's someone else. But my body refuses to relax even though I know I'm safe here—as safe as someone can be.

The heavy, deliberate cadence echoes off the walls. Each step is a solid thud, bearing the weight of the body, making the floorboards creak just enough under his imposing posture. *Camillo.*

It took me less than a week to distinguish between the footsteps of the brothers. A habit built over the years from the will and need to survive.

There's a knock at my door. I shove the album under my pillow before slowly opening it.

"Back so soon?"

My hand trembles around the doorknob. I can't look at him, and I don't trust my voice.

"Rosa?"

"Yes, Mr. Camillo?" I mumble, looking down at my sneakers. I don't want him to see my puffy eyes or the lingering redness from crying on the way home. He'll ask unwanted questions.

He steps closer to me, filling the hall with his masculine scent. It lulls some part of my brain and causes my tight shoulders to drop. I swallow thickly, praying he'll just walk away.

He doesn't. "Did something happen?"

I shake my head.

"Are you sure? You didn't rush back just to make dinner, did you?"

"No," I lie, my voice thick with tears. I clear my throat as quietly as possible. "Everything is fine, Mr. Camillo."

"You're sure?"

"Yes."

His hand twitches at his side, and I hold my breath, waiting to be grabbed or worse. This is exactly the kind of questioning I can't handle.

"Did you go anywhere fun?"

I flinch as if I've been struck and stare up at him. Why does he want to know that? The alarm bells in my head sound.

I try to school my features, to keep the frantic worry off my face. He's just being friendly. He doesn't know anything.

"I'm sorry?"

"Did you do anything fun? While you were out."

"No."

His dark brow arches as he tilts his head. For once, his hair isn't tied back at the crown. Instead, the thick, glossy strands tumble around his face, framing the sharp angles. He's as menacing as he is beautiful.

But it's the flicker behind his dark eyes that makes my insides flutter in a way I can't quite pinpoint. He's watching me, observing me, and my skin prickles on high alert.

Each slow passing of his eyes feels like an embrace heating my skin.

My palms are sweaty, and my tongue feels swollen in my mouth as I stand there dumbly, watching him. I shouldn't enjoy the way having his eyes on me makes me feel.

"So, you just walked around the city all day?"

I suck my lip between my teeth. I don't want to deliberately lie to him. There's no telling what will happen to me and this job if he finds out everything. But I need to protect Ethan. I need to protect myself. "Yes. That's what I did."

The half-truth sits heavy in my chest, but I know what these men are capable of. They're monsters wrapped in attractive packaging. Beautiful, yet deadly. And I've learned my lesson so that I trust no one but myself.

Camillo and his brothers may have warmed up slightly to me being here, and they may have not raised their hands to me, but there are worse ways to destroy a person.

"Oh," he responds.

His hand moves, and I step back on instinct, flinching. I watch as his hand flexes, and his gaze hardens for a brief second before he drags it through his hair, pushing it back.

"Are you sure nothing happened?"

"I'm sure." I hear the waver in my voice. "I just need a few minutes before I start dinner."

He rubs the back of his neck and nods. "Sure, yeah. Of course."

I dart into my room and close the door behind me, sinking to the floor. My heart is racing under my T-shirt. I need to get a hold of myself before I start on dinner.

With a wobbly exhale, I stand on shaky legs. Collapsing on the bed, I stare at the ceiling, trying to calm my frantic heart. 'What ifs' bounce around my head before I can stop them.

What's going to happen if they learn about Ethan? What happens if Grayden finds where we are? I can feel the stuttering breaths and the tightness in my chest. Each inhale is shorter than the last, and I can't quite fill my lungs.

I squeeze my hand tight enough that my nails bite into my palm. And as the sting of pain slices through the panic, I finally manage to gulp down a lungful of air.

Once my hands stop shaking and I can properly stand back up, I make my way to the kitchen. I just need a distraction from my thoughts, and I'll figure the rest out later.

I stop in the doorway, my brow puckered. Camillo is sitting at the island and tapping away on his phone. Usually at this time, he's gone, arriving back just in time for dinner to be served.

Maybe he's making sure I'm still doing a good job. I busy myself around the kitchen trying to figure out where to start. Luckily, I prepped some food last night, so tonight's meal shouldn't be too hard.

Camillo clears his throat, and I nearly drop the bowl of defrosted chicken at the sudden noise.

"What are you making?"

I take a calming breath before answering. "I thought I'd make that paella you said you liked so much."

He nods and sets his phone down. "Can I help?"

It's not the first time he's offered to help me. The hairs on the back of my neck stand up, and I can't help wondering if he thinks I can't cope with the job. "No. Thank you."

"Okay."

An uneasy silence fills the room.

"You didn't need to come back so soon. We could have just gotten takeout. You should enjoy your day off."

"I don't mind."

"Right." His deep voice drops off, and he ducks his head, picking up his phone again.

Why is everything so awkward between us now? It's almost as if our dinner together didn't happen...

"Rosa?"

"Yes, Mr. Camillo?" I ask over my shoulder as I wash the rice.

"Just Camillo is fine."

"Of course."

The sound of the running water echoes around the quiet kitchen. "About earlier."

I turn toward him, brows pinched. Did I do something earlier? Did I forget something? I run through the possibilities.

"Outside your bedroom." The way he looks at me sends a jolt of electricity down my spine. My legs squeeze together. I shouldn't find him as attractive as I do. I shouldn't think about him the way I do when my mind drifts.

I know what kind of man he is. I should run the other way. But now that he's shown an interest in me, I can't seem to move. Doubt plagues me, and I'm almost certain I'm reading too much into the attention he gives me.

"I'm sorry if I made you uncomfortable, Rosa."

My mouth parts, but I can't seem to find my voice.

"I just... You see, you just looked...uh..." Again, his hand drags through his hair before he meets my gaze again. "Actually, never mind. I'm just sorry."

Another pregnant silence fills the kitchen as I stare at him.

I should say something. Tell him something to erase the pained expression that's creased his face.

"Do you want something special for dessert tonight?"

The smile that lights his face knocks the air from my lungs. Gone is the brooding man, and in his place is something otherworldly. Some dark angel, ethereal and hauntingly beautiful. I lick my lips.

"Do you know any good recipes for lemon drizzle cake?"

"I do, actually."

"Really?"

I nod, unable to help the small smile that tugs on my lips. He leans closer to me over the counter. "Have you always been this good at baking?"

I shake my head. "No, I'm not very good at it."

"That's not true. Do you enjoy baking?"

Do I? No one has ever asked me that. No one has ever considered my feelings or thoughts before. I tuck a loose strand of hair behind my ear and offer a sheepish shrug before moving back to preparing dinner. "I suppose. Well, yes."

"Do you have a favorite dessert?"

"I like lemon sponge cupcakes. But I..." I swallow the words back. He doesn't need to know the tumultuous relationship I have with food, the nausea that builds when I stare at a meal knowing that I'm adding to a problem, or the bile that burns my throat when I slip and indulge too much.

Telling him any of that would just ruin the surprisingly light atmosphere and companionable conversation here in the kitchen. "I like simple desserts," I add.

"Cool. Is there anything else you like to do? Hobbies or something?"

"No. I don't have anything like that."

I watch the confusion on his face. How he draws his brows together before something dark flickers over his face. It's gone in an instant.

"How about a favorite movie? Or books to read? You don't have to spend all your time looking after the house, especially not on your day off."

"Half-day," I remind him with a smile. "Plus, I don't mind."

He hums, and the rumbling sound sends a wave of pleasure through my body.

As I busy about the kitchen, to my surprise, the conversation doesn't stop. It's not invasive. Instead, he's talking about things he enjoys and making small talk.

For every question he asks me, I tentatively ask him one in return—like I can chip away at his hardened exterior little by little. I want to ask him more, pry deeper, but I don't want to ruin the fragile tether between us with my naivety.

"It smells delicious." He sighs as he stretches his long legs out.

And for once, I don't dismiss the compliment. Instead, I watch him, my lips tugging into a shy smile in response as I clean up the counter.

This is different. He's different. Softer with me than anyone else in this house.

And it terrifies me in the best way possible.

CHAPTER 14

CAMILLO

I'd completely forgotten about the dinner party that Marco planned for tonight.

Arriving home, the presence of the guests with my brothers alerted me to my lapse in memory, and I had to excuse myself, rush upstairs, shower, and throw on a suit for this meal with one of our underbosses, together with his wife and daughter.

As we sit around the dinner table, I look at the woman across from me. My brothers are hoping to set me up with her to strengthen the bond between our families.

Of an impeccable background, she's what people would call beautiful. She has stunning features and is slim yet with big boobs—fake, obviously, given the way they bob up out of her dress.

As Rosa clears away the main course, Marco gives a loud cough into the silence and lasers a deadly look toward me.

"Oh, er, sorry, what did you just say?" I reply to her mother who hasn't stopped yapping since the moment she entered our mansion.

"*I said*," she says a little too forcefully, "that our daughter is extremely bright. We've never had her tested, but she must have an extremely high IQ. She's just finished a beautician's course, you know."

No one says anything. I mean, what the fuck am I supposed to say in response to this shit? I clear my throat. "Um, that sounds...fulfilling for Sheila."

"Sheena," her mother snaps.

"Oh, yeah, Sheena...," I echo, trying to avoid looking at the woman in question. I scramble for something to say to fill the awkward silence. "Is Sheena, er, short for something?"

Her mother gives me a beaming smile. "Of course. It's short for Sheenalina."

She must be joking. "Really?" I reply with a chuckle.

"Yes, really. I wanted to call her Serafina. But my bitch of a sister used that name for her baby before I could."

"Oh," I say weakly.

"And then, I wanted to call her Evangelina. But my cunt of a cousin decided to use that name for her kid before I could."

"Oh, um, dear..." I mutter.

"And then, I wanted to call her Clementina. But my other sister—"

"Let me guess," I interrupt," hoping to bring her boring as fuck story to an end as quickly as possible. "Your ho of a sister used that name for her baby before you could."

She narrows her beady eyes at me. "*Are you calling my sister a prostitute?*" She looks like she's about ready to rip off my head.

Marco gives another loud cough. "No, he's not. *Right, Camillo?*"

"Er, right. I was just trying to continue the theme of your story."

She hoists her bosom up—which is, quite obviously, just as fake as her daughter's. "Well. I wasn't letting anyone else use my next choice of baby name. So, I came up with something completely unique. That way, none of my fucking family could claim that they'd always loved the name and that it'd been their first-choice baby name for as long as they could remember. And, guess what? It worked! Because no one used it for their baby before I could."

"I wonder why," I mutter, earning me a sharp glare from Marco.

I just give him a small shrug of my shoulders. I mean, what the actual fuck?

"Anyway, Sheena's amazing IQ means that she's the most amazing beautician in Chicago," her mother continues, puffing out her ample chest with pride. "She can do all sorts of make-up looks. She's in high demand for Fratellanza weddings and parties."

"Does she know how to clean up blood and wounds?" I blurt out. Fuck, what made me just say that? And why is my mind flashing back to the day Rosa helped me take care of my injured brothers?

Sheena looks the sort of woman who definitely wouldn't get her expensive clothes and perfect manicured nails ruined by dealing with a man like me. Whereas Rosa… Man, those tight white T-shirts she wears, clinging to every tempting curve of her breasts, which clearly aren't fake, and hips that I'd love to grab and—

Alessio gives me a sharp kick under the table.

"Will I have to deal with blood and stuff like that when I marry you?" Sheena whines in an irritatingly nasal tone.

And Rosa, who's just served the dessert, takes a sharp intake of breath when she hears the word '*marry*'.

Of course, she doesn't know that's the point of this meal—well, she does now.

When my older brothers suggested a little while back that this underboss's daughter would be a perfect match for me, it sounded like a feasible plan.

But something's changed since then. And that's why I can't summon up any enthusiasm for the woman sat in front of me who's wearing an expensive designer dress and has the face and body of a catwalk model.

***

Thank fuck that stupid dinner is over. Well, almost—Sheena is using the powder room while her parents wait for her in the entrance foyer.

After saying our goodbyes, Marco excuses us, saying that we have an urgent matter to attend to.

And then he orders me to follow him into the office.

"What the fuck was that?" Marco snarls after he slams the door shut. The office is nowhere near the foyer, so now Marco can shout as loud as he likes, knowing that there's no chance of them overhearing.

"What was what?" I mutter.

"You know what I'm talking about. When we mentioned Sheila to you before, you liked the idea."

"It's *Sheena*," I correct him.

Marco looks ready to murder me right about now. "Sheena, Sheila, Sheenalina, or whatever the fuck her name is, would make a decent wife. If you weren't interested, you should have said that before the damn dinner. Now, we've offended her father, and that's the last thing I need right now."

I rub the back of my neck. "I don't know, Marco. In person, she seems a lot less suitable. So, you may as well tell that irritating old bat of a mother that it's a no go."

Turning on my heel, I know that I have to talk to Rosa tonight and explain everything. I don't know why, but I don't want there to be any secrets between us—and I don't want to hurt her in any way.

CHAPTER 15

ROSA

Marco asked me to cook for and serve at a dinner party for his business associate's family tonight. It was only three extra people, so it wasn't too much extra work, and I was anxious to make everything perfect.

But then I hear those words from the woman called Sheena: "*Will I have to deal with blood and stuff like that when I marry you?*"

My lungs gasp for oxygen. But nothing reaches them.

Not able to think, I dash to the powder room and lean against the basin.

My thoughts are going at a hundred miles an hour.

I know I should be working, but I have to try to process what I've just heard.

But I still can't believe it—despite hearing them clearly all talking about it. *He's going to actually be marrying that woman...?*

He's never mentioned any of this to me. Not a single word. How could he do this?

I know I'm only the maid here, but the way Camillo's been with me, the way he took me to dinner, and the things he said to me...

After all that, I think that his marriage to Sheena is a fairly big, huge, substantial, ginormous thing for him to forget to mention.

I choke back a sob. Looking at myself in the mirror, my colorless expression stares back at me.

I'm pale and ugly—there's nothing special about me.

While that other woman, she could be a model—she probably is in her spare time—because she's absolutely stunning.

But there's something that's even worse, and that's the part that really gets to me...

It's that she's half the size of me. No, I'm not being honest with myself. She's more like a *quarter* of the size of me. She's definitely a size zero.

And that means he was lying to me all along when he said—no, insisted—that he prefers his women to be curvy.

How could I have been so stupid to fall for his empty words and promises?

How could I have ever believed that he really wanted me?

The same thoughts keep going around and around, but I know I have to get back to the kitchen. Finally composing myself, I open the door.

And I run straight into...

Her. Miss Skinny Minnie. I thought my evening couldn't get any worse—but fate hasn't finished with me yet.

She looks down at me, a sneer dancing across her expression. "Stay away from him!" she hisses.

"What?" I stutter. "I'm sorry, I don't understand—"

"Of course you do. Do you think I haven't noticed the way he keeps looking at you?"

"You must be mistaken. I'm just the maid here..."

"Just the maid?" she snaps. "Stop with the stupid lies. I can tell that you're much more to him than just an employee. But he's mine, do you hear me? Mine. It's been planned for ages, and I don't need a fat girl like you waltzing in and trying to steal my man."

I open my mouth, then shut it, completely lost for words.

"Do you think he would want to be seen in public with someone like you?" she snarls. "He's rich and powerful, and he needs someone like me by his side. Someone who looks the part. *Someone who doesn't stuff her face and actually bothers to look after herself.*"

She laughs as she looks me up and down. "You'd only make him a laughing stock. Everyone would know that he was only with you because he feels sorry for you. Why else would a man like him be seen with someone who looks like you?" she spits.

Her words slice into me. I wish I could just put them down to her being a mean girl, but I know what she's saying is true.

Because I could never fit into his life.

He can have any woman he wants. And, of course, he would choose someone like her over me—someone who's thin and skinny.

Because that's the very least a man like him deserves.

***

I'm gripping the edge of the kitchen counter. Thank God, Sheena and her family have left now. I try to move, but the events of tonight just keep replaying over and over.

I can't believe that he brought that woman here. And even worse, I had to serve them dinner, pretending to be nothing more to him than the maid.

But now I realize that's what I am to him—just the maid. And I'll never be anything else.

I hear his footsteps approaching. "Hey," he says softly, stepping into the kitchen.

His voice is soft, concerned, but I don't turn around. I'm not ready to look at him, not when my emotions are still so raw.

"Hey," I murmur. I can't look at him and instead occupy myself with the dirty dishes as they taunt me about the awful dinner and everything that's just happened.

As he takes a step closer, I can feel the warmth radiating from his body, but it doesn't comfort me like it usually does. His voice is low as he speaks. "I'm sorry, Rosa." His tone is sincere and genuine, and it tugs at my heart, even though I don't want it to.

"For what?" I ask, finally turning to face him. I wish that he could say something to make this all go away. But I know that's not going to happen.

He looks genuinely pained. "You should never have been put in that position tonight. *I* should never have put you in that position. I'm sorry." He takes another step closer, reaching out to take my hand.

But I pull away. Because I can't let him comfort me after that.

He lets his hand drop to his side, his expression filled with regret. "I didn't invite her to hurt you. I swear, it wasn't like that. Marco arranged this dinner ages ago—before I'd even met you—and I completely forgot all about it until I arrived home tonight and found Sheena and her family here. It's totally my fault. I'm so sorry, Rosa."

I want to believe him, but then I remember the way she smiled at him—and the hurtful words and insults she said to me outside the powder room.

"It's not like that between us," he insists, his voice practically pleading now.

"But you're marrying her..."

"No," he says firmly. "It was just a dinner for us to meet and see if we would get along. It was all set up before you were hired. If I'd remembered about it, I would have called it all off. Because you're the only one I want to get to know now."

I'm silent for a few moments. "I felt invisible tonight," I confess, my voice barely above a whisper. "Like I didn't matter. Like I was watching from the sidelines."

His eyes soften, and when he reaches for me again, he puts his hands around my face in a gentle grip.

"Rosa, you're not invisible to me..."

Tears prick at the corners of my eyes, although I try to blink them away. I don't want to cry in front of him.

"I'm so sorry I made you feel like you didn't matter," he murmurs in a gentle tone. "That's the last thing I ever wanted."

I nod, grateful for his explanation and believing what he says.

And that should be an end to it—we should be able to go back to getting to know one another.

But what happens next means there's only one option left open to me—and that's to quit.

CHAPTER 16

ROSA

The piece of paper feels heavy in my hand.

And each step forward feels like my feet are tied to lead bricks. But I keep on walking.

This is the right thing to do.

This is the *only* thing to do.

I thought things were back on track after that awful Sheena dinner.

A bitter laugh chokes at my throat.

Sheena—if only someone like her was the cause of my worries now.

The day after the dinner party with Sheena's family, my mind started working overtime. And I haven't been able to think about anything else since.

Because the worst thing happened.

I spotted one of Grayden's men, Kane, staring at me from his car as I waited for the bus.

Just the thought of the sly smirk on his face sends an icy chill rushing down my spine.

It's happened again and again over the past week—Kane's balding head and leering eyes catching my gaze in the supermarket, his looming figure watching me from across the street as a cigarette lights his face. Nausea sweeps through me at the memory.

If they've found me, then it's only a matter of time until they find Ethan.

And I can't let that happen.

I won't let that happen.

I can't stay here anymore.

They can't protect me—despite how desperately I wish they could. Despite the flutter in my stomach whenever I catch Camillo's eyes roaming my body in the kitchen. Despite the memory of him calling me gorgeous.

I remember the way his gaze held mine after he took me out for dinner, how his heat surrounded me, how his sandalwood scent filled my senses. He'd been so damn close.

But it's all the more reason to leave.

I won't bring trouble to their doorstep.

My hand trembles as I knock on the door.

"Come!" It's barked just as all Marco's orders are. A command to be followed with no objection or hesitation.

I crinkle the paper in my hand before I can take a calming breath. I have to do this.

"Sit." He doesn't even bother looking up from the papers on his desk—and I don't think I want him to.

I slide into the chair and will my body to stay still and keep from fidgeting.

My eyes are unfocused as I stare at the polished wood of the desk.

He collects the documents he's looking at into a neat stack and sets them aside. His eyes flick up to mine. "What do you need, Rosa?"

Somehow, I find a buried nerve of steel in my body. Because I know that this is what I have to do.

My gaze lifts. I extend the piece of paper toward him. "I appreciate everything that you've done for me—that you've all done for me. For giving me a chance."

His gaze skims over my letter before snapping up at me. "*You're resigning?*"

The shock on his face startles me. I've only ever seen Marco less than collected once before, and that was when he was bleeding from several places.

"I'll be leaving in one week," I say quietly. Even though I wish I could just flee straightaway, after everything they've done for me, I know I have to give them time to find a replacement. I just have to be extra vigilant for the next week—and pray that Grayden doesn't find Ethan.

Marco leans back in his chair. His arms are crossed over his broad chest. He doesn't say anything. And I'm not sure if that's worse than him yelling. "Why?" he grits out.

"I'm sorry?"

"Why do you want to resign?"

The calm mask of his face makes me shiver. It's a calmness before the storm. I can see the fury etching into his face. The way his hands tighten under his arms and his jaw clenches. My mouth opens and closes soundlessly.

"I asked you a goddamn question, Rosa!" he yells, finally snapping.

I wipe my palms on my jeans. My chest rises and falls rapidly, and I can't meet his gaze anymore. I can't tell him. I can't tell any of them. "I'm not the right fit," I mumble.

"And?"

"I'm just trying to save us all the trouble of this not working out—"

I jump out of my skin and leap out of the chair as the door bursts open and crashes back against the wall.

Camillo and Alessio rush in, both wide-eyed and panting.

"What the fuck is wrong with you two?" Marco snarls.

"I tried to stop him," Alessio rasps as he grabs Camillo's arm to hold him back.

"And why is he barging in anyway? Forgotten how a door fucking works? Or you know, knocking? I know we taught you manners when you were growing up."

"You can't fire her." Camillo glares at his oldest brother.

I know I should leave and let them handle this privately. But I can't move. I'm rooted to the spot, spine straight and heart pounding.

"And why should I care what you think?" Marco demands.

"Get the fuck off me!" Camillo shakes off Alessio. "I'm not going to do anything." Camillo strides closer. My chest twists painfully as his scent envelopes me. "She's the best damn maid we've had," he snarls, only just keeping his voice from yelling. "She cleans this place so that it looks like a palace, she cooks the best food and bakes the best cakes I've ever eaten, and she's even memorized Alessio's anal closet system—"

"It's not ana—"

"Enough!" I flinch at Marco's raised voice and the loud thud of his fists coming down on top of the desk, rattling the wood, as he tries to regain control over the whole derailed conversation.

"Think about this, Marco," Camillo growls in a dangerous tone.

"I'm quitting." But I'm not sure they've heard me. I clear my throat and speak louder. "I've just handed in my resignation."

"What?" Camillo blurts out.

Don't look at him. Don't break. This is the only way to protect everyone. To keep Ethan safe.

"You mean I chased after his ass for nothing?" Alessio whines.

"Maybe if you worked out more, you wouldn't be so winded," Camillo barks before turning back to me. "Why didn't you say something when we came in?"

"If I could have got a word in, I'd have told you," I say quietly.

"Rosa." His voice is soft, begging me to look up at him. Weak as I am, I cave and lift my chin. His eyes search my face. "Is this because of the other night?"

"What happened the other night?" Marco demands.

"Nothing," Camillo says, his eyes never leaving me.

"I just have to leave..."

"Why?" Camillo asks.

"A great question," Marco clips. "Again, had you not barged into my office, I'd have an answer to this."

Camillo gives him a glare before turning his gaze back at me. "Rosa?"

But I don't have an answer. I was going to figure out what to tell him after I'd spoken to Marco. I've been wracking my brains for whole day, scrambling around for a way to explain my leaving to Camillo, but I've come up short every single time. "Personal reasons," I murmur.

When Camillo realizes that I don't intend to expand on this, he backs up, an icy mask of indifference shuttering in place over his features.

My chest seizes.

But a curt nod jerks his head, and he shoves his hands in his pockets. "Right. Of course." Despite the coolness of his voice, his eyes swim with disappointment. But as quickly as it appears, it's shuttered behind another layer of ice. His jaw works before he turns and leaves the room.

Alessio looks toward me. "You should reconsider, Rosa," he says quietly, and the genuine tone in his voice takes me by surprise.

He turns and also walks away, leaving me once again alone with Marco.

Marco's intense gaze is fixed upon me. "I agree with Alessio. But if your mind is made up, I won't stop you."

"It is."

He nods with finality, indicating that he's accepted my decision.

I don't wait for anything else. I spin on my heel and make for the laundry room.

While some people can't do anything when they're upset, I'm the opposite. There's something about cleaning and housework here that calms me and makes me feel safe.

This is for the best.

Because if Kane follows me here, Grayden will know exactly where I am. And then, he'll drag me back to hell himself.

***

After dinner, I need some time alone. My heart gallops in my chest as I tuck a loose strand of hair behind my ear.

Sitting in my room, the need to make sure Ethan is safe pumps through me like a compulsion. I could phone to check up on him. But I need to *see* he's safe. Because Kane following me has sent my anxieties into a tailspin. I'll just have to be extra careful and take more precautions than normal.

An hour later, I'm almost there. I pull the coat I'm wearing tighter against my body, fighting against the chilly air as it whips down the street. There's been a recent rain shower, and it feels like it might rain again soon.

The flickering streetlight cast the area in a soft yellow glow. There's no one on this side of the street, and the silence is deafening.

I'm nearly at the corner of Kori's street when my hair is yanked back by the root.

My yelp echoes around the barren street.

"Found you," a voice hisses into my ear.

Hot, rancid breath washes over my neck and smothers me with the smell of alcohol and cigar.

Every bone in my body locks into place as I freeze with fear. He's found me. *Oh my God.*

"Do you really think you're smarter than me, you stupid bitch?" Grayden snarls.

Another rough yank. My feet slip out from under me on the slick surface of the alley I'm being dragged into.

"Please," I beg, my fingers clawing at his as I try to dislodge his hands.

But it's no use. He's stronger than me. He's more powerful than me in every way.

"Do you think it's funny to humiliate me?"

I can feel my hair rip from my scalp. "N-no..."

"Do you know what this has done to my reputation? How much you've fucking embarrassed me? After I gave a fat bitch like you a chance?"

His fist collides with my side, knocking the air from my lungs.

I gasp before the hard, dirty alleyway collides with my cheek.

My stomach lurches when the toe of his handmade loafer collides with my gut.

"I'm the fucking laughingstock of the country club! All because of your stupid stunt. People are fucking whispering shit about me!"

"Please," I mumble, curling into myself. "I wasn't—"

Another rough yank on my hair.

And I scream before I can swallow the sound.

"Shut the fuck up!" The cold metal of his watch collides with my jaw as the smack of his hand jolts my head to the side.

The metallic taste of blood coats my tongue.

"No one's coming to save you, you ugly bitch. You belong to me. Remember? You're fucking mine."

I cry out as he kicks me again.

"Where the fuck is my son? Where have you hidden him?"

Another smack. I feel my lip split.

"Fucking answer me! Where did you take him?"

I twist in his grasp, frantically trying to break free from the iron vise he has on my hair.

Dirt coats my knees as I drop face first to the ground. Another kick to my stomach. And I'm gasping.

Broken shards and rocks dig into my palms as I crawl forward.

Everything hurts. I can taste the salty tang of my tears and blood on my upper lip.

A sharp yelp leaves me as Grayden drags me back into the alley by my ankle.

I kick, managing to connect with his jaw.

He hisses, and I scramble away. The hard cement of the sidewalk crashes into my knee. But I manage to get to my feet and stumble down the street.

"Wait!" I scream to a bus. "Please! Wait!"

By some miracle, the driver stops just long enough for me to slip onto the bus.

It's nearly empty at this time of night. Finding a spot in the back against the window, I sink into the worn upholstery. My hands tremble in my lap as tears leak from my eyes. I curl inward, trying to take up as little space as possible.

The walk from the bus stop back to the Marchiano estate goes by in a blur of painful steps.

I don't recall if the guards spoke to me or if I slipped past them unseen. I don't remember walking down the hall and throwing up in the bathroom.

Seeing my reflection in the mirror is what breaks my trance. The woman who stares back at me is filthy and with hollow and vacant eyes. Covered in dirt, tears streaked down her face, and blood crusted down her chin.

I swallow hard and do my best to clean up. Beneath the grime, my lip is cut and swollen, and a bruise is blooming around my eye and cheek.

I think that everyone must be asleep by now, but the murmur of a voice down the hall makes me tremble. I cover my mouth to hold in the sob that burns my throat. I can't let any of them see me like this.

They'll ask questions I don't want to answer.

I press my ear to the door and wait.

When a long time has passed and there's been no more sounds, I tentatively open the door and rush toward the kitchen in the darkness.

My sigh of relief fills the air as I quickly bundle some ice in a dishtowel.

"Rosa?"

I freeze.

Oh God. Of all the people to see me like this, it'd be *him.*

"Did you go out?"

I start to shake my head but then suddenly stop because of the pain it causes. "No."

"Are you okay?"

"I'm fine," I say as evenly as possible. "I just needed a glass of water. Have a good night."

"Wait."

I can't breathe, my body trying to shrink into itself.

He looks toward the refrigerator where I was getting the ice from. "Were you getting something to eat?"

I shake my head.

"Have you eaten?" His hand slams against the wall and fumbles as he searches for the switch.

I wince as the bright light floods the area. And I can taste bile in the back of my throat as I try to shift my body away from him.

But his gentle fingers wrap around my arm, making me flinch away with a whimper in pain. He slowly turns me toward him.

But I can't look at him, my gaze looking down at my scuffed sneakers coated with dirt from the alleyway.

"*What the fuck happened?*" His words are a harsh whisper, and I can feel tears welling in my eyes.

If I open my mouth, I know I'm going to crack and break into a million pieces and never be able to put myself back together again. I fist my hands, ignoring the sting of my nails on the scrapes and cuts of my palms.

"Rosa."

The single word is harsh. It demands I look at him. But I can't.

His shadow looms over me, cornering me against the island, the hard edge pressing into my already bruised back. I whimper again before I swallow the sound.

He eases back just slightly. "Who the fuck did this?"

The words are a low, dangerous rumble. He's angry. His body coiled tight, like a predator about to strike. This is the man everyone talks about. The beast who prowls the nights.

But his anger isn't directed at me...or I don't think it is.

"Tell me."

I shake my head.

"Rosa." The sound of my name from his lips softens something inside me. He's lifting my chin gently, but I feel the stiffness in his muscles.

I can't help but look up at him.

And the growl that rips from his lips makes the air whoosh from my lungs. "Tell. Me. Who. The. Fuck. Did. This. To. You."

My vision blurs as I look into his dark eyes. A sob strangles me even as I bite my lip to keep it back.

I can't do it. I can't break. I can't shatter. Ethan needs me whole and well. If I shatter now, there'll be nothing left of me.

Camillo searches my gaze, his thumb brushing the tender bruise along my cheekbone. "Please... Please, tell me."

The words crack his voice and, with it, the dam of my emotions. My legs give out, and I sink down onto the hard floor.

Crouching in front of me, Camillo caresses my hair away from my face and cups my cheek. "Tell me who did this, Rosa. I just want to help. Please." His voice is unnaturally soft now, layered with some thick emotion, "Please let me help you."

CHAPTER 17

CAMILLO

Fury. It's an emotion I know well. Usually, I'm able to channel it into doing something useful, but right now it's calling the shots.

Red. It's the only thing I see as I sit across from Rosa in the kitchen while she tells me that the husband she left is responsible for the state she's in.

White. My knuckles are pale and bloodless from how hard I'm clenching my fists under the table.

Her hand shakes as she holds a glass of water, sloshing some of its contents onto the table.

Each word from her lips seals this fucker's fate. I'm going to make him pay. There's no doubt in my mind.

I want to hear him scream. I want him to beg for mercy.

I want his last shuddering breath to be done in agony.

I want to watch the life drain from his face. And for him to know that the hell he's going to rot in for eternity will be a paradise compared to the torture I inflict.

"I was trying to protect Ethan."

I snap back to the kitchen. "Ethan?"

"I... He's my son." She takes a deep breath. My hand curls around her trembling fingers, trying to give them a soft reassuring squeeze. The action is stiff and probably useless, but I need her to know that she can lean on me. That I want her to lean on me. Where the fuck that's coming from, I don't know, but that doesn't make it any less true.

"That's why you were quitting?"

Her head bobs, and the urge to caress her face grips me. I shove it down. The last thing she needs is for me to press into her wounds.

"He's staying with a friend. I was on my way to see him." I can hear her voice crack, and my heart clenches in my chest. The pain in her voice is like a knife to me. Slicing at me bit by bit. "I need to know he's okay."

"I'll make sure of it. Right now, you need to rest."

"I can't! I need to get Ethan to safety."

"I'll make sure he's safe. I swear on my life nothing will happen to him while there's a breath left in my body. I need to talk to my brothers."

Her hand clutches onto my forearm, and my body tightens. It's the first time someone other than my family has clutched onto me like this. The first time in a long time that someone's touched me without expecting me to come swinging. And I don't understand the feelings that are surging through me.

Her desperation is rolling off her in waves as her hand trembles against my skin. "No one else can know! Please—"

"You're safe here. I promise. But I have to tell them."

I watch her gnaw her already raw lip, and my mind begins to formulate the perfect plan to get the fucker who did this to her. How fucking dare he lay a goddamn hand on her.

"What will Marco do?" she whispers.

"I don't know," I tell her honestly. "But you're safe with me—and I'll make sure that your son is too."

Without letting go of Rosa, I use my free hand to get my cell out. I hit speed dial to each of my brothers in turn. Marco detests being woken up, but I don't care—he can chew me out later.

"I need you. Now. Kitchen." That's all I say when Marco answers.

Then I do the same with Alessio. "Kitchen. It's urgent." Then I hang up.

We only have to wait a matter of moments before we hear footsteps thundering down the staircase.

My brothers burst into the kitchen.

Both are bare-chested, their muscles gleaming under the electric lights.

Marco has a knife in each hand, his teeth bared. Alessio is brandishing his revolver. Both are ready for battle.

As Marco's eyes fall on Rosa, they widen with shock—and something else.

Anger.

"What the hell happened?" he snarls as he stands there in just his boxers, his muscles tensed, and his razor-sharp knives still fisted in his hands.

Rosa is plastered to my side, cowering from the fierceness in his words.

My jaw ticks, and I grip her hand a little tighter. She's not mine, but I'm damn well not going to let anything happen to her.

"Rosa has a son. He's in danger." I explain in as few words as I can what Rosa's just told me.

"What the fuck!" Marco roars, making Rosa jump out of her skin.

"You're angry," she chokes.

She's right. He's fucking furious.

I know Marco too well. It's not how she thinks. "It's not that you lied about having a son," I say gently. "It's because you've been separated from him."

I can see the pain in Marco's eyes. He's a dad now, and the anguish of being separated from his kids is something he's going through at this very second with the women and kids forced to stay in Italy.

Alessio is standing with his arms folded across his chest and his gray sweatpants slung low on his hips. "Tell us everything," he says. "Start at the beginning."

With a reassuring squeeze to her hand, I urge Rosa to tell them.

This time I can't hide the rage that bubbles through me when she talks about what happened. About the night he cracked her rib and her fleeing with her son. About tonight in that fucking alley.

A rough hand drags down Marco's face, and he curses under his breath.

It's a fucking mess, but I refuse to let her face this alone.

"We're bringing him here," I growl in a fierce voice that brooks no argument. "Rosa's son. He's coming here. Tonight." I catch Marco's eye. And he gives me a small nod. I can see the determination behind his gaze—he's just as angry as I am.

"He's okay where he is, but I just need to check on him. I can't impose on you." Rosa's voice is tiny. "I'm sorry. I don't want to be a problem."

"I'm not going to repeat myself, Rosa," I say in a low voice.

"But—"

"We'll keep you both safe until this shit is sorted," I grit out.

Her sob echoes around the room. And I swallow hard. I want to pull her into me and rock her. Comfort her in some way that's new and terrifying all at once.

But I don't know how.

Between hiccups and gasps, she thanks us all, over and over.

We should be treading extremely carefully due to the business relationship we have with Rosa's father. But I can't do that, not now that I've learned about all this. "About the business side—" I start.

"Fuck that," Marco snarls. "Just get her boy to safety. That's all that matters—that her and the boy are here with us and safe." Conor Davis has derived his wealth from a variety of business assets which include a pharmaceutical company. And through his plant, we've been able to produce more drugs in the States after problems getting product from Colombia due to more government crackdowns. And with Grayden Devlin being his son-in-law, things have the potential to get very messy.

I give him a nod of gratitude. Marco can sense this is important to me—and I can always count on the support of my brothers when I need them.

"Let's go and get the boy," Marco says, already barking orders down his cell phone for soldiers to meet us at the main gate.

"Ethan," I tell my brother. "His name's Ethan."

"Ethan," Marco echoes. He gives a brief nod, and then, he's gone.

I can see the uncertainty in Rosa's face. It's understandable after everything's she's been through. She doesn't know who she can trust.

"Nothing will happen to your son. My brothers and I will make sure of it. Give us ten minutes to organize everything, and then we'll be ready to leave. We'll need you with us—Ethan doesn't know us, and I don't want him to be scared. Are you up for another journey tonight?"

"Yes," she whispers, her eyes shining. And I can see that the conviction behind my words is enough to give her some reassurance.

While Rosa cleans herself up and gets ready to leave with us, I stride into the office to talk to Marco.

"I want his fucking head," I snarl.

"If I say no, you gonna do it anyway?"

"I. Want. His. Fucking. Head." I repeat the words, leaning forward so my fists are braced on the desk. "With or without your permission."

"Thought so. And her?"

"What about her?"

Marco shakes his head. "I'm not telling you not to do it. Just be careful, and for God's sake, think it through before you do it."

I drag a hand through my hair, disheveling the thick strands. I hate how I feel around Rosa. Weak and out of control.

And yet, it's the most liberating feeling I've had in a long time.

I really don't know if I should be taking relationship advice from Marco. After all, he got Juliana to marry him by kidnapping her after a bloody wedding. He's always been impulsive and a maniac; however, even that was pretty unhinged for him. But striding to the door, I linger at the threshold, letting out a deep sigh. "Thanks, man."

As he nods in reply, my thoughts are already turning to how I'm going to make Grayden Devlin pay for ever laying a finger on Rosa.

A grin stretches across my face at the thought—because I want him ruined in every sense of the word. I'm going to make a plan as soon as the opportunity arises. And he's going to learn just what it means to fuck around with what's mine...

CHAPTER 18

ROSA

"Is this...really necessary?"

I'm in the backseat of a black SUV driven by Alessio, with Marco in the passenger seat and Camillo sitting beside me. And as I look around us, I can see a convoy of half a dozen identical SUVs filled to the gills with their armed soldiers. And while I'm extremely grateful for their support, I can't help worrying that I'm putting them to a huge amount of trouble.

"I'm not taking any risks when it comes to your son," Camillo growls. He takes my hand and gives it a tender squeeze. "Ethan's too important to take any chances," he adds in a gentler voice.

We pull up outside Kori's house. I've rung ahead to let her know that we're on our way, so she's expecting us despite the late hour.

Camillo and Marco accompany me to the front door, one either side of me. Their soldiers are keeping watch, eyes and weapons trained in every direction. Please God, can Kori's neighbors all be asleep and no one look out their windows...

I ring the doorbell, and a few moments later, the door opens.

Kori, dressed in her pajamas, gives a slow whistle as she sees the SUVs lined up on the street and the armed men. Ethan is clinging to her leg, hiding as best he can until he sees me.

"Momma!"

My heart stutters as I scoop him up, plastering kisses to his face and forehead repeatedly as tears leak from my eyes. He's whole. He's untouched. He's safe. Grayden hasn't got to him yet.

"Thank you," I say to Kori, still clutching Ethan in my arms. "I don't know how I'll ever be able to repay you for what you've done for me."

"As soon as I woke Ethan up with the news that you were coming to get him, he's been so excited, but we're going to miss him." She squeezes me tight after she hands me Ethan's backpack and stuffed bear. "If you need anything, call me. And keep in touch."

"I will."

"Nice to meet you." Kori nods at the stoic statues of Camillo and Marco before we take our leave.

On the way back to the estate, Camillo rides in the front passenger seat, leaving Ethan to sit with me in the back.

My heart is in my mouth as we drive. Does Grayden know what we're doing? Are his men in the shadows, watching and waiting to grab me and Ethan? Even with the Marchianos and their soldiers surrounding us, I can't help thinking that this isn't over.

During the drive, Ethan holds my hand and snuggles tightly into my side, not wanting to let me go, and I relish the feel of his tiny body against me.

When we get back to the mansion, I breathe a small sigh of relief. As the puff of air leaves me, the tension in my body starts to recede a little. This is happening. It's actually happening.

I carry Ethan into the living room, and gently, I set him down, kneeling before him. "Are you okay? Did you eat? Are you tired?"

He startles as he catches sight of someone behind me, and his eyes widen. I know who it is without turning around. I can feel him every time we're in the same room. The air turns electric and wild. My body has a mind of its own when he's around. *Camillo.*

Ethan's tiny fists grip at my pant leg as he jumps up and cowers behind me.

"It's okay, honey," I soothe. "They're not going to hurt us."

I look over my shoulder to where Camillo leans against the wall, arms crossed over his chest. Imposing and domineering as ever. But the way his shoulders fall and the slight upturn of his lips tell me this is him relaxed. He's giving me space, but he's still close enough for anything I might need.

"These are Momma's friends. We're going to be staying with them for a while." My hand soothes over the back of his head. "Okay?"

Ethan bobs his head. I press a kiss to his forehead and stand back up.

"Are you hungry?" I ask Camillo. He and his brothers are up at this late hour because of me. "Do you want me to make something to eat or get you a drink?"

He shakes his head. "Not for us. But if Ethan is hungry, go ahead and fix him something. Then you can put him to sleep in my bedroom."

"Oh, that's not necessary," I say quickly. "He can come in with me."

"You've only got a single bed."

"I can sleep on the floor. I don't mind."

"I would put you in one of the guest rooms, but the only furnished ones are in the north wing of the house. I want you near us so that we can protect you." Camillo's voice is insistent.

"But—"

"I'm not taking no for an answer," he says firmly.

I look down at Ethan. "Are you hungry? Do you want something to eat first, or do you just want to go to sleep?"

"Just sleep, Momma," he says in a soft voice.

"Okay, come on, honey, let's get you cleaned up and settled in bed."

We follow Camillo up to his bedroom.

He starts to move some of his things out of the way.

"I'm sure we'll be just fine in the spare room," I start to say.

He pauses, a box of his gym equipment braced against his shoulder. "No." He's being oddly stubborn about this. "You'll have this bedroom from now on. And tomorrow, I'll set up the spare room next door for Ethan."

"I can't take your room."

"You're staying in here. End of story. We can't keep tabs on you if you're in another wing of the house."

"But this is *your* room."

"And now it's yours."

I grab his arm, watching the muscles flex beneath my touch. I drop it quickly. "This isn't fair to you."

"This is for the best. My room is central to the house. Someone trying to break in has to climb to the second floor and go past Marco's and Alessio's bedrooms. It's the safest place for you and Ethan. Plus, there's nowhere next to your current bedroom where we can set up a bedroom for Ethan, and he'll want to be close to you at night."

The guilt of kicking Camillo out of his own room is still nagging at me.

"Rosa." He stands before me, the box settled down by his feet. "There's no point in arguing, okay? It's fine. I promise." He leans down a little, meeting my gaze. "Just sleep in here. Please?"

The way his voice softens makes my legs turn to jelly and my stomach flutter. He's not like this often, and those fleeting moments are usually reserved for his family. "Okay," I whisper.

Bringing Ethan into Camillo's room, I help him with a quick rinse of his hands and face, and then settle with him into the bed. The sheets are clean because I changed them this morning.

As I lay there, stroking Ethan's forehead as he falls asleep, I look around at the room that I've cleaned and tidied so many times. It's spotless now—very different than how it was the first time I saw it. Camillo still struggles with tidiness, but a daily once-over by me has been keeping the room looking good.

As I stretch out in his huge bed, I feel guilty that Camillo will be in my cramped single bed tonight. He's huge, and there's no way he's going to be comfortable.

I stay awake until I hear Ethan's breathing even out. And only then can I relax and let myself fall asleep as well.

***

The next morning, I dress Ethan in one of the spare outfits the clinic had given us that Kori packed into the backpack. It's shabby and a little small, but it's clean and will do until I can sort something else out.

I open the bedroom door to take Ethan downstairs. But I'm startled to an abrupt halt.

Because our way is blocked.

By a huge, muscled body.

Camillo is on the floor outside the door.

He's instantly alert, springing to his feet, his gaze darting into the room behind me. "What's wrong?" he blurts out. "Is everything okay?"

"We're fine. But did you sleep out here last night?"

"Yeah." He shrugs at my surprised expression.

"But—"

"I had to make sure that you and Ethan stayed safe," he says firmly.

I felt bad before when I thought he'd be spending the night in my cramped single bed, but now, I feel awful knowing that he spent the night sleeping on the floor. And I also feel something else—because he did this to keep Ethan and me safe.

"I feel bad that you slept on the floor," I say softly.

"Make it up to me by making my favorite pancakes for breakfast," he says in an easy tone, and I can't stop myself from grinning.

The pancakes and bacon are ready by the time Camillo and his brothers come down to the kitchen and sit around the table.

Ethan only met the men briefly last night. And this morning, he clings to me, his tiny hands grasping the edge of my skirt, his brown eyes big and wide.

I bend down beside him, brushing a strand of his fair hair out of his face. I can feel his grip tighten, his small body pressing closer to mine "It's okay, honey," I say softly.

He nods, though I can see the fear lurking in his gaze. He's only four, and everything about this arrangement is unusual, new, and overwhelming.

"Are you hungry, honey?" I ask, rubbing his back soothingly.

He shrugs, still holding onto me as if letting go might make everything around him disappear.

I pick him up, his little arms wrapping around my neck, and lower him onto the seat next to mine.

He keeps his eyes downcast, his tiny fingers fiddling with the hem of his T-shirt.

"This is Mr. Camillo, Mr. Marco, and Mr. Alessio," I say as I point to each of the men in turn.

"Mr. Camel?" Ethan murmurs very quietly with a scrunch of his brow. "He's a camel and has two humps?"

Camillo's not known for being easygoing, and I'm pretty sure that if anyone else had just called him a camel, he'd be seeing nothing but a mist of red. But hearing the words from this tiny person in front of him just makes his lips tug up in the corners with a grin.

"Yeah, Camillo is a bit hard to say. But my nephews and nieces call me Uncle Millo, so you can call me that as well."

"Oh no," I say quickly. "He'll get used to Mr. Camillo with practice—"

"I insist," Camillo says firmly. Then he jerks his thumb at his brothers. "And you can call them Uncle Marco and Uncle Alessio." Then, he thinks of something else. "And Rosa, please cut the 'Mr.' and sir thing with us all; we're just Camillo, Marco, and Alessio from now on."

My eyebrows shoot up, but his brothers simply nod in agreement.

"Do you like pancakes?" Camillo continues.

But Ethan doesn't say anything and instead huddles into my side.

I give an apologetic look to Camillo.

Camillo's brow furrows as he outright ignores the food on his plate—a complete first for him. I can tell he's trying to think of a way to break the ice with Ethan.

"Here comes Mr. F," he announces, giving his best attempt at a friendly smile. But for some reason, it comes out more like a grimace—and makes him look a little scary. And Ethan must think the same because he buries his face into the sleeve of my shirt.

But Camillo's not one to give up easily. "He's a Chow Chow dog," he says, gesturing to the huge dog who's approaching. "And he might look like a grizzly bear, but he doesn't eat people—the only thing he eats is everyone else's food which, by the way, he's always stealing."

Ethan's gaze widens in panic, and he clutches at my arm.

"It's okay, honey," I reassure him. "The dog is friendly and won't hurt you."

But Ethan won't be comforted, and he spends the whole meal clinging to me and refusing to eat.

"Camillo," Marco barks, startling not only me but also Ethan. "Let's go. We've got stuff to handle at the casino."

"Now?" Camillo says.

A silent exchange between them happens, and Camillo's posture changes instantly. He nods at his brother before turning back to me. "We'll be back before dinner, Rosa. Our men have got the whole estate guarded and monitored. No one can get in or out without us knowing. You're safe here. But if you need me—for whatever reason—just call my cell."

I nod at him, grateful for everything he's doing.

"See you later, Ethan," he says more gently.

And I can't help noticing the hurt that flickers over Camillo's face when he doesn't get a response from Ethan. I try to explain. "It will just take Ethan a little time to get used to being here."

After breakfast, I bring Ethan through the house with me as I clean. As I tackle the kitchen first, he sits at the counter, legs swinging. "Here, honey. Momma has to do some cleaning and housework, so I need you to be on your best behavior for me, okay?" I hand him some paper and a pen for him to draw with.

Ethan spares me a small tentative smile. And throughout the day, I don't dare move away from his line of sight, instead taking him with me from room to room as I work.

In the late afternoon, I'm back in the kitchen and preparing dinner. My knot of anxiety and worry loosens, and something inside me melts, seeing Ethan here with me.

I heard the men return a couple of hours ago. They must be working in the office or be down in the gym because they haven't come into the kitchen. No doubt they'll wander in once they start feeling hungry.

I find myself sitting at the counter beside him as I chop vegetables, just soaking up that he's here with me again. My lips press to his forehead before I turn back to my job. I refuse to let the Marchianos think that my son is a distraction. If they did, they might send us packing.

Ethan's tiny hands keep touching my arm, as if he's making sure that I'm still there next to him. My heart aches when I think of how much he must have missed me when I had to leave him with Kori.

A while later, my thoughts are interrupted. "Rosa?" Just the sound of my name from Camillo's lips makes my heart gallop in my chest. It's like it's something decadent and forbidden. I shouldn't like it as much as I do. But for someone so intimidating, he's only ever shown me kindness and gentleness. "Smells great," he says as he and Marco enter the kitchen. "Can you take a second? I need you upstairs."

"Yes, of course." Wiping my hands on my apron, I look at Ethan, but seeing him there, I'm unable to move my body away from him.

"He'll be fine. I'll stay in here with him to make sure," Marco says.

As comforting as Marco's offer should be, I still find myself hesitating. He wouldn't hurt my son. I know that deep down. But after everything that's happened, I worry each time I let Ethan out of my sight, fear sinking its icy claws into me.

Ethan's body goes rigid, and I swallow hard. The wide, fearful expression on his face keeps me rooted in place.

"It'll only take a few minutes," Camillo assures me. "Ethan can come too, actually."

My brow puckers as I look up at him, the harsh angles of his face softening. Reaching my hand out for Ethan, I grip it tight, not sure what to expect as we go upstairs.

The fleeting feel of Camillo's hand on the small of my back calms the nervousness that swims through my veins. But it does nothing to stop the frantic beating of my heart or the butterflies that have taken flight. If anything, it causes them to accelerate.

I freeze in the doorway to the room next to Camillo's. Alessio is putting a final screw in a bed that resembles a red racing car. Until today, this room has always been empty. But now there's also a dresser, nightstand, a toy chest, bookshelves, and a small cozy couch.

"You should have listened to me in the first place," Alessio complains to Camillo. "I told you that you had this piece the wrong way around, but as usual, your stubborn ass refused to listen to me. There, it's all done now. I swear it would have been quicker to put all this furniture together myself instead of having your and Marco's clown-like input."

"You and your brothers did all this?" I murmur in a small voice.

"Yeah."

"But why...?"

Camillo shrugs. "For Ethan."

"I'll see you at dinner," Alessio says over his shoulder as he takes his leave. But all I can do is look in stunned silence at the room they've set up for my baby boy.

Then I also see several bags and a handful of boxes, just waiting at the side of the room. I step toward them. "What are these?"

"We... I..." Camillo rubs the back of his neck, looking away. "It's some toys and new clothes for Ethan. Shoes too. Marco and I thought he could use them."

"What?" The word tumbles from my trembling lips. It's too much.

"He didn't come with anything but a backpack and his stuffed bear."

I spin to face Camillo. "This is too much," I choke out. I watch his throat work over a lump as his gaze moves over me, something vulnerable shining in his dark eyes. My heart stutters.

"It's nothing."

"I'll pay you back. Every cent."

"Absolutely not."

"You can deduct it from my pay, plus something for Ethan's rent and food."

Camillo's brow lowers, shadowing his eyes. "No."

"Please. This is very generous, but you didn't need to do any of this."

"I know. But we... *I wanted to.*"

Why does that make my insides turn to jelly? What is it about seeing this hardened man soften that makes my insides come roaring to life?

The urge to pull his face down to mine and plant my lips against his grips me tightly. I make a small step forward before catching myself.

I watch as his muscles tighten beneath his shirt, his sleeves rolled up like usual, showing his strong wrists and forearms. It'd be wrong to move closer. He's just being nice. He's always just being nice.

"I don't want to be a charity case or some sort of leech on you."

"The fuc—" He pauses, eyes bouncing between Ethan and me. "The *duck* you are."

I chew the inside of my cheek to keep from smiling at his correction. Since moving in with these men, I've yet to hear them censor a single one of the curses that come flying out of their mouths with alarming regularity. It's endearing to see the effort he's making in front of Ethan.

"But where are you going to sleep?"

"The bedroom I mentioned in the next wing."

"You're already letting me bring my son to stay here with me. We don't need any more. You didn't need to go to all this trouble..."

"It wasn't trouble at all. Really."

The sincerity on his face melts me even more. Those flutters turn into a hurricane, and my stomach swoops as I squeeze my legs tight. "I'd still like to pay you back. Please."

"Just keep making those cupcakes and all the meals, and we'll call it even."

I purse my lips, although I can't help a smile spreading across my face. Whatever he says, I'm still going to find a way to pay him back every cent.

"Go on and look through it. The associate at the store said it should all fit, but if it doesn't, we'll return it and get the right size." His voice is soft, barely above a whisper, meant just for me to hear—a tenderness creeping in that he's only letting me see.

"Thank you," I exhale.

The corner of his lip kicks up, and I can't help matching it with a shy smile of my own. I turn and gently guide Ethan toward the bags and boxes. I'll find a way to pay him back. To show him how much this means to Ethan...and to me.

***

I knock at the office door to let the men know that dinner is ready. They troop in and take their seats at the dining table.

Dinner is pretty much a repeat of breakfast with Ethan barely looking up and being too nervous to eat. But at the end of the meal, I have to say something before the men leave. "Thank you—all of you," I say quietly. "For letting me bring Ethan here and for everything you did today for us."

Marco gives me a nod before pushing his chair back and heading with Alessio toward the office.

Camillo's dark eyes lock on mine.

And my throat runs dry.

Something lingers in his gaze, but I can't quite pinpoint what I'm seeing. Warmth and something else...

***

I've just tucked Ethan in when I hear a noise from somewhere in the house.

All the men are out, and they said they wouldn't be back until much later.

And that can mean only one thing: *someone's in the mansion who shouldn't be.*

My heart starts to race.

I need to ring for help.

But my phone's in the kitchen.

Should I stay hidden up here?

Should I just hope that whoever it is doesn't come into this room?

Will the guards come before the intruder gets me?

Oh God, what do I do?

I snatch up Ethan's bear for some reason—he's comforting. And I tiptoe back to my bedroom to get some sort of weapon.

But I can't find anything that looks useful. And I just grab the nearest thing.

I take a deep breath. And I step back into the hallway to get to a phone. I need to ring Camillo. Or ring the guards.

But as I turn the corner, I run into *him.*

His gun is pointed at me.

And I'm about to have a heart attack.

My lungs can't suck in any air.

His eyebrows snap up. "*What are you doing?*"

"I thought you were an intruder or a serial killer or something," I exclaim with a loud exhale as I realize it's Camillo.

He tilts his head to one side. "I *am* a serial killer, kind of..."

Jesus, he's right about that. "I mean, I didn't realize it was someone from the family creeping around down here. I thought you were all out."

"I was, but I came back to get something before I have to go back out."

"To do what? Actually," I say quickly, "don't answer that."

He gives me a strange look. "Why are you holding that?" His head nods at the can I have clutched in my hand.

"I thought the intruder might think the hairspray bottle was a baseball bat given that the lights are off..."

He raises a brow. "A baseball bat?"

"Well, it *is* a jumbo sized can..." I try to make myself sound more convincing than I feel.

"Uh huh." He tilts his gaze to the side. "And what about the teddy bear? Was he going to protect you when you went up against the intruder?"

"What? Uh, no..." I snatch the bear behind my back. "He was just, er, for moral support..." Could I sound any more ridiculous? "Oh God, just shoot me now," I mutter.

He looks down at his gun and then back up at me.

My eyes widen. "I don't mean for you to actually *shoot me*. I just meant that..." My voice trails off. I just meant that I want to disappear the hell away from this man and the fumbling mess I'm making of this situation.

"It's okay, Rosa," he says in a soft voice. He carefully takes the hairspray and bear from my hands and leads me back to my room. "You're safe here, I promise."

And there's something in the way he says those words that makes me feel safe—makes me feel protected. And I see that same look in his eyes as I saw at dinner. And it's something that has my body heating and my breath picking up.

CHAPTER 19

CAMILLO

I get up this morning after spending the night sleeping outside Rosa and Ethan's bedrooms, just as I have every single night since Rosa first brought Ethan here.

While Marco and Alessio go for a workout in our mansion's gym, I have breakfast with them both, and as we eat, I can't help but notice Rosa and Ethan flinching at the slamming of a door down the hall.

As soon as breakfast is over, I text both my brothers. "Meet me in the office. It's important."

They arrive immediately. "What's wrong?" Marco barks as he slams the door shut behind him.

"That." He looks at me in confusion. "And all the other door slamming the pair of you seem to do all day long."

"You're just as bad, especially when you're a grumpy ass first thing in the morning," Alessio retorts.

"No, I'm not. I've stopped slamming doors since..."

I don't finish what I'm saying, not wanting to admit to my brothers that I've been making an effort to be quieter around the house for the sake of Rosa and Ethan.

"And it's not just the doors. It's all the shouting down the phone," I say as I look at Marco. "And all the stomping around the house," I add as I switch my gaze to Alessio.

I scowl at my brothers. Irritation licks through me, bubbling through my blood. "I get everyone's wound up with the feds still being all over our asses and the women and kids having to remain in Italy for the time being. But you need to be a little more conscious of the loud noises you're making around here."

"Here? What, you mean like *in my own home?*" Marco snarls.

"Yes. I want..." I take a deep breath. "I want Rosa and Ethan to be comfortable."

Marco just continues to glare at me. He's not very good at taking into account other people's feelings.

I drag my hand over my hair and try to make them understand. "They scare easily. You know, after everything they've been through. I just want to make things easier for them."

The only thing I care about right now is Rosa and Ethan not being scared and not flinching. And once I explain this to my brothers, they get it.

"Okay," Marco says with a nod.

"Got it," Alessio adds without further argument.

And I know that my brothers will do this because they can sense how important it is to me.

A week. It's only been a week since Rosa was reunited with Ethan. The change is palpable in her. She hums more often now, singing when she thinks the house is empty and it's just the two of them.

But the moment one of us enters the room, Ethan's smile drops from his face and Rosa only flashes a tentative smile before getting back to work.

I fucking hate it.

I hate how much I crave seeing her smile and hearing her sing. Anything from her is a glorious gift, and I spend the rest of the day thinking about it over and over. It's a distraction I can't afford right now, but one that won't go away.

***

Ethan sits across from me this morning, finishing his pancake, eyes downcast.

I've tried to talk to him, but he simply blinks at me, his chest rising and falling too rapidly. Worse is when he hides behind Rosa or the furniture in the house when I enter the room.

It's not personal, I repeatedly tell myself.

It's *his* fucking fault. Grayden fucking Devlin.

And just like that, another reason to skin him layer by layer is added to the ever-growing list. Marco's warning still swirls in my head, stopping me from doing something too rash—because I don't want to ruin what I have with Rosa, although I'm not sure exactly what that is.

"Was something wrong with breakfast, Camillo?" she asks.

"Huh?"

Rosa stands beside Ethan, fingers brushing back the soft waves of his hair from his face. She's motherly and affectionate, and my chest warms as I watch her with her son.

She looks down at my plate. "You've hardly touched your food. Was there something wrong? Do you want me to make you something else?"

"No." I look down at the half-eaten pancake. My mind's too preoccupied to even enjoy the fucking perfectly cooked breakfast. I rub at my jaw, managing to put a smile on. It feels strained and fake. "It's great. It's just work stuff." I shovel a few more bites into my mouth to prove the point.

I've got too much going on in my head. And I can't tell her what's bothering me even if I wanted to. Because I don't even understand it myself.

As I walk away, I try to formulate in my mind what's going on. It takes me a while. And when I figure it out, the realization bowls me over.

I want Ethan to like me. I want him to laugh and relax in my presence.

Rubbing at my sternum, I hope I can make the tightness in my chest go away. Since when do I give a shit about anyone who isn't my family?

I don't even enjoy my nieces and nephews this much. I love them and will spoil them rotten during the holidays and birthdays, but this need with Ethan is different. I feel protective of him as I do his mother. Some urge to stand between him and the world nags in the back of my mind constantly.

But I don't know what to do.

I don't know how to connect with Ethan—or with kids in general. They're breakable and small. Worse, Ethan is so quiet and timid that I'm not sure I know how to break through to him.

I rise from my chair and freeze in the doorway. "It was delicious, Rosa. Thank you."

I school my features before entering the office. Marco is behind the desk, while Alessio lounges in a chair with a laptop open in front of him. They look engrossed in whatever it is they're dealing with.

"What do you need?" Marco clips.

"Advice?" I don't sound too sure.

His eyes lift from the paper, a dark brow arched. I never come to my brothers for advice.

Alessio's eyes bore into me before he jerks his chin to the free chair beside him.

"Uh…" I wasn't expecting to talk to both of them at the same time.

"Out with it. I don't have all day," Marco barks.

"This was a bad idea," I say, starting to rise from the chair.

"Sit," he growls.

"Gonna call me a good boy if I do?" I fire back.

Alessio's lip twitches, but Marco's fierce expression has me looking away as I sink back into the chair.

"Now, what is it?" he says in a terse tone.

My lips move, but I find it hard to get the words out. "How…" I wince, shaking my head, unable to look at either of my brothers.

Alessio sighs with impatience. "How what?"

"How do you get kids to like you?" I blurt out.

Alessio snorts, looking at me like I'm a freak—as if I don't already know that.

"What kind of question is that?" Marco grits out.

"A serious one?" I try.

"How do you act with our kids when they're here?" Marco clips.

"I don't. Or not well. You guys are usually there most of the time. I don't have to do much around them."

"You literally babysat them for us before they left," Alessio interjects.

"Yeah, but for what, a couple of hours? I bribed them with a shit ton of candy and sat them in front of the TV. Anyway, it's not as if they all really like me."

"Of course, they like you," Alessio says in a confused voice.

"I've got three words to say to you," I reply. "Maximo. Shampoo. Superglue."

Marco sighs. "My son likes your sense of humor. He thought you would find it funny in the same way he did. I get that his actions were a bit misplaced, but I'm telling you, the kids all like you."

"I don't know." I shrug with a heavy sigh. "This feels different, somehow..."

Marco cocks a brow. "You mean with Ethan?"

"Yeah," I say with a large exhale. "So, any advice?"

"Well, for one, stop doing those smiles at him," Alessio advises.

"Huh?"

"Yeah," Marco agrees. "It makes you look like a serial killer. And it's creepy as fuck."

I scowl at them both. "You're fucking with me, right?"

"No, we're not," Alessio adds with a straight face.

Breathing through my nostrils, I rub the back of my neck. I'm not a big smiler at the best of times, but my nerves in front of Ethan are making it difficult to even smile properly. I don't want to fuck things up, but things really aren't looking promising for me so far. "Okay, stop with the weird smiling. What else?"

"Quit with those jokes that aren't even funny."

"What jokes?"

"Like when you said that Mr. F is like a grizzly bear and steals everyone's food. Ethan looked terrified at the prospect."

"Oh, come on," I say as I glare at them. "I was just trying to break the ice."

"Do you want our fucking advice or not?" Marco growls.

"Okay. Fine. I'll stop with the jokes. But what else...?"

"Play a game with the kid? Watch a movie? It's not that hard."

I bite back a groan. "It is that hard when the kid flinches every time something unexpected happens. I want him to like me, not to have a fucking heart attack each time I speak to him. It's just not that easy with him."

Marco considers what I've said. "What's the kid actually like?"

"No clue."

"So, find out, and go from there."

"I know a few shows the kids watch all the time and don't shut up about," Alessio adds, his eyes lighting up with a soft smile. It's not the hardened expression I know him to wear daily. It's something else—a rare sight, and something that only appears when he's talking about his wife and kids.

"You just need to find something to talk to him about," Marco says.

I chew at the inside of my cheek as I rise from the chair. I don't think that their advice is going to really help me. But none of their kids are what you'd call mousy, so maybe they're the wrong people to ask.

"Need anything else?" Marco asks.

"Nope. That was it."

They share a look, and I can't quite figure out what it means. I don't like it, but I don't have the time to waste here.

"Don't forget we have a meeting at the casino," Marco reminds me.

"I know."

"I'm serious," he growls.

"I'll be there."

"On time."

"Do you want me to set an alarm? Or maybe you'd like to follow me around all day to make sure? I'll be there, don't worry." It's important we all present a united front for today's meeting at the casino. I'm not going to mess it up.

Marco nods, satisfied, and I fly out the door and down to the gym. My body is wound too tight to focus. I need to let out something before I explode. I'm too pent up and worried to be around anyone.

The sweat drips down me, clinging to the strands of my hair that hang in my face as I collapse onto the bench. I inhale sharply before pulling my phone from my pocket. My finger hovers over the name before I bite the bullet and push it down.

"What's wrong?"

"Uh... Hi to you. Nothing's wrong. I just..." Fuck. Asking for help shouldn't be this hard. I should be able to figure this all out on my own. But I don't know the first thing about kids, and I haven't got a clue where to start.

"Camillo?"

"Sorry. I just need some advice."

I hear my cousin, Lorenzo, settle into his chair as the creak of leather sounds over the speaker.

"And you're asking me?"

"Yeah. I asked Marco and Alessio already, but their advice wasn't helpful. It's about kids."

He pauses for a few moments. "Did you knock someone up?"

"What? Fuck. No!" I drag a hand down my face and lean forward so my elbows rest on my knees. "It's complicated."

The next twenty minutes are me filling Lorenzo in on the whole Ethan situation. I purposely leave out the fact that I want to impress Rosa and that I want to show her I can be there for both of them. From the amused tone as he asks questions, I'm sure he already knows.

"So, any advice? Because I know how Clara was pretty quiet and withdrawn when she was younger." Clara is Lorenzo's oldest daughter. He had a lot of issues with her after his first wife died, and it wasn't until he remarried that things started to improve for his family—although things were pretty rocky with his new wife to start with, especially as it was an arranged marriage. It's hard to comprehend everything he went through when you see how happy he is with his wife now.

"Yeah, I think I can help."

I pace, making mental notes as Lorenzo offers some suggestions. Crafts and games. Read stories together so that we have something to talk about. Take it slow—baby steps. Let Ethan dictate the interaction. Talk about what we're doing instead of asking direct questions. Keep it all low key so as not to increase his anxiety.

It's all solid advice. I can do this. *I hope.*

"Is she pretty?"

"What?" I bluster.

"The girl you're trying to impress, Camillo?"

"Wow, look at the time," I say in a rush. "I gotta go."

Lorenzo's laughter fills my ear, and I can't help the smile that spreads across my face.

"Good luck."

"Thanks, Lorenzo. I owe you."

I make a mad dash to my room, knowing Ethan and Rosa are downstairs still. After a quick shower, I dress for the meeting at the casino, my mind whirling. On the way back, I'll stop to get the necessary things.

I feel my heart racing in my chest. Because if this doesn't work, and if this blows up in my face, I don't know what I'm going to do.

***

I'm standing in the living room, and I see Ethan hovering in the doorway. His small hands are gripping the doorframe while he looks into the room through his eyelashes.

He's still skittish around me, and I want to make this work for Rosa's sake, but more than that, I want Ethan to feel comfortable around me. I've got Lorenzo's advice now, but I still need to take that first step. And although ways to break the ice keep running through my mind, none of the ideas ever seem quite right...

I look at what's caught Ethan's attention. Mr. Fluffy is lying on the rug in front of the fireplace. Although the dog is a lazy greedy guts, he's also gentle, patient, and cuddly. Could he be the way to reach Ethan?

I crouch down onto my haunches next to the dog, rubbing his ears, and then I look up at Ethan. "Hey, Ethan," I say, deliberately keeping my voice light. "Have you petted Mr. Fluffy yet?"

Ethan barely moves, but his eyes flicker from me to Mr. Fluffy and back again. He follows this with a slight shake of his head, just a tiny movement, but he doesn't take a step forward. I can see the hesitation in him, the uncertainty. "He's friendly, you know," I continue. "He loves meeting new friends."

I bring my hand down to pat Mr. Fluffy's side, and his tail thumps against the floor, his eyes half-closed in contentment. In this relaxed state, I'm hoping that maybe Mr. Fluffy will help put Ethan at ease. "You can come closer if you want. You don't need to be scared of him," I add. "He's just like a big fluffy teddy bear." I make sure not to liken him to a grizzly bear this time.

Ethan still stays rooted by the doorway, not moving a millimeter, and I can tell he's torn between wanting to trust me and wanting to stay as far away as possible. Inhaling a deep breath, I remind myself that this will take time. Building trust isn't something that can happen overnight.

"Do you know what Mr. Fluffy loves?" I say, trying a different approach. "He loves when people give him belly rubs. And I bet he'd love one from you."

Ethan's big brown eyes widen a little. "Really?" His voice is barely above a whisper.

"Really," I say with a nod. "He won't hurt you, I promise. If you want to, you can come and sit next to me."

Ethan stands there, frozen. But then, very carefully, he tiptoes into the room, as if he's not entirely sure this is a good idea. I just stay where I am, letting him come to us on his own terms. Mr. Fluffy senses the tension, and lifting his head slightly, he wags his tail slowly.

Ethan reaches us, and I can see the uncertainty in his eyes. "It's okay," I say in a quiet, gentle voice. "You can put your hand out and let him sniff it. He likes it when people do that."

Ethan hesitates, but then he reaches out. Mr. Fluffy sniffs the offered hand, his wet velvety nose nudging against Ethan's fingers. Then, unable to help himself, the dog licks Ethan's hand with a quick soft swipe of his tongue.

Ethan gives a tiny giggle—a sound that makes my heart swell—and before I know it, he's sitting down next to Mr. Fluffy, and his tiny hands are running tentatively along the animal's fur. And as the time passes and Ethan starts to relax, his movements become a little more confident. "Can I give him a belly rub now?" he whispers.

"Sure," I nod. And I watch as Ethan gives Mr. Fluffy a careful touch on his tummy, the dog instantly rolling over onto his back and wagging his tail with enthusiasm, eager for more.

I sit back and let them bond, feeling a small sense of relief. This is a good start—a tiny step toward something more. I know there's still a long way to go, but for now, I'm just really relieved and happy to see Ethan smiling.

***

I sit too straight and too rigid to appear natural as Ethan sits across from me.

His cards are fanned out on the coffee table across from my own, the deck separating the two. Rosa is cleaning somewhere down the hall.

Over the last two weeks, I've slowly made progress. I've made my steps light and quiet. I've lowered my voice, being calm and gentle as I speak to him. I let him decide when and for how long we interact. And today's the first day he's allowed Rosa to leave without rushing after her.

"Any blues?"

Ethan shakes his head. He still won't say much, but I do get his fleeting smiles across the table at mealtimes. Each one knocks the wind out of me, making me feel like I've won the fucking lottery. Like mother, like son, it seems.

I draw a card, adding it to the line of cards.

"Any greens?" he whispers.

I slowly scoop the three cards together and slide them toward him. That's all he needs to win the hand. Did I let him win? Maybe, but the way his eyes light up loosens something in my chest. The raging beast inside me relaxes, and pride eases it back like a balm.

At that moment, Rosa comes in and sets down a plate of crackers and cheese beside Ethan. To my surprise, she also sets down a small plate of cookies—made specifically for me with chocolate protein powder, rolled oats, and peanut butter. It's become my new guilty pleasure.

"Thanks, Rosa."

"Momma, I won against Uncle Millo." Ethan smiles up at her.

"You did?"

He beams at her, showing her his winning pile of cards.

"Great job, honey. Eat up now. It's gonna be a while until dinner." She bends down, giving me a perfect view of her plump ass, to press a kiss to Ethan's head. My eyes track her as she walks back out of the room to finish up whatever chore she was doing.

"Would you like to stop for the day?" I ask Ethan. This the by far the longest we've interacted, and I don't want to push my luck.

His lips purse, and his forehead wrinkles in thought. "No."

I blink. I bite back the smile that threatens to pull my lips up. Progress. It's slow, but it's progress.

"A different game?"

Instead of answering, his eyes fall to the plate of cookies, and my brow arches. "You can have one if you want."

He doesn't move, and I slowly push the plate toward him. "I won't eat them all," I tell him. I would, but he doesn't need to know that. I'll just grab a bar on my way to the casino tonight. "It's okay."

He tentatively picks up a cookie, adding it to his plate. That uncomfortable feeling in my chest burns, and I rub at it, clearing my throat. I take a cookie myself, giving what I hope is a comforting smile before popping it into my mouth.

He nibbles on his, testing it out. I hate how tentative he is with his food. How unsure he is.

Silence fills the space. This is normal. I've come to accept it. Ethan continues to munch on his food, and I watch him as I polish off another cookie.

"Can we…" He stops, looking down.

"Can we?" I prompt, my voice as soothing as I can make it.

"Can we walk around?"

"The house?"

He nods.

"Sure. You didn't when you first got here?"

Another shake of his head.

"Well then, you've missed the best part." I slowly stand from where I've rested on the floor for the last hour. "We've got the best playroom for miles."

My knees and joints are stiff from sitting so long, but it was well worth it. My hand extends down to his small figure, and I wait for him to decide if we're going to hold hands or not.

He frowns. "What's that?"

"What?"

He points to the back of my hand.

"It's a tattoo. It's like a drawing on my skin."

Luckily, the hand that faces him doesn't display the more macabre of the artwork that crawls up my wrists and arms.

He stares at my hand for a minute before his tiny fingers latch onto mine. My heart stops in my chest, and I'm not breathing.

Something warm and sweet slides through my body. Some emotion I can't put into words but want to as Ethan squeezes my hand tightly. Damn if it doesn't feel so right.

I catch Rosa's soft smile and a shine in her eyes as she passes the room and sees us together.

Soon, I can tell that Ethan is getting tired. I suggest that we watch a movie, something calm and quiet so that he can relax, and he agrees.

I pick Ethan up and gently put him on the couch, tucking him up with a blanket as he curls up against the cushions.

Mr. F lumbers up and settles down next to Ethan, while I sit on the other side, keeping a little distance to give Ethan his space.

As the movie plays, after ten minutes, I notice that Ethan's eyes are drooping, and before long, he's fallen asleep, his head resting on Mr. F.

His little body is completely relaxed, one hand still tangled in Mr. F's fur. And the dog stays perfectly still, as if he knows that his job right now is to keep Ethan safe and warm. He's even taken to spending every night sleeping outside Rosa and Ethan's bedrooms with me as if he's reluctant to let Ethan out of his sight, and a part of me realizes how much the animal wants to take care of the little boy and make him feel comfortable here.

Maybe I was a little harsh before when Mr. F ate my lemon and coriander chicken—plus when he finished all the bacon before Rosa could cook me any. I know I'm a grumpy fucker at times, but there are also plenty of times when I buy toys for Mr. F and take him for walks, and maybe I need to up that a bit to show him my appreciation. Because I do appreciate Mr. F—he's a part of this family now, and it wouldn't be the same without him here.

At night, the animal even wants to snuggle up with me when we're both sleeping outside Rosa and Ethan's bedrooms. Maybe I'm going soft because I find myself looking forward to having his soft fur next to me.

And as I sit there and watch them both, I can't help but smile. Ethan's trust is still fragile, but this is another step in the right direction.

CHAPTER 20

ROSA

Camillo's deep voice rumbles through the room as I continue to polish the wooden bookcases.

Ethan is nestled beside him, focusing on the colorful pages in front of them. The sight alone brings tears to my eyes. But it's more than that. It's watching them interact that squeezes my heart so often and makes my throat run dry.

As if he can feel me looking at him, Camillo's eyes rise above the book. The smile on his face turns my body to a molten pool. It's the same smile he gave me before our dinner date—the one that transforms his face and turns me to goo on the spot.

He continues to read softly, and I turn back to my work before my heated cheeks can give away where exactly my head is drifting.

What is it about seeing Camillo with my son that ignites some part deep inside of me? There's something so unknowingly attractive about how soft he is with Ethan that it makes my heart race.

I try not to eavesdrop on their conversations—the fact that Ethan even talks to him, brief as it is, shocks the hell out of me—but I can't help it. I lean back, trying hard to make out all the words and relishing the fact that Ethan is getting more and more comfortable.

I know it's a dangerous line to walk, but I want him to feel as safe as I do here—regardless of how temporary it all has to be.

"Swimming?" I hear Ethan's voice pipe up.

I whirl around, nearly knocking the lamp to my left over. I catch it just in time and let out a soft sigh.

Ethan's looking right at me, his big brown eyes pleading to go.

A tentative smile pulls my lips up, and I nod.

The smile on his face lights it up, and my heart clenches. This is my little boy again—the one he should have always been.

"He's never gone swimming before," I tell Camillo.

I can't quite hear what he says, but Ethan bobs his head up and down and heads upstairs, leaving Camillo and me standing in the room.

"You don't have to do this," I start. "I can watch him while I clean."

"It's hot, and I could use the exercise. It's not a problem." His eyes travel along my body, leaving a heated wake in their path. "You can join us. You can spare some time, right?"

I shake my head. "I've, um, got a lot to get done."

The idea of anyone seeing me in a swimsuit, exposed to the world, makes bile burn the back of my throat. And as tempting as it would be to sink into the crystal blue water and relax, I'm supposed to be working.

Camillo nods and heads up the staircase too.

I make a beeline for the kitchen, a perfect window to the estate's yard and the pool within eyesight. I'm not too busy that I can't watch, but I don't want to be caught slacking on my job either. Despite Marco effectively dismissing my resignation, I don't want to risk it. I owe them too much.

A while later, the sound of a splash has me jerking my head up, anxiety gripping me. Ethan stands on the pool deck, life vest and swim trunks bulking him out.

Camillo shakes out his head, pushing the damp strands back from his eyes. Even from here I can see the water dripping off his sculpted muscles and sloping down the valley of his chest. All his tattoos are on display, the ink crawling along his back like smoke surrounding a beast.

The vivid lines and arcs highlight the dips and valleys of his broad back and bring his whole body to life.

His large hand reaches out toward Ethan before gently guiding him down to the deck, so that his legs dangle in the water. They're talking, but I can't hear their words despite the window being open.

Ethan's being well taken care of, so I drop my gaze back to the fruit before me. The platter is nearly done, and pitchers of juice and lemonade sit on a serving tray. The laundry is the last thing I have to finish, and it's running a cycle now. I could, if I wanted, go out there and dip my feet in.

I gnaw the inside of my cheek. I'd made the fruit platter and drinks assuming the others would join eventually. But so far, it's just the two of them.

Bonding.

The word slips into my mind, coating with honey. I don't hate it. In fact, I could fall into the sensation and never resurface. And that alone is a scary but tempting thought.

Shaking my head, I carefully balance the drinks tray in my hand and push out the door toward the yard.

Ethan's soft peel of laughter is like a piece of beautiful music. I set the tray down. He's splashing on the step, making small waves like he does in the bath. Camillo's large body looms next to him.

My knees wobble when Camillo's dangerous smile floats my way. His dark brow is raised in a silent question for me to join them.

I shake my head and dash inside. I can feel the heat crawling up the back of my neck and cheeks. The thought alone of being near him like that... it's more tempting than I want to admit.

When I emerge again from the kitchen with the fruit tray, Ethan is kicking his legs and bobbing in the water before they're both climbing out, dripping wet. Ethan rushes toward me before I can stop him.

Camillo gently grips his hand, and he murmurs something about running with wet feet. I melt a little at how caring he is toward Ethan.

Eyes wandering, I take him in. The broad expanse of his chest, the hard lines of well-earned muscles glistening with water. My tongue runs over my lips subconsciously before I can avert my eyes.

"Having fun?" I ask.

Ethan nods as he gives me a big grin.

"You didn't need to do this, Rosa." The smile on his face says he's thankful, though. "We're going to see if the others want to join in."

"I figured you'd be hungry and thirsty."

Ethan settles himself in a chair and reaches out for a piece of fruit before stopping.

"Go for it, buddy," Camillo encourages, toweling off his hair. "Have as much as you want."

Ethan settles back with a slice of apple. "Momma swim too?"

I can feel Camillo's gaze zero in on me without having to look. It makes my skin tingle and my stomach flutter. "Not today. I have to finish my work."

"After?"

"I won't be done until late, honey."

"You can take the time off," Camillo interjects, sounding just as hopeful as Ethan does.

"No, that's okay," I start, shifting my weight from foot to foot. "I need to get some clothes ironed. Anyway, I'll have some time before dinner to spend with Ethan."

"Rosa."

The firm sound of my name makes my knees shake. Locking them in place, I plaster on a smile. "Honestly, it's fine, I promise." And turning on my heel, I dash into the house.

The time passes slowly after that. Camillo and Ethan meander into the house after a while, and Camillo tells me that he's taking Ethan out for an ice cream.

I watch them leave, their laughter ringing in my ears, as I swipe a bead of sweat from my forehead.

It's so tempting to change and go for a quick dip in the pool. The muggy heat is stifling now. With a lack of central air, thanks to its maintenance today, the kitchen feels boiling.

Indecision races through me. If I'm quick, no one will even know. I can change and be back to the laundry in no time. It's all I have left to do before dinner.

With a quick glance over my shoulder and down the hall, I let my nails bite into my palms as I rush up the back stairwell to the bedroom.

I get changed into a black one piece that cuts high along my hips. The back is cut open, dipping low on the small of my back. It's the only one

I've found left behind by the previous maid, and so I put it on despite how much skin it shows.

I tiptoe down the stairs, stopping at the laundry room to check the machines. There's plenty of time for a quick dip.

I carefully lay the towel I've brought with me onto one of the lounge chairs and dip my toe. The cool water is like a balm to my heated flesh. My ankle, calf, and knee follow, and before I have any second thoughts, my body is submerged into the cool water.

The water drips from my hair, now mostly blond with just a bit of faded brown at the ends, before I smooth it from my face. It feels wonderful and better than I could have imagined. Sinking beneath the surface, I let my limbs fall heavy at my sides before breaking the surface once more.

This is the perfect way to stave off the heat. Just a few minutes longer, and then, I'll go back inside.

A short while later, after enjoying the water and feeling refreshed, I climb out of the pool.

My foot meets the decking.

And a shadow looms over me.

My heart chokes.

My gaze darts up to follow the towering lines.

And his broad chest fills my vision.

"I forgot my wallet," he says as he picks it up from the table by the sun lounger.

Heat crawls up the back of my neck. "Sorry," I mumble. I drop my gaze.

"For what?

Humiliation bubbles to life in my gut. Curling inward, I clear my throat. "I have laundry to finish."

"Rosa—"

I plaster on a fake smile, meeting his gaze. "I'll just get dressed..." I edge past him a little, praying he'll let me go and escape back to the safety of my bedroom.

Gently, Camillo's large hand wraps around my arm. "You don't have to go. You're allowed to be out here if you want. It's practically a sauna in the house while they work on the AC."

My anxiety soars. The world spins, and each breath comes in small little pants. I need to get out of here.

Tears sting my eyes, but I shove them away as I take off toward the door back to the kitchen, my towel forgotten as I run to the safety of the house.

A quick glance over my shoulder makes it feel like I've been punched in the gut.

His dark brows pull together, and his jaw ticks before something darker slides over his face. He takes a step closer.

The door to the kitchen is so far from me.

If I can just...

But I'm not going to make it before he gets to me.

I know he's not going to hurt me, but dread swells in my stomach.

My reflection in a window catches my attention. I'm paralyzed looking at it. My fists tighten, and I drop my gaze. It's better if I don't look. Quickly, I swipe at my eyes. How could I be so stupid? What was I thinking, wearing a bathing suit like this? And even worse, how did I think I'd be able to sneak around unseen?

Cover up, no one wants to see your rolls.

What is wrong with you? No one wants to see that!

Isn't that a little...tight on you?

Maybe you should stay inside, sis...

Hot breath tickles the top of my head as a warm hand wraps around my wrist, halting me. I'm frozen, paralyzed with fear.

"It's just me," he says softly.

The heat of him spreads over my body like a soothing hand running along my skin. My body wants to melt into his, but instead, I tense again. "I need to change."

I don't want him to see me like this. Skin all exposed. The curves of my body filling out the stretchy, wet material. The way my thighs touch and how much cleavage is showing are already mortifying enough.

"Look at me."

I close my eyes, turning around to face him.

"Rosa."

"Please," I whisper. "I need to change." I don't want to cry in front of him. But I know what I look like. I know how undesirable I am like this.

His calloused finger hooks under my chin, lifting my face.

Squeezing my eyes shut tighter, I plead with my breathing to even out and for my pulse to go back down.

"Did he do that to you?"

Opening my eyes, I blink. "What?"

"Your husband." The words growl between his clenched teeth. "The bruises on your back and arms. Are they from...before?"

Confusion sweeps through me. That's what he's upset about?

Although he's called me gorgeous before, that little voice in the back of my head keeps telling me he didn't mean it and was just being nice.

But right now, he's only zeroed in on the faded yellow and purple marks that are exposed on my back. He's not looking at the rest of my body—nor the size of me.

"Did he do this to you?"

The ferocity in his voice, the spark of anger in his eyes, makes my body tremble. Not from fear, but from something else.

"How could he mark something so fucking beautiful?" The warm breath of his words caresses my face as he leans closer, his forehead pressed against mine. I'm not sure he even realizes he's said them because the hardness of his face remains. "Tell me. He did this, didn't he?"

I nod, unable to find my voice.

But I know I don't have to be afraid of this man. The face he wears as the Marchiano enforcer is just a mask he wears to prove to the world he's the monster everyone thinks he is. But behind it is a man who's gentle with a broken boy...and even more so with me. A man who coaxes these feelings in me and makes me cling to every compliment that falls from his lips.

When his hold on me loosens a little, I take my chance and dash inside and up the stairs. My hands are trembling as I hastily pull on my clothing.

Then, as I lean against the closed door, I lock eyes with my reflection. Revulsion tears through me, followed by shame.

Who would ever love a fat pig like you?

The words Grayden said to me whisper again and again through my mind.

***

Since leaving Grayden, my parents have left me a number of voicemails and text messages. And although they were angry at first, my mother's been messaging me more lately, asking how Ethan and I are. I haven't dared tell her where I am, but I can tell that my parents' attitudes are softening—and, quite honestly, it's nice to have someone in my family care about me. Camillo and Marco refused to decrease my wages to take into account Ethan's bed and board, and every day I'm worried about what will happen to us because their charity can't last forever—and eventually, Grayden will catch up with us. He's already found me once, and I know it's impossible to stay hidden while I'm still in Chicago.

My mother's persuaded me to come for dinner at the family home tonight. I deliberated long and hard about whether I should go, but they're my family, and they're the only ones I can ask to lend me enough money to get away for good and start afresh.

On my evening off, I drop Ethan at Kori's house for a play date with Kristopher. He's so excited to see them again, and I want to talk to my parents without Ethan there.

At the agreed time, I arrive at the Davis family mansion, my palms sweaty as I climb the steps up to the front door. The maid shows me into the drawing room where my parents and my younger sister, Reagan, have gathered for drinks. "There you are, Rosa." My mother greets me with a kiss on each cheek, her familiar expensive perfume wafting through the air. "I'm glad you're here so that we can help you. We're your family, and we just want to support you to get your life back on track after recent events."

I breathe out a sigh of relief. I was so afraid that they would refuse to help me. "I'm so grateful for your help. I just need enough money to get Ethan and me away from Chicago and Grayden, and I promise I'll pay you back as soon as I can."

My mother's gaze slides from me to my father and back again. "Don't you think it would be better to return to Grayden so that you can give things another go? Grayden's been sick out of his mind with worry after you up and left in the middle of the night and took his son with you."

"He's *my* son as well. And Grayden hates both of us."

"Nonsense," Father grits out. "He's been looking everywhere for you, wanting to bring you home."

"He's even said he's prepared to forgive you this one time," Mother adds.

"*I've told you that he beats me and the last time he went for Ethan as well.* How can you think that I would ever return to a man like that and take my son back to live in that environment?"

"Really, Rosa." Mother sniffs. "It can't be that bad."

"Mother, how can you say that?" I cry. My only regret is that I didn't leave sooner. That I didn't have the courage to do something before if not for me, then for the sake of my little boy.

Her eyebrows knit together in a frown. "Well, you've never looked like you're suffering. I mean, you're *fatter* than ever. Surely, if things were as bad as you claim they were, you'd be looking thin and haggard?"

I'm left utterly speechless and unable to speak for a few long seconds. I thought Mother asked me here today to talk about helping me, but it's clear that her 'help' consists of trying to convince me to return to Grayden. A shudder runs through me. "He doesn't want us home to be a family together. He just wants us home so that he can punish us—so that he has someone to bully and beat. But I won't let him get near Ethan or me ever again—"

"For God's sake, she's being melodramatic as always," my sister interrupts impatiently. "She's always been the same—just an attention-seeker."

My mouth drops open. Reagan's always had attention lavished on her by my parents and everyone else. She's thin and glamorous; she has the sort of stunning looks that turn heads whenever she walks into a room and makes people want to talk to her. I've never begrudged my sister getting so much attention. But just once in my life when I need some of my parents' focus on me so that they can help me figure a way out of this mess and a way to keep Ethan and me safe, she doesn't even care.

"It's clear that you didn't bother to think about how this will affect Reagan's marriage prospects," Mother chimes in, instantly taking her side as always.

"And do you appreciate how much trouble we went to in the first place to arrange this marriage to Grayden for you?" Father adds.

"Because the men certainly weren't lining up to ask for your hand as you'll remember," Mother says. "Not a single man wanted you as his prospective wife."

I can't help but cringe as I'm reminded of my shortcomings.

"Reagan, of course, has always had lots of interested suitors," Mother carries on. "But then, she works hard to maintain her beautiful, skinny figure. She would never dream of embarrassing us by looking fat like you. But you just don't care—you let yourself go as soon as you became a teenager."

I feel like yelling out that I didn't. It wasn't my fault that I suddenly found myself with huge boobs, child-bearing hips, and a big ass.

"Do you realize what an embarrassment it is having to be seen next to you?" Mother says. "Having people think that I have a daughter who's fat, ugly, and lazy?"

I've heard variations of this all my life, but the tears still burn the back of my eyes.

"Grayden may refuse to do business with your father now. Please think carefully about how much trouble this is causing your family. Grayden has told your father that he'll forgive you, so the best thing for you would be to go home to him."

Tears are threatening to spill. "Excuse me," I mumble, "I need the powder room."

Rushing down the hall, I run into the powder room and lock the door behind me.

Taking deep breaths, I try to stop the tears, but they still fall.

I don't care that Reagan's more beautiful or more popular than me. Sure, I felt envious at times when I was growing up, but I've always loved Reagan and wanted her to have nothing but happiness in her life. But it's clear that she doesn't love me back—she doesn't love me as a sister should.

And it's not Reagan's fault. Everyone loves Reagan, right? Not just my parents, but everyone else as well. So, it must be me. *I'm* the one who's got something wrong with her—something that makes me unlovable. I shudder as I recall the awful memory of my wedding reception...

It's the reception now, and I look around and try to find where my new husband is. Shouldn't he be at my side and celebrating with me?

The day has been going well so far, and although he's been a little distant, I'm sure it's just because of how busy it's all been. But he's been gone for ages now. So many people are approaching me with their congratulations, and I can tell they're wondering like me where he is.

The reception is at my parents' mansion, and I excuse myself to go up to my room to freshen up. And as I pass the guest room, I hear a sound and then a giggle, but I hurry on by.

Someone must have snuck up here, but I don't need to know what my guests are getting up to in there. But then I hear a familiar voice...

"Oh yeah, just like that, oh yeah..."

"You know you won't get as good as this with your new wife," a woman puffs out...

I don't recognize the woman's voice, but I'd know the man's voice anywhere.

He's the man who I heard say 'I do' to me less than two hours ago...

My world stutters to a stop. It can't be... Despite it being an arranged marriage, I thought he would be happy with me. But then I hear his voice again...

"She's fat and ugly."

And mortification sweeps over me as I hear what he really thinks about me. How the man I'm to spend forever with really sees me.

And I think it can't get any worse, but then he adds the icing to the cake: "And I only married her for the money..."

And that's when I realized that the only thing that mattered to him was the business deal with my father—an alliance which was going to make them both a lot of money. But the cheating was only the start of what I had to endure with him...

After calming myself down as much as possible, I splash cold water on my face. I have to convince my parents to lend me the money I need. I have to make them understand how bad things got with Grayden. *I'm their daughter—they have to help me.*

I stiffen my spine and return to face my family. As I head back to the drawing room, I come to a sudden halt just outside Father's office door when I hear a familiar voice.

A voice that I never wanted to hear ever again.

Ice slides up my spine.

And I can't get enough oxygen into my lungs.

"I deserve a medal for putting up with your daughter," he snarls. "You're lucky I didn't demand that you take the stupid bitch back before now."

I'm terrified as I hear the voice of the man I've been running from...

"She's absolutely fucking useless in bed, you know," he snaps.

I can just about summon up the energy to peek through the crack in the door.

Thank God! He's not actually here. He's only on the speakerphone.

"She can't even suck dick properly." I cringe as I hear Grayden's clear hatred of me spew down the phone to my father. "You won't find another man who'll put up with her ways. She won't be a good wife to me, and she sure as hell can't be bothered to lose weight so that I won't be fucking repulsed by her body. She's a fat fuck, and she's a complete waste of space."

To hear him speak like this—to my father of all people—is absolutely mortifying.

I've tried my best with Grayden, but nothing I do is ever good enough for him.

"And now you're telling me that she's making up stories and lies that I beat her? For fuck's sake, she's a dumb cunt and completely unhinged."

Father is apologizing profusely for my behavior—I don't understand how he can believe Grayden over me. And he keeps saying that he hopes Grayden won't let my behavior ruin their business dealings. That's all he cares about—money and business.

Grayden says he'll be over in thirty minutes to collect me...

He's coming. He's on his way here. Now.

I know I have to get away. My parents are determined for me to go back to Grayden—but I can never do that.

I hurry to the back door. I can't stop my hands from trembling as I open it.

The click of the latch feels louder than a gunshot in the still night air.

My breath catches, and I freeze, listening for any sign that my parents have heard me.

Silence. My heart pounds so hard in my chest that I swear it's going to give me away.

I have to move. I can practically feel Grayden getting closer. The thought of his arrival—and his anger—sends a shiver down my spine. I can't waste another second standing here.

I tug my jacket tighter around me and step off the porch, my legs shaky and unsteady beneath me.

The night air bites through the thin fabric of my clothes. I should've worn something warmer, but I can't worry about that now. Every second I spend here is a second closer to him finding me.

I hurry forward, forcing myself to put one foot in front of the other. My breath comes in quick, shallow gasps, each one like a knife in my chest.

I need to get away, far away before he arrives.

My feet carry me down the familiar path toward the edge of the woods where the trees stand tall and menacing in the darkness. The moonlight filters through the branches, casting eerie shadows on the ground.

It's darker here, the thick canopy above blocking out most of the light, and it feels safer than the open streets. At least if he follows me into the woods, maybe I can lose him in the tangled maze of trees. *Please God, let me get away before he gets here.*

I stumble over a root, barely catching myself before I fall. My breaths are ragged, my lungs burning with the effort of running. I can't keep this up. I'm not strong enough, not fast enough. But I can't stop. Stopping means he'll catch me, and if he catches me...I don't want to think about what will happen then.

My thoughts race, frantic and disjointed. Every step feels heavier, harder. I'm not going to make it. He'll find me. *He always finds me.*

My legs buckle, and I drop to my knees, the damp earth cold against my skin. I press my hands to my face, trying to steady myself, trying to stop the world from spinning out of control around me.

Eventually, I make it back to the main road, and keeping to the shadows, I wait for what seems like a lifetime for a bus to come along.

And once I'm back at Kori's, I confide in her everything that's happened, knowing that I won't tell Camillo about any of this later. As far as he's aware, I've spent the evening at Kori's house, and I want to keep it that way. Because a part of me feels ashamed and embarrassed that my family's unwilling to help me—that there must be something wrong with *me* for them to treat me this way.

When Ethan and I catch the bus back to the Marchiano estate, I'm hypervigilant. Thank God I didn't tell my family where I'm living. Because today has told me loud and clear that they won't be helping me.

But another thing is also clear: that there's no escape. I know that now. I've known it all along. No matter where I go, no matter how far I run, he'll always be there, just a step behind, waiting to pull me back into the life I thought I could leave.

I'm trapped, caught in a nightmare with no way out. But for now, I just have to get us back to the Marchiano estate without Grayden catching me...

CHAPTER 21

CAMILLO

The image of Rosa in that little black one piece is burned into my mind.

The way it hugged each and every one of her curves, cutting high on her hips, and exposing a mouthwatering expanse of creamy thighs haunts my dreams nightly.

But it's the yellow and purple that decorated the slope of her back that prompts me into the gym today. My knuckles are bruised from where I slammed them into the brick wall of the house after she fled inside. The sting of it is dull now as it collides again and again with the bag.

Anger is a different beast altogether. It festers and sinks, settling deep down inside me. An old friend roaring to life once more.

As badly as I want to storm over there and repay him for every fucking mark on her body, I restrain myself. He's connected in a way that would be bad for us. There are ways around it—especially given where I sit in the organization. But with the FBI breathing down all our necks, it's not a risk I can take. *Yet.*

And it's this thought that keeps me going.

My heavy breathing fills the room as I wipe the trickles of sweat from my brow and gulp water from a glass. My imagination works overtime, conjuring different images of Rosa. Curled up on the floor of that alley with tears running down her face. Cowering beneath his hands. Struggling to free herself from his hold.

Memories of it still affect her. She was quiet and subdued after she came back with Ethan from her evening off—it's clear she finds it difficult to relax even when she has time off and should be relaxing.

The sound of shattering glass fills the room.

I look down, and I realize I've smashed my hand with the glass into the wall, blood trickling from my battered knuckles. The sting of it brings me back into the room. The haze of red fades, and in its place is something else, crystal clear.

Never again.

I won't allow it to happen ever again to her. She's going to learn how to defend herself. I'm here to protect her, but it's just in case for when I'm not around. My jaw ticks. The idea of her having to use it at all settles like a lead brick in my stomach.

Quickly, I clean off my hand and wrap it. Jogging into the kitchen where Rosa's busy chopping for a vegetable platter, I pause in the doorway. And leaning against the frame, I watch her. She never fails to take my breath away. To calm the demons prowling deep inside me.

"Rosa."

She looks up at me.

"How much do you have left to do today? And what's Ethan up to?"

"Just the food prep. Ethan is drawing in the lounge."

"Good. You're coming with me."

"What?"

"Finish what you're doing and go change. Something you don't mind getting sweaty in. Marco will keep an eye on Ethan."

She blinks at me, lips parting just a little. I watch as her tongue peeks out to wet them, and I can see the wheels in her head turning.

"Finish and change," I repeat. "I'll wait."

Fifteen minutes later, Rosa is standing before me in a baggy t-shirt, shorts, and her sneakers. I can't help how my eyes track over her body.

Every inch of skin sends another jolt through me. Even with her body hidden, I think of the curves beneath, just waiting to be lavished and explored. I shake my head, dismissing the thoughts.

I nod, holding open the gym door to her. "After you."

"W-what are we doing?"

The door to the gym clicks shut, and I guide her toward the middle of the room with my hand on the small of her back.

"I'm going to teach you how to defend yourself."

"What?" Her horrified squeak echoes in the room as she whirls to face me. Her brown eyes are doe-like, innocent, and captivating.

My lips stretch into a small smile. "I'm going to teach you how to defend yourself."

"No." Her head shakes furiously. "That's not necessary. I don't want to put you out."

I step in front of her as she moves to go back to the door. "It is."

"Camillo, I—"

"I don't like the idea of you not knowing the basics." And I hate the idea of someone else laying a finger on her without her consent—or the thought that she won't know how to fight back. Something inside her is willing to fight to survive. She's proven that much already. "Please? I'll feel better if you know just a few things. Just enough so that you can buy your time until I can get to you." I hold her gaze. "*And I will always get to you, I swear.*"

"Why?" She purses her lips before taking a calming breath, as if she's scared of the answer I'll give.

"Why am I doing this? Or why do I care?" I don't have an answer to the second question. I just know I do. Something in me wants her. Something in me needs her. And if this is how I can soothe that beast, then I'll take it. Every damn chance I can get.

She nods.

"I'm doing this because you need to learn. If not for yourself, then for Ethan."

"And the second part?"

"We'll go slow at first," I say, brushing off the question as I move further into our gym. Already, the floor is covered in thick mats. I pushed most of the equipment that might prove a problem out of the way. "Just something basic you'll practice every day from here on out."

"But I don't know the first thing about any of this."

"That's why I'm here."

Her eyes drop, and she tugs at the hem of her shirt. "Do we have to do it here?"

"Is there something wrong with the gym?" Is this some trigger I don't know? This is my sanctuary. The only place where the world fades, and I can just be me.

I watch as she tugs once more on the oversized shirt, pulling it and twisting the fabric between her fingers.

"Rosa, you can tell me."

Her bottom lip trembles before she clamps her teeth down upon it. "It's nothing."

The muscle in my jaw ticks. "No one else will come in here. It's just going to be me and you—if you're worried about that."

"It's not that." Her voice shakes, and my heart squeezes. "It's just…" Another firm shake of her head and the fisting of her hand at her side. "Nothing."

"It's not nothing. You can tell me—you can trust me." Do those words sound as desperate to her as they do to me?

"I don't want you to be…" The words barely reach my ears, too muffled at the end, as I strain to listen. "With all the mirrors and stuff. It's just going to be worse."

"They bother you?" I'm stunned as I suddenly understand the issue. She doesn't like the look of herself in the mirrors. Fuck, I don't want her to feel uncomfortable.

Gently, I tilt her chin up to me. Tears rim her eyes, and I bite back the snarl of anger rumbling in my chest. *What do I have to do to make her feel beautiful?* "Don't look at them. Focus on me. You can stay this way around, so you don't have to look at them, okay?"

She worries her bottom lip but nods. The battle isn't over by a long shot, but a spark of pride shoots through me before I can tamper it down. It's a step in the right direction.

"Good." Clearing my throat, I step back, my hand dropping down to my side.

Silence fills the room, and I desperately want to ask her the burning questions on my tongue, each one harder to swallow than the last.

Rosa has secrets, each one deeper than the last. And I have no right trying to pry them from her. It'd only fuel the obsession I have with her. And then she'd wake up to the monster that lurks beneath my skin and flee.

Slowly, I walk her through a few quick stretches, taking my time to admire the way her body bends and contorts.

Every muscle of my body heats. I tug at the loose collar of my tank top, watching the curve of her ass as she bends forward, finishing up the last rep.

Fuck. The image of me behind her, hands on her hips, watching as I drive into her... *Get a fucking hold of yourself.*

"Okay, that's good." My voice comes out hoarse, and I clear my throat. "Have you ever done anything like this?"

A firm shake of her head.

"We'll take it slow. If I do anything that makes you uncomfortable, you need to tell me." I hold her gaze, searching the brown depths of her eyes. "Understand?"

"Yes."

"Good."

I gently lift her hands up and slowly walk her through a few defensive maneuvers. How to ball her fist so as not to break her thumb. How to stand so she isn't easy to knock over. How to best use her body against someone twice her size. And how to use the heel of her hand to debilitate her attacker. There are so many things I need to teach her so that I know she'll have a chance if anyone ever comes after her again.

"Thank you," she pants, wiping the back of her forehead with the edge of her shirt, exposing her stomach just a little. It's a tease.

"For what?"

"This."

"Don't thank me yet. We're not even close to me being done."

She takes a step closer. The distinct scent of roses that follows her around envelops me. The softness in her features, the gratitude in her eyes, slices at me. Her hand freezes halfway between us before dropping down. "What's next?"

"The hard part." My body reverberates with excitement and fear. Putting my hands on Rosa shouldn't elicit such a feeling. But since that dinner date, since seeing her in that dress, my mind hasn't belonged to me anymore.

Slowly, I wrap my arms around her loosely, coaching her through how to break various holds. Again and again, we practice it, and every wiggle of her body against mine only fuels the fire within me.

When she masters a move, we switch it up and move onto another. The holds become firmer and tighter until she's struggling in my arms. Two taps of her hands mean I'll let go, but she powers through every hitch of her breathing to maneuver her body out of each hold.

My body's on high alert, continuing to examine her expression for any missteps on my part. Her lovely features are set, determined, and zeroed in on the motions we've gone over.

My hand circles her arm, and I inch her backward, looming over her. Her skin is soft under my calloused fingers as they grip just firm enough to make it a challenge.

She does all the right moves, but I've still cornered her. My hand circles her throat in a soft hold—one I fear is an overstep as her pulse races beneath my fingers.

She knows how to get out of this. We've practiced dozens of times now. But she's frozen.

Her chest labors against mine, her back flush against the wall where we've ended up.

Her tongue darts out over her lips, and my eyes zero in.

She's so damn close.

Right there, ripe for the taking.

Her panting breath fans over my heated skin.

Just a few more inches, and my lips would brush hers...

Would she taste as sweet as I imagine? I swallow loudly, watching as her tongue wets her lips again, slower.

Her pulse jumps under my hand. Her pupils bloom, and it's not fear eliciting this reaction. It's something else.

The grip on my hand slackens. And her body leans forward.

Fuck it. Pressing my lips against hers, I swallow the gasp of surprise that leaves her. And tongue tracing the seam of her lips, I dive in, claiming my taste of victory.

The hand on her throat moves to cup her jaw, angling her head into just the right position. My other hand cups her hip, pressing her into me.

Every nerve in my body explodes as I lean my hips into her. I know she can feel me, feel what she's done to me, and I don't give a damn.

Hungry for more, I devour her.

Gone are the gentle strokes of her tongue against mine, replaced by a claiming of her own. The spark that's so buried beneath everything flickers to life within her.

My fingers bury into the back of her hair, threading through the silky strands.

Her own nails drag tentatively up my arm, drawing a deep rumble from my chest. My teeth tug on her lip, capturing it, and sucking it between my own teeth.

Fuck.

I need more. I press closer, fitting my body against hers, my hardness pressing into her softness. Seeking more, needing more.

My fingers grasp her, holding her against me before they drift up under the hem of her tee. Toying with it as my thumb brushes the side of her rib gently, inching higher still.

She's addictive. From the taste of her to the feel of her body against mine. Nothing tastes or feels as good as she does.

I groan against her jaw as my lips trail down the column of her smooth throat.

Laughter from the hall makes me freeze. I can just make out the soft voice of Ethan beyond the door.

Wide eyed, Rosa looks horrified.

I pull back, gently dropping her back to the ground. Searching her face, I tried to find some inkling as to what's going through her head. Something to tell me that I wasn't the only one drowning just now—that it's not just me.

"I..." She clears her throat, pulling at her T-shirt to adjust it back into place. "I...uh..." She looks at the door and then at me.

And like the bambi she is, she skitters out of the door.

Braced against the wall, I let out a deep sigh. I'm well and truly fucked now.

Because one taste wasn't enough.

And I want more...

CHAPTER 22

ROSA

Absentmindedly, I touch the tip of my finger to my bottom lip. The ghost of his lips brushes mine, leaving a wave of arousal rocketing through my body.

My skin tingles at the memory of his hot breath along the sensitive skin of my neck. Every nerve in me exploded when he kissed me, leaving something utterly changed in its wake.

He'd wanted me. *Kissed me.* What if he actually—

I shake my head, dismissing that line of thought.

It was a mistake.

It had to be a mistake. We were just caught up in the moment from the work out with our adrenaline running high.

I'm getting my hopes up for something that doesn't exist. There's no way that he'd ever find someone like me attractive or interesting enough to keep around.

Camillo can have his pick of anyone. Women must throw themselves at him left, right, and center. Why would he bother with me?

And even if something did happen, he'd find my lack of bedroom skills a complete turn off. I shudder as I remember what Grayden used to say to me about that.

The vase I'm dusting nearly slips from my fingers. *Get your head together.* For four days now, I've thrown myself into my work, avoiding him at all costs. I've taken to the more labor-intensive cleaning tasks—the things that are probably more seasonal or yearly. I've been deep cleaning rooms that never get used and steam cleaning carpets in rooms on the other side of the mansion where no one will disrupt me.

When I come out of my bedroom in the mornings, he's still there with Mr. Fluffy, both sleeping on the floor outside the bedrooms to keep watch over Ethan and me. I shuffle past him as fast as I can after an awkward "good morning," focusing on patting the dog so that I don't have to look at Camillo. I've told him that he doesn't have to do this every night, but he refuses to stop. As much as he pretends to not like the dog, I can tell that Camillo has a secret soft spot for the animal, and I often catch him sneaking treats to him when he thinks no one's looking.

During the day, I'm in and out of the rooms before he even appears, especially at mealtimes. The food sits on the table, waiting for them, as I quietly make my way to another part of the mansion. I hear all about the funny jokes from Ethan later in the night. This is the new routine—I've told Ethan I still have work to do and will eat later.

Setting the vase back down, I quickly wash my hands and set about dinner prep. From a quick glance at the clock on the microwave, I've just enough time to get this done before Camillo comes back from the casino. And it's plenty of time for me to relive the way my body heated against his...

I can't believe how responsive I was to him. It was as if someone touched me with a live wire. His sandalwood scent fogged my brain and made me giddy as my stomach swooped.

I clear my throat. The more I relive it, the harder it is to remind myself that this is all a fantasy—one that continues to keep me up at night, my imagination running wild.

It was just a kiss. But I've never been kissed like *that*. Consumed so completely and fully that it lingers days later.

Shaking myself, I focus on the task before me. Ethan sits at the table quietly coloring, his legs swinging as he hums to himself, Mr. Fluffy next to him as his constant companion. They're best friends now, and Mr. Fluffy is determined to keep watch over my little boy at all times.

It's the most relaxed I've seen him since he arrived. And for that, I'm forever thankful to Camillo and his brothers. And because I don't want this to change, it's all the more reason to stay the hell away from Camillo until the awkwardness has settled.

I won't ruin things for us here. Not when things are finally feeling like they're right.

"I'll be right back," I say to Ethan, knowing he won't leave the table. Slowly, I make my way into the laundry room. The load still has a good twenty minutes to go. This will give me just enough time to finish prepping for dinner. Determined to finish well before anyone gets home, I hurry back into the kitchen.

"Hey, Ethan."

The voice freezes me. My hand hovers above the bowl of marinated chicken, and my breathing picks up.

So much for avoiding him. Dread swims in my stomach as I swallow thickly. This isn't happening. Why is he home early? Has something happened?

My heart races as I grab the bowl and pretend that I haven't heard him enter the kitchen. I don't spare a glance at the table where I know he's sitting now.

I quickly wipe my damp palms on my jeans as Camillo and Ethan continue to talk in soft voices—something about the game they played the other day.

I can do this. Just act nonchalant. It's clear we both regret what happened, and it isn't going to be repeated. Despite how much I wish it would.

We're both adults, and we can act grown up about this.

"What's for dinner?"

I glue my eyes to the counter, willing my heart to settle. But the fluttering has turned into a thundering gallop in my chest. "Chicken risotto, green beans, and a side salad."

"Sounds delicious."

I nod stiffly, turning back to the meal. Anything to keep my gaze from wandering over to the table.

"Can I help?" He's closer. The sound of his voice is louder, and the scent of him so near to me sends me spiraling back into the gym when his body was pressed against me. I squeeze my legs tighter together. "N-no. That's okay."

"Sure?"

"Yep," I squeak as I turn quickly, setting the pan on the stove.

He murmurs something to Ethan, but I can't quite catch what he says. Ethan's tiny footsteps echo as he leaves the room and goes up the staircase, presumably to get something from his bedroom.

The walls are pressing in. My chest constricts. I don't want to be alone with him. I can't face rejection anymore.

"Rosa?"

My fingers fumble with the burner knob, shaking too hard to be of use. Why am I so nervous? So awkward?

"Rosa?" His voice brushes the side of my cheek softly.

"Hmm?"

"Are you okay?"

"Fine, fine."

Camillo's warm hand braces my arm, and I freeze. "Is this about why you're avoiding me?" he asks in a low voice.

The pain in his voice slices through me. I don't know what to say. I'm being delusional about anything happening between us. I'm broken and useless, and he's a protective angel who doesn't lower himself to be with someone like me. "No."

Gently, he turns me to face him, his brow arched. His mouth opens, then snaps shut before he can utter a sound.

"I'm sorry for letting it get that far," I murmur. "For not stopping it sooner."

Something shutters over his face, and the stony mask falls back into place. I've seen it too many times when he and his brothers are talking—indifference. And I hate the feeling of it being directed at me.

"What?" he growls.

"The kiss," I whisper, dropping my eyes. "What I mean is, I get it. We can just pretend it never happened." I'm rambling. The words just spill from my lips without so much as connecting with my brain.

Confusion knits his brows together as he searches my face.

My eyes hit the floor, and I wring my hands together. "I know I'm not the ideal...anything. And you're...*you*. So, it's okay. We can just pretend it didn't happen and move on. No need to talk about it."

The warmth of his palm cups my cheek, lifting my chin so I have to stare into his eyes. The corner of his lip twitches as the shutter of cold indifference melts away. "Is that what you want? To pretend it didn't happen?"

My heart stutters at the expression on his face. "Don't you?"

"Fuck, no."

I blink at him. "What?"

"I don't want to pretend it didn't happen," he says. His words don't make sense. Why wouldn't he want that? Why would he even say any of this? To torment me? To mock me? But that isn't the Camillo I've come to know over the last few weeks.

"I don't understand..."

And that smile, the one that makes my knees turn to jelly, floods his face as his thumb brushes the apple of my cheek. "I can't and won't forget it. That's not happening for either of us. I refuse to let it. You and that kiss are all I've thought about for four fucking days, Rosa."

"Me?" I stutter.

"Yes, you. I don't see anyone else here I've kissed, do you? I mean, I haven't kissed Mr. Dog Breath over there, thank God," he says, jerking his chin in the direction of where the animal is slumbering.

I can't help a small smile, and I shake my head. But it doesn't make sense. "Why?"

"Why what?"

"Why can't you forget it? Why me?" His heat washes over me. His lips are just a hair's breadth away. It's so tempting. All it'll take is for me to rise on my tiptoes to press my lips to his. To claim them as boldly as he claimed mine.

"Because it was single-handedly the best kiss I've ever had."

"But..." I start as his thumb brushes across my bottom lip, his eyes tracking the movement. My cheeks heat, and my body trembles as anticipation flares to life within me.

"But nothing. You, Rosa. *You* have consumed every thought I've had for fucking weeks now. There's no one who haunts my dreams like you do." He presses closer, trapping me against the island. "I've had a taste, and I'm not about to let you go. I'm addicted. Don't make me forget you. Don't make me pretend. I won't be able to do it."

My fingers grip the fabric of his shirt to keep me from swaying. His sleeves are rolled up as usual, and I can't help my fingers from tracing up the muscles and ink on his beautiful forearms. Please don't let this be a cruel joke. Please don't let him shove me away and shatter the fragile shell of hope that's blossoming in my chest.

Beneath my fist, his heart races, mirroring my own. "I'm not that strong of a man, Rosa."

I can't find my voice, but I nod. The way he looks at me, the devotion and hunger that shine in his eyes, makes me shiver with excitement. No one has ever looked at me like this before.

"That's my good girl," he breathes. The praise in his words ignites something in me, coiling in my lower stomach. His thumb brushes my cheek again before he consumes my lips, sealing whatever bargain we've just struck.

He steps back, breathing just as ragged as mine.

The air is stifling now, crackling to life with electricity.

The smile on his face swirls my stomach, making it flutter and swoop with a myriad of emotions.

Once more, his fingers drift up to my lips, and I feel them pull into a stunned grin.

He wants me...

CHAPTER 23

CAMILLO

It's still early when I walk into the lounge, the sun just starting to come up. I'm on my way to the kitchen to grab a bottle of water before I work out, and I'm definitely not expecting anyone else to be up yet, so I'm surprised when I hear the faint sound of music.

Getting closer to the kitchen, I recognize the tune—it's Gilded Shelter, a band whose music I always seem to hear whenever I switch on my car radio. The music gets louder the nearer I get, and I see something unexpected as I reach the doorway.

Rosa is up earlier than normal, and she's moving around the kitchen with a relaxed and carefree rhythm. She doesn't spot me as I stand there, so I just stand back and rake my gaze over her, realizing that she's actually a really good dancer.

As I'm watching her dance like nobody's watching, I can't help the grin that tugs up the corners of my lips because she seems different like this—there's a lightness about her right now.

I stand in the doorway, not wanting to disturb her as she dances across the kitchen, collecting things for what I'm assuming is breakfast. She's multitasking and making it look effortless—chopping mushrooms and stirring a pot on the stove, all while keeping in perfect time with the music.

With some reluctance, I clear my throat quietly. She stutters to a stop in the middle of a spin, her eyes widening as she realizes she's been caught, and for a few moments, she looks mortified, and her cheeks flush a deep pink.

"Don't stop," I say softly with a smile as I step into the room. "You've got some moves there."

"I didn't realize anyone was awake," she blurts out. "I sometimes dance while I work because it makes the chores go by faster..."

"It's fine, Rosa," I reassure her. "More than fine, actually—I like seeing you dance."

She smiles shyly. "They're my favorite band. I couldn't help myself when their latest song came on."

After collecting my water and giving her a long, lingering kiss on her lips, I head for the gym, thinking how this woman makes me so happy every single fucking second of the day.

***

I'm listening to the radio in my car a few days later when they mention that Gilded Shelter is in town for their sold-out concert. And I get an idea...

I know tickets will be nearly impossible to get for such a popular band, but I have connections—people who owe me favors, people who can get things done. I make a few calls and ask around, and within the hour, I manage to get two tickets for tonight. I get them couriered to the casino, my insides lighting up at the thought of surprising Rosa.

Late afternoon, I return home earlier than normal and walk into the kitchen.

"Hey," she says. "You're early."

"Yeah." I don't even try to hide my grin. "I've got something that I want to give to you."

She watches me pull out the tickets from the pocket of my jeans and hold them out for her to see.

"Are these...?" she starts to say before her voice trails off.

"Tickets to the Gilded Shelter concert tonight," I finish for her. "I thought maybe we could go together."

She gasps, and her hands fly to her mouth. "I can't believe this! How did you get these?"

I shrug, trying to play it cool. "I have my ways."

Her eyes are sparkling as she throws her arms around my neck, and I find myself hugging her back, enjoying the warmth of her embrace.

"Thank you, Camillo." She giggles, a bright happy sound filling the room.

I pull back and look at her, feeling a strange sense of satisfaction at her reaction. "You deserve it," I say simply. "Now go and get ready. The others can have takeout tonight, and Alessio said he'll look after Ethan. We leave in an hour."

***

The energy in the arena is electric, and I can see the excitement radiating off Rosa as we listen to the warmup act. She's practically bouncing, her eyes wide with anticipation. When Gilded Shelter finally takes the stage, the crowd erupts into cheers, and Rosa joins in without hesitation. She sings along to every word and does more of those sexy moves of hers.

I find that I'm watching her more than I'm watching the band, and I like this side of her that I'm seeing, and I'm drawn to it in a way I hadn't expected.

After a while, I notice that she's stretching onto her tiptoes as she strains to see over the heads of the people in front of us. And without giving it another thought, I reach out and put my hands around her hips and start to move her.

Her head swings to me. "What are you doing, Camillo?"

"Lifting you onto my shoulders so that you can see better."

Her eyes widen in alarm. "You can't carry me on your shoulders. I'm too heavy..."

My brows knit together in confusion. "Of course you aren't," I say. "But—"

"But nothing," I growl. She's nothing compared to the weights I lift each day, and I raise her up as if she's as light as a feather.

She exhales a yelp of surprise, but then, she's laughing, her hands gripping my shoulders as she balances herself on me. From her new position, she's got a perfect view of the band, and I can tell by her reaction that it's the best seat in the house.

As the band continues playing song after song, even I start to enjoy the music and let go a little. Everything about the night is amazing, but the best thing by far is the woman on my shoulders who's singing her heart out with sparkling eyes. With her, I feel something I can't quite put into words, but it's there, growing stronger with every passing minute.

When the concert finally reaches its end, the band take their final bow and give a last wave to all the fans, and I lower her back to the ground. She's buzzing with excitement, and her face is flushed with happiness. We're about to turn to leave, but before we do, I find myself stopping her, my hand gently grasping her arm.

She looks up at me, and her eyes sparkle in the dim light of the arena. For a moment, I just drink her in, taking in the way her hair falls in soft blond waves around her face, the way her lips curve into a smile, and leaning down, I press my lips to hers.

She kisses me back, her hands coming up to clutch at my shirt as she leans into me.

And when we pull apart, the way she looks at me makes my heart race.

***

My labored breathing and trickling water fill the air as I brace my hand against the shower wall.

Every one of my muscles is tense and pulled taught. An image of Rosa trapped beneath me against the wall of the gym, her eyes wide, fills my mind. It's quickly replaced with the image of her pressed against the kitchen counter, the thought of her parted lips beneath my thumb sending a wave of electricity rushing through me. *Attraction, need, hunger.*

This woman is an addiction I can't quit. A problem that I shouldn't be indulging in, but I'm helpless to stop myself. The way she looks at me. Like I'm something more, something reverent almost, beckons the beast inside me all the more.

Even now, as the water runs ice cold over my body, I picture her soft smile and the feel of her lips against mine. My fist slams against the tiles of the shower as my release tenses every muscle in my body. This was supposed to clear my head, to make it so I didn't spiral into madness. But all it's done is wind me up further.

Head bowed, I let the water drip down my hair, my panted breathing filling the air. Whatever spell Rosa has me under has sunk its claws into me hard and deep.

Dragging my hand through the wet strands, I brush them from my vision as I shut the water off.

She was determined to brush off that first kiss as a mistake, believing some misguided notion that I could find her lacking—that she's not a handful of lush skin and heat beneath my fingers in all the best fucking ways.

Quickly, I dress, choosing a pair of dark jeans and a shirt, rolling up the sleeves as I make my way into the kitchen. The lack of humming from the other rooms tells me that Rosa is there, cleaning the oven, counters, or God knows what else. The entire mansion is spotless. How she continues to find things to occupy her time, I don't quite understand. My skin tingles the closer I draw, my hardness jutting against my jeans already, when the heady mix of roses and floral scents hits my nose.

Acutely aware of where she is at any given moment in the mansion, that scent clings to me. Wrapping around me, like some siren call. It's concerning how well I know her patterns in the house, how aware I am of her every moment of the day.

As I step into the kitchen, she's busy prepping lunch. Her body is turned so that she can watch Ethan who is playing quietly outside with some new trucks Marco got for him.

She's mouthwatering. Oblivious to my stare as I lean against the doorframe, my arms crossed over my chest, she's relaxed and at ease—and it does something to me. I rub at my chest, trying to make the sensation go away.

"Hey," I say in a low voice, pushing from the threshold toward the counter.

The spoon clatters to the countertop, and Rosa whirls to face me. The terror melts off her face, and some of the tension building in my chest goes with it.

"Hey," she breathes.

"Busy?"

Her gaze moves to the stove and back to me with a smile. There's that spark. Beneath that timid shell, deep down, there's something that wants to fight for whatever this is. "I..."

"I'm not taking no for an answer," I murmur. I'm closer now, nearly close enough to cage her beneath me. To put my fingers on those plump hips and bring her against me. My skin tingles with just the thought. "I was hoping"—my voice is lower, softer as I close the distance—"that you'd sit outside with me until dinner."

"Why?"

"Figured you, Ethan, and I could enjoy the backyard a little. You're working too hard."

"But I'm here *to work*." Something about that grates at my skin.

"You'll have plenty of time after to make dinner and do anything else." I'm desperate for her to say yes. I hate how weak I am around her. How easily I want to fall to my knees and plead for just a drop of whatever she'll spare. But I can't stop myself—even when I know I'm playing with fire. Let it burn, for all I care.

"It'd be nice for you to spend more time with Ethan." I don't know why, but it makes me ridiculously happy when I see her with her son.

Softly, my hand settles on her hip, feeling her tense beneath my hand before her body relaxes. It's become less frequent since I've started noticing it—since I've begun to touch her as frequently as I can. It's a small step forward. Like Ethan, she needs time. But I'm goddamn desperate to feel her at ease beneath my fingers.

There's something special about Rosa and Ethan. And I'll be damned if I let a single person harm them ever again.

That I'm having these thoughts should scare me—should terrify me to the bone.

But it doesn't. And that itself is far more terrifying than the emotions squeezing me tight at this very moment.

"I'm almost done with this," she tells me.

"Can I help?"

I know the answer before she even shakes her head. It hasn't changed since I started asking weeks ago. She's stubborn at the oddest of times.

"Are you sure, Rosa?"

"Very. It's nearly done. You two can eat. Then, we'll play."

"Us three."

"No, I'm not..." Her words taper off. "I'm not hungry."

"You didn't eat breakfast."

"I'm fine."

"Please, eat. Even if it's something small."

"I'll eat later."

"Rosa." My breath brushes the column of her neck, making goosebumps erupt on her arms. My hand dips past her hip and into the pocket of her apron.

Her fingers tremble as she wraps them around my hand, trying to stop me. It's a feeble attempt.

"Crackers are not a meal." The unopened pack crinkles as I place it onto the counter. "One small plate. That's all I'm asking.

"Okay," she whispers.

I smile against her skin, dropping my lips to her exposed neck. "Good girl."

She's so receptive to praise, and I can't help the smile on my face now. I'd praise her every hour of the day if she'd let me.

"You're distracting me." She sounds breathy.

A rumbly laugh leaves me. "That's the plan."

I want to make her feel how hard she makes me. My body is no longer my own. I want her to know that I respond instantly and unconsciously to her. That I'm helpless around her. That it's her body that excites me like this. Because *it's her* that I want.

Even when I shouldn't.

I back up just a bit. The surrounding air is charged and dangerous. Another step back and another, and I slide into a chair.

The flush on her cheeks and the shy smile she tries to hide send another jolt of pleasure through my body.

Whatever game I've just started, I'm determined to win.

And something tells me that I'm going to enjoy the prize more than ever before.

***

For hours, Ethan, Rosa, and I run around the backyard playing various games. The soft giggles from Ethan warm me just as much as Rosa's hand against my arm as she fights to catch her breath.

The flushed but content expression on her face burns into my memory.

And every bone in my body begs me to guide her into the house and finally take what I'd been fantasizing about for weeks now.

Will she taste as sweet as I imagine? Will she sound breathless, moaning my name?

Sliding into a lounge chair, I watch as Ethan and Rosa continue to construct a castle in the sandbox. Fort Millo, as Ethan had proudly named it with a timid smile my way, is starting to take shape.

The way he and Rosa both jump at any sudden noises burns a fire in my gut. It's getting better, but it's far from perfect. And I want it to be perfect.

Dusting herself off, Rosa tucks a loose strand of hair behind her ear. The golden halo of the setting sun behind her steals my breath away.

She's a complete goddess, every single curve of her.

Catching her hand, I pull her to me. And settling her body between my legs, I wrap my arms around her middle, dropping a soft kiss to her covered shoulder, then neck.

Her surprised squeak delights me far more than it should. And after a minute, she relaxes against my chest.

"Are you having fun?" I ask.

"Yes. And it's great that Ethan is so happy here."

The soft admission twists something in my gut. Sparking some urge to tear the world down for both of them. I'll enact my vengeance on their behalf before it's all over. They'll never know that kind of horror again. "Good."

Rosa watches Ethan closely. "I don't know how to say thank you."

"For?"

"This. For Ethan being safe and happy."

"You don't need to thank me or any of us."

"I do."

My brow crinkles. "I mean it. I want you both to feel comfortable here. I want you to relax, to enjoy yourselves."

Her head bobs, but I can still feel the tension in her shoulders against my chest. I don't know how to convince her of this. I don't know how to prove it to her. The words I want to say are buried so deep that I'm not even sure they exist. They're overshadowed by other things—darker things—things I hope she'll never have to see from me.

Because the moment she does, it's all going to come crashing down.

"Still, thank you," she says softly.

"You're welcome."

"This is nice."

"Yeah?"

"Yeah," she exhales.

I smile, resting my chin on the top of her head as Ethan continues to play. It feels right, having her in my arms like this. Natural in some foreign way I can't articulate. "Good."

Silence fills the space. I don't know how to broach the topic that burns my tongue. It's there, bubbling to be let out. "Rosa?"

"Yes?"

"Do I scare you?" The words come out in a soft whisper. The urge to know the truth, to know if I'm seeing something here that she doesn't in fact feel, burns hot through me. And the insecurity of it all makes a bead of sweat trickle down the back of my neck. Is she going along with this because I intimidate her? Or she feels obligated because of some fucked up notion she has after I gave her a job?

"No."

My heart stops. "*No?*"

"Well…" A slight shrug lifts her shoulders. "Sometimes. At first, yes. But not for a while now." She hesitates. "You're kind—and that's what really scares me."

"Me being nice to you scares you?"

Wordlessly, she nods, and I tug her closer. She doesn't elaborate more, and I don't force her. She's a survivor, and the trauma has left too many wounds to heal right now. A sentiment I know all too well. "I don't want to scare you... But I know I scare everyone."

"Only at first, Camillo."

A dry laugh leaves my lips. "It's my job to be a monster, to be a beast that keeps everyone in line..." My tongue feels swollen in my mouth as if the words are some buried secrets that I can't pry out.

I know what I am. I know the kind of image I show to the world. I know how others perceive me when I walk into a room. I relish the power it gives me. What I've made myself into over the years is no secret. The world wanted a monster, and I was more than happy to fill that role. But knowing she sees that in me is worse than any words or slurs thrown my way.

"I don't think you're a monster."

"You don't know me very well."

"From what I've seen"—her hand squeezes mine on her thigh—"you're not the worst out there by far. You don't hide who you are." Her nails drag over the lines along my forearm, making my muscles tense. My body jumps at the electricity that swallows me whole whenever she touches me. "You're not a wolf in sheep's clothing. You're just a wolf. Fangs, claws, and all. You don't try to be something else. And I appreciate that."

Her words ring in my ears. I swallow thickly, letting the soft hum of the world envelop us. Rosa leans against me further, a soft sigh leaving her.

"Rosa?"

"Yes?"

"Will you let me help you in the kitchen?"

It's not what I want to ask. But it's what falls from my lips. It's safer this way.

Her body tenses in my arms. "Why?"

"I like watching you cook. And I was hoping you'd teach me?"

She twists in my arms. Her blond brows are puckered, and her big brown eyes cloud with confusion.

Before I'm even aware of what I'm doing, my hand cups her cheek, keeping her from fleeing from me.

"But why? I'm not that good. I mean, you could have some chef teach you or someone who knows what they're doing."

"I don't want that. I want you to teach me. At least then, maybe I can give you a night off or something. And more time with Ethan."

I watch the wheels in her mind turn, working over why I'm doing this. I watch it all flash across her eyes. I hate how what's happened to her has sapped her confidence, making her second-guess and doubt everything. It's another tick in the reasons why her husband will be a dead man as soon as the moment presents itself.

I brush my thumb over her cheek with the lightest of touches. "Rosa, I just want to help. All I want is for you to have more time with Ethan. And for me to spend more time with both of you too."

She nods. "We can figure something out."

"I'd like that, Rosa."

Turning back around in my arms, her head lays against my shoulder, and I watch her fingers idly drawing along my tattoos, tracing the patterns as she keeps an eye on Ethan. The soft expression on her face warms something in my chest, sliding beneath the blackened bits of my heart to something that beats weakly beneath it.

She's going to hate it, but I'm determined to step up for her. To step in and help. Not because she needs it. But because I need to be near her like I need oxygen. I need her in my arms, next to me, within reach. And I plan on having my next hit of her very soon.

I smile, the plan formulating in my head.

CHAPTER 24

CAMILLO

I back away from the enormous bed as soundless as I can. The silky sheets no longer smell like me but like her, and I wouldn't have it any other way.

Ethan's small body rests against the fabric, exactly where I placed him, passed out already for his nap.

The door clicks shut softly behind me before I rush down the stairs.

I'm giddy—a word I never thought I'd say about myself, let alone experience, but I'm excited. The adrenaline is pumping through my body.

A soft hum guides me to where Rosa is diligently stirring a pot of pasta, the hearty smell of homemade Bolognese sauce filling the room and making my mouth water.

A grin tugging my lips up, I slowly make my way behind her.

She hears my footsteps because she's paying attention—she always is. I've learned not to surprise her by grabbing her. She's perfected that elbow to the sternum move we've practiced.

Despite the pride I feel over that fact, I hate how jumpy she is with me still—how anxious and uneasy she is before she takes a breath and relaxes.

"Rosa?" I announce quietly. My arms encircle her body slowly, softly.

She jolts, her eyes squeezing shut.

I stay still, letting my heat roll over her for a heartbeat, then another. She relaxes against me, and the tension in my gut eases. "Smells good."

"It'll be ready just after your brothers get home."

"Oh?" I don't love the fact that she knows their schedule as well as I do—that she pays them any mind at all. I want her all to myself. "What can I do to help?"

"No, I've got it."

I smile against the side of her face. "I wasn't asking, really. What can I do, Rosa? What else is left?"

"I've got it."

My arms tighten around her, and I drop my lips to the exposed curve of her neck. "I'm not asking, Rosa," I say with a low growl.

Her body melts into mine as her pulse leaps under my mouth.

I tug her closer, feeling the curve of her ass rub against me just right as she twists in my loose hold.

"You're distracting me."

"Good." My hands wander over her hip and up under her T-shirt. Goosebumps pebble upon her beautiful skin as I brush her stomach. My fingers trace up higher. "I'll just keep distracting you until you give me a job to do." My thumb brushes the underside of her breast beneath her bra.

"Okay!" she squeaks, her face and neck flushed red. "Okay. We'll make the bread and salad."

I step back. "Awesome."

I don't miss the shy amusement on her face as she shakes her head. It's progress. Little by little. "What's first?"

"Wash your hands."

I can feel the amused smirk tug my lips up. She's not demanding or forceful with the order, but it does something to me, nonetheless. A minute later, I stand beside her, clueless where to begin.

"So, we're going to cut the lettuce."

"Okay."

Her chin jerks to the knife between us. "I've already washed it and everything else we need. You just need to chop it up in bite-sized pieces."

Easy enough. I can feel her eyes on me as she watches my slow, tentative movements with the knife. It's nothing like how I'm used to handling them. This is different but in a way I don't actually hate.

"Those are too big."

"You said bite-sized."

Her lips purse. "For regular people, not barbarians."

"You clearly haven't watched my brothers eat," I mumble.

Her giggle echoes around the room, and the knife falls from my hand. My world practically stops.

"Did you cut yourself?" she asks with concern.

"No." I shake my head. "I just love the sound of your laugh."

"Oh." Her gaze falls to the ground as her hands twist the fabric of her apron.

Knife forgotten, I step closer. "It's beautiful." I tilt her chin up so she can see just how much I mean it. "I'll just have to make you laugh again to prove it."

Her cheeks flush, and those soft freckles along the bridge of her nose taunt me. Just one taste. I can have just one taste without getting carried away.

As if she's reading my mind, Rosa's pink tongue flicks out, tempting me. "We should finish," she murmurs.

"Right. What's next?"

I step back, watching as she quickly finishes chopping the lettuce into smaller pieces before adding it to the bowl. Step after step, Rosa guides me through the process. It's easy enough, but when she does it, she makes it look effortless.

The counter is covered in a mess. Flour dusts the surface from where it exploded when I added it to the mixer on high. Again, her soft squeal of laughter catches me off guard, stealing my breath from me. Relaxed, she and I worked side by side, as if we've done this our whole lives.

Domestic. That's the word that continues to flash into my mind over and over.

This is too domestic for someone like me. And yet, watching Rosa relax and talk to me with ease erases whatever doubt lingers in the back of my skull.

"Now, we just knead it."

"Knead it?"

"Yeah." She swipes her cheek with the back of her hand, streaking it with flour. "Like this."

She's so close. Closer than she was when we started. Her arms move as she kneads the dough in demonstration.

I smile down at her.

"You're staring at me again," she murmurs.

"I am."

"Why?"

Because, even covered in flour, she's stunning. I step closer, watching her eyes widen.

There's a flash of fear and trepidation, but something else also catches my attention. Desire and hunger sparkle there too.

I want to wipe away the bad and replace it with only the good from now on.

And the only way to do that is to take what I want. To finally cave in and drink my fill of her.

It's a colossally bad idea.

Anyone can walk in at any moment.

But the look on her face, flushed and delectable, spurs me on. It's like someone's lifted a veil from my eyes—I'm seeing clearly for the first fucking time in ages.

Her lips are glistening from where she's licked them. *Fuck.*

"You have a little..." My thumb brushes the streak of flour away, lingering against her skin, hot beneath my fingers.

"Oh?" she exhales.

The hold I have on my restraint slips as if I've let the chain go willingly. And my mouth swallows her gasp, a lovely sound full of need and surprise, as I claim her mouth.

Her trembling fingers clutch the cotton of my T-shirt.

I brace for her to push me away. But she tugs, pulling me against her more.

Whatever thread of control I had over my actions snaps like a rubber band. And I dominate her mouth with mine.

My hand clutches the edge of the counter to keep my body weight off her. The hand on the island cups her hip, then the back of her thigh, guiding her leg around me. And this allows me to nestle perfectly where I want to be. A groan slips past my lips at the contact.

My nose skims the column of her throat before I follow with my mouth, nipping and sucking at her tender skin.

Her head lolls to the side as my fingers gently grasp the hair at the back of her head, guiding her exactly where I want her.

Labored breaths fill the room as I continue to sprinkle her skin with kisses—laying claim to her so that no one else dares to come near her again.

It's not enough.

Her soft whimpers and uneven breathing aren't damn near enough.

My hand moves from her hair to the back of her other thigh, hoisting her up onto the counter.

Her legs automatically wrap around my hips.

I move against her as if my body has a mind of its own. The ache in my cock intensifies as it juts painfully against my zipper, and it's my turn to groan as her fingers weave into my hair. The feel of them is just right. Fucking perfect.

My fingers move to the inside of her thigh, inching higher with each stroke as I claim her mouth once more.

Each caress of my tongue against hers sends another jolt of need racing through my body. I need to have more.

I inch my hand higher, dragging over the seam of her jeans as her hips lift just slightly before I pause. I lift my gaze just enough so that I can stare at her.

Face flushed and her eyes turning hazy, her mouth is parted as she drags in a ragged breath. She's utter perfection.

"Tell me to keep going, Rosa," I murmur against her skin. "Tell me you want this as bad as I do."

Her beautiful breasts labor with every breath as my fingers continue their intense strokes through the denim.

Is she as eager for this as I am? Is she wet and waiting for me?

With another stroke from me, her head falls back with a small, strangled whimper. "Please..."

It's all the permission I need.

The pop from the snap on her jeans mingles with her gentle pants as I trail my lips down her neck.

Shimming the material from her legs, my hand caresses her now bare calves as I sink to my knees.

My gaze locks in on her lacy black panties. Her whole body is as sexy as hell. And my mind focuses on the one thing I want as I part her legs.

I don't give a fuck about anything else. It's only her that matters.

I want to learn her taste and drown in it.

I want to hear her plea and moan for me.

And I want to feel her touch as she begs for more.

The tip of my tongue presses to her clit through her panties.

Fuck, I can already taste her. And it's even better than I fucking imagined. It's a drug—and I want it from only her.

As she gives a soft moan, I caress my tongue there more forcefully.

My hands grasp her thighs before I can stop myself from pushing her thighs wider.

Gentle. I need to be gentle.

My hands relax against her legs. I move her hips closer to the edge of the counter.

And my tongue flicks over the tight bundle of nerves.

My mind drinks in the delicious sounds escaping her. Her cry of pleasure short-circuits something in my brain. I want to satisfy her and make her hungry for more.

"Oh God," she gasps.

I can't stop toying with her little bud. Her panties are wet, but I want them fucking soaking before I even contemplate removing them.

I trace lazy circles around her heated center, swiping back and forth, up and down, hitting from every angle I can.

Her body arches and hips lift as my fingers continue to caress up and down her legs. And her thighs wrap around my head snuggly and so damn soft against my heated skin. I'd suffocate on her if she'd let me.

My fingers inch higher with each pass, teasing her and myself with the possibility of sinking my fingers deep inside her pussy.

Finally, I ease her panties down her legs, lavishing her inner thighs with kisses and nips, until she's bare before me. Glistening and soaked with arousal.

I dive in like a starving man. My laps turn longer and faster. And my tongue teases her as I devour the taste of her.

Finally, blissfully, she grips my hair and holds me against her. And her fingers shake as her whole body trembles around me.

Her panting fills the kitchen. "Camillo..."

The breathy sound from her arrows a jolt straight to my cock. My name falling from her lips is going to completely undo me like some preteen who's just discovered what sex is.

"I...I need, oh God..."

I growl against her, dipping my tongue into her wet pussy as my fingers move to brush over her clit again and again.

She writhes beneath me as her fingers tighten. "I just...I need to..."

And as another strangled plea leaves her, the brush of my fingers against her bud turns into a firmer stroke. And she shudders around my mouth, pulling me against her.

I'm a prisoner to her, and I'd gladly never leave.

This is heaven, my face between her legs, listening to her cry out and come undone because of me.

But this is far from over...

CHAPTER 25

ROSA

The world shatters as Camillo's tongue works between my thighs, and my body has a mind of its own as it trembles in aftershocks. He's the first man to touch me like this and not make a negative comment about my body. And I don't want to focus on anything but the utter bliss flowing through my veins right now.

Hazily, I watch him rise from his knees. I bite down on my lip, trying to control my erratic breathing.

The smile on his face is wolfish, and my heart flutters in my chest.

"How long do we have until we need to make dinner?" he rumbles.

My body sags with deflation. It's over. That's it. One mind blowing orgasm, and he's had his fill. "Um, half an hour."

"Good," he clips.

I ease off the counter, my legs trembling still.

His hand grasps me. "Where are you going, Rosa?"

"What?"

"We're not done."

My mouth parts, and I don't know what to say, but I can't deny the utter thrill that his words send through my body.

He comes closer, pressing his body into mine. "Not by a long shot, baby." Two powerful hands grip the back of my thighs and hoist me once more against his body.

This is a bad idea. Anyone could walk in.

"Focus on me."

My eyes lock on his as he brings me to the pantry. Closing the door, he presses my body against it. A soft moan escapes my lips.

I lick my lips, my brain fogging as his mouth nips along my skin. "Wait."

He freezes.

"Are you sure you want this?" I ask him.

His brow furrows.

"I'm not the right sort of woman for you—"

But he silences me as his lips crash into mine, stealing my breath and silencing my doubts.

My fingers tremble as they work his jeans open. I'm possessed. Something else is guiding my body and controlling my movements. Someone who's needy for the man before her. For someone to see me, for me.

"Fuck," he murmurs against my throat, his hands working my breasts. "You're completely addictive, Rosa."

His voice is growly, making me instantly melt on the spot.

Pressing me against the door, he braces against the wood with one hand while grabbing my hips with his other.

"What if...what if I'm bad?"

"Bad? Impossible." His voice is hoarse with need—need for me—and sends a fresh wave rushing through my body. It's dark, heady, and so bordering dangerous that I'm sure I've forgotten how to breathe for a few seconds.

His hand grabs at my thigh, so I have to wrap my leg around him. He presses his hips forward.

With the way I'm open to him, he grinds his hardness right against my core. "That's all for you, baby. There's not a goddamn thing on this earth that'll feel as good as it will when I sink into you. Whoever the fuck told you otherwise is a goddamn liar."

"But..."

"But nothing. I don't give a fuck about what *he* told you. What I do care about is hearing those beautiful sounds you make right before you come. This time with me buried inside you."

His mouth lowers to mine, capturing my lips. I've never seen a man like this. So wound tight over me. My heart does a pathetic flip. "You mean that?"

"Every goddamn word, God as my witness. There's nothing you could do that wouldn't turn me on, Rosa. I want this. I want you. No, fuck that, I *need* you. Now be a good girl and help me."

Something inside me snaps. The rocks of anxiety that weigh down my heart shatter into a thousand shards of joy, and his words feel like freshly fallen snow—a cool balm to every broken thing inside me.

Love. That's what I'm feeling. "I need you too, Camillo," I exhale.

"Damn fucking right, you do. I'm making you mine right here and right fucking now."

He's as desperate for me as I am for him. I know it just by looking at him. But it's more than just the sex. This differs from the empty rutting Grayden would do. This is an affirmation that the real me has been seen. Camillo's seen the broken bits of me that match his own in some twisted, fucked up way. It's a bond we both feel. Tethering us together in a way that it feels absolutely right to be so reckless with him.

My fingers tug his boxers down, and his erection springs free. Hard and thick, the tip glistens.

Keeping me pressed against the door, Camillo takes a foil packet from his pocket, and his devilish smile makes my insides turn to jelly as he rips the top open with his teeth. And in one swift movement, he slides it over his cock.

His body presses me back against the door, his hand grasping my thigh as he lifts me all the way up.

"Fuck, Rosa, I've been thinking about this for weeks. Tell me you want me to fuck you..." He rocks against me, his voice dropping an octave as he caresses my skin. "Tell me you want me as badly as I want you. Tell me you want me to be the only one who fucks you this good."

I nod, unable to find the words as my mind blanks.

He holds my chin, running this thumb across my bottom lip, watching the motion like a man at worship. "Tell me, baby. I need you to say it."

"I want you. You and only you."

His forehead drops to mine, and I can feel him tremble against me as he takes a sharp, full breath. "I want to be gentle with you, Rosa. I want to worship you like you deserve, but I don't know how gentle I can be right now."

I drag my fingers along his jaw, guiding him to look at me. "Take me." Who is this woman? Where has the old shy, timid me hidden—and where can I lock the door to keep her there? Never before have I felt so wanted and free in my life. Never before have I craved someone in such a sensual way.

This is new.

Different.

He reaches between us, grinding the head of his cock at my entrance. The look he spears me with is anything but gentle. It's raw and open. And yet I'm not scared.

He pushes his hips forward, slower than I want, but it's just the right pace to make my whole body light up.

Lifting my heavy eyelids, I watch the control snap on his face, his expression frenzied. "Fuck, Rosa, you're so tight." He's panting now against my neck. "I'm not going to last long, but I promise I'll make it up to you later."

The promise sends a thrill through my body. He kisses me hard and devours my lips and tongue as he sinks deeper.

I don't know where he begins and where I end.

"Hold on, baby..."

I do as he commands. My nails bite into his arms.

He withdraws before slamming his hips forward. He sinks into me again and again, banging me against the door until it rattles.

My hands are all over him. I bunch the fabric of his shirt in a futile effort to feel all of him as he continues to roll his hips into mine.

Each hard thrust from him makes me moan louder and louder.

"Fucking perfect. I knew you'd be fucking perfect, baby."

I'm completely lost in him. This man is mine. The only one who'll ever look at me like I'm some prized possession in his grasp and not some broken toy.

The knowledge intoxicates me. This is what it feels like to finally have someone care. This is what it feels like to be wanted, just as I am.

Camillo doesn't relent even as we hear the front door slam shut.

I can feel his smile against my skin at the base of my throat.

And the rhythmic banging of my ass against the door only doubles.

His lips close around my throat, teeth grazing, biting down just hard enough. A thrill of something molten moves through me.

It's everything I've ever craved and secretly wanted. I'd given up looking for it. But I've found it with Camillo.

His mouth claims mine, his tongue thrusting into my mouth like his cock, branding me anew.

"Fuck, Rosa, you're gripping me so tight." He withdraws, slamming back into me again and again. "Are you going to come for me again, gorgeous? I want to feel you so tight all around my cock. Be my good fucking girl and come for me."

I whimper against him, my head pressed against the door.

And one final thrust throws me over the edge.

His entire body tenses over mine. Absolute pleasure consumes his face as he pumps inside me. Everything goes blank as I cling to him as he pushes me straight into another climax.

We're both breathing hard as Camillo gently kisses my shoulder. He pulls out from me and carefully arranges my clothes before he opens the door.

He calmly ushers me through the kitchen, and fingers laced, he guides me down the hall to the bathroom.

"Camillo." I grab his arm.

"Shhh. Let me take care of you, Rosa. "

My chest swells with that silly emotion again. *Love.*

I nod.

"That's my good girl. Now sit."

Obediently, I comply, dropping to the small chair in the bathroom as he dampens a flannel.

"If that's how cooking class with you is going to go every time, I think it's a good thing you kick me out."

I can't help but laugh as he gently drags the cloth over my inner thighs, warmth spreading through my body.

"You have a beautiful laugh. Beautiful everything." He's staring at me now. My heart thunders in my chest. Is it that easy to fall in love with someone? To want them to want you that badly? And with the way he's looking at me, I want it more than I've ever wanted anything else.

The smile on his face could light up the entire state. And it's a look that shows me something no one else sees.

CHAPTER 26

CAMILLO

Tugging a tee over my head, the sight of the rumpled sheets and discarded clothing brings a smile to my lips.

Whatever spell Rosa has on me is fully rooted into place, dragging me under each new wave, week by week, day by day. I spend most of my time away from the house, rushing to get back just to get my fill of her. It's completely out of character for me, but I don't give a fuck.

Loosely tying my hair back, I can't help the smile that plays on my lips as I tiptoe to the door.

I pause, lingering just beside it as I listen to any movement outside.

I'm certain my siblings are already dressed and downstairs, but better safe than sorry. My brothers don't need to know my private business.

The sound of soft chatter fills the hall as I make my way to the kitchen.

It's nothing unusual now to see Rosa and Ethan sitting alongside my brothers around the table—both of them filling some hole in my heart I didn't know was there.

As per usual, Ethan's plate is nearly clean while Rosa continues to pick at her small portion. It's progress that she even sits and eats with us, but there isn't a fucking bone in my body that doesn't want to strangle that man forever—for daring to make her feel less than she is, for damaging someone like her.

I slide into the open spot beside Rosa and give her a quick smile before reaching for the pot of coffee and helping myself to a stack of pancakes.

"Momma, when do I get to have a sleepover with Uncle Millo?" Ethan asks as he licks a bit of whipped cream off his fork.

"You want to have a sleepover?" I ask.

"Yes, please. Like you and Momma always have sleepovers after you put me to bed." He tilts his small head to one side. "When can I have one too? Please, Momma, please?"

Rosa splutters into her water glass, coughing violently. "W-what?" she exhales, her face bright pink.

I open my mouth. "I, er..." But my pancake lodges in my throat.

"We're not..." Rosa's voice is a panicked squeak. "I mean, what makes you think that, honey?"

"I hear Uncle Millo walking down the hall and you two talking sometimes after the lights go out."

Her mouth forms a perfect 'o'. And my cock can't help hardening at the sight.

"What do you two do?" he asks.

I can feel Marco and Alessio losing a battle to keep their laughter at bay. I can see that Rosa's mortified, and my eyes narrow to each of my siblings, willing them to shut the fuck up.

"You see..." I start to say, but how the hell do I explain this to a four-year-old?

Alessio's fist is jammed against his mouth as Marco fights hard to keep his face in that scary neutral mask he wears around the clock.

Rosa's hand fumbles with her glass of water, sloshing it against the sides before taking a long gulp.

"It's okay, Momma," Ethan pipes up. "I know not to disturb you. Uncle Marco told me that if I need anything during the night, I should go into his bedroom, and he'll get it for me. He and Uncle Alessio say that we need to let you and Uncle Millo spend some time together."

The tips of Rosa's ears turned bright red as the realization sweeps over her that my brothers are both aware of what's been going on between us.

For a kid who was skittish about being alone with any of us men, he sure has gained confidence fast around us all. And a feeling crawls through me—something like pride—at the thought of him being used to us. *Of him fitting in.*

I rub the back of my neck. I could try to talk our way out of this, but the reality is that there isn't a chance in hell I'm going to stop having these *sleepovers* with Rosa.

Because I'm well and truly addicted now.

Under the table, I give her a reassuring squeeze. And some of the tension melts from her shoulders as she relaxes into the touch. If we weren't at the breakfast table full of people, I'd give her a reason to relax further. With a mind of their own, my fingers trace a lazy line to the inside of her thighs. Clamping down on my hand, her thighs press together. I bite back a smile, choosing instead to focus back on Ethan's curious brown eyes and not his mother's glare.

"We play games," I offer. "Or work out sometimes."

"I'm sure you do," Alessio mutters into his coffee cup.

My foot collides with his shin under the table, earning me a fierce glare and a grunt.

'*Fuck off,*' I mouth as I feel Rosa's embarrassment roll off her in waves.

"What kind of games, Momma?"

"Oh, uh..."

"The rules would be too complicated for you to understand, Ethan," I say gently. "They're special games for, um, grownups."

"Oh." Disappointment sags his small shoulders.

Guilt washes over me, and I fight the need to rub my chest. It's bad enough my brothers are already smirking at me, but if they knew just how badly I'd break for this kid, I'd never hear the end of it.

Think. I can fix this. And end this horrible fucking conversation before Rosa melts into a puddle on the floor and never lets me near her again.

"But we can have our own sleepover sometime this week, Ethan. It'll be extra special. We can camp out in the backyard, watch some movies, and roast marshmallows. How does that sound?"

Rosa's eyes snap to mine. And the delight that sparkles in them forms a knot in my stomach.

"Really?"

"You bet. If it's alright with your mom."

Ethan's face swings to Rosa. "Please, Momma?"

"Ethan, honey..."

"Please?" he tries again. "I'll be really good. You can join us too!"

"I don't want to inconvenience you," she says to me.

"Not possible. It'll be fun." *It'll be fun?* What the fuck was that, and where had it come from? When have fun and kids ever been associated with me? I blatantly ignore Marco's unhinged jaw as I stare back at Rosa.

"Okay, sure," she murmurs softly.

I watch as her gaze drops to the table and that adorably shy smile lights her face. "Great. I'll take care of everything." And I start to make a plan inside my mind, determined to make this the best goddamn sleepover Ethan's ever seen.

I look across at Rosa again, and a small smile sparks in her eyes.

The way she looks at me... My chest does that weird squeeze, and I swallow back the lump in my throat. I don't deserve that look, but damn if I don't want to try to be worthy of it.

CHAPTER 27

ROSA

Ethan's little body snuggles closer into my side as I flip yet another page of *Peter Pan*. He's engrossed in the story as always, and I cherish these moments. A warm bed, food in his belly, and a boy whose smiles light up the room once again.

Safety.

A feeling of love.

Two things I didn't think we'd ever get again.

My voice falters, clogging with emotion. I don't want to think about any of this—about what's next, about how we're going to have to eventually move on from the generous offer laid out before us because it can't possibly be real.

Clearing my throat, I launch once more into the perilous adventure of the lost boys, placing a small kiss on the top of Ethan's freshly washed hair. He looks adorable in his white pajamas with pale blue teddy bears all over them—it's one of the sets Camillo insisted on getting for him when Ethan first arrived.

A knock at the door pulls my attention, and I look up to see Camillo leaning there. My breath stutters out as I watch him standing there with his shoulder braced against the doorframe.

His hands are tucked into the pockets of his jeans as a soft smile graces his face. It lessens the harsh frowns and brooding expressions that he normally wears. It makes him look more angelic than monstrous. The real Camillo, the one he doesn't think anyone can see.

"Am I interrupting?"

"We're reading *Peter Pan*," Ethan squeals. "Momma was just getting to the best bit." The body that was just nestled against mine, clambers toward the end of the bed with his stuffed bear as a sword. "Do you like *Peter Pan*, Uncle Millo?"

Camillo rubs the back of his neck and shrugs. "Haven't read it. I watched the movie, though."

"There's a movie?"

I nod, placing the book on my lap, my index finger saving our spot. This month's obsession is pirates. Anything and everything pirates. My lips tug up as Ethan attempts to speak like a pirate before falling into a soft pile of giggles.

"Sounds like you're having fun."

"Momma's the best at reading."

"Is she now?"

"Uh huh." Ethan nods as he sits back up. While he still sometimes tucks himself behind my leg or tries to be as small and unnoticeable as possible with the others, it's different when Camillo's in the room. They have some unspoken connection.

A connection that melts me on the spot whenever I see it.

"You should join our story time," Ethan announces.

"I, uh..."

"P-please?" But Ethan's single word is hesitant. Almost as if he's not sure if he's overstepped or misspoken and will be admonished for it. Memories of Grayden snapping at him for bothering him before bed, for just wanting a scrap of attention from his father, flash before my eyes, and my fingers tighten around the book in my grasp.

Camillo's eyes land on mine in a silent question of permission.

"Only if you want to," I say softly.

And Camillo instantly nods. In two long strides, he's beside the bed on the other side of Ethan.

Ethan pats the open spot on his left. "You can sit here, Uncle Millo."

"There's not a lot of room for me on your bed, Ethan."

I suck in a sharp breath. It's not meant as a dig at me. I *know* this. And I know I take up more space than I should. Even the king-size bed Grayden and I shared seemed too small with me in it—something Grayden always pointed out.

The conversation around me fades to the background as my mind tumbles over and over, the darker thoughts being dredged up by something so innocent.

"How about this?" Camillo murmurs.

I blink back into the room. Despite being a twin-sized bed, Camillo's maneuvered the mountain of stuffed animals—more gifts that he and his brothers insisted that Ethan needed—so that all of us somehow fit. His back is braced against the footboard, one leg on the ground while Ethan fits into the crook of his body.

Our legs brush, and Camillo gives me a knowing smile. "Okay?"

I clear my throat. "Yeah. Now, where were we?"

"Can Uncle Millo read, Momma?"

"Oh, I'm not sure if he has time..."

Ethan, his brown eyes wide, tilts his face up toward Camillo. "Will you read, please, Uncle Millo?"

Camillo looks uncomfortable, shifting on the bed, his body rigid. I open my mouth to gently tell Ethan not to push, but Camillo clears his throat and nods. "Sure. But no making fun of me, okay? I'm not going to be nearly as good as your mom."

I know he means it as a joke, but the way he says it, I can't help but wonder. Did someone used to mock him for not being good enough? Is that why he understands Ethan so well? Is that why he sees me? Why he silently understands how Ethan and I are so lacking in confidence and trust?

Ethan's small hand slips into Camillo's much larger one. "I'm not very good at it either," he says in a small voice. "But if you try your best, then you can be proud of yourself, and I'll be proud of you too, Uncle Millo."

The strained smile on Camillo's face melts, and a genuine one takes its place. My chest grows tight at the sight. I love watching them play in the pool or listening to the gentle conversations they have while I clean or do chores. It's just...perfect.

No, I know that it's more than that. *It's love.*

I've even been able to eat more lately, and not in that binge and fast cycle I was in before. I'm trying to sit down properly at mealtimes, although I'd be lying if I said it wasn't still a struggle.

"Alright. What happened before this?"

Ethan's expectant expression swings to me, and my expression quickly turns into another soft smile as I recount the previous happenings in the story to Camillo. The way he looks at me, though...

I feel seen.

I feel...*wanted.*

I tear my gaze away with a flush as he turns the page and picks up the story from where I left off.

These last few weeks have done nothing to slow the pounding of my heart when he's around. To calm the uneasy attachment I feel when it comes to him. And now, is he really reading my son a bedtime story? It's too good to be true.

As I listen to the story, Camillo's deep voice washes over me, sending waves of pleasure rolling through me. It's soothing—but it shouldn't be. It's a slippery slope, and I'm not sure I can stop myself. With anyone else, I don't think I could let go like this—open myself up.

Catching my eye, Camillo smiles, his hand rubbing along my calf in affection. I can feel the tension ebbing from all my muscles. Closing my eyes, I'm so relaxed that I could even fall asleep right now. Because I trust him with my son. I trust him with our lives.

Ethan's sleepy voice fills the room as he asks questions just like he normally does. My eyes close, and I listen to the two most important people in my life just be.

It's foolish to trust him so soon.

And it's even worse to allow him into my life in a way that will crush me when it comes shattering down like everything good ever has.

But I can't help it...

"Rosa?"

I hum in reply, unwilling to open my eyes.

"Rosa?" This time his whisper is accompanied by a gentle brush against my cheek. "Come on, let's get to bed."

"Ethan's gotta..." My words tumble into something incoherent as I force my eyes open. I blink into darkness which is illuminated only by the dim nightlight sitting atop the dresser.

Camillo's soft expression fills my vision as he brushes a stray strand behind my ear.

"He's out cold. I tucked him in and everything."

"You did all that?"

"I did. I didn't want to wake you until I had to."

I nod, pushing from the awkward position I fell asleep in and going into Camillo's embrace. Despite the sleepiness tugging me under, I smile into his chest. "Thank you."

"You don't need to thank me."

"Still, thanks."

"C'mon, sleeping beauty, let's get into a proper adult bed."

Fingers laced, Camillo leads me to the door before he pauses. Following his gaze, I see him looking at Ethan as if he's reluctant to let him out of his sight.

The expression on his face is one I can't quite make sense of.

It's vulnerable, open—but in a new way I haven't seen before. Something like fear etches into the corners of his mouth and forehead.

"C'mon. If we hover too long, he'll wake up." This time it's me who tugs us down the hallway, Camillo's heat pressing into my side me like a cozy blanket hugging me. I stifle a yawn as he flicks the nightstand lamp on.

He pulls the shirt from his body and exposes the ropes of muscle and beautiful lines of ink to my greedy eyes. I follow his lead in discarding my clothing onto the armchair. Sleepily, my fingers fumble around in the drawer I hope is mine, tugging on the nearest t-shirt, before I lazily walk toward the bed.

The smell of sandalwood fills my nose. And I realize it's not my shirt but one of Camillo's as it hangs off my body in a way mine usually doesn't. Not caring enough to change, I slip into the smooth sheets with a sigh.

The room darkens, and the bed dips.

"Tonight was perfect," I say in a soft voice.

"Yeah?" His large frame cocoons me from behind, pulling me against his chest, making me feel safe and secure. A large hand circles my waist, holding me against the planes of his body. It's a familiar position we've settled into over the last few days.

"Yeah." I nod into the darkness. "You should join us for bedtime more often."

His lips at the back of my neck send a soft shiver skittering through my body. "Anytime. It was nice. *Nulla è difficile per chi ama.*"

I love when Camillo speaks Italian. I don't understand it, but the rhythm of it is soothing. If I wasn't so tired, I'd ask him what those words mean, but sleep once more pulls me under as Camillo's deep breathing evens out behind me.

I relax into his embrace, feeling some sense of peace I never thought I'd ever feel—and which I know can't last...

CHAPTER 28

CAMILLO

The sound of my footsteps echo around the hall. I've struck out in each room I've gone in search of Ethan.

I pause, catching sight of Rosa sitting on the floor, knees tucked beneath her. Her brow is puckered in concentration, and that delectable bottom lip of hers is sucked between her teeth. I could watch her all day if I didn't have work to do or a promise to keep.

I gently clear my throat before entering the room—a soft signal to both Rosa and Ethan that I'm here. It's the best way to announce myself without either of them spooking.

Ethan's smiling face meets mine before his brow scrunches in a way that is nearly identical to his mom's.

"Hey, you two."

"What's that?" Ethan asks.

I look down at the mitt in my hand with a smile. "It's a mitt. Am I interrupting you?"

Rosa shakes her head. "No. We were trying to figure out this game. It's supposed to help prepare him for kindergarten or something, but..."

I step closer, peering over her shoulders, but all I can do is grimace.

Her soft lyrical laugh fills the room as she stares up at me. That sound alone could make me die a happy man.

"What?" I ask a little self-consciously.

"You look as confused by it as I am," she giggles. "I'm glad I'm not the only one who thinks it's too complicated."

"I'm not the smart one of the family. You're better off asking Alessio if you want help with that."

Rosa shakes her head. "I think we'll just stick with the good old-fashioned ABC memory games. And you're plenty smart. You were the one who figured out that thing with the oven last week."

Hearing her call me smart feels weird. A good weird. A weird that I could get used to.

But deep down, I know it's just idle flattery, even from Rosa. I'm the brawn, the muscle. No one comes to me for plans or ideas unless it involves busting someone's kneecaps. But when Rosa says something like this, I almost believe it. Almost.

"What's a mitt for?" Ethan interrupts with a quizzical look.

"Baseball, of course." I smile. "I remember you said you wanted to learn the game. Since I've got the day off, I figured maybe we could spend some time together and I'll show you. I promised, after all."

New things have the potential to be hit or miss. Ethan's come out of his shell around me, laughing and asking to do things or play games, but I can see still the trepidation in his eyes every time. "But you can say no and spend the day with your mom if you want."

"It's okay, Ethan," Rosa encourages. "If you want to go outside with Camillo, you can. I'll be inside for a bit to finish some work. I can always join you both outside after."

"Is it hard?"

"Baseball? Nah, in fact, I think you're gonna love it. But we can do whatever you want while your mom works."

Offering to watch Ethan flows effortlessly off my lips. It's some compulsion I'm not sure I want to fight. Spending time with him is important. Not just to Rosa, but also to me.

I watch as he tentatively moves to grasp my hand.

"Why don't you go slip your shoes on, and I'll meet you at the back door?"

"Okay!"

Ethan dashes off toward the mudroom, leaving Rosa and me alone. I step closer, closing the space between us, before capturing her lips. Waking up with Rosa in my arms every morning is better than any fucking work out or drug on the market. Nothing makes me feel like she does.

Her breath, labored from just one kiss, warms over my face as I pull back.

"Come out when you can?" I whisper.

She nods, and I capture her mouth once more, taking her bottom lip between my teeth. The small sound from her is swallowed by me while I fight the urge to throw her over my shoulder and show her just what she does to me without even trying.

Instead, I step back, exercising some herculean control over my dick and body. Her glazed expression sends my body thrumming with need. Soon. Not soon enough, but soon, I can sink into her once again.

"Don't overwork," I order, capturing her lips once more, before breaking away with a smirk and a playful swat to her ass as she moves away. Without seeing her face, I know that delicious pink color is painting her cheeks, and her beautiful lips are slightly parted. My girl knows what she's missing.

I walk with Ethan toward the back of the mansion and the mudroom, the little boy bouncing on the balls of his feet.

"Ready?"

"Ready," he chirps.

I guide Ethan toward the side of the house where Marco, Alessio, and Lorenzo are already setting up. Ethan stops beside me, gripping my sweatpants nervously.

"Hey," I start, bending down to be eye level, "they're just here to have fun with us. They'll set up while we go over the basics. Is that okay?"

"Are they going to play with us?"

"Yeah, if you want."

To my surprise, Ethan nods. I stand with a smile and lead him on.

A tight nod is all I give the guys as we get closer.

"Okay, buddy, you ready?"

"Uh huh..." He's nervous, rocking on his small feet as my brothers and cousin approach, sporting our red family baseball jerseys.

"Okay, first, safety."

Marco moves slowly behind me, extending the helmet and jersey for Ethan to take.

The little boy glances at them, then at me.

"These are yours."

"Mine?" he squeaks.

I nod. "You can take them. I'll help you put them on."

"Does Momma have one?"

"I think I can persuade her to wear one too." The thought of Rosa in a jersey with 'Marchiano' on the back does something to me. And the image of her alone in it with nothing underneath does something even more. I clear my throat, reminding myself that I have an audience who can clearly see everything going on.

His fingers move over the threaded embroidery of his name on the back. "That's my name," he says in awe.

"Sure is. Now you're one of us."

The look Ethan spears me with nearly knocks me over. It's like a sucker punch to the gut, and I'm left hanging on for dear life to stop me from falling apart.

No one has ever looked at me the way he is—like I'd just given him the world on a silver platter. Like I'm some sort of superhero.

Suddenly, little arms shoot up and wrap tightly around my waist.

Awkwardly, I kneel, unsure what to do.

Ethan's never hugged me before.

And I'm paralyzed with fear of fucking this up.

"*Help*," I mouth to Alessio, who only shakes his head while miming a hug.

My heart races in my chest like a fucking racehorse. Slowly, I pat his back gently with a shaking hand before giving him a slight squeeze.

"Thank you," Ethan exhales.

"Anytime, buddy. Anytime..." My feet are frozen in place, and I'm too shellshocked to do or say anything else.

Marco, seeing this, clears his throat as he steps up toward Ethan. "Now that you're properly dressed, let's get your helmet on," he says gently.

Ethan tentatively lets Marco lead him to the bench, where my brother swiftly clicks his small helmet into place before flashing me a thumbs up.

I clear my throat, trying to dispel the tightness in my chest. "You good, Ethan?"

"Yeah," he nods.

Alessio claps me on the shoulder. "You're getting there, Millo," he says quietly. "Just keep on with what you're doing. He's opening up to you as you win his trust."

I give my brother a grateful nod, and then, I walk to stand beside Ethan who's now fully prepared for his first swing.

***

A few hours later, I turn to the little boy. "Okay, Ethan, ready for something new?"

With a nod, he moves to the marked spot. His hand tightens around the plastic bat, which only hours ago trembled. We've spent nearly all afternoon practicing with him, hitting ball after ball. But now, it's time for a few low and slow lobs to really step it up.

"Remember," I start from where I'm crouched beside him, "eye on the ball, and swing when you're ready."

"What if I miss it?"

"Then, we'll try again."

"But..."

"But?"

"No one is gonna laugh?"

"No one is gonna laugh," I promise him. "In fact, I bet you we're all gonna cheer for you, regardless. And I'll tell you a little secret." I lean closer to him. "Uncle Alessio over there can't swing for shi—um, salt. He's got a lousy swing." And Ethan's soft giggle nearly has the same effect on me as his hug did.

I give Marco the signal and watch him slow pitch the plastic ball toward Ethan. His eyes squeeze shut as he swings. The crack of plastic on plastic splits the air, and Ethan's brown eyes widen with surprise.

"I hit it?"

"You hit it."

"I hit it!"

An eruption of cheers follows with a few whistles.

"Let's try again."

Repeatedly, Ethan hits ball after ball, the smile on his face growing with each cracking sound of the bat making contact. They only roll a few feet from where we're positioned, but that's not what matters. It's the fact that he's doing it.

Pride and something else moves through my body. Something I'm not sure I even know how to describe.

Affection.

Warmth.

Family.

Another crack of the ball hitting the bat snaps me out of my thoughts, and I smile. A new lyrical cheer hits my ears as Rosa's voice mingles with the guys' cheers, pulling my attention from Ethan's little dance. The look she sends me makes my heart race.

"Did you see that, Momma?" he squeals.

"I sure did."

"Kid's a natural," Alessio chimes in.

"We'll have you running bases in no time," I add.

"Really?" he says with wide eyes. The pure joy on Ethan's face as my family continues to praise him settles into something hot and thick in my stomach.

We continue practicing with Rosa watching us. And Ethan's tense, tiny shoulders relax more and more as time passes. And his laugh bubbles through the air when Marco hauls him up and runs the bases piggyback style, high-fiving Lorenzo once he's back on solid ground.

Comfortable. He's comfortable—or more comfortable—than he's ever been in the last few weeks. And that makes standing out in the blistering heat, burning my neck to hell, completely and totally worth it. The smile on his face is worth it alone, and the hot, syrupy feeling through my body is something I'm not ready to give up.

But beneath the joy simmers my anger. How could anyone ever make such a small, precious person feel so fearful and distrustful? How could anyone ever take someone so sweet and break them like they're worthless?

My fist clenches at my side. But I don't have time to think about that. Right now, I just need to focus on Ethan. "Do you want to keep going?"

"Please?"

"As long as you want, Ethan. As long as you want."

"Do you think Momma will try?" he asks with hope in his voice.

"I can ask her."

And his wide grin warms my gut as I make my way to where Rosa sits.

"He's laughing," she says in a voice full of wonder. "Actually laughing."

"Yeah, he is."

She shakes her head with a small, dreamy sigh.

Tugging her closer, my arms wrap around her waist as I stand behind her, watching Ethan hit another ball a few inches further than the last time. His fan club goes wild, causing him to break out into another little dance.

"He wants you to try," I say softly.

"To try? What, baseball?"

"Yeah."

"I don't know the first thing about what to do."

"I can show you."

"Okay, but in a few minutes. This is his moment to shine."

With my chin resting on her head, Rosa leans into my chest like she belongs there. She does, whether either of us will admit it or not. Her fingers thread with mine.

"Thank you."

"For what?"

"For trying with him. For just being you."

Yet again, this woman slices me to my knees without even trying. To be seen as something other than some bloody-knuckled brute is rare—nonexistent, really—and yet, Rosa sees something.

I squeeze her tighter. I don't know how to tell her what I want...

To tell her that I'd do anything in my power to keep her and Ethan with me forever. Even when I know they're not mine to keep.

To tell her that I want her not just to warm my bed, but also for something else—something that would heal the broken and damaged bits of me.

The words lodge in my throat.

I'll only fuck it up if I try.

Things are going so well right now. The thought of losing her or Ethan is enough to make me pause. To make me swallow the emotions bubbling inside me.

I won't risk messing it up. Not until I know for sure that she feels the same way about me...

CHAPTER 29

ROSA

Frosting dots my cheeks, and the sweet smell of freshly baked cakes fills the calm night air of the kitchen.

The house is peaceful—in a way it isn't during the day. Despite the quiet that seems to engulf the estate while the Marchianos are busy doing whatever underhanded deals need to be made or taking care of their businesses, the house still feels lived in and bustling. But now, at two in the morning, it's a different kind of quiet. One that used to unsettle me, but now only brings a soft sense of belonging.

We are safe here.

Camillo and his brothers make sure of it.

I'm in their debt for something I can't possibly pay them back for, ever. But this is a small step in the right direction, as insignificant as it feels. A smile tugs at my mouth as I finish scripting the frosting across the top of the cake.

The large island in front of me is covered with cupcakes in various flavors. I know better than to bake the favorite flavor for only one of the brothers. It's childish how they fight and pout over it, but it's also harmless—I've learned a lot about these terrifying men since I started working here.

After everything they've given Ethan and me, the least I can do is bake a birthday cake.

The clock down the hall chimes loudly, and I stifle a yawn. Swiping the back of my hand to my forehead, smearing more frosting there, I admire my handiwork. The mount of dishes looms behind me, reminding me of what staying up so late has produced. But it'll be worth it to see the surprise once everyone is up.

Ethan's tiny body is curled up on the bench of the breakfast nook, fast asleep. He didn't want to go to sleep without me upstairs with him, but he soon fell asleep when I tucked him up on the cushions with his stuffed bear and a warm blanket.

A yawn escapes from me as I continue to, as quietly as possible, clean up the mess I've made. If I can finish soon, I can still get a few good hours of sleep without anyone the wiser.

As quickly as I can, I wipe down the counter, having hidden the surprise birthday cake in the pantry for the morning.

It's the closing door that alerts me that Camillo is finally back from whatever assignment he was given to deal with. We don't talk about that often. It's not my business to poke and prod him when he comes back, lips drawn into a grim line or exhaustion etched into his features, his knuckles almost always sporting some kind of fresh bruises and blood.

I know he thinks I don't see it or notice. But my eyes are wide open to the darkness that swallows him whole. Yet, he doesn't scare me the way Grayden's violence always did.

My lips tug up into a smile. Beneath that hard exterior is something vulnerable only I can see. It's revealed in flashes here and there—something broken that fits perfectly with all my own jagged pieces.

"Rosa?"

I straighten, putting the spatula back in the drawer before turning to face him.

"What are you doing up?"

"Ethan couldn't sleep," I lie smoothly, hoping he won't see through it or the frosting crusted along my hairline, and hoping that for once, my voice doesn't falter. "I got him a glass of hot milk. I was just cleaning up."

I can feel his body heat even before his arms encircle my body from behind. His distinct sandalwood scent fills my nose, and I lean further back. He pulls me closer, breathing in deeply. The way he clings to me mends something within me I can't quite understand.

"Tired?" he murmurs.

I melt against him and nod. Without another word, Camillo steps back and carefully lifts Ethan's sleeping body, then carries him up to bed.

The excitement of tomorrow running through me causes a smile to tilt my lips as I climb the staircase behind them.

After we tuck Ethan in, we tear off our clothes and climb into bed. And it takes less than a second for his body to wrap around behind mine. His lips find the juncture of my neck.

Despite my exhaustion and sleepiness, one brief touch of his lips and glide of his tongue across my skin makes it all vanish. Desire races through me.

"Mmm...why do you taste like frosting?"

I bite my lip to keep my smile from spreading. "You'll see in the morning."

He hums against my skin, his large hands gripping my hips and dragging me further against him. "You made something?"

"Maybe."

"I can always find a way to make you tell me."

I smile into the dark. And a thrill of need and want rushes through me at the idea. "Oh?" The warmth from his mouth washes over my throat and makes goosebumps pebble my skin.

His lips part as he continues to kiss against my jaw, my neck, up to my ear. "You sure you don't want to tell me?"

His low voice caressing my ear only heightens the feeling building in my belly. A part of me wants to cave in—but another is far more interested in finding out his methods for making me spill my secret.

My heart pounds in my chest and thunders against my ribs as his fingers skim lower and lower.

What is it about this man that makes every rational and reasonable thought flee from my head? It makes me feel reckless and in control all at the same time. But I only feel like this with him—like Camillo is slowly but surely mending something in me, putting me back together kiss by kiss.

"I can be really persuasive," he whispers against the side of my neck.

"I don't want to ruin the surprise," I manage to gasp out.

And the haze in my head takes over as his rough hands trace a path down my body, igniting the heat within me.

Reaching my legs, he pushes his palms between them, forcing my thighs apart.

And his fingers skim over my skin as he nuzzles my neck.

The anticipation grows as I feel his warm breath on my ear, his deep voice sending shivers skittering down my spine.

"I've been looking forward to this all day," he whispers against me. "Looking forward to having you in my arms and stroking your sweet pussy..."

Pressing myself against his mouth, I hold my breath as I feel his fingers start to inch their way closer to where I need them.

My body trembles with each touch from him. And my eyes flutter in blissful anticipation as I silently beg him to touch me where I need it the most.

I let out a moan as he traces over my slick outer lips and growls at what he finds there. "So wet. You're such a good girl for me..."

My breaths are shallow as he keeps one hand there while the other moves over my throat, then down to cup my breasts.

"Such perfect tits," he exhales as he rolls a nipple between his rough thumb and finger, making it instantly harden into a peak.

With every touch, I gasp and tremble with pleasure.

He pulls me tighter into his embrace, his muscled body spooned around me as his hands keep playing with my body.

My head presses back against his shoulder. And I let out a small whimper as his finger swirls around my clit for the shortest second before returning to caress my inner thighs.

I close my eyes in anticipation, willing his hand to return to where I want it, needing it so desperately.

"You're already dripping wet," he rumbles into my ear, his tongue teasing a trail down the side of my neck as he licks and nips at the skin there.

My breath hitches as his fingers dive between my lips again and circle my clit.

I can feel the tension building from within. My panting intensifies.

And I reach behind and grab onto his thighs for support.

His forearm is grasped around my waist, so tight that I couldn't escape even if I wanted.

One of his hands is massaging my clit with firm fingers while the other pinches and tugs at my hard nipples, making my nerve endings scream out for release.

And as a powerful orgasm rushes through me, I start screaming out and try to push his hand away.

But he refuses to stop until every last drop of my pleasure has been wrung out of me.

Gasping for air, I collapse back against him as he wraps me in his strong arms and whispers to me. "Perfect, Rosa. You're just perfect."

***

While Camillo helps Ethan to dress, I get things ready for breakfast. I want everything to be perfect for Marco's birthday.

When Ethan comes down, hand in hand with Camillo, he lets out an excited squeal when he sees not only the birthday cake but also the cupcakes I've baked in everyone's favorite flavor.

Camillo, however, has a different expression as he watches Alessio and Lorenzo digging in. He grunts, his lips pursed. "I get you baked for Marco since it's his birthday and for Ethan because he's a kid, but why did you also bake for *them*?" he asks as he lasers a look at his brother and cousin and jabs a finger in their direction.

"Jealous, are you?" Alessio asks with an arched eyebrow.

"No," he says a little too quickly.

And I can't help but bite my lip to keep from giggling as he grumbles under his breath.

As we settle down around the table, his hand comes to rest on the top of my thigh.

"Are you going to make all our favorites on everyone's birthdays?" Alessio asks, a hopeful look in his usually serious eyes.

"If you want, of course."

"I'm glad I've got a meeting here this morning," Lorenzo adds as he picks up another cake.

"Camillo mentioned you'd be joining us for breakfast this morning," I say in a shy voice.

"It was really nice of you to think of me and bake my favorite flavor too," Lorenzo smiles.

Heat creeps into my cheeks at the praise being flung my way this morning. It shouldn't affect me like it does, but still, I can't quite wrap my head around it. Or the fact that Ethan and I now fit so seamlessly in with them. It feels like a dream I haven't woken up from—one I'm not certain I want to.

Camillo's warm hand cups my face, turning me toward him despite the presence of his family. The heat crawling up my neck is only partly because of embarrassment. His dark eyes search mine as if he can see straight down to the broken shambles of my soul. I squirm a little beside him, uncomfortable with the idea of him seeing how broken I really am inside.

I know he won't judge me, but what I am is unfixable, and I want to hide that part of me a little longer. He's seen too far down as it is.

"I still can't believe you made us cupcakes too," Alessio says around a mouthful of cake. "You spoil us, Rosa."

"What's all this?" Marco's voice cuts through our chatter.

"Happy birthday!" Ethan pipes up, scampering around the table to give Marco a shy hug.

"Thanks, buddy," he says.

"Momma. I'm full now. Can I go play and tell Bernie Bear all about the yummy cupcakes?"

"Sure, honey," I say with an indulgent smile at him as I watch him skip away.

I watch as the others give birthday greetings to Marco. It's an open display of affection and warmth. And it sends a jolt of longing straight through me.

"Happy birthday, bro," Camillo says.

"Thanks," Marco murmurs as he heads for the hot pot of coffee before freezing. "*What the fuck is that?*"

My hands shake at the growl in his voice.

"A birthday cake?" Lorenzo mumbles over the rim of his cup, his brow arched. "Rosa made it."

Marco's body spins to face me.

And I fight the urge to sink against Camillo.

Fury is etched into Marco's dark eyes, his upper lip curling in a snarl.

"I..." I swallow hard. "I wanted to surprise you with a cake."

Eyes narrowed, he strides toward me.

Camillo jerks up and stands between his brother and me. "*Marco.*"

"Move," Marco orders.

"*No.*"

The temperature in the room plummets.

No one dares move as Camillo and Marco clench their fists.

"Move, Camillo."

"*No.*"

"This is a shit time for you to grow some balls."

The hard clap of Camillo's hand into Marco's chest makes me wince.

"I'm sorry," I mumble, easing from my chair gradually.

My breathing is coming in small pants.

Anxiety winds tighter and tighter around my chest.

"I just wanted to do something nice for your birthday," I whisper. "I didn't mean to upset you."

My chin wobbles, and I bite down hard to keep my lips from trembling. Tears blur my vision.

Why is he so upset? Does he not like cake? Have I messed up and misunderstood something important here? And now, to make things worse, Camillo is squaring off against Marco. *I've ruined it all.*

My hands tremble against me, my coffee cup long forgotten on the table. I stand with my eyes downcast.

"I'll—excuse me," I stutter, moving past the looming figures in the middle of the kitchen.

Guilt claws through my body, tearing me apart with its talons, shred by shred.

"Rosa, wait—"

But my feet carry me into the hall before Camillo can even finish his sentence.

Nausea swims through me as I try to keep the tears from falling. Hands braced on my thighs, I bend forward, trying to get as much air into my lungs as I can. It's futile, like sucking through a broken straw.

Why am I even crying? He didn't say he hated it. But it's clear I've overstepped some mark. I just wanted to do something for his birthday. To provide Marco with a small thank you for everything he's done.

But I can't even do that properly. And now I'm responsible for messing things up between Camillo and Marco. *Me.*

"What the fuck is wrong with you?" Camillo's bellow in the kitchen rouses me from my stupor. My breathing turns frantic, small gasps peppering the air.

A muffled reply hits my ears, unintelligible over my gasping breaths. My arms wrap around my body tightly as I try to stop the sob that clogs my throat.

"Rosa?" I hear the echo of my name. I don't know if one or several moments have passed, still frozen to the spot and unable to move.

"I'm sorry," I mumble, my words soft, barely above a whisper.

"Hey." Camillo's face fills my blurry vision, and concern battles rage as he scans my face. "There's nothing you need to be sorry about."

I will the tears back, clearing my throat. "I didn't mean to upset him. Or for any of that to happen."

"Marco was just...shocked. He's not used to someone else making the birthday cakes or anything. He's seen it as his job since our parents died—were killed. He's always felt guilty about our mom no longer being around. Marco and Alessio practically brought up me and our youngest two siblings after our parents were killed." His words come out through clenched teeth.

"I didn't know."

"I know. He won't admit it, but he handled it all wrong. But it's okay, I promise."

I want to believe him, but I can't. I nod, not trusting my voice to stay even.

He leads me back to the table. I follow, keeping my eyes down. I can't look the others in the eye. I've overstepped my position here, and I'm the reason Camillo and his brother nearly came to blows. In the months I've been here, I've never seen them like this with each other.

The atmosphere is charged, and Marco's seat at the table is now empty. I don't dare ask where he's gone so that I can apologize to him—not that it'd do any good to fix all the damage I've done.

***

The morning goes by in a haze, my thoughts tumbling over one another as I absentmindedly clean and do laundry.

As I mop the ground floor, I freeze outside the hallway, catching the brief conversation inside Marco's office.

"You need to apologize."

"Since when do you get to tell me what to do, Camillo?"

"You're being an asshole. More than usual."

"Is that so?"

"Yeah."

I shouldn't be listening to this; it's a private conversation.

"Rosa was just trying to be nice."

The mop nearly drops from my hand at the sound of my name. I really shouldn't be listening, but my feet won't move.

Someone sighs, and I can almost picture Marco and Camillo both dragging their hands down their faces, mirroring each other. There are so many small things like this that always remind me that they're siblings.

"I just..." Marco starts to speak, and I hear another longer sigh. "It's hard to forget what happened."

"I know," Camillo says more quietly. "They were our parents. We'll never forget what happened to them and how they left us."

"It's even harder to accept we've got people who love us now," Marco continues. "A *family* who care about us." There's another pause and what sounds like drinks being poured. "I know we've always had each other—always will have each other—but there's always something around us. Guilt? Sadness? I don't fucking know, but it clings to us like a second fucking skin no matter what I do. I've tried hard to do what I could for you all."

"We were dealt a shitty hand..." Camillo's voice is low. "You did your best."

"But I didn't manage to fix it, did I? It was Juliana, Cate, the kids." Another lingering pause. "Rosa and Ethan too. No. Don't give me that look. You're not as subtle as you think you are. We're also not stupid. I see the way you look at her. They *all* make us a proper family. They get rid of that shit that haunts us like ghosts."

Camillo's reply comes in a mumbled response I can't quite pick up. Their voices continue softly for a few more minutes.

I shake my head and back away from the door, then wander down the hall. But the sound of the doorknob turning sets my spine tingling, and I hurry my step, mop and bucket handle clenched in my fists as Camillo and Marco leave his office.

But the air around them is different. Less charged. Lighter.

Marco claps Camillo on the back before they part ways.

They seem to have made up. I breathe out a sigh of relief and head back to the utility room to change out the mop water.

"Rosa?"

Startling, I knock over the half-filled bucket into the sink with a small, muttered curse. And my heart lodges in my throat.

I turn to face Marco. "Y-yes?"

"I didn't..." He clears his throat, stuffing his hands into his pockets. "Earlier," he grits out. "You making the cake was thoughtful. I didn't get a chance to tell you."

Is this his way of apologizing?

My brow puckers, unsure. "No one should have to make their own cake on their birthday," I say quietly. "I didn't know. What I mean, I wasn't aware that making all the cakes was your thing and a sort of tradition for you. I'm sorry I overstepped."

His jaw ticks, but he nods. "Things change when we bring new people into the family. It's not a bad thing. See you at dinner."

All I can do is nod mutely, unsure what the feeling fluttering inside me is. It's different from the way Camillo makes me feel. This is something else entirely. Something that warms me differently.

Family. This is how a family is supposed to act. Do they really consider Ethan and me as family? Or is he just being polite to make up for what he said earlier?

Family.

The word settles against my skin, leaving me confused and hopeful. And I know that it's a dangerous combination because danger will always be waiting for me in the shadows...

CHAPTER 30

CAMILLO

The conversation in Marco's office replays in my head repeatedly.

Family. A fucked-up f-word that I guard like a rabid dog.

And yet, the word is broken to me all the same.

But by some miracle, we still have something. Something imperfect, with jagged edges and tattered holes, but it's something. And it's something that includes Rosa and Ethan in every single version of it that plays in my head.

My stomach rumbles as I enter the kitchen. Thanks to some fucker trying to be smart, I missed both lunch and dinner.

But even worse, I missed getting to spend time with Rosa in the kitchen before it was all finished, hearing about all the things Ethan had to tell me. To say my mood is sour is a gross understatement. I hate missing those moments, soaking up all I can with both of them.

That asshole is no longer still breathing. It's the very least he fucking deserves.

Heading through the open door into the backyard, I round the corner and glimpse Rosa lounging in a chair on the deck. Nestled into her is a sleeping Ethan.

Absentmindedly, her fingers run through his hair as she stares up at the night sky riddled with stars, the soft illumination of the half-moon haloing around her. It bathes her in its glow like the goddess she is.

The smile that stretches my face feels foreign and yet natural all the same.

It's a smile that only comes out when she's around. Like I can't help reaching for something I'll never be able to keep. Knowing I'll be burned in the end should make it less appealing. It should deter me. But it doesn't. I dig in deeper with each day she remains mine.

Softly, I pad over to her, pressing a soft kiss to her head. She jolts slightly before easing back into the chair.

"You're out late," I murmur.

"Stargazing and catching fireflies. Ethan wanted to wait for you to get home to read him the rest of Peter Pan." She smiles at me, and I can't help but match it. "I think you've successfully replaced me with bedtime story duty."

"Sorry."

Her laugh is gentle. "Don't be."

I want to tell her I don't know jack shit about kids or what I'm doing. I want to tell her that if it'd been anyone but them, I never would have taken that second look.

But I don't. The words don't form on my lips because I'm afraid she might laugh at me. Emotions and I don't mix.

Never have. Never will.

Somewhere along the explanation, I'll fuck it up, and that'll be it. Maybe it's selfish, but I love the way she looks at me. Like I'm someone she's proud to be with.

"I can put him to bed so you can finish your tea," I offer before my brain can process what I've just offered. It happens more frequently when I'm around her. Like I've forgotten everything about who I am and what I do. But I know that's a lie.

It's because of her. *It's me trying to be something worthy of her—of her and Ethan.*

"I can do it."

As she starts to move, I shake my head. "You worked today, yeah?"

"Yes?"

"Then let me. You deserve a few minutes alone."

"I'm fine. I don't want to put you out or anything. You just got back from...wherever it was you were. I can carry him up."

I ignore her, gently lifting Ethan into my arms. He weighs nothing. "Be a good girl and finish your tea. I have plans for us after."

I watch as her skin flushes, and her bottom lip gets sucked between her teeth in a way that tells me her mind has slipped into the place mine constantly seems to go when I'm around her. I'm worse than a fucking teenager. But with her, it's impossible to think of anything else.

The house is quiet as I walk the halls, clinging to the fragile body in my arms like it's some priceless jewel. Ethan's breathing is soft and even against my shoulder. This unnecessary and terrifying urge to keep him protected pounds through me with each step I take. I shouldn't feel like this—whatever the hell *this* is—so soon. And about a kid?

But somehow, both he and Rosa have slipped in past every single defense and wrapped themselves around me.

I'm not sure if I hate the idea or if I want more.

I tuck Ethan in quickly and flick off his light before making my way back down the stairs and out to where Rosa still lounges.

"That was fast. I barely finished my tea."

"We can stay out a little longer. It's a nice night." For Chicago anyway. It isn't too blustery, and the balmy air has cooled slightly as we inch closer and closer to the fall.

I nudge her over on the lounger until we're sitting side by side, nestled just right so that her plush body meets every hard edge of my own. I itch to feel her skin under my fingers, to skim over it and explore every inch. Every rational action of my body disappears the moment the pads of my fingers skim her smooth skin.

Rosa's breath hitches as my fingertips continue their leisurely path along her exposed leg. The way she fills out every inch of clothing she wears only taunts me to remove them. Even now, just in her simple denim shorts and T-shirt, she's absolutely mouthwatering.

My hand moves further inward, feeling the way her skin pebbles and reacts under my touch. It's a high I can't get enough of—and if I don't stop now, I'm certain the guards and soldiers patrolling the grounds are in for quite the show.

And as entertaining as the thought is, I want Rosa all to myself. "Rosa."

She hums a response, her head leaning against my chest.

"Done?"

"Yes."

It's a breathy response that sends a jolt straight to my cock. "Perfect."

I waste no time sliding from behind her. And before she has a chance to move, I scoop her up with ease, wrapping her legs around my waist.

Swallowing the gasp that leaves her, I claim her mouth. Tongues clashing, I devour her like she's my last meal. And as my hands knead the back of her thighs, I grasp her to me. I adjust my grip on the back of her thighs as my hands skim under her shorts to grab her ass.

"I can walk."

"You can..." My words break as I claim her lips, her jaw, her throat, anywhere and everywhere I can get a taste of her. Sweet and delicate. "But I like this better." I give another squeeze to emphasize my point.

Her head tips back, exposing the column of her neck and more to my trailing lips. "Okay..." There's a hint of something in the word, broken only by her breathy sigh. "I like it when you pick me up." Her soft admission echoes around the silent halls, broken only by our panting breaths.

"Yeah?"

Nodding, her fingers drag against my scalp, and I grip her all the tighter. Holding her against me so she can feel just how badly I want this. How badly I need this.

"It makes me feel good..." I steal her beautiful words with another bruising kiss, pressing her into the door to the bedroom. *Our* bedroom. It hasn't been mine in weeks. That thought alone sends another jolt through my body.

Pride surges through me, battling it out with the hunger bubbling in my gut. My body is on fire. My hips press into her all the more, canting against her as I fumble with the doorknob.

"I'd carry you everywhere if I could," I growl into her ear as the door springs open.

Once more I hold her against me, groping at her with each step as if I can devour her whole.

The door slams shut as I kick it behind me. Keeping the softness of her pressed into the planes of my body, I can't find it in myself to care we might have woken my siblings. They'll live. But I might die if I can't get my fill of her—if I can't make her feel as amazing as I feel when I'm with her.

I lower her to the floor, hands skimming along her body. I back up a space. Then, with her pupils dilated, she watches me shed my jeans, revealing my black boxers that strain against me.

I catch her gaze in mine. "Undress for me, Rosa."

A flush spreads across her cheeks. "What?"

"Take. It. Off." My voice rumbles through my chest as I watch her body tremble with excitement.

I make myself comfortable on the bed, watching the show before me.

She pulls the top from her body, exposing the emerald green of her bra.

And with a quick flick, the button of her shorts opens, exposing the matching set of panties, making my cock jump as it begs to be released from its confines. Soon...but not until I've had her come on my tongue.

I can't take my eyes off her. *She's fucking perfect.*

I hold her gaze as she peels the denim from her shapely legs and discards it behind her.

In the dimly light room, I skim over her thigh and hip.

Her hands still while mine continue to explore the soft inside of her thighs. "I didn't say to stop, Rosa..."

My touch tears a moan of desire from her as she reaches behind her to unhook her bra. The fabric flutters to the ground.

Greedily, my eyes rake over her flesh, shamelessly taking in my fill of her.

Her nipples harden into peaks as she watches my tongue swipe over my lips.

I trace up her sides. "You're beautiful..." My fingers glide over her heated skin in slow, languid swipes. "So fucking beautiful."

Her head falls back as my fingers dance around the swell of her breast, teasing her nipple with each swipe of my thumb.

"Panties too, Rosa..."

Her breathing comes in short, erratic pants as her hands deftly move to the flimsy fabric covering her from me.

Enraptured, I track her fingers as they hook into the waistband and expose her mound to me.

My mouth waters. "Perfect..."

I sit back on the bed as her heavy-lidded eyes move over my body.

Reaching behind me, I pull the black tee from my chest, baring the hard planes of well-earned muscle to her.

I motion to her, beckoning her to me.

Dropping to her hands and knees, she moves toward me slowly.

But I shake my head. "Up here."

"What? But we've never—"

"Up here," I repeat.

She whimpers at the demand, and I bite back a groan of my own at the sight of her prowling toward me.

She straddles my lap and closes her eyes as her softness brushes against my cock. But I have other plans.

"No, Rosa." I smile at her, licking my lips. "I mean up here. I seemed to have skipped dinner."

She stills. Her eyes wide. "I... You don't have to..."

"I want to," I growl.

The pink of her cheeks deepens, her gaze turning away as she swallows thickly. "But...I'm...too heavy."

"Bullshit."

Her eyes snap to mine, brow furrowing. "I could suffocate you!"

"What a fucking way to go."

"That's what Grayden said to me—that I might suffocate him—when I suggested it once. I'm serious, Camillo."

"So am I."

"But—"

"If you bite that lip one more time, Rosa, I'm going to drag you up here myself and bite it for you."

"You don't care about how heavy I am?"

"Care? Baby, the only thing I care about is how many times I can make you come. Now bring that perfect ass up here and sit on my face before I take matters into my own hands."

I can see the want and the war in her mind, glazing her brown eyes and making my cock strain all the more.

But the uncertainty seems to linger. Finally, her fingers curl into the sheet before she nods. She trembles a little as she continues up my body. Her knees press into the pillows above my shoulder.

And my hands grip her ass and haul her to my mouth.

Her body tenses as I press my tongue into her slick folds and nudge that tight bundle of nerves.

Circling around her clit, once, twice, three times.

She jolts suddenly, trying to lift herself off me.

My fingers dig into her hips, keeping her captive against my mouth. I press a kiss to the inside of her thigh. "It's okay, Rosa. Just let go."

I close my mouth over her bare sex again. Every part of me wants to devour her like the starved man I've become.

A moan ripples from her lips, and as she relaxes over me, I grip her harder.

I swirl my tongue around her clit and caress up and down her beautiful thighs. The thought of sinking into her makes me ache. I swipe at her heated center while her hips rock against me.

"Camillo..."

I tease at her clit as her thighs clamp around me. Nothing else matters but bringing her to a sweet climax—and doing it all again and again until the whole damn house hears us.

Something primal beats in my chest. And I want the world to know she's mine.

I devour her. I fuck her with my tongue, sucking at her clit until her sounds of pleasure fill the room like the sweetest music I've ever heard.

Thighs shaking, her moans are deeper now, less restrained, and her body melts over me.

"Camillo, I'm going to—" A sharp scream breaks her sentence as she shatters around me.

But I can't stop. I keep lapping at her, drawing out her orgasm even further.

But this is far from over. One down and several more to go.

Gently, I push her onto her back and tug my boxers off.

My fingers fumble around in the nightstand until they brush the foil packet. Tearing into it, I watch her full tits heave with each breath as she comes back down from her high.

The hazy look in her eyes makes me even harder until I can feel pre-cum at my tip.

My lips nip at her sensitive flesh as she gasps and mewls under my tongue.

I need more. I want her wrapped around me—all those lush curves pressed against me. And I want to feel her clenching around my aching cock.

Capturing her lips, I take what's mine. She throws her head back as I push her thighs apart and rub the head of my cock against her entrance.

And I drag it through her slit, teasing her.

Her fingers lace behind my neck as her hips roll against mine. Begging for more.

My fingers trace a path along her full, beautiful body. Capturing her plump lips with mine, my kisses are fierce and dominant.

I trail kisses down her throat and over the swell of her bare breasts.

"You drive me fucking crazy..." Taking one of her nipples into my mouth, I suck greedily and listen to the increasing urgency of her moans.

With each grind of my throbbing cock over her sensitive entrance, she writhes against me. She needs this just as much as I do.

"I'm going to make you scream for me again," I growl as I push inside her.

She cries out, her pupils dilated, and I revel in the tightness that surrounds my cock.

Pulling out, I plunge into her again, her walls becoming even slicker with each thrust.

I increase the depth. And her pussy grips me, sending pleasure rocketing through me.

In her big brown eyes, I see intense desire and need reflecting back at me. And picking up the pace, I savor every sensation as I push deeper into her without restraint.

With one arm supporting my weight, my hand roams along her body—teasing, stroking, and caressing every inch of her skin.

As our bodies move in perfect sync, I know that she trusts me with the most intimate part of herself—and I'm going to make sure she experiences nothing but pure bliss in return.

When she's with me like this, she's no longer the same shy woman. Her captivating gaze meets mine, and I'm lost in the depths of her desire.

My rough fingers reach down between us and caress her clit to bring her to the brink of ecstasy. "I love playing with your sweet pussy," I groan in a voice thick with pleasure.

Her response is a breathy moan, making me ache for her even more.

I take her nipple into my mouth and suck and nip at it until she cries out, savoring the way she arches beneath me and begs for more.

And as I pump relentlessly inside her, she shatters into ecstasy. She's screaming my name and writhing beneath me.

I continue massaging her clit until she begs me to stop. And even then, I refuse until she is completely spent and satisfied.

Lying with her in my arms, I tell myself to remember that this won't last. But even that's not enough to make me stop now...

CHAPTER 31

CAMILLO

The next morning, we lie in my bed together, and Rosa's finger plays with the empty space along her ring finger. The exact spot that the gaudy band should be.

It hasn't escaped my attention she doesn't wear it. I hadn't seen it on her finger the first time we met, either. I didn't ask then, and I'm not about to ask now. It never feels right to bring that looming blade above our heads. To bring *him* up.

The fact remains that she's a married woman—even if she has left her husband.

My hand tightens at her hip, needing to feel her beneath my hand. A compulsion to make sure that this is real.

"You're quiet," she whispers.

I look down at where she lies in my arms. The comforting familiarity is exciting and yet terrifying at the same time. This is different for me. Strange and unknown.

My lips press to her head where the strands are a golden perfection and no longer covered in cheap dye. I prefer her this way. Cheeks flushed, lips slightly swollen, and her blond hair fanned out around her gorgeous face. "It's still early. You should go back to sleep," I murmur.

"So should you."

I shake my head. I'm too wound up. My head is a spiral of thoughts that I don't know if I want to face. The emotions are a beast all of their own, but something in my chest beats to make Rosa mine. To have her as mine in a way that no one else can take. And that means dealing with that fucker.

Luckily, he's stayed in his lane and left her alone for now. On my orders, our men have been keeping a close tab on him—and on Rosa when she's out.

I want that fucker's head on a silver platter.

But that isn't possible right now. Because of Grayden's connections—specifically due to him being Conor Davis's son-in-law. Conor Davis is very important to our business right now, and we need to keep him on side.

I want to gag at the thought.

If our business dealings weren't an issue, Grayden would already be six feet under, and I wouldn't have to worry about how to make Rosa mine permanently. Instead, he hides behind others and plays his stupid games.

Why we ever wanted to bring Conor Davis, his pharmaceutical company, or his shitty money into the business, I'm not sure, but I'm not about to argue that point to Marco or Alessio. This is the way our world works. Roles need to be played. And questioning my capo isn't in mine.

My fingers trace along her hand, stilling her fingers. I want to tell her everything racing through my mind.

To explain just how badly I want her.

I nuzzle into her neck, my hands tightening around her as if that can somehow let her know. Because if I hold her tight enough, she'll be mine. And then, maybe I can keep her...

It's a foolish thing to want, to even dare to dream about.

"Are you mine, Rosa?"

I have her body, that much I know. But do I have her heart? Do I have her?

"What?"

She rolls in my arms to face me, her brown eyes clouded with emotions I can't place.

"Are you mine?"

"I..." That tempting lip is sucked between her teeth as she looks at me. "Yes?" It's not a statement from her, but a question.

I don't know the answer I want from her, let alone myself, but that isn't it. I don't want any doubt from her. I don't want to fear that she'll slip through my fingers. I don't want her to question it in any way. I want her to know. I want her to hold on all the tighter. "You can't really be mine as long as he's...there." My eyes drop to that bare space on her fingers, slightly lighter than the rest of her sun-kissed skin. I want to replace it with something of my own.

The urge is a slap to my face.

I want her to be mine fully. Unequivocally mine.

Her fingers cup my face. It's a soft touch I'm not sure I deserve. "I don't know how to sort that mess out."

"You can divorce him."

"I can't." It's a soft admission. One I'm not even sure I've heard correctly.

Fire burns hot and out of control in my chest.

She shakes her head. "He has all the power and money. I don't have that."

"We have money. We have lawyers. Use them."

"It's not that simple."

"Isn't it?" Why can't she see how simple it could be? My heartbeat pounds through my body as I stare down at her. My brow furrows. "You don't want to divorce him?"

"What?"

"You don't want to finally be rid of him?"

"Of course I do." My nostrils flare as she scuttles back from me. A look of outrage lights her beautiful features. She shakes her head again. She gets out of my bed, her body moving around the room and gathering the discarded clothing to occupy herself. Her hands tremble with each piece. "It's not as simple as hiring a lawyer. It's complicated."

"Explain it to me."

"Why are we talking about this?" she whispers. "Why does it matter?"

That's the million-dollar question. The one that I keep circling around and around. Why does it matter when I have her here with me? What does it matter if she's still married?

My tongue traces my teeth, and I take a deep breath. "It matters to me."

"I can't do it." She tugs on a T-shirt, a gray one of mine, and the sight of it is distracting enough. My eyes crawl over her legs, moving to how the shirt swallows her whole and brushes the top of her thighs. Messily, she piles her hair on the top of her head. "He'll take Ethan from me if I try."

"What?" My eyes snap to hers, glossy now with a fresh sheen of tears.

"He'll take my son. He has all the power in that situation. He'll do whatever he can to take him from me. I could hire the best lawyer in the world, and it wouldn't matter. He has power and pull. I can't ever risk that happening. *I can't.*"

"We have power. We have pull. My brothers and I, we can figure it out."

"It's not the same kind of pull." Her words pierce my chest. She's not wrong. But it still stings. She perches on the edge of the bed. "I want to be rid of him, but I can't. I can't risk my son. I can't risk the court giving custody of Ethan to that monster. I can't do that to Ethan." She's kneeling now on the bed, pleading with me to understand.

But her words ring in my ears. *Not the same kind.* The pull that separates us from them. *The kind that divides her from me.*

"I'm yours," she breathes, settling herself on my lap. Soft hands cup my face as she searches my eyes. "I'm yours. You have me. Completely."

But I don't.

"Please." Her words are soft, her gaze falling from my face. "Say you understand? I have you, and you have me. That's all that matters. Right?"

"I do." My thumb brushes her cheek, watching her eyes flutter closed. But the words are hollow, meaningless.

She might not have said it in so many words, but the rejection still stings. It slices through me like acid. And bile burns the back of my throat.

She's not mine to keep.

The voice whispers again and again in the back of my head.

I've always known that. I knew it the moment I kissed her. The moment I tasted her and claimed her body. I knew that I'd never be able to hold on to her. Because that's the way the world works.

I'm not like *them*.

I'm not like *him*.

He's powerful in a way that stems generations and reeks of nepotism. He's connected and threaded into the high society of Chicago. I'm...none of that. People don't know my name the way they do theirs. I'm the shadow lurking against the wall, barred from entering. And I'm lesser because of it.

My chest tightens uncomfortably as the feeling settles over my skin.

"Camillo?" Her lips graze my jaw and neck.

"I should get up," I tell her as I push the covers back.

Her brow furrows as disappointment and hurt briefly flicker over her features.

I take her in my arms. I can feel the heat in her body, but it's not enough to distract me from my thoughts. I keep hearing that voice in the back of my head that continues to haunt my nightmares. I'm not good enough—and nothing can change that...

I kiss her forehead where it wrinkles as I shove the thoughts and feelings that bubble in my gut down. They don't belong here right now.

Because I have this woman in my arms, pressed against me, demanding my attention. For now, it's enough.

It has to be.

I'll worry later. And I'll deal with the rest later.

"If we don't, we'll never leave this bed. Plus, I have a meeting at the casino this morning."

"Oh?"

"I'll be back before lunch," I assure her, pecking the corner of her lips. "Then we can finish this and watch that movie Ethan wanted."

I ease her from my body. Each of my muscles are wound tight with some push and pull I don't understand.

I need the gym. I need to work out my frustrations to see the bigger picture. I need to figure this shit out. To find a way to be part of her world. But for me, it's an impossible task...

"I'll meet you down there," I murmur, heading toward the shower, each step stiffer than the last.

And all the while, the voice in the back of my head tells me that I can't fix this...

CHAPTER 32

ROSA

The atmosphere of the house has shifted.

It's different. Buzzing with excitement and anticipation.

It's palpable as I set down breakfast in front of Ethan. My thoughts haven't stopped tumbling since the other morning with Camillo.

Divorce.

He made it sound so simple when he brought it up. It's anything but. Grayden is too well connected, too entangled into Chicago's world of money and power that he'll find a way to ruin me and take Ethan away.

And he'll take Camillo down with us.

There's no quick solution. Money can't fix it like Camillo suggested.

And yet a part of me yearns to see it happen—so that I can be Camillo's in body, heart, and soul.

It's a fantasy, of course. A pipe dream that keeps me up when he's fallen asleep.

He asked me if I was his. I want to be, but that fear in the back of my mind won't go away. What if he gets his fill of me? What then? What's my backup plan?

"So, what's the plan?"

The conversation at the table snaps me back to the present. The family is returning from Italy today—well, Marco and Alessio's wives and children are; Debi and Danio have decided to stay a little longer in Italy. The threat from the feds has finally been dealt with, so it's safe for the family to start coming home.

"They'll land in about an hour," Alessio says. "We'll pick them up and get lunch. Then, I'm not sure."

"Then we'll clear out for a few hours so that you two can spare us the nightmares." Camillo's taunting smirk doesn't quite light his face like it usually does.

"You're not any better," Alessio replies.

"We'll make sure food gets delivered to your room."

"You're hilarious," Alessio says in a dry tone, but there's a spark in his eyes—something warm and longing.

"Thanks for noticing," Camillo quips.

"Rosa." Marco says my name like an order. I've gotten used to it, but it still jolts me in my chair—I'm too preoccupied with my own thoughts.

"Yes?"

"Can you prepare a special dinner tonight, please? I'd appreciate it."

"Of course. What did you have in mind?"

"I've left a list."

"What the special dinner for?" Ethan pipes up.

"The family is coming home," Camillo says gently to Ethan. "They've been, uh, away on vacation."

"More family?" Ethan asks around his bite of eggs. I can see the anxiety bubbling in his eyes. New people, despite how comfortable we've gotten here, bring unexpected challenges. Loud sounds and new temperaments to learn.

"A few more. Every bit the traditional big Italian family."

"Should I make sure their rooms are ready?"

Camillo's brow scrunches. "No. They're already as clean as a whistle. You don't have to do anything extra, Rosa." He leans closer to me, his lips pressing to my temple. "They're going to love you."

The conversation around me blurs, as does the rest of the day. Despite what Camillo said, I spend a little more time in the rooms than normal. There's not a speck of dust to be seen, nor a single item out of place. I even give Camillo's room an extra special tidy, even though I know none of the new arrivals will be going in there; although, to be fair, Camillo has been making a big effort lately to be tidier—putting clean clothing away instead of flinging it onto the floor, throwing away his car magazines once he's read them, not leaving empty drink cartons in the room. As I originally suspected, he's actually a pretty clean person—it's just clutter that's his downfall.

That evening, around dinner, I listen to everyone as they catch up on all the news of the women and children. And after helping to tidy up, I opt for some one-on-one time with Ethan, leaving the family to catch up with one another.

***

Both Juliana and Cate have welcomed me with open arms and appear eager to get to know me. Ethan is nearly always whisked off to do something with the other kids, with a quick glance at me to make sure it's okay. It eases some of the tightness in my chest and gives me a weird feeling of warmth inside me to see him tentatively making friends.

The conversation is pleasant and loud with excitement, like it always is each morning now. Today, like the last few days since their return, there's not much for me to do. Cate insists on handling mealtimes while Juliana is happy to take care of most of the cleaning. I help where I can by tidying the rooms, but I've taken a step back, careful not to step on their toes.

My eyes lift and land on Juliana. Marco's beautiful wife has stunning blue eyes and swishy black hair. Both she and Cate are kind and warm, and the women ask questions about Ethan and me to get to know us every chance they get.

And then there are the conspiratorial looks we share at dinner as the men talk gruffly about business problems and the clubs and casinos. I've never had friends outside my immediate family, let alone women who actually seem to want me around. My heart squeezes at the effort they're making with me.

I push back my chair. "I should get started on my work." There's not much for me to do, but I need to do something. I need to feel like I'm contributing.

As I pass with my small caddy of cleaning supplies, I watch Ethan quietly coloring beside a few of the younger kids. It warms my heart to see it, but the small flinches every time one of the older children yells breaks my heart. It's better than it was when they first arrived back from Italy. And slowly, he's breaking from his shell. He smiles often now, and when he and Camillo are alone, the energy he has triples.

After cleaning Camillo's bedroom and bathroom, I turn down the hall to one of the guest bathrooms. But the guest bathroom is spotless. Someone's already cleaned it this morning.

Turning on my heel, I grip the caddy tightly, and numbness spreads through me as I reach and take in the now vacant and spotless kitchen. Not a speck of dirt or dish to be cleaned.

Heaving out a sigh, I replace the caddy and catch sight of a small piece of paper on the counter. It's a note from Juliana inviting me to join them all tonight for a BBQ outside, plus an additional note at the end to say that they've already taken care of the grocery shopping for the meal.

Every responsibility I have has been taken and handled. Braced against the counter, I will myself to push past the worry that's worming through me. And racing alongside it is gratitude for including me. I don't understand what's wrong with me. This jumble of emotions billow in and out like a ship's sail as anxiety swirls within me. Numbly, I move through the kitchen, wiping a spotless glass as my mind spins around the stark facts staring me in the face. I move from room to room, straightening the already neat and tidy areas again and again on autopilot.

Because without something to show how valuable I am, there's no reason to keep someone like me around.

***

In the evening, I sit in the backyard with everyone. The men see to the BBQ while the women chat and the children play.

The buzz of nature and laughter fills the balmy Chicago air. I should be enjoying it. I should soak it up for all it's worth. But I can't. My fingers fidget in my lap as conversation surrounds me. I nod and smile at the right moments.

Even the warmth of Camillo's fingers playing with the loose hair at my shoulder absentmindedly does nothing to soothe whatever crack has fractured open inside me.

Time ticks by, minute by minute, as the sun drops low behind the tree line that surrounds the property, an easy conversation bouncing between the others. With a feigned yawn, I excuse myself.

Camillo's room—my room—is bathed in the fleeing golden rays. My skin itches as the tears I managed to keep away tonight threaten to spill past my eyes.

"Rosa?"

I stumble to my feet at his voice through the door. Trembling, I fiddle with the bed covers as if I'm getting ready for bed.

The door clicks shut. I can feel the heat of him before anything else. It's comforting, and yet it scares the hell out of me.

"Rosa?"

"Hmm?"

"What's wrong?" Camillo's soft whisper strangles me further.

"Nothing..." I gnaw my lip, hoping he won't pick up on why I can't meet his eyes. He'll know I'm lying if I look at him. But this isn't a problem he can fix. "I'm just tired."

"Rosa, look at me."

Reluctantly, I turn around and muster one of those practiced smiles. One that crinkles around my eyes to make it appear genuine despite it being anything but.

"What happened?"

"What do you mean? Everything's fine. I enjoyed the BBQ. You should go back and join the others."

"Not before you tell me what's going on." The arch of his brow is all I need to see to know that he's not buying my acting. Another thing to add to the list of things I fail spectacularly at. "Tell me," he whispers firmly, tilting my chin toward him. Those deep brown eyes of his searching my own for some hidden answer.

The words lodge in my throat. My gaze darts to the side. I don't want to cry. Furious, frustrated tears gather regardless.

"Rosa." His voice caresses over my face as he leans toward me, forehead pressing against mine.

I squeeze my eyes shut, banishing the sting.

"Please, baby?"

Those two words crumble what little resolve I cling to. "I'm not needed here anymore," I choke out.

"What?"

"You don't really need me anymore now that everyone's back."

Camillo jolts like I've slapped him. Something flickers across his face. A feeling bubbles into my gut as rejection fizzles to life in his eyes, hardening the warm chocolate of his irises into steel. "You want to leave?"

I'm unable to look at him. "You hired me to do a job. With everyone here, there's no point. I don't want to overstay my welcome."

"Rosa," he breathes into my hair, before pulling back. "You don't have to leave just because there's nothing to clean or cook. You can't possibly overstay your welcome here. Because you *belong* here."

Those eyes, now warm once more, search mine as he towers over me. They sparkle with some emotion that makes my stomach flutter.

"You have a place here." His thumb swipes over my bottom lip before cupping my chin. "Ethan has a place here. So, you're staying. Even if you're not needed to clean or cook as often."

"Okay," I exhale with a smile.

And Camillo's lips tilt up into a knee-weakening grin before he claims my mouth. "Good. Do you want to go back down?"

"I'd rather stay here, if that's okay?"

"Even better."

And I can't help the soft smile as he pushes me back onto the mattress.

Camillo's lips along the column of my throat banish the thoughts, leaving a welcome blankness.

I lie back on the bed, trembling with desire. He crawls over me like a predator, drawn to me with an intensity that makes my emotions spin out of control.

I watch him as he peels off my clothes and then his. His hands spread my legs, his lips kissing all the way up from my calves to my inner thighs.

I'm consumed by the intoxicating scent of him and the sight of his hard desire for me.

I feel his hands gripping my ass and hauling me closer to his mouth.

And then he holds my thighs wide open as his hungry tongue devours my pussy, sending shivers down my spine.

I try to pull away as the tension builds. But he won't let me, intensifying his teasing and sucking on my clit until I can't even control my moans.

Every lick along my seam brings me closer to the edge...

And when I finally reach it, I scream out in pleasure, my whole body shaking under his tongue.

His guttural sounds vibrate against my core, his tongue swirling over my clit before pushing into my entrance and making me arch my hips up into him.

I feel myself succumbing to the pleasure again, my mind hazy, yet my body responding eagerly to every touch.

His fingers tease my tits and tug at my long nipples, pulling more moans from my lips.

I push my breasts into his touch, unable to resist the pleasure coursing through my body. "Camillo..." I whisper, my voice husky, feeling utterly desired and wanted by him.

"Get on your hands and knees—show me your pussy," he commands, pulling me up onto all fours and positioning himself behind me, entering me with an intensity that leaves me breathless.

I let go completely. I'm his in this moment—physically and emotionally.

"I want to possess you, claim you, make you mine in every way possible," he rumbles into my neck.

With every thrust into me, I push back against him, needing him deeper inside me.

Every inch of him is pounding against my walls, driving pleasure to every single nerve ending, his balls slapping against my pussy with every thrust.

And when we reach our climax together, it's even more intense than ever before. "That's it, baby," he growls. "Come for me..."

Afterward, we lie panting, and he scoops me into his embrace, stroking my hair back from my forehead as he presses a deep kiss to my lips.

I feel content and fulfilled. He's captured not only my body but also my heart and soul.

For a few long minutes, we lie there in a blissful state. And as his hands caress me, any doubts fizzle into a blissful state of mind fog. I sink into it, welcoming the distraction, wanting it to stay and drag me under so I don't have to face the reality looming in the distance.

CHAPTER 33

CAMILLO

I'm a caged animal. Prowling along the mats in the gym, my form moves back and forth.

Sitting on the bench silently in front of me is an informant. And he's brought me nothing but more bad fucking news.

"Leave."

"Sir," he starts.

I whirl around to face him, my teeth and claws out. I'm looking for a fight. Anything to keep the beast sedated so that I can think.

His hands fly up in surrender.

"You did your fucking job. Now fucking leave."

Scrambling to the door, he flees.

I continue to prowl. I can't see her like this—wound up and pissed off. It'll only scare her. I've spent too many weeks hiding this part of me from her.

She's delicate and soft. The moment she sees me for the monster I am, she'll run from me. They always do. My chest aches with the haunted and disgusted looks of others. The sting of it steals my breath away as I rub at my sternum as if I can physically make it go away.

My fist clenches, sending a sharp throb through my knuckles. "Fuck." I drag a hand down my face, taking a deep breath in and hissing it out. Repeatedly trying to find some semblance of calm.

Rosa will be here any minute for her self-defense lesson. A weekly excuse to spend more time with her and to sink into her with the mirrors behind us. Who knew such a timid woman would enjoy being such an exhibitionist? My body thrums with the memory of Rosa wrapped around me, our bodies slick with sweat and reflected in the mirror so I could see just how I filled her...

She's mine.

I need her like I need oxygen. Like my soul needs some shred of humanity to cling to before I tip over into a blackened pit of sin.

She's mine in a way no one else has ever been.

And yet she's not.

Not completely.

I have her body. I have her attention. I even think I might have won her heart. But I can't have her completely. I can't show the world just who she belongs to...*belongs with.*

"Fuck," I snarl, whirling a tight jab into the canvas bag to my right. It teeters on the hook, creaking from the force.

Divorce is clearly off the table if our conversation was anything to go by. He's old money and full of lies, connections, and deals to get whatever the fuck he wants. I have the power and the ruthlessness of the Fratellanza behind me, but it's not enough. Fighting fire with fire will only engulf us both to ruin.

I won't risk my family being exposed like that. I won't make a sloppy mistake in a rigged system. Rosa's right about one thing. We can't fight him in court. Not that I'd planned it ever making it that far. As far as I'm concerned, Grayden Devlin is a dead man on borrowed time.

"Sorry," Rosa pants from the door, breaking the dark turn my thoughts have taken—the only path they seem to take when it comes to Grayden and his worthless life.

"Why are you out of breath?" The sound of her panting steers my thoughts in a different, more welcome direction.

"I just got back from the store. The line was crazy, so it took longer than I thought. I didn't want to be late for this, though." A sheepish smile spreads over her face. Warmth soothes over the tightness in my muscles, replacing the ice-cold fury that threatens to drag me under.

"You didn't need to rush."

She smiles at me, the meek shyness she always has finding its way onto her face. It's beautiful—but another stark reminder of just how far apart we are. She's innocent and angelic. I'm not by a longshot—because a dark soul doesn't find a halo at the end of his blackened rainbow.

Gently, I wrap her hands, letting the silence envelop us. It's the distraction I need, her body pressing into mine as I listen to the sound of our shallow breathing.

But it doesn't break the wall around me.

The warmups blur by, but before we even start the actual lesson, I can't help pushing Rosa up against the mirror.

She starts to say something, but it's only a weak protest—because she needs this as much as I do.

Silencing her with a finger to her lips, I hum against her neck as I lick up the column of her throat. "I need you now..."

Her beautiful body fills my palms as I drag her hips into mine, pressing her luscious curves against me.

"You're utterly irresistible." I tug off her clothes, only just stopping myself from outright ripping them.

I run my tongue along her heavy tits as I see every inch of her nakedness in the mirrors around us.

Spinning her around, she braces herself against the wall as I kneel down, spreading her legs as I position myself beneath her.

My mouth waters at the sight of her glistening pussy.

I lick along her slick lips and tease with the tip of my tongue as she grinds herself on my tongue.

I know what she wants—and what I need. I latch my lips around her clit, sucking so that she moans loudly for me.

The sweet taste of her only fuels my hunger and hardness. And I push my tongue inside her and show her what I plan to do when my cock penetrates her.

I feast on her, my hands caressing her delicious thighs.

"Please, Camillo... I need to come..."

I deny her, enjoying every single second of worshipping her body.

With each swipe of my tongue, she grows more breathless and desperate.

And one last thrust of my tongue inside her makes her finally explode in pleasure and convulse around me.

But I'm not done yet and push up to my feet. Her breasts are full and perfect for my mouth to explore. I tongue her ripe nipple, grazing it between my teeth.

And snaking my hand down over her belly, my finger traces back along her slick entrance as she arches into my touch.

After teasing her clit with my fingers until she's whimpering, I hitch her up against the wall and wrap her legs around my waist.

Meeting her eyes in the huge mirror at our side, I trail my gaze down her body, feasting on the sight of the goddess before me. "See how fucking gorgeous you are," I growl, grinding my dick against her slick seam and loving how she loses her inhibitions when we're together like this.

Sinking into her entrance, I take a moment to admire the beauty before me—her skin glowing and her eyes bright with desire.

I want to savor every touch and taste of her as if it's my first time with her.

And unable to hold back any longer, I plunge into her and take her hard and fast.

This is my favorite place to make love to her—watching our reflection in the mirror so that I can admire how perfect she looks with my cock inside her.

As I pound again and again into her warmth, she keeps begging for more.

Her pleas fuel my desire. I hold her in place as I move with urgency, driven by the need to give her another orgasm.

And when she finally comes undone again, unable to contain the sounds escaping from deep within her, it's all I need to let go and join her in ecstasy.

I continue to please her until she can't take any more, her cries echoing throughout the room before we slump against the wall, panting and spent.

And kissing her deeply, my heart beats rapidly, and I know I don't want to ever let her go.

But it's as if the world is whirling past me as I watch from the sidelines like a spectator to my life...

"We only have a couple of hours until everyone gets back from the zoo," she says as she gets dressed and checks the time.

"However will we fill the time?"

"None of that." She raises her blond brows at me as I step closer. "We're supposed to be working on those holds."

"I thought you hated those?"

"Better safe than sorry. You wanted to do this, Camillo, remember?"

"Maybe I changed my mind."

"I haven't." Her voice is soft as I step closer, and invading her space, I can nearly feel her tremble. "I don't want to be helpless again..."

"You aren't helpless, Rosa." Her gaze meets mine, and the softness nearly does me in. I don't deserve the look of reverence she gives me. Like I've saved her somehow. "You were never helpless. *You're a survivor.*"

"But now, I stand a chance in case something goes wrong." Her voice is timid.

"The only way that'll happen is if I'm dead," I say with a low growl.

She blinks at me, clearly startled at my admission.

But I'm not holding it back from her. Not anymore. If I want her to be mine, she needs to see *me*.

The thought terrifies the fuck out of me. And I'm hit by another ice-cold splash of water that she's too good for the likes of me. But I can't stop now that I've said it.

I brace for her reaction. For her gasp of horror. Her brow knits, and her eyes search mine, looking for something.

"The only way someone is going to lay a finger on you is if I'm gone. I will easily kill any man who tries to take you and Ethan from me."

Her lips part. "Camillo..."

My body goes rigid. I know that tone.

Softly, her hand cups my cheek. I lean into the warmth. Eyes closed, I let her ease some of the darkness brewing inside me. Taming the roaring beast that lurks beneath my skin. The light of her cocoons me.

"Camillo, you don't need to do that."

"I do. I need you to understand..." I'm fumbling. The words have me tongue tied. "I'm not a good man," I breathe finally, forehead against hers. "I don't deserve you. I won't ever be worthy of you. But I want *you*—more than I want anything else. But I need you to understand that I'm going to do whatever I need to do to make sure you're safe."

She says nothing.

I can hear my pulse racing in my ears. The blood roaring as my chest constricts. It's an intense confession. The closest I can get to telling her how I feel. I open my eyes, looking down at her. "That means taking care of your fucking husband."

"Taking care?"

"If we can't fight him legally, there are other ways."

"You mean..." Her voice drifts off, silence filling the gap.

"I have a plan." This is a goddamn bad idea. But she deserves to know.

I've had a plan for a while now. One that's been formulating since she walked back into the estate, face swollen and beaten. A new beast rumbles to life in my body. One built of brimstone and fire. One that craves blood in payment. It's settled into my mind and only solidified.

With the FBI off our backs now, the Fratellanza are once again untouchable. I can finally hit him where it hurts. I can repay every single mark and bruise that marred her perfect body until even hell won't know what monstrosity has landed on their doorstep. Until the taste of copper fills the air and the beast I am is satisfied.

He'll never hurt Ethan or Rosa again.

And that thought beats as hard and solid as my heart.

She wriggles from my grasp. "*No.*" Her head shakes furiously. And her eyes flash with something I can't pinpoint. *Is she finally seeing me for what I am?*

"No?"

"You can't." She clears her throat, wrapping her arms around her body.

Her words dig the blade in my chest deeper, twisting and serrating my insides. I blink. Pain spreads through my body as I stare at her. The look of horror on her face is mixed with something else, but I'm not sure what.

My hands fall to my sides. It takes every fiber of my body to remain upright. Knees locked, I stare at her, watching her features contort and brow furrow. She's pacing now, her arms still tightly wrapped around her middle. "There has to be another way..."

I can't hear the rest of what she says over the roaring in my head. Over the sound of the fracturing of what little is left of my heart, the jagged pieces crumbling into dust within me.

She's staring back at me now. Eyes wide and mouth trembling. I can see the disgust woven into the fleck of golden yellow amongst the warm brown hues of her irises.

I disgust her.

The thought repeats over and over again.

"Rosa—" I reach toward her.

But she flinches. And my hand drops back down.

"Camillo, promise me you won't do it."

I don't make promises I can't keep. I stare at her. She's only a few feet from me now, but a chasm stands between us that might as well be the Grand Canyon. My throat works around a lump as I try to find the words to make it go away, to drown out the feeling that overwhelms me.

She steps closer. "Please?" Tears rim her eyes. Tears over the monster she realizes I am now. Over the realization of just whose bed she's been sharing all this time.

Ice fills my veins. She finally sees the nightmare I am. Every bit of the broken, mangled monster that the gossipers have told stories of. Why wouldn't she? I've just offered to kill her husband—to make her mine, utterly and completely.

My chin jerks. A tight nod is all I offer. Because it's not a promise I'm willing to make.

Despite the coldness that washes over me, I will do whatever I can to get her out from his grasp. Away from his poison. And if that means dirtying my hands, so be it. And even if it means destroying the world for her and myself, I'll do it.

"We should get started." I move past her to the gym bag.

Rummaging around for extra wrap, my mind tumbles over everything. I knew it was too good to be true. I knew the moment the mask came off, she'd see the monster everyone else believes me to be. I'd hoped she'd see past it. I'd hoped she'd never look at me the way she just has. I wanted to be better for *her*. To do better by *her*. But that isn't my nature.

I've known it since the moment I saw her in that church—*I've known that I'd ruin her.*

***

Laughter fills the room as we all sit around the table for dinner this evening.

Marco shoots me a look of concern, but I just send him a small nod to let him know that I'm okay.

"Camillo?"

I snap back to reality. Rosa's hand is on my thigh. The table is empty except for her. "Where did...?"

"Everyone left a while ago. Are you feeling okay?"

I plaster on a smile, squeezing her hand. "Fine. Guess I zoned out a little. We should probably go up to bed."

"Okay." I watch as she gnaws her bottom lip, eyes closing. When she opens them, there's something shimmering in her gaze. "I'm sorry."

"Sorry?"

"For earlier."

A hollow laugh leaves me. "Don't be. It's fine."

"It's not. You don't understand—"

"I do."

"*No.*" How the word leaves her lips freezes me in place. Timid, shy Rosa has never sounded more determined since I've met her. Her chin wobbles, just a little, betraying how she really feels, but she meets my gaze with a steel behind her eyes, the brown lit with a fire.

"No?"

"I just..." She sighs, seeming to gather her courage. "It's complicated. But what you were suggesting, what you said, I just think there's a better way that doesn't involve *that*. And we'll figure it out. Together."

As comforting as her words are intended to be, they don't dispel the bubble of hopelessness that's blown up inside me. How could someone like her love a monster like me now that she's seen the beast within me? How could I have ever fooled myself into thinking I wouldn't drag her to hell by keeping her with me?

"Together." Mindless, I repeat the word before changing the subject. "Let's get Ethan to bed, huh?"

"Camillo?" she says with a tug on my hand. "You understand, right? This isn't... It's not about *him*. It's because I don't want you to take that risk. I can't—I won't let you do that for *me*. Violence isn't the only option here."

But it's the only one I understand. It's the only way to ensure he can't harm her ever again. If I want her the way every bone in my body desires, then I can't allow him to keep breathing. She's right about one thing, though. It isn't about him at all. It's always been about *her*.

And the creature that lurks in the darkness of my subconscious is out for blood.

And I won't be satisfied until I have it...

And although I think things have taken a turn for the worse between Rosa and me, I never imagine what happens next, and it's so bad that it makes her want to leave me...

CHAPTER 34

ROSA

I'm doing more cleaning of rooms, although they clearly don't need it, when I pass the office. The door is slightly ajar, and the three brothers are in there. And they're having an angry conversation.

Putting my head down, I hurry past—whatever's going on, it's none of my business. And I'd rather not know the details of their business dealings.

"Mrs. Giordano came over today and told me that her Felicity is pregnant!" Marco yells. "She's absolutely furious. What the fuck, Camillo? How could you let this happen?"

I freeze. Ice crawls through my veins as the words register... *Furious. Pregnant. Camillo.*

"And what the fuck were you doing, Alessio? You should have been keeping an eye on him, making sure something like this didn't fucking happen."

"I'm not his babysitter," Alessio drawls. "How far along is the pregnancy?"

My feet move unconsciously. I peek through the crack in the door.

"She says eight weeks."

My breath stutters in my throat. *Dear God. Camillo and I have been sleeping together for longer than eight weeks...*

"Look, give it some time." Camillo shrugs. "She'll get over it."

Jesus, he's been sleeping with someone else at the same time as I've been sharing his bed...

"Get over it? Are you kidding me, Camillo? She's already demanding child support. And the scan says it's fucking triplets!"

Bile burns the back of my throat. *Triplets*? She must have gone for an early ultrasound. I know from one of my cousins that her doctor identified her twins at a six-week scan...

I know Camillo would have been with other women before me. But I can't believe that he would sleep with other women while we were actually together.

Does he see me as just a fling? One of several women that he has on the go at once? Because we've never really talked about our status. But it's just that I thought I was more to him than a casual thing—I thought that he felt the same way about me as I feel about him...

I close my eyes and try to inhale through my nose. It's like I'm drowning in everything that's happening—his betrayal, the lies, the future that I thought we were building together. And it's like a whole house of cards is collapsing around me.

How could I have been so stupid? Tears roll down my cheeks. Humiliation and incomprehension consume me. I should have known that what I have with Camillo was all too good to be true. I should have known that he wouldn't be serious about someone like me—didn't Grayden tell me all along that there was something wrong with me? That I was lucky that he had even agreed to marry me because no other man wanted me?

I peek through the crack of the door.

"She'll be demanding child support for God knows how many years," Marco grits out.

"At the end of the day, it's just money," Camillo replies, not looking or sounding the slightest bit sorry. "There's no point stressing about it..."

But I can't listen to any more of this. I just can't.

I dash down the hall to my old bedroom.

And shutting myself inside, I sink onto the bed, putting my head into my shaking hands.

My heart is racing out of control in my chest, beating so loud that I think I can hear it. I feel like I can't breathe, like the air is actually suffocating me.

The words I heard keep echoing in my mind, replaying over and over until they blur together into one confusing, painful mess.

***

I know that Ethan and I can't stay here any longer, but I can't get myself moving to start packing and thinking about where we're going to go now. Back to Kori's maybe?

I don't know how much time has passed when I hear the door handle turn. I quickly wipe my tears, not wanting Ethan to see me upset

But it's not Ethan.

It's him.

"I was looking for you." His smile falters when he catches sight of my face. "Hey, what's going on?"

I turn toward the bathroom, needing to get away from him, but he catches my arm and turns me toward him.

"Rosa?"

I try to swallow the knot in my throat. "I heard it all," I croak.

"What?"

"I heard everything you and your brothers said in the office."

"You did? Look, um, it was an accident..."

"An accident?" I choke out a bitter laugh, though nothing about this is remotely funny. It's absurd, ridiculous. How can someone be with one woman, but at the same time fall into another woman's arms and accidentally create life? Triplets, no less.

Triplets.

The thought twists in my stomach like a knife. I feel sick. Nausea churns inside me. I thought I knew him. I thought we were solid, that our relationship was something real, something worth holding onto.

His brow crinkles as he looks at me, and he's silent for several, long seconds. "What exactly did you hear?" he asks.

"I wasn't eavesdropping. The door was ajar—Marco was yelling, and it was impossible not to hear it. Please don't pretend. I know that you've been seeing someone else." My voice cracks. "And I know that she's pregnant now."

"You think I got someone pregnant? But I haven't—"

"You've gotten Felicity pregnant!" I practically yell. "With triplets. Please don't lie to me. I thought I meant something to you! But now I know you've been seeing someone else..." To my mortification, I can hear the sob in my voice.

I pull away from him and sink down onto the bed once more as the strength ebbs from my knees.

He kneels in front of me, cupping my face in his hands. "Rosa, I don't know what you think you heard. But let me explain."

"There's nothing you can say—"

"Mrs. Giordano came over today because she's found out that Felicity, her dog, is pregnant by Mr. Fluffy."

I blink once. Twice. Three times. "W-what?" I stutter.

He nods. "Alessio and I had lunch at their home a couple of months ago as we had some business to talk over with Amadeo Giordano. And I had Mr. F with me because I was supposed to take him to the vet afterward."

"But it sounded like... Marco said she was furious..."

"Felicity is Mrs. Giordano's pride and joy. I think she loves the dog more than she loves her own children. You see, Mrs. Giordano breeds dogs, and she thinks we've ruined her plans for Felicity to have purebred puppies with her next litter."

"You mean...?"

Camillo starts chuckling. "Yeah. And Marco's blaming me because he reckons that I should have been keeping an eye on Mr. F."

I can only stare openmouthed at Camillo whose chuckle has turned into a full belly laugh. And I find my own lips tugging up into a grin, and soon, I'm clutching my stomach as my laughter hurts my sides.

As our laughter finally subsides, I let Camillo take me in his arms and kiss me. And I let him comfort me.

And although I believe his explanation and can see how I completely misconstrued the situation, I still have the foreboding that something bad is going to happen between us. It's almost like a premonition...

CHAPTER 35

ROSA

The conversation around me is light and airy. Plans to take the kids out to the park after breakfast are being made, but I'm only half listening.

The last few weeks have turned everything inside out and upside down, leaving the ground beneath my feet unsteady and unsure.

"What do you think, Rosa?" Cate's smile startles me back into the conversation.

"I'm sorry?"

"We thought we'd leave in about an hour or so, try to beat some of the traffic. Are you still joining us? It would be great to spend some more time with you."

I shouldn't. Despite how helpful everyone's been, I have a job to do—if you can consider cleaning an already clean house a job.

"It'll only be for a few hours. Just to get the kids to run off some energy and to kill time while Mr. Fluffy is at the groomers nearby," Juliana adds in a friendly voice. Her brow puckers. "Not hungry again?"

"Are you sure it's not my cooking?" Cate laughs as she gathers the empty dish of scrambled eggs to drop off at the sink.

"No!" I rush to assure, clearing my throat as heat crawls over my cheeks and neck. "You're both great at cooking. It's just, I'm..." My tongue feels heavy in my mouth, but I plaster on a smile. "I'll grab something in a bit before we leave."

Guilt gnaws on my insides at the lie. The thought of eating turns my stomach sour as I remember what my mother used to say to me: *You're better off not eating. It's not like your body can't handle it.*

"I'll finish clearing the dishes," I offer, jumping from the table. Anything to banish the words that worm into my subconscious. Dizziness rolls through my body, and I grip the table.

"Rosa, are you okay?"

"Fine. Just, um, I just stood up too fast." I smile off Juliana's concern.

She and Cate exchange a look, but thankfully, I make it to the sink before either of them can protest. I've made it a point the last few days to always volunteer to do the dishes. I make myself useful rather than idly sitting by.

Black hedges my vision, and I hastily blink it away.

Three days.

I've gone three days without eating much. A glass of water. A stick of gum here and there to try and curb the awful pangs and cravings as I try to trick my body and mind. Longer sessions in the gym on the treadmill—which is really hard when the lack of food is causing headaches and making me feel so fatigued and sluggish. It's hard to hide at dinner what I'm doing. It's hard to find excuses as to why I'm picking at my plate even though the food always smells and looks delicious.

My stomach clenches in on itself, and I double over at the sink. Three sharp breaths hiss through my teeth until the feeling subsides. Hunger pains.

Tears prick my eyes as I right myself and quickly finish cleaning.

The tremble in my hand worsens, as do the dots along the edge of my vision.

***

I end up getting to the park an hour after the others.

I sit at the picnic tables with Juliana and Cate as we watch the children run around in the sunshine, climbing up the slides and relaxing on the swings.

"It's been really great that the guys had you to look after them," Cate says softly.

"We were worried sick when they kept going through one maid after another," Juliana adds. "It was already stressful having to flee to Italy and be separated, and it was made worse thinking that the guys weren't being looked after back here in Chicago. They can get a bit intense when the pressure's on. Marco can get a bit...aggressive," she says carefully.

I keep quiet about my own initial experiences with her husband.

Cate sighs. "He sure can. And Alessio, when he's stressed, he gets pretty controlling. But it sounds like you made the mansion feel like a home for them while we were away, and we're truly thankful for that."

I flush a little at their words. "It was no problem, really. I needed the work, and I was just doing the job they hired me to do."

"Working for the Marchiano brothers is more than just a job," Juliana giggles. "And after Savona left, I thought they were going to be without a maid until we came back."

Cate bites back her grin. "Alessio told me about the agencies laughing in their faces when they asked them for a maid. It was the men who were lucky to get you."

Camillo's told me a little about Marco and Alessio's relationships which started out as arranged marriages. Although Marco and Juliana's wedding turned into a bloody wedding, while Alessio forced Cate into marriage with him.

It sounds as though things didn't start well for either of these women. Which is hard to believe when I see the couples now. But from what Camillo's said, politics in the mafia world are complex and fraught with power plays.

"We were pretty much strangers to our husbands when we married," Juliana says. "It's surprising that out of all the brothers, Camillo is the one to meet someone by himself."

The conversation instantly reminds me of Sheena, but I quickly shake my head to dismiss all thoughts of that awful woman.

"Anyway," Juliana continues, "we just wanted to say thanks for looking after Marco, Alessio, and the house. We really do appreciate it and appreciate you. I know it made Marco happier that he had Ethan to spoil and play baseball with. Our sons are really hyper at times, but he missed them for sure."

Cate's brow furrows. "Alessio was practically going crazy not being able to see the children for so long. The way he talked about having Ethan there and the mealtimes with you guys, it had a calming effect on him and gave him some of that family time these guys really crave and need to keep them grounded in this crazy world of theirs."

I look over at Ethan playing with the children. Maximo is holding out a ball to Ethan with a smile, and Xander is talking intently to my little boy about some cartoon they were watching earlier.

I'd really like Ethan to have siblings one day. Seeing how he is with the other children affirms my view that he needs people his own age to mix with. He needs to be a child and do all the normal things children do. And he deserves to do that all without the weight of the world on his tiny shoulders.

***

By some miracle, the running around after the kids doesn't make my hunger worse. And by the time we get back to the mansion, the kids are worn out, and the little ones are tucked up in their beds for a nap.

If I can just make it to the gym, I can work in another small run before doing some more cleaning. Sluggish, my feet move down the hall. The room spins, but I push on.

"Rosa?"

My body snaps straight as I plaster on a smile.

"Where are you going?"

"I thought I'd get in a quick run before I start on the bedrooms."

Camillo's eyes are searching, tracking over my body as if he can see the damage within. As if he knows something I've yet to voice.

I tug my oversized shirt subconsciously, pulling it down more to cover the tops of my chunky thighs.

"I was on my way to get lunch, Rosa. Are you hungry?"

Yes. "No. We ate lunch at the park."

"You did?"

I nod and fight back another wave of dizziness.

"Rosa?"

I brace my hand against the wood paneling of the hall.

He's in front of me in two long strides.

"When did you say you ate?"

I mumble something offhand. Shoving three crackers and a single cube of cheese into my mouth hours ago isn't what he's talking about. But it was the smallest amount I could get away with while Juliana and Cate watched me like hawks.

Do the girls know? I shake my head, dismissing the thought. Of course they don't.

"Rosa?"

"It was at the park." I clear my throat. "I think I'm just going to lay down. The heat must have gotten to me."

Camillo doesn't move.

Under his gaze, I squirm. If he looks too long, will he see what everyone else sees?

His eyes narrow, but he steps back, allowing me to pass.

I take three steps before the floor tilts under me.

And a warm hand catches me around the waist.

"Fuck," he growls.

"I'm okay...just dizzy." I wriggle from his grasp, feeling tears prick my eyes. How can he even bear putting his hands on me?

"*Rosa.*"

And the soft brush of my name cracks something in me. I fist my hand into his T-shirt. Burying my face into his chest, I will the tears to remain locked away. How can he be so gentle with me? How can he treat me like this when I look how I do?

"What's wrong? Fuck, baby, I can't fix it if you don't tell me."

He *can't* fix it.

I'm wrong for him. Always so fucking wrong.

I pull back. "You can't fix it."

"Like hell I can't."

"I just..."

Camillo tugs on my hand, guiding me through the hall and up the stairs. The door clicks shut behind us as he gently takes me to sit on the edge of the bed. Kneeling before me, he cups my face. "You just?"

A few moments beat between us. "Aren't you embarrassed by me?" I whisper.

That I've managed to ask the question surprises me. But I cling to it. I need the answer. I need to know if I'm just as worthless as I feel—and as Grayden and my family have always made me out to be. I'm too fat and too short. My thighs touch too much. My boobs are too big. My stomach isn't flat like the women who fill the rooms of Chicago high society. My hair isn't the right shade of blond. My eyes are too flat...

"Why would I be?"

"Look at me. I mean, really look at me. I'm not..." Anger spikes in me, and I clench my fists in my lap.

Not like them. Not beautiful.

"You're not what?"

I shake my head, losing my confidence. "It doesn't matter."

Calloused fingers grasp my chin gently, and he keeps my face from turning away. "It matters to me."

"I'm not...anything." The sneering whispers have followed me all my life. The way I've longed to be like the other women in my family. Slim. Lithe. Willowy in ways that fabric drapes from me instead of pulling taught and bunching oddly. The way I long to be smaller and take up less space.

"I don't understand, Rosa."

I open my mouth to answer, but I can't get it out.

"What the hell happened at breakfast? Or was it at the park? Did someone say something? Do something?"

"No."

"Rosa." His thumb brushes my cheek. "Baby, I don't know what's going on with you lately. I haven't seen you eat a meal in days. And don't lie to me—please don't lie about it. Cate and Juliana have noticed too. I'm worried about you. I just want to help."

"I'm not...beautiful."

"You are."

"I'm not. Look at me!" I push his hand away as some spark of indignation dredges to life from the depths where it's been shoved down.

"I am looking at you," he says gently.

"You think this is beautiful?" My hand gestures to my midsection. I hate that I'm still so insecure about my weight. I hate that I sound so needy and weak. "I—"

His lips crash into mine, cutting me off. It's soft and yet desperate all the same. It sucks the air right out of me.

Pulling back, Camillo looks deep into my eyes. "*You* are beautiful." His hands grip my hips and then the back of my thighs. "*These* are perfect. You are a fucking goddess."

A bitter laugh escapes me.

"The fact that you have some goddamn curves on your body is nothing to be ashamed of. You, Rosa, are nothing but gorgeous. Just like this."

I try to wriggle from his grip, but he holds me all the harder. "That's not true, Camillo."

"It's a fucking fact to me."

His words steal my breath as I look at him. Really look. Heat flickers in his eyes as his chest rises and falls.

"You think you're heavy? Baby, you weigh less than what I lift on my bad days. You think I want some model who barely eats when we go out to dinner? That couldn't be further from the truth. There isn't anything about your body that doesn't drive me fucking wild. I can't keep my hands to myself. You make me fucking crazy, baby. You and only you. I fucking love this." He palms the plush of my hip. "It gives me something to hold on to when I'm claiming what's mine, when I'm worshipping you. And this." His hand skims down to cup my ass. "I love this too. Every inch of you is mesmerizing."

Tears are now running down my cheeks.

"What do I need to do to make you see that you're beautiful? What do I need to do so you believe me?" Because whatever it is, I'll do a million times over until you believe me."

My heart is thrumming too fast...

"You skipping meals and starving yourself stops—right here and right now. There isn't a single thing wrong with how you look. *Not to me.* I want you just like this. Tummy, thighs, hips, ass, and all."

I'm unable to comprehend what he's saying. *He wants me? Like this?*

"But…"

"No buts, Rosa. I mean it. You are beautiful, breathtaking, exquisite. You are a goddamn goddess."

I clear my throat, trying to get rid of the tears from my voice. "I want to believe you," I say quietly.

"Then do it."

"It's not that simple."

"You're right. It's not. We'll get help. You can talk to someone, and I'll spend every goddamn breath I have in the day reminding you just how beautiful you are." His head drops to my shoulder. "Just…please stop starving yourself. I just found you…"

"O-okay."

"Okay?"

"I'll stop skipping meals."

"And you'll talk to someone? We can make it so it's discreet. No one but you and I have to know."

Again, I nod. Help. Talking to someone. Is it really that simple?

Camillo's lips brush the juncture between my throat and ear, offering a distraction. But my mind continues to race. It's not easy to change years of ingrained habits and how I see myself. I cling to him tighter, willing the voices that whisper in my head to fade. Because I know that with the support of this amazing man, I'm determined to get better.

CHAPTER 36

CAMILLO

My hand slams onto the nightstand, blindly looking for my ringing phone.

A growl of displeasure rumbles through me when it clatters to the ground. It's too fucking early for this.

Rosa stirs beside me. Blinking back sleep from my eyes, hand tightening around her waist, I try to keep her nestled in my arms as I reach down for my phone. But the screen staring back at me is blank. "What the fuck?"

The ringing continues, and Rosa looks at the other nightstand, confusion knitting her brows. Because her phone vibrates against the polished wood surface, the screen lighting up.

I loosen my grip on her as she scrambles across the bed to reach it. "Hello?" Her words are a groggy, barely-there whisper.

At four in the morning, her sleep-laced voice is a new kind of drug. My fingers tingle to touch her skin. I've made it my personal mission to make sure Rosa knows just what she does to me at all hours. To see herself through my eyes every fucking chance I get. Watching her break before my eyes shredded me in a way I don't want to admit. Any ice between us thawed in an instant, and I was left on my knees ready to pay whatever price was needed to save her.

I want to show her that I'm not the brute I've made myself into, despite every instinct telling me otherwise. I don't want her looking at me like that again. I rub at my chest, the hollow feeling yet to dissipate.

A sharp gasp snaps my attention back to her.

The smooth sheet gathers at her waist, exposing my T-shirt she threw on before we fell asleep last night. The sight of her in my clothing nearly undoes me, but I zero in on the tremble of her hand.

"Rosa?"

The phone hits the bed, and she gives me her back, inching toward the edge of the mattress.

"What's wrong?"

Silently, she stands.

I jump out of bed, my feet tangling in the sheets. "Shit," I mutter as I stumble toward her. Gently, I tug her toward me, watching her shoulders shake in a silent sob. "Rosa, what happened? Who was that?"

"My mother."

"Did something happen?"

She nods. The tears rim her eyes, but she doesn't shed them as she looks up at me. "I have to go home."

"What?"

"I have to. My dad—I just..." She doesn't get a full sentence out.

"Something happened with your dad?"

"He passed away."

I freeze. From the bits and pieces of her home life she's shared over the months, her relationship with her parents is still a mystery to me. It's a hard topic for her to broach. A sea of conflictions that leaves me wondering if she even knows herself. Numbly, she walks toward the ensuite.

"When do you need us to leave?"

"Tomorrow afternoon. My mother said to come then."

"Okay," I nod.

"Wait, *us*?"

"Where you go, I go," I say in a strong voice.

"I—"

"I'm not going to let you deal with this alone, Rosa. And I'll make sure while we're there, my men discreetly monitor your family's mansion and the immediate vicinity to make sure that you and Ethan are safe from Grayden." Her body is framed by the light of the bathroom, but even shadowed as it is, I can tell she's gnawing on her lip. I step closer, kicking the sheet from my feet. I tower over her, tilting her chin up. "And I'll be by your side. You have me to support and protect you. All of us will."

"Thank you," she whispers.

"Not needed. I'll take care of everything on our end." She doesn't move, her mind elsewhere. I know that look. I know that feeling eating her alive. I brush her lips, breaking the spell her thoughts have on her. "It'll be okay."

And she gives the smallest nod as she turns from me.

***

I tug at the sleeve of my dress shirt, leaning against the SUV outside the Davis mansion where Rosa's family resides. But it's a useless gesture to make myself presentable, not that it matters.

It hasn't changed in the five years since I last saw it. The semi-circular drive leads to sprawling grounds with manicured grass and a Victorian era mansion. Everything about it is grandiose and meticulously kept—yet ice cold and unwelcoming.

We're here so that Rosa can see her family. The black dress she wears hugs every inch of her body. It's modest and elegant, the neckline cut in a square line, exposing the beautiful freckles of her skin that have come out since she started spending more time in the backyard with Ethan and me. Her blond locks are glossy and full as they shine where they're caught by the weak rays of sun.

She smiles softly down at Ethan. "Okay, honey, we're here now. Let's go in and see Grandma and Aunt Reagan."

Ethan's round eyes look at me, and I wink, extending my hand to him. He grasps it tightly and nestles into my leg.

I look to Rosa. "I'll keep an eye on him."

"Thank you."

"You don't need to thank me, baby."

Steeling herself, Rosa takes a deep breath and lifts her chin. Emotions shutter over her face before she clears them away.

I lace her fingers with mine as we walk up the stone steps.

She stops in front of the grand door. I bring our joined hands to my lips. But the small smile on her face slips off as soon as an elderly man opens the door.

He wordlessly escorts us in. The foyer is grand and dotted with elaborate floral bundles. Men and women adorned in black and dark grays, their tailored suits and Chanel dresses screaming their wealth, fill the space. They've obviously all come to pay their respects having heard the news.

"Rosa?" We hear her name called, and Rosa freezes beside me.

The hand that grips mine tightens before she plasters on that fake smile. I hate it. I hate when she uses it, but I know when to keep my mouth shut. Now is not the time. And I know from what she's said that seeing her family again is going to be difficult for her.

A woman bursts into sobs as she embraces Rosa. "I..."

"I know," Rosa murmurs, dropping my hand to wrap her arms around her mother.

They linger for a moment before breaking apart, and the woman's gaze drops to Ethan, although she doesn't bother to greet her grandson. She dabs at her eyes while her gaze skims over Rosa quickly. A flicker of something—judgment, perhaps—flittering over her before her sharp eyes land on me.

I stand at my full height, chin lifted. I have nothing to prove to any of these people.

And yet I want to.

I want to prove to the world that I belong here for Rosa's sake.

"You..." Her mother mutters at me, shaking her head, dismissing whatever she was about to say. Turning on her heel, she beckons onward. "Rosa, you and Ethan can follow me. Your *friend* can mingle."

My jaw ticks at the slight snub. Rosa nods quietly, her mouth set in a firm line.

It shouldn't dredge up that taunt in the back of my head—but it does. It's like the last few months haven't mattered, and I'm back sitting in the church pew watching the world slip through my fingers.

Ethan's hand tightens on mine, and I can feel him cling to my leg all the more.

Anger, red hot and boiling, fills my veins, and the room full of high-society sneers and whispers only makes it worse. Something roars to life in my chest.

Protect him.

Protect Rosa.

From what I'm not sure, but I'm almost certain it's from the people that surround us.

I kneel, not caring that my pants touch the ground and the fabric is dirtied.

The murmurs swirl around us, but my focus zeroes in on Ethan as he buries his head into my sleeve. "You're okay, buddy. Your mom will be right there with you. And I'll be right here waiting."

"Rosa, come now," her mother admonishes in an impatient voice.

"Ethan, it's okay, honey." Rosa's voice is gentle toward her little boy.

I give Ethan's hand a squeeze. "As soon as you're done, I'll be here, and we can find somewhere else to go without so many people, okay?"

Ethan very slowly drops my hand and moves to his mom's side. She takes a breath and mouths *thank you*.

After watching them turn a corner and disappear from sight, I drag my hand down my face. I need a fucking drink. My eyes narrow on a large group of men and women, older than me by at least a decade, who stare at me wide-eyed.

They jolt and turn away quickly as I arch a brow.

Hushed whispers fill the air from their little group, the sneers and mocking laughter only prickling my skin more.

Playing with the cufflinks of my shirt, I squeeze past the bodies. Not a single person seems to be affected by the passing of the man. A testament to what kind of person Conor Davis really was. I'm certain of the fact that the world is better off without him.

Leaning against the bar, I throw back the whiskey, letting the burn soak up some of the fire gutting me now. Now and then my gaze lingers on a group too long. The difference between them and me is a blunt reminder that I don't belong here.

I tower over most of the people in attendance, making it impossible for me to blend into the crowd. Their appearances are immaculate, adorned with pocket squares and worn expressions. I slouch while they stand straight; their voices come out refined while mine is only able to rasp and rumble as I order another drink from the bartender.

I pick up the new glass and give the crowd my back. Watching them makes me sick. Picking up my whiskey, I move away from the crowd.

"And she showed up with some thug instead of her husband." A cluck of a tongue is followed by a soft laugh. "Conor was right to marry her off—even if it didn't do her any good."

I freeze to the spot, my hand tightening around the tumbler.

"And to think, Cyndie has to deal with *that* on top of Conor's passing. What was Rosa thinking? Has she no shame?"

"I'm just hoping Grayden doesn't show up. Imagine."

Each sentence curls my fingers tighter around the glass until I feel it shatter in my grip, sending ice and liquid dripping onto my hand.

The gossipers gasp, eyes wide as they gaze at me with unabashed horror.

The room closes in. My chest tightens.

Freak.

Monster.

Animal.

Murderer...

Each label is a bullet in my armor. Another crack in the chain of my restraint.

"Sir."

I snap my eyes to the attendant who is holding out a towel. Snatching it from his outstretched hand, I notice the way he gulps thickly, his eyes avoiding mine.

I swallow back the comment that burns my tongue, tossing the bloody towel back at his chest. He's just a kid working at some fancy ass party for the elite.

I glare at the women gawking at me, my lip curling into a snarl. They're lucky it's public and daytime; otherwise, I'd show them just how thuggish I can be. I've never raised a hand to anyone who didn't deserve it, especially not a woman, but I'd gladly make the exception to prove my point. I stalk toward the door.

I fucking hate it. I hate how they look down their noses at me. I hate the disdain they don't bother to conceal.

Turning on my heel, I move through the house and to the front entrance where a few lingering guests dot the stone steps.

I inhale deeply through my nostrils. What the fuck was I thinking? Coming here now?

I don't belong in this world. I don't belong near her. *I don't belong with her.*

The ugly truth of it settles against my skin, its barbs sinking in and ripping at me. My gut tightens. It's nothing I don't already know.

Knowing that Rosa is caught up in the crossfire of their unpleasant gossip makes my body shake with anger. My fists curl tightly, the scars on my knuckles whitening.

Fucking snobs.

I sink onto the cool stone step, head in my hands. But the cool air does nothing to keep the demons at bay. It does nothing to chase the inferno rising in my chest.

I suck in a breath, then another, willing myself to calm the fuck down.

My phone vibrates in my pocket, and I gladly take the distraction.

I read through the text. It's a loose end that needs dealing with. And I realize it's the perfect way to let off the dangerous steam boiling inside me. It's a fucking fairytale ending to this shit show of a day —because it's a safe way for me to let the beast out. I quickly fire off a reply.

"Camillo?"

Shoving my phone back in my pocket, I stand to meet Rosa in the doorway. She lingers in front of another woman. She's taller than Rosa by a few inches, but younger in her appearance. And she has the same shade of blond hair, perfectly styled, and the same nose. Her sister, no doubt.

But that's where the similarities end. This woman is much thinner, lacking the mouthwatering curves her sister has. But the biggest differences are the pinched, unsatisfied look on her face and the bitter curl lacing her lips. Besides Rosa, she barely warrants another glance.

I'm in front of Rosa in an instant. "Everything okay?" I cup her cheek and tilt her face. Tears line her eyes, and my heart squeezes.

She opens her mouth, but the woman behind her speaks first. "This is a private event—*for relations and select friends of the family.*" The way she speaks makes it clear that I'm neither of those things.

I search Rosa's eyes, trying to find the answers, ignoring the woman behind her. "I'll go, Rosa, if that's what you want. And I'll be back when you're ready to leave. But only if you say so."

"She doesn't need you lingering around. You've stirred up enough trouble as it is."

Nostrils flaring, my eyes snap to the woman. "I'm not fucking talking to *you*."

The indignant gasp she gives makes me roll my eyes, but I can't help but notice I'm attracting unwelcome attention from people standing nearby.

Rosa trembles beneath my hand, pulling my attention back to her.

"Rosa?" I say quietly.

Her fingers curl around my hand on her jaw, squeezing me tightly. "I'm okay, Camillo."

"*Rosa.*" Her sister speaks in a warning tone, and it takes every ounce of self-control I have not to shove the woman into the house and slam the door so Rosa and I can be alone.

Dread swells in my chest. I know what comes next. Bracing for the impact, I straighten my spine, trying to reinforce the walls around my heart.

"We'll be okay, Camillo. We have to stay here for a few more hours, just to help my mother. I don't want to cause trouble for anyone."

My stomach dives, and a small breath shudders out. Forehead pressed into hers, my eyes close. I suck in a deep breath of her scent.

I'd hoped she'd do the opposite. That she'd put up a fight—do anything to keep me here. But I should have known better. A bitter laugh bubbles in my chest, but I push it down before it can escape. "Okay," I mumble.

My hand drops. I force myself to let her step back from me.

The manicured nails of her sister curl around Rosa's shoulder like claws. She gives me a slow once over before her lip curls again.

"Call me when you're ready," I clip before lowering my voice. "My men are keeping an eye on the mansion and grounds so that you're safe from Grayden." And turning on my heel, I don't give Rosa a chance to take her words back—to keep me here.

My body vibrates with rage. Hazy red flares to life in my vision as I cross the lawn in a few quick strides to the SUV. Yanking the door open, I drop into the driver's seat.

"Fuck!" My hands tighten around the steering wheel. It feels like someone has put my heart into a vise. It stings, watching her turn her back on me like that. Knowing that no matter what I do, no matter how hard I claw myself up, it doesn't matter.

But it's my own damn fault for thinking I could have something more. Isn't this what I deserve?

The tires squeal as I tear from the curb, dialing Alessio's number as I go. It rings twice before he picks up. "I'm heading there now. I'll deal with the fucker. Have him ready."

"Camil—"

I hang up before Alessio can protest or pester me with questions. Torturing a snitch is just the type of therapy I need right now.

And it'll take my mind off the fact that they've all been right. Every voice that haunts my nightmares and subconscious was right about me. I am a monster.

And monsters don't get happy endings...

CHAPTER 37

ROSA

Every bone in my body is exhausted. Ethan's compact frame is sprawled out on the covers of the bed, and his suit, the one he picked to match Camillo's, is rumpled.

I sigh, shaking my head as I brush the blond strands from Ethan's forehead. I don't quite know how to tell him we'll be staying here.

I eye my phone on the table next to my purse. I want to text Camillo. To tell him to come back and pick us up now. My fingers itch to dial his number, but I know it'll cause problems with my family.

"Rosa!"

I wince at Reagan's sharp knock on the door as I glance at Ethan. One beat, then another, and I push from the mattress and to the door. "Shh," I whisper to my sister, closing the door behind me. "He's taking a nap."

"Good. He won't get in our hair. You're needed downstairs."

"Ethan's been perfectly behaved today, and he always is," I clip, irritated at her implied criticism of him. But she's not listening, and I sigh and watch as she struts down the hallway toward the stairs. I stiffen my spine and hold my head up high. The crowd of family, friends, and acquaintances—people who would have found it a personal snub not to be invited today—still linger among the lower level of the house. People who sat by and watched with their fake smiles and pleasantries while my life was sold away years ago.

I enter my father's old office. The smell of cigars lingers in the air, the smoke woven into the imported rug like a second layer. It's a smell that haunts my nightmares, alongside Grayden's rancid breath. My mother dabs her eyes as she leans into my sister's embrace.

"You need me?"

"Yes." My mother lifts her chin, though it wobbles. "We have so much to do before the funeral at the end of the week. I just—" A sob breaks her voice.

"What can I do to help you?"

"Well, you can start by getting everyone out," Reagan clips. "I can't do it—I have a nail appointment. And it's clear Mother's distraught."

I blink.

"Then you can call the relatives to inform them of the funeral date. Then you need to contact the lawyer about the will Daddy left."

"Mother hasn't done that yet?"

"Rosa," Reagan admonishes when my mother once more makes a strangled sob, "This isn't easy for her or me. *You* left the house, so you wouldn't understand the pain *we're* going through right now. Try to look at it from our point of view. Stop being selfish."

"What?" It's Camillo's voice in my head that spits the words back. *Selfish? Me?* A fire ignites in my belly, knowing just how he'd want me to stand up for myself, to call them out on their bullshit, as he'd put it.

"It's the least you can do after causing such a scene earlier."

"I didn't mean to cause a scene."

"But you did. It's so very typical of you. What in God's name were you thinking bringing someone else here today?" Reagan hisses. "You're *married*, or have you forgotten that? How do you think that makes us look? Makes *me* look? Did you think about that before you invited him here?"

"I'm sorry." I wince as my apology comes out quickly. I've become so used to apologizing all my life that it's hard to not do it automatically like I just have. "I just—"

"And look how you're dressed," she spits. "You might as well put a sign on your back to announce to everyone that you're hooking up with a common criminal. It's all anyone could talk about today. And now, people are going to think I'm like that too—and I can say goodbye to getting a good marriage proposal, all because of you. You know, there's a reason Daddy was so reluctant to do business with *them*."

I feel like pointing out that Camillo told me that our father had been easily persuaded when they increased the financial incentive—our father had morals unless there was a large sum of money involved. But the words lodge in my throat because our father's just died, meaning it's not appropriate to be arguing like this.

"You only ever think about yourself. The very least you can do is help Mother out now."

My mouth gapes open. "Is that how you both feel?" My gaze swings to my mother as she sits behind my father's large cherry wood desk.

"We have an image and reputation to maintain, Rosa," Mother sighs. "I thought you understood that. All that time with Grayden and you still haven't learned anything. Everyone saw that thug with your son today. What kind of role model is that for your boy? I know you and Grayden are having *problems*—he came to see your father about it after you ran off—but it all reflects so poorly on our family. Anyway, your help is needed here right now. You can't possibly expect me to see to everything myself..."

My mother has never appeared small in my life. But looking at her right now, she looks like a shell. Self-medicated, her eyes are hazy and lined with unshed tears. She's lost in her grief. As much as I want to defend Camillo and my life with him, now is not the time. But I'm determined to sit down with my family once the funeral is over and talk to them about everything and set the record straight.

"Okay. I'll stay if you need me to."

"Start with the lawyer," Reagan orders. "Aunt Annette is getting antsy to see if Daddy left her anything." Reagan's chin is held high as she moves past me toward the door. "Oh, and make sure you find something more appropriate to wear for the funeral. I'm sure there's something more suitable in your closet. You can't carry off something so clingy, not with your big size and all."

I bite back the retort on my lips as the sound of her too high heels on the wood fills the room, and I watch her leave the room before I sag into the chair across from my mother.

Her eyes laser in on me. "What's going on between you and that Marchiano, Rosa? The truth."

He's the man for me, but saying that right now seems like it'll cause more problems than it'll fix, and I can tell my mother's not in the mood to really listen to anything I have to say. "It's complicated."

She lets out a terse huff of air. "So, the rumors are true then. Whatever did I do to deserve this? And from my own daughter." She stands with a dismissive shake of her head. "I need to lie down. See that the guests are taken care of."

There are a million things I want to say to her. There are a million things I *need* to say to her. But it'll have to wait until after the funeral.

I don't know how long I sit in the office. I don't know when I throw that awful picture of my father and Grayden shaking hands at our wedding against the wall to watch it shatter. I don't know how long I numbly move through the motions of contacting my family's lawyer, setting up for the reading of the will, and ushering the last guests out.

Finally, when I trudge back upstairs, I find Ethan sitting on my bed, quietly drawing with a pencil on some random papers left in my old bedroom. I walk over and sit by him, placing a kiss on top of his head.

"Are we going home, Momma?"

Home. That's what the Marchiano estate felt like. My heart squeezes in my chest as I shake my head. "Not yet. We're going to stay here for a bit. Grandma needs some help for a while."

His brow furrows, and his lips draw into a small line. "What about Uncle Millo?"

"We can call him if you want."

"But he was supposed to read the end of Alice in Wonderland tonight."

"We might have a copy in the library downstairs."

"But it won't be the same, Momma. We were going to play baseball again and go in the pool as well." Tears well in his eyes, and his lip wobbles. "We have to go back."

"It's only for a few days, honey."

"But what if..." His gaze drops. "What if...something happens?"

"Happens?"

"To you? Uncle Millo isn't around to look after you and me."

My heart breaks into tiny pieces as I clutch Ethan to my chest. He's still affected by what happened with Grayden—and I'm not sure if it's something that he'll ever get over. And I feel so damn guilty for that. "We'll be okay for a few days, baby. I promise. We can call him every night if that's what you want."

"Now, Momma?"

Exhaustion weighs every bone of my body down as Camillo's face flashes into my mind. My chest squeezes, and I rub at my breastbone to ease the feeling. I saw the brief flicker of hurt in his eyes when I told him that he didn't need to stay—and it gutted me. I just didn't want for anyone to be uncomfortable, including him. "He's probably working still."

"Can we try?"

I nod, grabbing my phone. "Okay, but if he's busy, we're not going to interrupt him. Then it's time for dinner, bath, and bed."

Ethan nods as he huddles up to me. "With video?"

"We'll see."

The phone rings once before Camillo's gruff voice fills the room. "Ready to come home, Rosa?"

"Momma, video," Ethan urges, tugging at the sleeve of my dress.

"Are you busy?" I ask in a small voice.

"For you? No."

"Ethan would like to video call. Is that okay?"

"Give me a minute." I'm not sure where he is, but he seems to be walking into another room. Then his face fills my phone screen, enough that I can't really see his surroundings. There's a fresh purpling to the left side of his jaw as if he's been hit.

"I can be there in twenty minutes, Rosa; we didn't need to video call."

"Momma," Ethan says, and I angle the phone toward him. "Are you going to do baseball without me?"

Camillo gives him a smile over the screen. ""No, buddy. I wouldn't do it without you."

I let them talk for a little while and then interrupt. "Ethan, baby, why don't you go wash your hands before dinner? I'll make sure you can say goodbye before I hang up."

"But I—"

"Please." I level my best mom-gaze at him.

"Okay, Momma." I watch as he scampers off.

"Rosa, shall I come and get you both now?"

I can't look at his face. I can't watch that shutter fall back into place again. "I need to help my mother with the funeral preparations."

"Okay...?"

"I have to help here. We have to stay here until then."

"Oh."

"Just until the funeral. Mother's a wreck, and, well, Reagan isn't much help either. They're my family. You understand, right?"

He clears his throat. "I get it. Of course. I just—" He shakes his head, dismissing whatever he was going to say. "Can I help anyway?"

"Thanks, but we'll be okay." I let out a breath. "I appreciate it, though."

Ethan rushes back from washing his hands. "Is Uncle Millo still there?"

"Yeah, buddy, I'm still here."

"Can we call again so you can read when I go to bed?"

"Ethan, he might be busy..."

Camillo's laugh fills the room. But it's not his usual laugh. It's different. "Sure, I can do that. But I've got some work to finish. I'll send you a text when I'm home if it's not too late. And Ethan? I'm not going to forget you or do anything I promised without you, okay?"

"Okay. Bye, Uncle Millo." Ethan waves.

"Bye, buddy. I'll talk to you when I can." He sounds strained, though he's putting on his best mask. "Rosa, I'll get one of my men to drop over a bag with clothes for you and Ethan. And my soldiers will keep watch over things while you're staying there. I have to keep you safe."

The silence beats between us. "Camillo?" I say quietly.

"Yeah?"

"Thank you. For everything."

"Of course. I gotta go." He pauses, dragging his hand down his face. His knuckles are wrapped, but I can just see the fresh bruise peeking out. "I'll talk to you later."

Both Ethan and I wave Camillo goodbye, but I can't help the pit that forms in my stomach. The undeniable sense that there's far more I should have said to him weighs my limbs down as I lead Ethan down to the kitchen.

Reagan's words swirl around in my head. She's never been one to pull her punches. And if she sees Camillo in the way she described—as a common thug—then most of the world we reside in does too. But they don't know Camillo like I do. Except even I can't deny that there's a darkness that lingers around him. Around all the Marchianos. Something that should scare me and tell me to stay away. And yet, I can't.

Even as we make our way down the staircase, I can't shake the feeling that something's wrong. The way he looked at the end of our conversation—it was slightly off.

Maybe it's better that Camillo's not here after all. I can blend in until this is over. I can take up as little space as I can and hope it all goes so fast it won't even matter. Except it always does matter, and it always will...

CHAPTER 38

CAMILLO

It's been a couple of hours since Rosa told me that she's staying with her mother until the funeral. The groans of the man beneath my boot echo around the darkened warehouse. The single construction light illuminates his body and the mess I've made, getting the answers we need.

The moment I'd felt my phone vibrate, I'd pummeled him to the ground. Now I wish I'd ignored the call all together. I'm more wound up than ever, knowing that Rosa is by herself and without me.

My hand throbs every time I flex it, but it's a welcome sting. Anything to keep the taunting laughs replaying in my mind and pit in my stomach from swallowing me whole.

"You look pissed," Alessio tells me.

"Thanks for pointing out the obvious," I snarl. "Anything else you'd like to comment on, or do you want to get this shit handled so we can get home?"

"Was that Rosa?"

"No, it was Jesus. And he said that nosy brothers don't make the cut to see the pearly gates."

He tilts his head to one side. "Bad news?"

"Nah, it was like a warm fucking hug. What do you think?" Surely, he can tell from my expression that it wasn't good news—and that I don't want to fucking talk about it.

"Camillo—"

"Unless you wanna go a few rounds with me, don't start, okay? I don't want to deal with Cate getting on my ass about messing up your face or some shit."

Picking a fight with Alessio isn't going to make this go away. It isn't going to make Rosa decide to come back home where she fucking belongs. It isn't going to get rid of the black pit that's devouring me little by little the longer I let my thoughts run wild.

"Look, Alessio, you can finish this off. I've got other stuff to do." I shove past him and toward the busted door of the warehouse. Abandoned and forgotten, somehow the building and I have too much in common for me to want to stay much longer. The clean-up crew will sort the place up after Alessio finishes what he needs to do. My job here is done.

"Millo."

"What?" I whirl on my heel to face him.

"Don't go back to her like this."

"I didn't ask for your advice."

"I mean it..."

My shoulders tense. "She's not coming home today, so no problem there. Any other questions you wanna ask, or am I free to go?"

His sigh fills the vast area, and I take my leave without another word. My body thrums with adrenaline and emotions I don't know what to do with. My already battered fist connects with the sheet metal on the outside of the warehouse as a curse flies from my lips.

My phone pings.

Quickly, I scan the text. My body wilts against the wall, and the anger bubbling through my veins cools with a single picture. Ethan. He's wearing the extra black T-shirt we packed earlier in case he got his clothes dirty, staring back at me with Rosa's shy smile behind him. The caption makes my heart stop: *Dressing like Uncle Millo.*

A slow smile creeps across my face as I save it to my phone. The goodnight text lights up my screen, and my chest turns into a vise.

I want to believe that it's only for a few days. But some part of me knows that's wishful thinking. And that voice grows louder and louder until all I can think is that she's slipped right through my fingers. I don't belong in her world. I don't deserve someone like her—and it's clear I'm not the only one who thinks so. I saw the looks everyone was giving me. I saw the talons of her sister's hand digging into Rosa's shoulder and the disapproval etched into her sour expression.

Would she disapprove even more if she knew what really was going on between me and her Rosa? Would she turn her nose up if she knew what Grayden had done—and would do again—to her sister?

My hands tighten on the steering wheel further as I zigzag recklessly through traffic to the estate. I haven't been back since Rosa and I left this morning. I ignore the soft conversation coming from the kitchen.

"Camillo?"

I pause on the first step of the staircase at Marco's voice. "I'm tired."

"Look—"

And I know from his tone that an interrogation is coming my way. I love my brothers dearly. I appreciate them having my back, but right now, sticking their noses where they don't belong is the last thing I want to deal with.

I don't give him a chance to say what he wants to, jogging up the stairs and into my room. The door slamming behind me echoes in the stillness. The flowery scent that clings to her fills my lungs when I take a deep inhale. It stings and soothes all at once.

The man who stares back at me from the mirror is a familiar stranger I haven't seen in months. My hair falls in loose waves from the knot at the crown of my head. A fresh bruise decorates my jaw, and there's blood all along my collar and neck. Eyes wild and hands clenched, the man before me is every bit of the monster I wish I wasn't.

"Fuck!" My voice comes out as a roar.

My knuckles slam into the mirror. And I spin on my heel, disregarding the pieces that clink to the ground.

The knock at my door isn't surprising. But I don't answer. Ripping the shirt from my body, I crumple it up into the corner and head to the bathroom.

Another louder pound on the door keeps me from starting the shower I so desperately want.

"What?" I growl, yanking it open.

Cate and Juliana stand before my door. Cate's hand is raised to pound on the wood again. They blink, and my tongue runs along my teeth. I'm going to get a fucking earful for waking the kids, but I can't bring myself to care. "Is Rosa okay?" Juliana asks.

"Fine."

"Are she and Ethan hungry? We saved food," Cate adds.

"No. They're not here."

Both women stare at me, and I swallow. I don't like that look. "What?" I ask slowly, very aware that my knuckles are dripping onto the dark wood floor and the mirror behind me is in a cracked mess. What's seven years of bad luck when I'm already living a nightmare?

"Nothing. We'll let you clean up," Juliana says, steering Cate away with her. Their hushed whispers don't carry as they make their way back down the hall.

My door clicks shut, and I sink to the ground. I drag a hand down my tired face, feeling all the pent-up emotions slink out of me, leaving me utterly deflated.

My phone pings again. But something tells me it's not Rosa. And yet the hope that flares within me is the only thing that gets my ass off the floor to check. But the hope that's flickered to life withers into ash in seconds. It's a simple confirmation that the job is done and Alessio is on his way back home. Tossing my phone to the bed, I move into the bathroom. Each movement is tight and controlled.

By the time I've showered, exhaustion pulls at my body, and I flop onto my bed to sink into the bliss of oblivion.

***

"You'll tell them if they need anything to call?" Juliana says.

"Yes."

"And you'll tell Rosa not to worry about anything here?" Cait says quickly.

"Yes."

"And you're sure...everything is okay?" Juliana adds.

"For the millionth time today, yes. Are we done?"

Both Cate and Juliana cross their arms. And I have to remind myself that my brothers would kill me if one single hair was out of place on their heads. As frustrating as having them in my business is, knowing Rosa has their support means the world to me.

Before either can come up with another list of things for me to tell Rosa, I make my escape out into the garage. The drive back to the Davis mansion is far from easy.

Rosa's text came in bright and early, asking if one of the soldiers could drop off more clothes for her and Ethan, including more black outfits for her. They obviously need more stuff in addition to what I sent over two evenings ago. I decide to take the bag myself. And the mere thought of seeing her and Ethan clicks something into place for me. But I don't dwell on that because she's not back...and she might never be.

The Davis drive is lined once more with cars and drivers in pristine outfits. I park and stride up the steps to be met with a quiet nod and direction of where to find Rosa.

"*No*. Not like that," I hear Reagan criticize as I approach.

"Sorry," Rosa murmurs. Her apology to her younger sister grates on my nerves as I hear Rosa stutter the words out. My fist clenches tighter at my side as I clear my throat.

"Why are *you* here?" Reagan hisses.

"Rosa asked for some more clothes."

Rosa's by my side in an instant.

"Why on earth did you ask *him* here?" Reagan sneers down her nose at me. "You could have just purchased more clothing from the store. *That would have been preferrable.*"

The heat of Rosa's hand on my body calms me like nothing in the world. It's terrifying and yet exactly what I've needed ever since she decided to stay here. She ushers me down the hall.

"Everything okay, Rosa?"

"Yes. It's nothing. Thank you." She smiles, taking the duffle bag from my shoulder. She presses in closer, smiling at me. Her usual beautiful rose scent is missing as I drop a kiss to the top of her head. In its place is something else. Something high end and expensive. It's not Rosa at all.

"Of course," I murmur.

"I miss you. Ethan does too."

Something frayed and raw inside me calms, and I pull her closer. "I miss you too. It's not the same at the mansion without you."

"Juliana and Cate are probably managing just fine without me."

"I wasn't talking about the house cleaning, Rosa." My voice drops, and I lean closer, pressing into her. "I'm talking about *you*. The house feels empty with you here and not next to me. So does my bed."

That delicious blush creeps across her cheeks, her tiny smile telling me that she's pleased by my words. And the beast inside me roars with victory, some primal neanderthal part puffing my chest out with pride. It's only ever like this with her...

"Where's Ethan? I figured I could spend a little time here with you both before I have to head to the casino."

The ease that lights her face flickers. Her hesitancy gives me pause. And the delight I just felt freezes in its tracks.

"I don't have to stay, Rosa."

"It's not that. I mean, I'd love for you stay but..."

I drop her chin and move back so that the air seeps between us. I try not to let it sting too much. "Got it. Was there anything else you needed?"

She takes my hand. "Camillo, I—"

"Could you two not do that right here?" a nasal voice snaps. "We have guests, and no one needs to see that."

My muscles bunch, and I remind myself that despite the kind of man I am, I'd never hit a woman. Though Reagan's grating demands are pushing me closer and closer to reevaluating that sentiment.

"Reagan, can you please just give us a minute?" Rosa grits out in a firm tone.

"Fine. But don't take too long. You know there are more important things to deal with."

I exhale as I listen to the sound of her heels clicking on the floor as she walks away. When I glance back to Rosa, her bottom lip is caught between her teeth, and I can see her body shake just slightly. Rage surges to life inside me.

"Rosa?"

"It's fine. C'mon, we can talk on our way to the backyard. Ethan's there."

I nod as she threads our fingers together, and I squeeze her hand. As we leave the hallway and pass the office, I note the men patrolling the ground like clockwork. Ethan is outside quietly playing in the grass. On the porch, a stern-looking woman watches over him.

"I can take it from here, Hildie," Rosa murmurs softly.

"Of course, Miss Rosa."

As she passes, Hildie narrows her eyes at me, and I arch a brow. Is everyone in this damn house so fucking stuck up?

"Momma, when—" Ethan's question halts as he jumps up from the grass. "Uncle Millo! You came."

Tiny arms wrap around my leg before I bend and wrap him into a huge hug. "Hey buddy. You've been having fun, I see."

"No." His admission is small and quiet, and I shoot a confused look to Rosa. "Can we go back home now?" he asks in his small piping voice.

"Not until this weekend, honey."

"I can take Ethan out of your hair for a few hours if you need me to."

Rosa shakes her head. "No, it's okay. There's not much else for me to do today."

"Rosa!"

She sighs. "Hold on."

I nod as she goes and sees what her sister needs.

"I don't like it here," Ethan murmurs.

"Yeah, me neither," I admit, watching Rosa in the doorway as Reagan animatedly waves her arms around until Rosa nods. My eyes narrow when Reagan's glare lands on me.

Rosa walks back over and slides back into her chair carefully.

"Everything okay?"

"Fine. It's just that there's some more stuff I have to handle now. Thank you for bringing the clothes, though."

"I snuck in a few toys too," I tell Ethan, smoothing his hair back from his forehead, "including Bernie Bear."

"You brought Bernie?" He flings himself into my arms and looks up at me with a wobbly bottom lip. "Thank you so much, Uncle Millo. I've missed Bernie as much as I've missed you."

His big brown eyes are identical to Rosa's, and his tiny voice pulls at the fragile strings that are barely holding my heart together.

"Rosa!" Reagan shrieks again from the doorway.

"I should probably go," I say.

"But——" Ethan starts.

"I've got to get going to work, buddy." It's a lie, but I say it for Rosa's sake. Whatever Reagan is throwing a fit over is making the atmosphere awkward for everyone.

Ethan hugs me tightly, and I hate the emptiness crawling into my chest when I let go of him. *When the hell did this tiny person manage to sneak inside my heart and wrap himself around my emotions?*

I follow Rosa silently until we're at the front door.

"Thank you, Camillo," she says softly.

I tilt her chin up toward me. "Anytime. If you need anything, you call me. I don't care if it's 3 a.m. and pouring rain. Call me." That small smile I haven't seen since I arrived fills her face. I press my lips to her forehead. "Are you going to be safe here?" Despite my top men monitoring the Davis residence every single second of the day, it's still weighing on me. "What if Grayden shows up and tries to do something, but I'm fucking across town?"

"We have private security as well as your men watching the place. My father had a falling out with Grayden which led to Grayden punching him and fracturing his cheekbone, so the security guards have been instructed not to let him anywhere near the mansion or our family."

"You're sure?"

"My father was the one who'd have sent me back to Grayden, so I'll be okay here."

I pull her closer to me, burying my nose into her hair. She might not have that rose scent that drives me wild, but she's still mine. *I hope.*

I tighten my hold on her and close my eyes. I don't want to fucking do this. Leaving her feels like ripping out my heart and losing a limb all at the same time. But it has to happen.

I step back, watching her eyes rim with tears. Without thinking, my thumb brushes against the apple of her cheek. "I'm a phone call away."

"I know. Oh, I almost forgot. My wages came into my bank account this morning. And I'm very grateful for it and everything else, but...well, I don't need your family to pay me anymore. My father left me some money."

I should be ecstatic that she's finally realized she's not just the maid to me—or to my brothers. She's part of our family. And she's been that since I kissed her that first time. But the money from her father means that she and Ethan can start afresh somewhere if that's what they want... And I'm left numb as the realization hits me.

I stare down at her. Of course, she wouldn't want to stay in Chicago. Now that she has the means to get away from Grayden for good, she'll take it. I should be happy. A better man would be. I should be supportive, but the ability to breathe is getting harder and harder.

"*Rosa!*"

Her head jerks in the direction of her name. "I have to go. I'll call you tonight, okay?"

Somehow, I manage to nod. And watching her as she hurries away, I claw at the top button of my dress shirt as if unbuttoning it will allow me to take a full breath. Fuck. The world tilts on its axis, and I struggle to get air into my lungs. They just won't expand. I can't imagine my life without her and Ethan in it. Fuck. Fuck. *Fuck.*

I stumble toward my car. The moment I slip into the driver's seat, my phone rings, but I don't look at the name on the screen before I ignore it. I'm needed at the casino or warehouse, but the thought of going to either of those places only makes me want to hurl. Turning out from the driveway, I ignore where I'm needed, and instead, I head in the completely opposite direction.

CHAPTER 39

CAMILLO

"Where the fuck have you been?"

I drop my bag on the floor. Two days ago, I left the gym, but I was no calmer than when I entered it, so I found another outlet for my anger.

"You didn't fucking answer your phone," Marco carries on. "And you didn't show up at the casino last night." He's looming in front of me, eyes narrowed.

"I needed to blow off some steam."

"And you couldn't be bothered to let anyone fucking know? We thought..."

My brow scrunches. The look on Marco's face is foreign. His brow is etched with lines, and he looks like he hasn't slept in a few days given the bags under his eyes. He's worried. The expression knocks some of the frothing rage from me. "What happened, Marco?"

"Someone hit the warehouse. We thought—"

"What the hell is wrong with you!" Alessio storms into the lounge, murder in his gaze as he heads toward me. Behind him, Cate and Juliana and the kids follow, worry etched into their faces.

My heart clenches. *Shit.*

"Office. Now." Marco's expression is fierce.

I follow wordlessly. It's been two days. And I haven't been able to stop myself from seeking out trouble. Needing to feel in control of my life. Needing to be ruthless and physical—just like the way the world sees me. Like *she* sees me.

With demons clawing at my skin, I'd visited a list of people who needed a reminder of what the Marchiano name meant, what the Fratellanza meant. I'd left without a word to my family. I'd thought it'd be a distraction. Something to stem the bleeding of my heart as it poured out. All it'd done was give me more time to think—about Rosa and Ethan. About losing her. And losing him. About how ill-suited I am for her.

From the moment I laid eyes on her, I always knew she'd never be mine. I'm not a good man. And yet I've deluded myself into thinking I could have her—have them both. I've done nothing in my past to deserve someone like her by my side.

The thought of sleeping in my bed, surrounded by the scent of her, was enough to make me ill. I'd turned off the side of the road and lost what little was in my stomach before I decided it wasn't worth it to continue down that line of thinking. Instead, I lost myself in the feel of flesh beneath my fists, the coppery smell of blood, and the high of an illegal boxing fight to drown my sorrows.

"Sit."

I drop into the chair. "Marco, I—"

"I talk. You fucking listen." This isn't my capo talking now. It's my brother. And somehow that makes this worse. At least with him taking on the role of capo, I could pretend and explain away my absence as being due to work demands. But I can't do that with him as my brother. He'll ask questions. Poke his nose into my business.

"What the fuck is going on? You don't just go out and act like that without telling us! We thought—"

"I wasn't thinking. I'm sorry."

"You're *sorry*?"

"What do you want me to say?"

"I want a fucking explanation. Where the fuck were you? And why have you come home smelling like a damn bar? I want to know what the fuck made you think going dark on us was a good choice. Fuck, Camillo..."

He sags into the chair, staring up at the ceiling. The soft mutter under his breath makes me feel bad. It's not so much an admonishment as it is the worry easing out of his tightly wound body. The man sitting before me looks older, his nerves frayed. The lump in my throat is hard to swallow.

"Well? I'm waiting."

I don't have the right words to tell him what's going on. Whatever storm is still raging inside my chest hasn't calmed at all in the last two days. There's no cure that'll soothe the darkness which is eating up my self-control. "She's not coming back."

His brow scrunches. "Rosa?"

I nod.

"She actually said that?"

I heave a sigh. "She told me she doesn't need the job here anymore. Her father left her some money, so she's got options now. She can leave Chicago for good."

"Uh huh."

"What?" I exhale, dragging my battered hand down my face.

"I swear to God, Millo, if you weren't my brother—"

"Comforting as I know that your threat's gonna be, let me stop you there. Look, I'm sorry I worried you, *all* of you. I just needed a distraction."

"You've got a phone for a fucking reason."

"Yeah. Yeah, I got it. Are we done?"

"Not by a fucking longshot." I sink further into my chair, buckling up for the longest lecture of my life. You'd think I was fifteen again, having started yet another fight in school, and not a fucking grown man with the way Marco rips me a new one. Eventually, once he's said his piece, he sits back, his face no longer reddened with anger. He looks tired. "So, that's it? You're just going to let her leave without a fight?"

"What?"

"You said she wasn't coming back. And you're letting her leave?"

"It's *her* choice. Plus...she doesn't want someone like *me*."

"Someone like you? What the fuck does that mean?"

I purse my lips, waiting for him to catch up with what I've spent the last two days coming to terms with. I can't keep her. Keeping her means hurting her, and that thought makes my stomach roil. She deserves the chance to be free and happy. To start afresh away from Chicago and that piece-of-shit husband of hers.

I'd only ruin her. Trap her here in a world that would tear her apart. The judgmental looks and whispers would only grow. She deserves better.

After all, that's what devils do, isn't it? Corrupt the pure things in life just for the hell of it.

I've always known deep down that whatever beast I am, I'm not made for a happy ending.

"She deserves the chance to be free." I'm not looking at Marco as I say the words. My gaze is on the dark view outside the window. The barest hint of Chicago's skyline skims the horizon as the deep darkness of the night starts to chase away the dusky tones of sunset. The inevitable change settles something in my gut. An acceptance of some kind.

"And if she wants to stay?"

"She won't. There's no reason she'll stay with us." I want to add *with me*, but I don't. "We're not the right kind of people for that."

"Bullshit."

A bitter laugh bubbles in my throat, and I lift my gaze back to Marco. He doesn't get it. As much as they tried to protect me, it wasn't enough. "It doesn't matter. It's how the world works, Marco. After the funeral, she'll be back to collect her things and get away."

"Are you going?"

"Going?"

"The funeral, dumbass."

"I... No."

"You should."

"I really shouldn't."

"Not looking like you just stumbled out of a fucking dive bar and smelling like one, no. But you should go."

"Why? I've made enough problems for her just by showing up at her family's home. She doesn't want me there."

"Did she say that?"

"No. But she didn't say the opposite either."

"Millo," Marco huffs, "go take a damn shower, change, and go to the funeral. If anything, do it to just show your respects to Rosa. I think you owe her that much."

The look Marco levels with me isn't one I see on his face often. In fact, I'm not really sure what to make of it. But it's clear that if I'm not going to go because of Rosa, he's going to make me.

I sigh. "Fine."

"Good. Now if you fucking ever do that shit again, being my little brother isn't going to save you from getting your ass kicked."

My mouth twitches. "You'd throw your back out, old man."

"Go."

I let the door close behind me. Alessio, Cate, and Juliana are all huddled together when I emerge. It's clear they're waiting for details, for some explanation to ease the worry they felt as sharply as Marco had. But unable to talk anymore for now, I decide I'll have to fill them in later.

***

This is a terrible fucking idea.

I should have fought harder against this when Marco strongarmed me into coming.

St. Hyacinth's Basilica is packed. But unlike the last time I was here, the church isn't decorated in delicate pink and white. Instead, people in black and dark gray line the pews, their soft murmurs punctuated by a few stray sniffles, while floral arrangements fill the space with their sickly scent.

My eyes sweep the area, noting the security. From the messages I've received from Rosa and Ethan, I know they haven't had any unexpected visitors or contact.

"Uncle Millo!"

Ethan's little shout echoes through the somber atmosphere. And I feel the laser stare of eyes on me. Weaving through the line of mourners, Ethan's small body rushes toward me. My heart hammers in my chest.

As self-conscious as I feel, I can't ignore him. I can't turn him away. *I don't want to.*

I squat down as his arms fling around my neck. That hollow feeling in my stomach grows, and yet something in my chest clicks into place. Acid burns my eyes and throat at the contradiction.

"Hey, buddy."

"Momma said you weren't coming."

"I…"

"I told her you would. Then we'll go home, right?"

I avert my eyes, not wanting to crush the kid's spirits. Rosa's watery gaze levels on me, and a small tentative smile pulls at her lips. *She's beautiful.* The days away haven't changed that. Bathed with the soft light from the stained glass haloing her perfect body, she's mouthwatering. Despite the modest black dress that seems to hide her curves, she's easily the prettiest here.

"*This was supposed to be a closed ceremony.*" The loud comment snarled from Rosa's mother hits my ears as I rise back to my full height, Ethan gathered in my arms like he belongs there. The tutting response from Reagan seems to fill the room like a wave.

"C'mon, buddy, let's get you back to your mom."

"You'll sit with us, right, Uncle Millo?"

I shake my head, "Not this time. You should sit with your family."

"Oh." Ethan's gaze drops, and my heart seizes in my chest. Fuck. "Unless your mom says it's okay," I add quickly. Anything to rid that sharp pang I feel and the look on his face.

"Cyndie," I say to Rosa's mother, giving her a small nod. "The Fratellanza extends its condolences for your loss." I grit out the words with reluctance—because that man deserves nothing of mine or my family's sympathies. But I'm not doing this for them. I'm doing it for Rosa.

Cyndie's tight lips twist, and I watch Rosa's sister straighten up a little more.

I look at Rosa's face, pink from the scene my arrival caused. "You came," she says softly.

"Yeah."

"Can he sit with us, Momma?"

"No, that wouldn't be appropriate," Cyndie snaps before Rosa can respond.

"It's okay. I'll find you later," I jump in, not wanting to cause a scene, and I set Ethan down next to Rosa.

Her breath hitches when my fingers trail along her arm in passing. "Okay," she says softly as she shoots me an apologetic look.

I step away, letting out a deep breath.

"What the hell was that? I can't believe you, Rosa." Reagan's hiss circles around me as I settle into an empty pew in the back.

The service is more than Conor Davis deserves. A choked up Cyndie stumbles through her eulogy of Conor and their life together. Even Reagan puts on a show for all the church to see. It doesn't escape my attention that Rosa isn't included in this. My hand fists at my side.

Soon, it's time for the burial. But the chilly air does nothing to chase the feelings in my stomach away. The soft patter of rain that drizzles the area only seems to heighten the dark feeling inside me—the feeling that I don't belong here.

Conor's black lacquered coffin is lowered into the family plot, and Reagan's exaggerated sob hits my ears. It lingers and festers as the murmurs continue to make their rounds. *Brute* and *thug* are mentioned more times than I care to count.

But my attention is zeroed in on Rosa. Curled inward under the umbrella she holds, her fingers twist together, and she doesn't hold anyone's gaze longer than needed. Fire licks my veins at the image. Rosa deserves to grieve however she wants, but something tells me this isn't her choice. It's *theirs*.

Back at the house, people mill about in conversation, reminiscing about Conor, Cyndie, and Reagan's life as some happy family, of all Conor's accomplishments in his life. My elbows brace against the bar, my back resting against its ledge as I watch the crowd.

"Who'd have thought she'd open her legs for that brute?"

The words snap my head in that direction, my hand tightening on the tumbler in my hand.

"From what Grayden's said, she's a bad lay. She must be good at other services, if you know what I mean."

"I doubt it. Have you seen her? She's a fat bitch. She'd put off any man with a body like that..."

Their boisterous laughter has me seeing red. The sound of cracking glass echoes around me as I slam the drink on the bar top. "What did you say?" My voice comes out as a growl.

Their grins fall from their faces in unison as I tower over them.

"You don't s-scare us."

I arch a brow at the stuttered declaration. I most certainly do.

"You can't do shit to us," the other slurs, pressing his pudgy finger into my chest. "Touch us, and I'll get my lawyer to sue you for everything you're worth."

My eyes drop to the digit pressing into my Italian suit, then back up at the man.

Hastily removing his finger, he lifts his drink with a feeble smile. "Plus, we're just having a laugh. Anyway, once you get tired of the mousy bitch, we'll gladly take her off your hands."

I squeeze my fist tighter at my side. My self-control is slowly slipping out of my hands. "Keep Rosa's name out of your fucking filthy mouth."

The man laughs like I've said the funniest joke. It's a bad mistake on his part. And he knows it the moment he feels and hears the crunch of his nose beneath my fist.

Chaos erupts around me as our bodies crash into the ground.

Each ragged breath seems to bring more rage than clarity to me.

I lunge at him again as my hands tighten their grip.

The slippery, viscous liquid of blood coats my knuckles as the haze of red turns even more intense.

Rough hands try to grab me.

But I rip myself free, my hands circling the throat before me until his cough and gasps are all I hear.

CHAPTER 40

ROSA

"*Camillo!*" I shriek. His body freezes. And rough hands yank him back.

"You animal!" a woman yells. "Harold! Oh, Harold, are you okay?"

"You're psychotic!" another man says. "He just attacked him!"

"You're going to regret this," Harold wheezes, gripping at his throat. "Not even your thugs can protect you now."

"Throw him out of here!" my mother demands.

I start to rush toward him, but Reagan snatches my arm, her nails digging into my skin. "Just let him go. This is Daddy's funeral, for God's sake. If he can't behave, of course he's going to be thrown out. Don't cause any more of a scene by running after him, Rosa."

My step falters, and I'm frozen in place, unable to know what to do for the best.

Everyone is speaking in shocked whispers, and my mother is dabbing at her eyes.

Camillo's eyes drop from my wide eyes to the ground. And he doesn't protest as he's hauled away from the scene.

***

The last few days since the funeral have been exhausting. I'm in the kitchen, doing the washing up. For someone who's grieving, my mother seems to be throwing quite the event tonight.

"Hurry up, Rosa. We don't have all night, and we're running out of clean dishes."

I wince at the sharp voice of my sister, and I can't help the bitter thoughts from skittering through my mind. *This is why my mother has staff. Why am I doing this?* But that's done nothing to stop my mother and sister from coming in every ten minutes with a new demand. As I scrub at a stubborn stain on a coffee cup, my mind wanders over what's been said since the funeral...

"You should be thankful we've haven't disowned you after what he did."

"You can't be thinking of leaving, surely? Mother needs your support while she's grieving."

"Well, if you really want to make up for what that thug did at the funeral..."

The porcelain cup clatters into the sink as I startle.

"Rosa! I heard a crash! Is everything okay?"

"Yes, i-it's fine."

"Those were a gift from your father!" My mother's cry fills the kitchen as I wince. "You stupid girl! Do you know how hard it'll be to replace it? How could you be so thoughtless?"

I swallow as my eyes drop to the ground. Her heavy sigh reminds me of when I was a child. One wrong step and I'd be met with a lecture about how no one would love me if I couldn't do and say the right thing.

"I see some things haven't changed," she snaps. "See that it's tidied up and replaced. I have guests to deal with."

Sagging against the counter, I make a start on the next stack of cups.

After finishing all the dishes an hour later, I make my way up the stairs. Each step feels like I'm being dragged down, like overcoming a mountain with rocks attached to my ankles.

Softly, I open the door and scan the room for Ethan. His small body is engulfed by the blankets, the teddy bear brought by Camillo snuggled close.

My heart clenches. My phone sits on the nightstand, untouched. The text I sent Camillo after the funeral still remains unanswered. The small little check mark tells me he's read it at least—read that Ethan and I have to stay here a little longer as my mother still needs me. The ache inside me as I stare at the phone, willing it to light up, is too pronounced, too physical as I rub at my sternum.

For days now, I've wanted to call him. To hear what happened at the funeral to cause him to act like that. *To know if he's okay.* But that unanswered text has stopped me, and I don't know how to fix this thing between us.

Whatever rift has grown between us is wedged in place. A short time away from him, and he's probably realized he's better off without such a mess up like me. So, despite the despair that shreds my insides, I flip my phone over.

There are a few texts from Juliana and Cate asking when we'll be back and talking about setting up activities for Ethan to do with the other kids once we've returned. But I can't answer them right now.

I squeeze my eyes shut as I curl up on the bed, careful not to disrupt Ethan. Hugging the pillow, I feel the emotions drag me under.

"How Grayden ever put up with you is beyond me."

"How selfish can you be? Mother is grieving, Rosa, and you're just worried about some thug."

"Are you sure you want to have another piece of cheese? Everyone's watching..."

The words swarm around me, each slicing against my skin until I'm bleeding raw. Every single one tearing away whatever armor I've built up over the last few months.

Of course, they're right.

I am nothing.

Not to them. Not to Grayden. So, why would someone like Camillo see me differently?

Smothering a sob into the pillow, I press my face into it further.

The fantasy of what I thought I could have with him shatters into a million pieces before I can stop it. The foolish brief flicker of hope that Camillo would want me snuffs out like a precarious candle in a hurricane.

The radio silence is enough for me to take a hint. All those tender moments with him, the way he accepted me and Ethan so completely, are blown away. The soft whisper of needing me, wanting me, swirl around me before stabbing at my heart repeatedly.

I always knew it would happen. A man like Camillo would never want something so broken like me for long. I'm not the person who soothes those demons that roar to life in his head; I cause reasons for them to flare up instead. It was only a matter of time until he realized this.

I wanted to believe he didn't think like that. But another painful stab squeezes my heart.

Pulling my head away from the pillow, I stare up at the ceiling. Loneliness gnaws at my stomach, sharpening the bile and acid that bubbles within. I haven't eaten much since the funeral. I'm trying so hard to remember to use the techniques I learned at therapy, but the tutting responses from my family every time I so much as sip a cup of tea are making it so hard. Not talking to Camillo only adds to the anxiety, turning anything that touches my tongue into ash.

For once, I thought I was enough. He made me feel like I was worth something.

Just Rosa. As is.

But I'm wrong.

A bitter laugh leaves me as I swipe at my eyes. If there's anything I'm good at, it's being wrong, being inadequate, being the problem. At least there I excel. It's the only thing everyone can seem to agree on.

I press a kiss to Ethan's forehead and lie back down, trying to distract myself from the darkness sinking into me as my eyes drift close.

Maybe in another life, things could have worked out. Maybe if I'd had more time to win him over, to transform myself into something he wanted to keep, to show him just what I have to offer, and to tell him I'm not afraid of him the way others are...

But what good would that do? The thought in my head doesn't sound like me, but its hold on my mind is too hard to ignore.

It wouldn't change anything.

"Rosa!" It's Reagan's voice. I furiously swipe my tears away. Any sign of weakness, vulnerability from me, and they'll pounce like the vicious animals they are, ripping my already tattered and worn away shield to shreds. "You're needed downstairs, Rosa!"

Slowly, I open the bedroom door.

"Finally! I thought I was going to break a nail pounding on your bedroom door. You can't just sneak off like that. What if someone needed something?" She tuts loudly. "You can't expect me or our poor mother to deal with anything while we're grieving. It's really quite selfish of you, you know. *So, hurry up.*"

I spare Ethan one more glance before I slip out the door and past Reagan without a word. Seen and not heard, that's how I survive here. That's how I please them. Take up as little space as possible and hope I can melt into the walls.

And I hate myself for it. I hate myself for not being stronger, for not being able to stand up for myself. But it's so hard. It's not just a case of thinking it and doing it. Because every time I try to defend myself, my mother and Reagan make it seem like I'm being selfish and self-centered and only thinking about myself. And anything I say in my defense just makes their barbs worse.

I just can't win with them. Deep inside me, I know what they're saying isn't true, but that they think it in the first place stabs at me and makes it so difficult to stand up for myself. I know it's what the therapist terms as self-esteem issues, but right now, I don't know how to get back on track—back to a place where I'm stronger again.

It's like flipping a switch. The routines of the woman I once was click back into place. And the woman I was becoming with Camillo and his family vanishes like she never existed at all.

CHAPTER 41

CAMILLO

I return to the mansion after dealing with a debtor. It didn't need to be done today—*but I needed it*. I needed the feel of warm blood on my knuckles. I needed a distraction after the funeral and Rosa's text that she's staying at her mom's house.

I walk through the mansion's front door. I'm home.

The house is quiet now, an unfamiliar stillness that feels like a heavy weight on my chest. I can still hear the echoes of Rosa's soft voice and Ethan's small footsteps. But they're just memories now, hanging in the air like smoke that suffocates me. They're gone. I know that. But I still can't believe it. And I don't know if it'll ever sink in.

As I look around myself, everything feels surreal. And the only thing that runs through my mind is the first day I drove Rosa here. And then I think about the first time I saw her smile, the first time I heard her laugh...and the first time I realized I was in love with her.

The house is so empty without her and Ethan. *Ethan.* Just the thought of his name makes my heart ache with such an intensity that I think it might burst. I scrunch my eyes shut, remembering the first time he wore his Marchiano baseball jersey, the first time he hugged me, and the first time he gave me that beautiful, unconditional love of his.

No, this isn't home anymore. It can't be my home without them here. I'm left just a shell of a man without them. I feel homeless, loveless...worthless.

I pause in the doorway of our bedroom, and it's like I'm frozen there. Reminders of her are everywhere—the smell of her perfume on the sheets, her hairbrush forgotten on the side, a book she was reading on the nightstand. But so much also feels different so that it no longer feels like the cozy nest we had together.

Rosa asked in her text if I could send over some more of their clothes and things. My brothers and Lorenzo are in the living room, sorting through the toys, but I can't move. I can't step out of this room and leave it all behind. My brothers are trying to help, but their presence only underscores how much I need them—because I'm barely holding it together. They move around the house, carefully collecting items that belong to Rosa and Ethan, placing them in boxes with a tenderness that I can't bring myself to emulate.

The thought of packing up Rosa and Ethan's things, of folding away the life we had, it's unbearable. By doing that, it's like I'm erasing us, piece by piece, until there's nothing left but a skeleton of a man who doesn't know where to go from here. I hear Marco call my name, his voice firm and reassuring. He's always been the one who holds it all together. And I know he's just trying to do that for me right now, but I can't help feeling like I'm slipping through his fingers.

I walk into the living room, and it's a mess with toys everywhere—the majority belong to Marco's and Alessio's kids, but alongside those are a small pile of the ones belonging to Ethan. Alessio is taping up a box, his jaw tight. He looks up at me as I walk into the room, and for a moment, he just stares at me. I can see the sadness in his eyes and the concern.

For a moment, I watch the way his hands move, careful and precise. He's always been like that, methodical, focused. It's comforting in a way to see him so steady when everything else feels like it's falling apart. But it also makes me realize how lost I am, like I'm drifting away while they stay anchored.

Lorenzo hands me another box, and I take it without a word. I lift the flap, and taking a glance inside, I see more of Ethan's toys, small and colorful, but they feel heavy in my hands. I can't help remembering the way his face would light up when he played with them, the sound of his childish chuckles filling the room. I rush to close the box, not quite trusting myself to keep it together if I look any longer.

Marco picks up from under a chair a small toy model of a red Ferrari. The toy car is one of Ethan's favorites, the one he used to roll across the floor with that sweet, determined look on his face. I reckon Ethan is going to grow up to love cars as much as I do. I hold it in my hand and let the cool metal press into my palm, and for just a moment, I'm transported back to the day when I bought it for him, his delighted giggles filling this very room while Rosa gently scolded me for spoiling him. Closing my eyes, I try to hold onto those sounds, but they slip through my fingers like fine grains of sand. "Do you want to keep this one?" Marco asks in a quiet voice.

I just shake my head, forcing myself to open my eyes and look at him. "No. It belongs to Ethan," I say, my voice barely above a whisper. "He should have it."

He nods and places it carefully in the box I'm clutching. As I watch him do it, I feel a strange mix of emotions. One part of me desperately wants to cling to these things, to keep them here in the hope that it will somehow make them return. But the other part of me knows that holding onto these objects won't bring the people I love back.

I slump down on the couch. The house feels foreign now, like it's not really mine anymore. I run a hand through my hair, trying to steady myself. The grief is too big, too overwhelming.

Marco sits down beside me, not saying anything, just there. Just his presence next to me is comforting, but it also makes the emptiness inside me feel even bigger. I don't even know what to say to him, how to explain the hollow ache in my chest. So, I don't. I just sit there, the two of us side by side in silence.

Lorenzo carries down the two bags with Rosa and Ethan's clothes that Juliana and Cate packed for them. "This is the last of it," he says, his voice strained. For once, he isn't the terse, authoritative mafia boss that the world always sees; Lorenzo went through a lot when his kids' mom died, and I can tell he feels an empathy for my situation—he understands what it feels like to lose everything.

I nod, not trusting myself to speak.

"I'll put them in the car," Lorenzo says.

"No, wait!" I grit out. Leaping to my feet, I stride into the laundry room and collect something for Ethan. His Marchiano baseball shirt. Even though he won't be needing it at the Davis residence, I want him to have it. I *need* him to have it. I want him to remember that he was, and still is, a part of our family. He's one of us—*forever*.

Folding it carefully, I trace my fingers over the threaded embroidery of his name on the back. Then I place it in the bag and zip it up, trying hard but failing to keep the sting from the back of my eyes.

Lorenzo, Marco, and Alessio load the boxes and bags into the car, and I stand there watching as a soldier drives it away, taking pieces of my life with him. The house feels empty now, as does my heart. And I don't know how to fill that emptiness, how to be whole again when the best parts of me are gone.

So, I just stand in the middle of our living room, letting myself stare at the remnants of a life that feels like it's been ripped apart. My mind starts spiraling into the worst possibilities. What if they don't come back? What if this is it? The thought terrifies me. I can't imagine a life without them even though over the last hour, I've been packing away their things like this is the end. I struggle to breathe as my chest tightens, but I can't let myself break down. Not yet. Not in front of my brothers.

"They'll come back," Marco says, coming up behind me and gripping his hand around my shoulder. He's trying to offer some reassurance, but there's an uncertainty in his voice that mirrors my own.

I don't respond. I can't, because I don't know if he's right. God, I want to believe him, but the truth is, I just don't know what to do next and how to make things right.

I stride off, saying that I need some time to myself. And walking to the gym, I close the door shut softly behind me.

A few months ago, I would have said that nothing could make me feel like this.

Nothing could make me feel this sad.

But standing here alone, I can't do anything.

Except fall to my knees.

And let the tears leak from my eyes and scatter onto the ground until I'm sobbing.

As my heart breaks into a million pieces.

CHAPTER 42

ROSA

"Now, Rosa, we need to talk about some *things*..." My mother's voice barely registers as I sit at the dinner table.

I push the food on my plate around. Each day passes slower than the last. The gnawing of my stomach makes my sip of water taste sour.

"To start, the Botanic Garden Board will be here for a luncheon tomorrow. I expect you to be present in my time of need and to help out where I need it, Rosa."

I watch Ethan from the corner of my eye as he silently finishes his plate. "Do you, er, think it's appropriate to be holding so many events so soon after the funeral?"

"These women were there for me in my hour of need," she snaps. "It's the least I can do to thank them." But I know that the real reason she's having all these events is to gloat over how much money our father left in his will. "Now, we'll have to gloss over the whole *thing* with you, Rosa."

I lift my gaze, unable to help the pucker of my brow. "What thing?"

"You being with that thug," Reagan replies. "It's all anyone is talking about. We certainly don't need to add any more embarrassment to our good name."

My mother nods. "And the fact that you were his servant as well as sleeping with him. It reflects poorly on us. With your stooping so low, people will think we're broke or something."

"And Ethan will simply have to disappear—we can't possibly have him at the luncheon."

"*I'm sorry?*"

The harshness of my tone snaps my mother's eyes to me. "You simply can't watch him when you're supposed to be helping me. I would have thought that much is obvious. Hildie can watch him for a few hours, so you'll be free to see to the list of things I need you to do today."

"I can do both," I grit out, my knuckles white as I grip the glass in my hand. Anger simmers within me. "Ethan's no trouble," I say firmly, "and his place is by my side." I look down at my little boy and give him a reassuring smile and a comforting squeeze to his hand.

My mother's eyes narrow at me. But I'm not backing down when it comes to Ethan—ever.

And silence stretches between us until my mother and Reagan rise from the table and leave.

***

Ethan watches me as I stand in front of the mirror, smoothing my skirt down for the millionth time.

The soft knock on the door has me sucking in a deep breath. "Come in."

I expect to find Hildie with a tray of Ethan's favorite snacks, but when I turn around, I'm met with my mother's pursed lips.

"You're not wearing *that*, are you?"

I look down at my knee-length skirt and fitted blouse. It's smart and elegant.

"*Change.*"

"W-what?" I say, unable to stop the stutter. I hate that the backbone I've gained over the last few months disappeared so quickly almost as soon as I returned here.

"If you insist on not taking care of your body and embarrassing this family because of it, you'll dress in something that is a lot more suited to your shape—something that will cover up all your flab and rolls of fat."

The familiar burn at the back of my eyes makes me drop my gaze, and the sigh of my mother feels like a slap. "You should have brought more appropriate clothing with you instead of what you've got used to wearing as that thug's whore." She steps into the room, giving Ethan's little body a wide berth with a disdainful curl of her lip. "And have you been following the diet I gave you?"

A harsh laugh strangles itself in my throat. The diet in question is nothing but the loss of anything joyful about food. A small crumb-like portion that's just shy of starving me compared to the opulent dishes my mother and Reagan dine on.

"Or are you sneaking food? If you're not going to care about what you look like, Rosa, how on earth can you expect anyone else will treat you with respect?"

My mouth opens and closes.

"Hurry up and get changed." She wrinkles her nose as she runs her gaze over me. "Something that isn't so tight and trashy. And not that hideous T-shirt you insist on wearing around the house either. The thought that someone will know it's *his* is unacceptable."

Camillo's black T-shirt is my lifeline. Mixed into my clothing, it's the last thing I cling to as a glimmer of hope. It doesn't smell like him anymore, but sometimes I delude myself into believing it does while it clings to my body in sleep.

"Just find something. Tomorrow, I'll make sure the chef knows you're on a new, stricter diet and get a trainer in. If you won't fix the problem, I will."

The door closes, and as Ethan continues playing on the bed with his teddy bear, I slump against the dresser, staring at my reflection in the mirror opposite.

"You know, if you really cared about this family and our image, you'd have taken Mother up on that surgery. Then, we wouldn't be dealing with your problem right now."

"Why are you so selfish, Rosa? It's embarrassing having to explain to everyone why you look the way you do..."

A part of me whispers that she's just doing what she thinks is best for me. That it's justified because of how I look.

But the other part knows that's a load of bullshit...

"You're beautiful, Rosa."

"Everyone was staring because you're stunning. Probably questioning why a knockout like you is with me. Not the other way around."

"Fuck me, Rosa. How am I supposed to focus right now when you're dressed like fucking perfection and looking sinful...?"

The words jumble together. The harsh jabs are vicious. But it's the soft soothing balm of *his* voice that wraps around me. A comforting armor, not without its holes, but it's a shield that makes the other words fade away.

My gaze looks blindly at the woman who stands before me.

Weeks flash before my eyes in a matter of seconds. Weeks of Camillo's arms wrapped around me as he whispers how breathtaking I am while his hands grip at my hips and body like he can't get enough. Weeks of sincere compliments from Juliana and Cate about a new pair of jeans or shirt I bought. Weeks of feeling welcomed and embraced as I sat around the dining table with the whole Marchiano family. Weeks of my son and I being loved by people who were, until recently, strangers to us.

The ache in my chest throbs as I continue to stare. Wishing more than anything that I was in a room with dark walls and dark wood floors. With a bed that's too big even for me. With the bright windows and the gym bag tossed in front of them. With the scent of sandalwood wrapping around me and welcoming me home.

That's what it was. *Home.*

I cover my mouth before slumping down onto the bed.

Why can't I just ignore what everyone else wants? Why do I always feel guilty for disappointing my family? And why can't I just put myself first for once? It's been ingrained in me my entire life that I need to put other people first—my parents, my sister, Grayden. But what about me? What about what I want—what I need?

Ethan's tiny arms circle around my neck, and he clings to me. "I don't like it here, Momma," he whispers. And the only things I can see are Ethan's fallen face and slumped shoulders.

And as I see this all, my heart breaks and shatters into a thousand pieces.

Fire rises in my chest as I watch the little boy who's blossomed over the last few months shrink back into his shell. One I fought tooth and nail to coax him from, and one that Camillo and his family helped to bring him out of.

When I compare how Ethan is now to how he was amongst the Marchianos, I know which boy I want him to be. I want to see my son laugh. I want to watch him bloom and run around the house like a child should. I want him to be somewhere where he doesn't have to tiptoe around or make himself small. He deserves to be loud and laugh whenever he wants. He deserves better than whatever scraps I was given as a child.

And I find myself comparing the cold demands and awkward silences of the Davis mansion with the loud laughter, warm conversations, and love of the Marchiano estate.

That's the sort of childhood and upbringing I want for my son. That's the sort of life I want for myself. I don't know why I always find it so hard to stick up for myself and put myself first, but I know that I can't let myself or Ethan suffer by staying here any longer. Ethan deserves better. He deserves so much more. And knowing that gives me the strength to do what I do next.

"I don't really like it here either," I admit softly through a sheen of tears. "We just had to be here to help Grandma and Aunt Reagan." I can now see that as each day goes by, my mother and Reagan's actions are sapping away his confidence—just like they've done to me my whole life.

I have to be strong for Ethan. But also, for Camillo... If I can't be strong for myself, I have to be strong for the people inside my heart.

I pick up my phone and dial Camillo.

He answers after half a ring. "Rosa? Are you and Ethan okay?" His voice rushes out in concern.

"I'm sorry I didn't stand up for you against my family, Camillo—"

"What are you talking about, Rosa? I should be the one apologizing—I've caused a scene at your family's home twice now. And in front of Ethan of all people. I'm so sorry. I would have rung, but I thought you wouldn't want to talk to me...especially after you didn't come back to me after the funeral."

"My mother needed me to stay for longer and help out with some other things."

"Are those things...finished now?"

"No."

"Oh." And I can tell his disappointment—and his want for me.

I'm fed up with doubting myself—and I decide to throw caution to the wind. "But I don't care, Camillo. She can manage without me. I'm coming back today. Do you think, um, you could give me a ride?"

"I'll be there." I can hear the smile in his voice. "Just tell me when and where, baby."

"I'll be ready to leave at 4 p.m."

"I'll be waiting with my car outside the house."

"No, Camillo. I want you to come inside."

There's a stunned silence from his end.

"Camillo?"

"Are you sure?"

"I've never been surer of anything in my life. I want everyone to see the man I'm with—the man I'm proud to have at my side." And for the first time ever, I toss aside what my family might think. I'm doing this for me. *For me, Camillo, and Ethan.*

"I'll...be there, baby." His voice breaks, and I feel myself tearing up at the thought of seeing him soon.

After hanging up, I shoot a grin at Ethan. "Come on, we've got to pack..."

***

When it's time for the luncheon, I make my way downstairs with Ethan and lift my chin as I enter the garden.

Nerves threaten to make me hurl the tiny amount of food I ate earlier. I've been feeling weak, dizzy, and downright terrible. And I know I can't go on like this. I have to get my eating issues under control again. For me, and for Ethan—so that I can be a good mom to him.

It's now or never. My feet freeze on the patio for a second. Doubt tugs me under.

But Camillo's words block them all out like some bullet proof shield. If I don't do this now, I'll never do it.

As soon as my mother sees me, she marches up. *"What are you wearing?"*

"You told me to change."

"Yes, but..." An approaching guest means there's no time for her to finish what she was about to say.

My hand smooths down the front of Camillo's black T-shirt which I'm wearing with a belt and over a pair of capri pants Juliana helped me pick out. It hugs my body and curves, yet it's smart and classy.

For the first time since I arrived here, I feel powerful and in control. I don't risk losing my nerve as I turn on my heel. If I let her jump in, she'll tear me down.

I find my place on the seating plan and find a spare chair to pull up beside me. We're sitting in the corner of the garden, practically hidden by the large plants surrounding us. I really don't understand why my mother even wants me here if she's determined to keep me as out of sight as possible. But I know the answer—she wants me here in case she needs to quash any potential rumors that I've returned to my maid job.

Over the luncheon, not a single person has said a bad thing about my outfit. A few of the younger ladies even compliment me—although it's to the tutting disapproval of a couple of the older ones. But for once, I brush off the negative comments and let myself focus on the positive ones. That's the sort of people I want to surround myself with—people who are kind and encouraging. And as I do this, I keep on repeating to myself the messages that I've learned in therapy.

The therapist talked to me about cognitive restructuring through addressing my negative core beliefs. She said that I should build my self-esteem by broadening my definition of self-worth to include non-appearance factors like my achievements, skills, and moral values.

I've learned so many other things from her as well, and I need to get back to focusing on those techniques.

And I need to get back to surrounding myself with people who will help me in this journey. Because that's what it is—a journey. Things aren't going to change for me overnight or at the click of my fingers. But to be strong enough to make this journey, I have to take these first steps.

I look down at my empty plate where a few crumbs from the finger sandwiches I'd nibbled on remain. Pride over something so small and insignificant rushes through me like a bullet. It's more than just defying my mother or eating something small. It feels like the chains that are strapping me down have loosened just a tiny bit.

It's not fixed. I'm not fixed. But it's Camillo's voice in my head that pushes me on. That leads me through the darkness.

At 4 p.m. on the dot, I see Camillo arrive and walk over to me.

And a small smile spreads across my lips, unable to be contained. Because he's the man I've been waiting for my whole life...

CHAPTER 43

CAMILLO

FOUR HOURS EARLIER

"What's so interesting on your phone, Millo?" Marco asks.

"What?"

But before I can say anything else, Alessio chips in. "He's probably watching some por—ow, fuck!"

I raise my brow at my family gathered around the table for lunch. Beside me, the two empty seats remain, delivering an uneasy reminder that they're gone. Two people who mean the fucking world to me. Two people who wrapped themselves so completely around my heart that, with them gone, I feel like I've lost a part of me.

"You haven't looked up from your phone since you sat down," Marco says.

"Something we should know?" Alessio chimes in.

My eyes slide to those empty places.

"Have you...tried to talk to her?" Juliana asks.

Following the funeral and the fuck up I made, I've spent the last week cleaning it up. Harold Covington, the asshole I punched at the funeral, made good on his word and pulled out all the stops in his attempts to get back at me.

He used every underhanded tactic in the book, but he forgot who I was and what power I carry in this city. The news of the scandal that suddenly engulfed his hedge fund brought a little satisfaction to me. Served him fucking right for running his mouth about my woman. But it didn't fix things between Rosa and me. Not until her phone call twenty minutes ago.

When I spoke to her, relief I didn't deserve to feel had pumped through me. It wasn't a fix. I wasn't sure I could fix it. But fuck, I wanted to try.

"She called me just before lunch."

"And?" Cate asks eagerly.

"And I talked to her."

A round of eye rolls.

"Well, what did she say?" Juliana says.

"And what did you say?" Alessio adds.

"And are they coming back soon?" Cate asks.

"Let him talk," Marco orders over the rim of his glass.

"She said...this afternoon, they'll be back."

I don't miss the way Marco's eyes meet mine. I can read the silent question on his face without even trying: *Once she's back, is she staying for good?*

I shrug in answer. I don't know, but I sure as fuck hope so. Inside me, the constant doubts claw each flare of hope into ribbons. It's killing me. I know that I have to talk to her properly once I've brought her back to the mansion.

"Good," Alessio comments. "It's not the same without her."

"You just miss her cooking," Cate laughs at her husband.

"We all do," Marco adds.

God, do I miss her cooking. But it's more than that. It's the sound of her humming in the kitchen. The way she looks when she's relaxed and having fun. The way she dances as she cooks. I just miss *her*. Her smell. Her laugh. Her shy smile. The way she blushes at the smallest compliment. The way she stares at me like she can't believe I'm real.

"I hope you manage to work things out," Juliana says softly.

I nod, gazing back down at my phone, my eyes looking at the photo of Rosa, Ethan, and me, again and again, wondering if we'll ever be that happy again.

***

The last four hours since Rosa called me have lasted an eternity, and each one has made me even more fucking nervous. I've gone so far as to clean my room, picking up all the clothes and car magazines that dotted the floor, plus put fresh sheets on the bed. Alessio had a field day while watching me at work.

But sitting here in the lounge, waiting until it's time to leave and trying to act like I'm not about to throw up, is harder than I thought.

"Stop looking at the clock." Juliana grins from where she lounges, reading a book. "Won't make it go faster."

"Don't you have something to do?"

"Nope." She pops the 'p' at the end, giving me a wide smile.

I mutter a curse under my breath. "Can you all wait somewhere else, then?"

"Someone needs to make sure you don't fuck it up between now and when you pick her up," Marco says, fiddling with the buttons on his shirt sleeve.

I roll my eyes. "Your confidence in me is heartwarming, really. I'm touched. But I've got this. So, please, can you kindly fuck off?"

Marco looks at me carefully. "Are you sure, Millo? I cleared my diary for this afternoon so that I could drive you to the Davis mansion."

I give him a grateful nod. "Thanks, but I'm sure."

Marco pulls his wife up, and they make to leave. "Okay, we'll find something else to do. But just call if you need me."

Juliana gives my shoulder a quick squeeze as she passes, and I listen as they make their way upstairs—no doubt to fuck.

The sudden emptiness of the room is unbearable. I drag a hand through my hair, pulling it up, then down, then back up before I start to pace the room.

The paperwork from our lawyer sits on the table. It's not ironclad, but it's a start, and that's all that matters. She asked me to find another way...to be the better man. And I'm trying.

Grayden might have power through his wealth, but if there's anything I've learned over the last few days, I'm going to stop at nothing to show him what genuine power looks like.

At 4 p.m., I pull up outside the Davis mansion and make my way inside. A maid directs me to where everyone is.

I stride into the garden, rubbing at my jaw, my heart lurching into my throat. Wiping my palms on my jeans, I try to will myself to calm the fuck down. Panic swells through my body, and I feel like I've lost every brain cell I own.

Consulting the seating plan, I find who I'm looking for. And when I see Rosa and Ethan, I lose the ability to breathe.

Her beautiful eyes lock onto me. I freeze mid step. Every muscle seizes up, and I forget how to function. The white noise in my brain is drowning me. And also anger—because I can't help but notice that Rosa and Ethan have been seated in the furthest corner, out of the way as if her mother is ashamed of them.

"Fuck it," I mutter, striding toward her. As she takes a few steps forward, I pull her close to me, any resolve to let her dictate this flying out the window.

The smell of her, roses and sweetness, fills my nose and every empty part of my body that's been bleeding since the funeral. It feels like fucking home.

I look down at her. Her chest labors in the T-shirt she's wearing—*my T-shirt*—with each second that passes.

My hand cups her cheek, thumb stroking her smooth skin. So much for taking it slow. "I've missed you... Both of you."

"Are we still in trouble?" a voice pipes up from lower down.

A startled chuckle leaves me as I kneel. Ethan stands tucked against Rosa's leg. He looks smaller than he is, different. My chest pounds with anger. *What the fuck did they do to my boy?* "You weren't ever in trouble, buddy."

"But—"

"I messed up, Ethan. I did something wrong. Not you or your mom. I didn't know how to handle everything. I need to work on that. And I'm going to work on it—for you and for your mom. So, it's on me. And I'm sorry." I look up at Rosa. "I'm really sorry. My home is your home. And it's been your home for a while now. If you want it…"

Rosa's sharp intake of air has me stilling. Have I already messed this up? Have I already overstepped?

Shit. Shit. Okay. Backtrack. I can fix this. "What I mean is… I mean you guys are, uh…" I take a deep breath, keeping my gaze fixed on Rosa. This is not going as I planned. Words aren't a strong suit of mine.

But I need her, them both, to know just what I feel like without them. *And that what I need is them.* "If you want to stay with me forever, you can. Please stay."

"Can…we really stay?" The hesitancy of Ethan's question breaks my heart.

Both of us look up at Rosa.

And I can see the fresh sheen of tears in her eyes as she nods, making Ethan relax, his small body crumbling a little on itself with relief.

I smile widely at them both.

And then she reaches up on her tiptoes and kisses me, right there in front of everyone. It's long, lingering, and needy. And we don't stop until a nasal voice interrupts us. "What in God's name is the meaning of this, Rosa?" her mother hisses, marching up to us with Reagan on her heels.

Rosa lifts her chin up. "Ethan and I are going home now—with Camillo."

Cyndie's face turns practically purple.

"I hope you're not serious, and this is your stupid idea of a joke," Reagan snaps.

Rosa looks them in the eye. "Camillo has shown me more kindness and respect in the short time I've been with him than either of you have shown me in my entire lifetime." Her voice is quiet yet firm. "I'm not saying this to hurt you. Because it hurts me even more to say this—to have to admit aloud that you haven't seen me as being worthy of your love and kindness."

"What would a barbarian like him know about kindness?" Cyndie splutters.

"He knows a lot. He's brought Ethan out of his shell, he's brought me out of my constant state of fear, and he doesn't disapprove or criticize at every turn. *He makes me feel that I'm good enough. Like I matter. Like I'm not invisible.*"

"You're being utterly ridiculous."

"No, I'm not." I can tell that Rosa can hardly believe that she's actually saying all this to her family. And as I listen to her words, I'm so fucking proud of her. "I want to be with people who'll support me, stand up for me, love me. I want to be around people who'll build me up rather than tear me down. Criticism and disapproving comments from strangers is bad enough, but from my own family—from the people who are supposed to love me despite anything—it cuts me to the core and makes me want to cry out from the pain of it. You've always made me feel like I'm not good enough. But I'm telling you right now that I am. I'm good enough. I'm not the problem. The problem is your shallows standards and your constant obsession over appearance and reputation."

"We've done everything for you," Cyndie spits.

"Everything for me? You've ignored me, belittled me, and made me feel like nothing. You never supported me when things became horrendous and dangerous with Grayden. Every time I've needed you, you've made me feel like a burden."

Reagan rolls her beady eyes. "Stop being so dramatic."

Rosa takes a deep breath. "I'm not being dramatic. I'm communicating my feelings and hurt to you. I've tried to be a good daughter and a loyal sister, but it's time for me to let go and move on with my life. It's time for me to put myself first for once—and put my son first. He deserves that. *I deserve that.*"

Rosa starts to walk away.

"You stupid girl, Rosa. You can't—"

But before Cyndie can speak any further, I have to say something to this awful woman. "Nobody puts Rosa or my boy in the corner—*ever*," I growl in a low, dangerous voice.

Cyndie's mouth opens and closes like a goldfish while Reagan can only stare wide-eyed at me.

And without another word, I scoop Ethan into my arms and lace Rosa's fingers with mine, leading them to my car—and taking them home with me.

***

"C'mon, let's go play." Ethan tugs my hand and Rosa's as soon as we arrive back at the Marchiano estate.

"Actually, buddy, can I talk with your mom for a bit? Why don't you head into the playroom and find us a game to play for after?"

His little arms cross over his chest, and for a blink of an eye, I see my posture and expression mirrored at me. "Okay, Uncle Millo. But not too long."

"Promise."

Once he's out of earshot, I rise and meet Rosa's eyes. "I owe you an apology. A big one."

"No, you don't."

"I do." I lick my lips. "How I acted at the funeral, and what I did there. And in front of Ethan." I can't look her in the eye as a reminder of her horrified expression fills my mind. "I fucked up. Big time."

"Camillo..."

"Please, let me finish, Rosa." I'm almost begging her. I'm tempted to drop to my knees and plead with her just to make sure that she really does stay for good.

I rehearsed the whole goddamn speech in my room, but now that I'm face to face with her, I can't remember a damn word of it.

"I..." I clear my throat, scrubbing my jaw. "It won't happen again. You deserve someone who isn't a wild beast at the drop of a hat, especially in front of Ethan. Who doesn't lose his temper and pummel rich assholes. I know that... I just..." Fuck, this is harder than I want to admit.

But that ache in my chest, the one that's ripping me apart from the inside out at the idea of her walking back out that door, is killing me little by little.

I drop my eyes. "I'm not the best man...or even a good one. I might never be. *But God, do I want to be it for you.* It's not in me to change easily. I'm the way I am because I need to be. My family depends on me being able to do what I do. But with you, Rosa, it's different. It's always been different. I don't want to be the brute or thug when you're around. I want to be the man *you see*. I sure as fuck don't want people gossiping about me or you. And I don't want people hurting you or making you doubt yourself just because they've seen you with me."

Rosa steps closer to me, her head tilting back to meet my gaze.

I cup her face in my hands. "All the things people say about me. All the things I've done... I don't want you to be ashamed of me. Or hurt. Or worse." But I'm fucking selfish. "A better man would let you slip away. Let you live a life where you're safe and away from danger. A better man wouldn't be selfish like me. He wouldn't do the things I do and call it love. Because that's what this is. *Love...*"

I haven't ever admitted it out aloud before.

"Rosa, my obsessive need to be near you, with you, in you...it's all because I'm in love with you."

"I want to keep you here. With me. Because this is your home as much as it is mine. Because I—" The words are thick in my throat. Love. It's not a word I thought I'd ever say. When it happened, I'm not sure I know.

The moment I laid eyes on her in that fucking wedding dress perhaps, but the fact remains that my heart is in her hands even if she rejects me. Even if she decides to pack up her things and leave.

"My heart is yours, Rosa. *I'm* yours. I..."

"Camillo." Rosa's soft voice draws my attention back to her.

"Yes, beautiful?"

Her lip twitches at the corner. "Can I say something now?"

There's still so much I have to tell her. Still so much I need to explain or try to explain. But I nod, letting her go.

"Good." A deep breath leaves her.

I tense, bracing for the news she's going to tell me. Every bone in my body is telling me to run. To put as much distance between Rosa and me as possible. Because a man like me doesn't deserve someone like her. Because this weakness she causes in me scares the absolute shit out of me. I've built myself to be a man of power. Of strength. But I would crumble to my knees just to hear her say she feels the same way I do.

My heart thunders in my chest as I wait for her to continue, acutely aware that her fingers are curling around the soft cotton of my T-shirt. Their slight tremble is the only thing telling me she's nervous or scared.

Her eyes bounce around the place. "I leave for a few days, and this place is just...well, it's a mess."

Confusion knits my brows. "Huh?"

"Clearly, you guys need a maid. So, I've decided Ethan and I are going to stay."

I blink. Searching her eyes, I wait for her to fill in the rest of that statement. It's incomplete. *She'll stay until when? For how long?*

"If you'll still have me? Have us?" Her voice trembles, soft and unsure.

"For how long?" The words scrape out of my throat. If this is just a temporary thing, I don't think I'll survive.

"There has to be a limit?"

"No, of course there doesn't. I just..." I rub the back of my neck. "You said you wouldn't need the job here anymore."

"I don't." Her honesty feels like a sucker punch. How have I messed this up so badly? "When I said that, I just meant I didn't need you to pay me for my work. But this is my home now, you said so yourself. Juliana, Cate, all the kids, Alessio, even Marco. And you—especially you. *You're home. This is our home.*" And I should have stuck up for you more in front of my family. I shouldn't have let them speak to you like that or throw you out. I'm so sorry, Camillo. I need to start putting first the people who matter to me—you and Ethan. And I've got to let go of the people who won't ever change or accept me for the person I am."

"I should have answered your text, Rosa. But what about the rest of it? The funeral? The embarrassment I caused you?"

"We can embarrass my family together. I'm great at it." Her lip twitches again, and I see a soft sheen of tears in her eyes. "I don't condone violence. But I understand why you did it. You want to protect your family. You want to protect *us*. How can I fault you for that?"

"If I told you what I've done in the past, you'd take off for the hills and never look back. But I'm trying here. For you and for Ethan."

"You are when it matters, Camillo." And that smile I've been craving so much over the last few days graces her gorgeous lips.

This woman. Whatever I've done to deserve even a scrap of her heart, I'll forever be thankful.

"I really am sorry, Rosa." I rest my forehead against her, breathing in her scent once more. "I'm working on things. I've finally realized that not everything has to be solved with fists and blood." I swallow the lump in my throat that threatens to choke me. "And I want to prove it to you right now—prove that I'm trying to be a better man."

I pull away gently, leading her toward the table and nodding to the stack of papers there.

"What's that?"

"Read it."

Rosa gingerly picks up the packet and flips through it. Her face contorts as her brows pucker downward. "Camillo, is this..."

"I told you I'd find another way." I clear my throat. "While you were with your family, I was doing this. Our lawyers are the best in Chicago. They know a specialist who helps people escape abusive situations, and she's agreed to help on the case. We've been working on it already, and we have more than enough leverage to ensure that you'll stay safe and that Grayden can't take Ethan from you—*ever*. He has money, probably much more than what your father left you, but so do we, and I can assure you that he'll run out before we ever do."

"I don't know what to say..."

"You can look it over later. I included our lawyer's direct line and the specialist's number so that you can speak to them and ask questions. Her assistant apparently went through something similar, so she's also listed in case you want to speak to someone who's been in the same boat as you're in now."

"Why did you go to all this trouble?"

"You know why." I hope.

She stares at me, searching my face for something.

"I'm in. I'm all in, baby. With you. With Ethan." I hold her gaze, hoping I appear calmer than I feel. My heart is pounding in my ribcage like it's trying to break free of my chest, as though it wants to make a run for it before Rosa can crack it open more than she already has. "I'm not good at this. In fact, I think you know I'm terrible at all this..."

Emotions are a weakness I've always thought I couldn't afford. Weakness gets people killed in my line of work. It makes them exploitable. But they're also the reason I'd wage a war on every fucking rich asshole in this city who utters a word against anyone I care about. And I realize now that these emotions that strangle me, that drag me under, don't make me weak when it matters. They give me strength.

"For you, Rosa, I'd do the impossible if you asked me to. I meant what I said when I told you I'd never be a good enough man. I'm who I am. But for you? For you, I'm trying to be this version you see."

The room is still. Anxiety bubbles through me as I worry I've said too much. She's just back—but have I already pushed her away again?

I've opened my heart and left it beating and bleeding at her feet. Is she going to kick it away? I can't look at her...

She sniffs.

"Rosa?" I lift my gaze once more.

She wipes at her eyes, smearing whatever makeup she had on. No doubt another stupid requirement for her fucking family. Another deep breath, and she holds my eye. "Thank you. That's what I want to say to you. And I can never say that enough."

"You're thanking me?"

She steps closer to me, cupping my cheek with her hand. In this position, we're eye to eye, and her beautiful honey brown eyes glisten. "I am. Thank you for that." She nods to the documents. "And for saving me. You don't have to try to be some version you think I see. You *already* are the man I want."

"I'm not."

"You are." Tears cling to her lashes, and her bottom lip wobbles.

Softly, I brush them away with the pad of my finger. "I'm not. Don't say that, Rosa. We both know I'm not."

"Yes, you are," she insists. "You've done nothing but show me and my son kindness. You've done everything you can to make me fall in love with you when I was nothing. Why else would you do all that, find a way for me to be free from Grayden, give us a home and a family, if you weren't a good man?"

I press my forehead to hers and sigh.

"You protect your family, Camillo. You'd do anything to keep them safe, and we were lucky enough to make that cut."

My heart aches with the weight of it all. With the words I've longed to hear from someone—and with my love for her. And my fear that I'm not good enough for her crumbles as I listen to her.

"You might be a monster to everyone else, Camillo. But to me, you're a guardian angel."

"You're too good for me."

Her hand circles my neck, and I close my eyes, clinging to her. I'm drowning, and she's my lifeline. Whatever I did in life to deserve this woman, I wish I'd done it sooner.

"I'm all in, Camillo. *If you want me, want us, we're yours.*"

"Mean it?"

"Yes."

The soft way she looks at me cracks me in half. Cupping her cheek, I pull her lips to me, and for the first time in God knows too long, I feel like I'm finally home.

She sighs against my lips, and I angle her head, deepening the kiss. Her fingers curl into the fabric at my shoulders before sliding into the roots of my hair.

If we had more time, I'd take her right here and now. I'd show her just what my words mean. But anyone could walk in, and worse yet, we're keeping Ethan waiting.

"Rosa," I murmur against her lips as I slowly pull back.

That shy smile plays at her lips. "I like how you say my name."

I grin. There's that spark I've missed. One I thought for sure was snuffed out forever.

Her soft laugh is like nothing I've experienced. Euphoria and bliss are all wrapped together in some drug I can't quit.

My hands slide over the back of her thighs, tugging her closer into my body. "I should welcome you home officially, but I think Ethan might get a little suspicious if we disappear.

"Later?" she says.

"As soon as he's down for a nap, beautiful, I'm going to worship you like you deserve."

The shiver that rides through her makes me strain against my zipper. Lacing our fingers, I will myself to calm the fuck down. Without warning, I scoop her up into my arms to carry her into the lounge where Ethan is waiting for us. Her squeal of surprise vibrates against my chest. "I can walk. You don't have to..."

"I know. I want to. I've missed having you in my arms."

Her sigh brushes against my neck, and I drop my lips to her forehead. And nestled into my arms, it feels like my world has righted itself back on its axis...

CHAPTER 44

ROSA

Things have started to improve ever since I returned to the Marchiano estate. I'm seeing the therapist again, and talking through my anxieties and insecurities is helping. It's going to be a long road, but I'm learning to not see myself as being defined by what I eat, what I look like, and what work I do around the house for the family. There's more to me than those things. *I'm worth more, and I deserve more.*

It's not an easy shift of mindset to make, but I'm determined to keep on with this journey I've started, and with Camillo and the others behind me, I feel stronger than I have in a long time. I want to be healthy in not just my body but also my mind.

I check my phone again. Camillo's lack of response to my last text to him is making a weird feeling gnaw at my belly. A dismissive shake of my head sends my blond strands from side to side. *I'm safe here.*

The house is quiet without Juliana, Cate, Ethan, or the other kids around. Despite their begging for me to join them at the movies, I had to take a raincheck because the lawyers for the divorce will be calling this afternoon to go over how things are proceeding.

It should make me feel at ease knowing that there's nothing that Grayden can do to ruin this for me. There's nothing he can take from me anymore. I'm out from under his thumb.

But an uneasiness I can't shake grips me tightly.

I tell myself that Camillo's at the casino with his brothers, and he's just busy with work. I must just be missing him—as if waking up, limbs tangled together, these last two weeks hasn't been enough time for us to catch up.

I pause as I pass the small den where board games and other toys litter the place. The kids had been so excited to go to the movies they'd left it a mess. A soft smile tugs at my lips as I start to gather the toys and neatly stack them back on the shelves.

I might not be the hired help anymore, but cleaning and doing things for the people I now call my family makes me feel needed.

The soft pad of footsteps down the halls isn't an unusual thing anymore. The security here has always been quiet and unseen, but they've beefed it up since everyone returned home. A safety precaution.

It should scare me. These men are every bit of the monsters the world makes them out to be. Ruthless, with blood on their hands, they've earned their reputations. But behind closed doors, they're different. A good different.

But the sound of those footsteps is slightly off. Enough that it tickles my mind and sends the hair on the back of my neck rising.

I shake my head again. It's just my old habits resurfacing.

As I focus on finishing the den, I hum to myself and let my mind drift to the man who's helped me rebuild my life. The way he looks at me. The way he looks at Ethan. Like we've hung the moon and stars, and he can't believe we're his.

I dust my hand on my jeans as I straighten.

Hot breath brushes the back of my neck.

And my blood turns to ice.

"Did you really think I'd let you go?"

My stomach plummets.

"Nothing to say, whore?"

How? Why? When? My heart hammers against my ribs.

And every piece of self-defense Camillo taught me blanks from my mind.

"If I can't have you, Rosa, I'm sure as fuck not going to let him have you. And when I'm done with you, I'm taking my goddamn son."

His powerful hand grabs the back of my neck.

I struggle against his hold.

But he only tightens it. And the cold wood floor crashes into me.

Grayden's face is red. He looms over me. His lips are curled into a sneer. And the acidic smell of alcohol wafts from him.

The bile inches higher up my throat. I scramble back, hitting the back of the couch. "Please—"

"Please?" His hard laugh fills the room. "Please *what*? You think I'm going to fall for your fucking waterworks?"

His boot connects with my ribs. And the air pulls from my lungs in a harsh gust.

"*You're a worthless fat bitch.*"

Another slam of his leather clad foot connects with my stomach.

I roll to my side. But two powerful hands grab my arms.

I kick and wildly try to create some distance between us.

I just need to get into a room. Somewhere I can lock the door and wait for help.

My heel connects with his jaw. There's a satisfying crack.

His hands drop. And I crawl across the floor as fast as I can.

But a hard yank on my ankle sends me sprawling back into the hard floor.

"I'm going to send you and that Marchiano fucker a message. He thinks he can beat me? That he can have what's mine?"

"P-please," I plead. But it's no use.

Another quick kick to his shoulder, just like Camillo taught me. I scramble back up.

My bare feet slip along the floor.

And I knock over the lamp as I scramble down the hall.

I rush to the kitchen. I just need a weapon—something until security comes.

If they come.

My frantic breathing fills the room. I duck down to hide behind the island. The butcher block of knives gleams like a saving grace just feet from where I crouch.

But the thud of his boots down the hall means I freeze.

The salty taste of tears hits my tongue as I lick my dry lips.

"Come out, *whore*. No one's coming to save you. My guys took care of them all."

All of them?

My heartbeat drowns my ears. I rack my brain to remember the moves Camillo drilled into me. *Anything is better than being a victim again.*

I just need to buy some time...

The sound of his steps stops.

"I wonder if he has to fake it as much as I had to," he sneers. "If I'd have known you'd spread your legs for just anyone, I'd have passed you around my friends and made a pretty penny off of you sooner."

He's closer now—I can tell by the way his voice echoes off the walls.

I squeeze my eyes shut. It's now or never.

I lunge for the knives, my fingers curling around a beautifully crafted handle. The evil look in his eyes sends bile racing up the back of my throat. It's the same look I've seen a million times...

"What are you going to do with that?" His head tilts to the side with the taunt. "I'm your husband. You can't kill me. I *own* you."

The butcher's knife wobbles in my hand as I hold it between us. "Leave. Now. I don't have anything you want."

"Wrong."

A step closer.

"You took fucking *everything* from me. I'm supposed to forget that?"

I tighten my hold on the handle, slowly walking backward. "I didn't."

"You took my son. You whored yourself to the men who tried to ruin your father." His laugh is deranged. "You've been a fucking waste of breath since I married you!"

He steps closer.

Then closer.

My back hits the edge of the counter.

I'm blocked in.

"Put the knife down," he sneers.

"*No.*"

"I thought I beat that fucking attitude out of you. Put it fucking down."

I let out a strangled cry and lunge at him.

The sharp edge slices into his shoulder. And his howl fills the room.

The back of his hand connects with my cheek. "You fucking bitch!" Metal clatters on the floor. And the coppery smell of blood makes me gag.

Dizziness makes my world blur. I push from the counter and rush into the foyer.

But I'm too slow. A scream rips from my lips.

Two slippery hands circle my throat.

The polished wood slips beneath my feet. And Grayden's body clamps down over me.

This is it.

I always knew he was going to take my life. His hands tighten around my throat. I claw and scratch. But darkness blurs my vision. I buck and twist just like we'd practiced. But his hands are too strong.

"You're a worthless bitch. I should have asked for money when I agreed to marry you. Your father fucking owed me, and I was given a useless whore like you?" His words are hissed. My hands push against his shoulders and into his wound, but it's no use.

The room floats around me. Like I'm no longer in my body. My eyelids droop with the lack of oxygen. My eyelashes fuse together with my tears.

"I'll take everything once you're gone, bitch."

I can't breathe. Dots take over my vision.

I know this is it. And I make peace with it. I'd finally gotten a taste of what happiness feels like.

And I can die knowing I had it all for just a little while...

My eyes close.

And I know they're not going to open again.

My only wish is that the men come home first. *Ethan can't find me, please God, oh please God...*

Air rushes into my lungs.

The pressure on my throat vanishes. And I gulp down lungfuls of air as fast as I can.

My eyes crack open. And I barely register what I'm seeing.

A figure in black looms over Grayden's body.

"Camillo," I croak as my eyelids droop.

And as I try to stay awake, all I hear are Grayden's whimpering pleas, alongside the crunch of bones. Again and again. Until the pleas go silent...

The next thing I feel is warm, strong hands around my face.

"Fuck!" Camillo's roar fills the house. "Rosa?"

But I can't answer as darkness pulls me under again.

"Rosa!"

I can't move. I can't speak.

"Fuck! *Fuck!*"

The heat I felt a moment ago vanishes. And I try to reach out toward it, needing its comfort.

But I'm being dragged under.

Camillo's voice echoes in the distance. "Get home. Now!"

A soothing hand brushes the side of my cheek, cupping it. "*Please, Rosa, please! Ethan needs you. I need you...*"

His words fade in and out as I'm dragged deeper and deeper into the void...

***

A warm hand brushes my temple, smoothing the strands of hair away from my brow. "Please...Rosa."

I open my mouth to say something, but the dryness of my throat makes it come out as a raspy sound. My eyelids crack open, and my gaze squints into the soft, warm light of a table lamp. Soft silken sheets are wrapped around my body.

I blink, trying to clear the blinding dots away.

"*Fuck.*" It's a soft, breathy sound of relief, and it's quickly followed by some muttered words in Italian I don't understand. "*Nulla è difficile per chi ama.*"

"Camillo...?" My voice is hoarse, and I rub at my throat, wincing at the sting.

"Shh, baby." Camillo's worn expression meets my face. His thumb brushes away the tears I didn't realize were there. His lips press to my forehead. "It's all over now..."

Over?

I struggle to sit up a little. The pillow behind my body helps, but the room spins as I do. Camillo's gentle touch supports me until I'm upright. The T-shirt that drapes over my body isn't mine, and it's not what I was wearing this morning.

"What...?" I grab at Camillo, horror picking up my heartbeat. "Where's Ethan?"

"Safe. He's safe." Camillo covers my hand with his own. "I got to him before he could see what happened here. He's with Juliana and Cate for now."

The questions burn the tip of my tongue, but a soft knock on the door stops me. "Camillo, your brothers want you to eat. Oh, thank God..." Cate's eyes widen and her voice breaks as she sees me. "I'll let the others know that you're awake," she says softly.

Camillo doesn't even look at her. His dark eyes roam my face, over and over, cataloging. "Shit, Rosa," he murmurs, pressing kisses all over my face. "Fuck, I'm sorry."

"Sorry?"

It's then that I see the dried blood on his knuckles. Mine? His? "What happened?"

"We can talk about it later."

"No. Now."

"Rosa."

"Please? Is he...?" I swallow, my voice dropping. "Did you kill him?"

"Yes."

I nod, unsure what to say.

"I'll leave you alone." He stands before I protest and makes it to the door.

I stumble out of bed after him, my limbs tangling with the sheets. "Wait!" I clutch at his arm. His muscles tense under my hand. "Why are you leaving?"

"You need to rest, Rosa."

"Camillo—"

"Please don't do this Rosa," he says in a quiet, hoarse voice.

The way he talks breaks my heart. I clutch harder. "Don't what? Tell you that you did what you needed to? That you saved me?"

"But I..." He shakes his head, sending the wavy strands bouncing about. It's messier than normal. A telltale sign that he's raked his hands through it repeatedly. He can't meet my eyes.

"*Saved my life*," I insist, willing my voice to stay even. "If you hadn't shown up, if you hadn't had stopped him, I'd be...dead." I swallow the lump in my throat. "If you hadn't stopped him for good, he would have just tried again. And again. And maybe when Ethan was with me. You've saved us both."

"You shouldn't want me around."

My hand cups his stubbled jaw, as I stand on my tiptoes so I can meet his gaze. "But I do. My son and I are safe *because of you*. You did what you needed to do to protect us. I will never fault you for that."

His body sags, and exhaustion is visible on his face, along with lines of worry.

My heart aches. "You. Saved. Me," I repeat, hoping it'll get past whatever walls he's left up between us.

"You never should have been in danger. If I'd just got his ass thrown in jail the first time, maybe this never would have happened."

"He'd have found a way out."

"I don't want you to think I'm a monster, Rosa."

"You aren't one."

"I am. I've never cared what others thought of me. But I care what *you* think. Because I'm not sorry he's dead. I'm not sorry I killed him. I'd have done it months ago if I knew this was going to happen. There isn't a line I won't cross for you or Ethan."

"That doesn't make you a monster."

"It does. I don't care I took his life. But I know you do, and that fucking kills me."

I'm silent for a few moments before carrying on. "I've just been hoping for something that was a fantasy the whole time. I hate violence—hate it with passion. But now, I see that it's a necessary evil sometimes. It should scare me how easily I've come to that conclusion. But it doesn't. It was wishful thinking that Grayden would ever leave us alone if we fought him in any other way. You did what needed to be done, Camillo, and that's the end of it. It's not the only option most of the time—but in this case, it was. I don't..." My voice breaks. "I don't think you're a monster for doing what you did. Please say you understand, Camillo?"

He closes his eyes briefly. "I understand, Rosa. I'm just so fucking thankful that you and Ethan are safe."

"Me too," I murmur against his lips. "Now, I'm starving. Can I have something to eat and maybe a cup of tea? Has anyone cooked?"

His forehead rests against mine. "Cate did. It's not as good as your cooking, though."

I pull back with a smile and slowly hobble back to the bed. Everything aches, but I'm alive.

"Rosa?"

I snuggle into the bed again, smiling at him. "Yes?"

"I don't deserve you. But I'm going to do everything I can to keep you."

I pat the bed beside me. It's no use arguing that he's already done enough. Neither of us is completely fixed. We're both a little broken in our own ways. But together, those broken pieces seem to fit like we were made for each other. "Then let's start right now..."

CHAPTER 45

ROSA

I stifle a soft groan as I sweep up the last of the broken vase from the den. The soft rays of morning light fill the room. It's a mess. Blood smears and puddles in certain spots, but I make a point not to look too long at it.

I don't know where Camillo and his brothers moved Grayden's body. It's better that I don't.

"Rosa?"

I blink, shaking the thoughts from my mind. "Yes?"

"You don't have to do this."

"I know, but I want to." I already owe Juliana and Cate big time for managing to get the kids up and in their rooms without seeing all the carnage.

Camillo's large body slides behind mine, his warm hand cupping my hip tenderly. "We can handle this. You should be resting."

It's the same argument he's given me over the last hour. First in the kitchen, then in the foyer, and now here. "I will. Once this is done. And I did tell you I wanted to make breakfast."

His hand holds me tighter, but not painfully as he's aware of where the bruises and scrapes are. His lips ghost along my throat to the juncture behind my ear. "You can make breakfast without having to clean the whole damn house."

I suck in a breath, trying to banish the fog in my head that his nearness brings. "Please let me do this."

"Okay." His soft heated puff of air against my skin has it pebbling with goosebumps. Cleaning is now the furthest thing from my mind.

He steps back, letting the cool air rush in, stealing the heat from my body. And we work in a companionable silence from then on until it looks as if nothing ever happened. But when I close my eyes, I can still see the vases and lamp shattered on the ground and the drag marks smeared through the blood.

"Rosa."

"I'll be okay."

Tugging gently on my hand, Camillo pulls me toward him until I'm in his lap on the plush sofa, his dark eyes searching mine.

"I just need to give it time. I'll start to feel better." I try to sound confident. Because despite the pit that fell in my stomach when Camillo admitted he'd killed Grayden, I feel lighter. *I feel free.*

Camillo's thumb brushes my cheek, and I lean into the heat of his hand. "I know you will. But it's okay if you're not right now."

Tears sting my eyes, and I squeeze my eyes tighter. I'm done crying for a man who wanted to kill me. I'm done mourning a life he should have given me. And yet, that doesn't stop the soft trickle from the corners of my eyes.

"*You're safe, Rosa.*" The words are murmured again and again against my temple before Camillo kisses my forehead, my cheeks, my mouth. Replacing every terrible memory I have with something else. I cling to him as he holds me. "You're safe, I promise."

"I know." I rest my forehead against his, opening my eyes. His dark eyes soften as they hold mine.

I'm not sure how long we stay like that. Something between us has shifted, though neither of us has said a word about it.

"I love you, Camillo." The words are barely above a whisper. I'm not even sure he's heard me. They just came out. But I mean them. I am in love with this brutal man before me. I'm in love with every part of him, even those that scare me to death.

His hands on my hips tighten, pulling me closer against his chest. His fingers thread into my hair. My heart thumps wildly as my head fogs. "Say it again, Rosa," he whispers.

"*I love you, Camillo.*"

His mouth tugs upward, and the hardened mafia man before me transforms once more into that boyish guardian angel who first swept me off my feet. "Fuck, I could hear that all day," he growls. A laugh bubbles out of me. "You mean it, Rosa?"

"I do."

He closes his eyes and just breathes in deeply. Once more his lips claim mine, deeper and hungrier than before. His large hands move around my hips until I'm grinding against him, panting with need.

"*Fuck.*" The word is gruff and needy. He's just as affected as I am every time we touch. "When I thought you'd left me and weren't coming back, and then, when you were lying there on the floor yesterday..."

His eyes squeeze shut tightly, and he grips me all the tighter, like he's scared I'll vanish into thin air.

"Shit..." His calloused fingers cup both sides of my face as he looks directly into my eyes. "I'm not good with emotions and words, Rosa. But after how close I came to losing you, you better get used to me telling you how much I love you every single fucking day and night. And I'll go to war and back with the devil himself just to keep you here so that I can keep telling you." He sighs deeply. "*Nulla è difficile per chi ama,*" he murmurs against my hair."

"What do those words mean? I keep hearing you murmur them." It's something I've been curious about for a while.

"They mean '*nothing is difficult for those who love*'. They mean that I'll always do whatever I can for you because I love you."

Everything in my body melts, and I lean my forehead against his, keeping us eye to eye.

"I think I fell in love with you the first time I met you, Rosa."

His bruised and battered hands drop to the back of my thighs as he lifts me flush against him. I can feel how hard he is for me. My legs circle his waist as he carries me toward the hall with a wicked gleam in his eyes.

"I love you," he whispers against my neck as he sprinkles it with kisses. "I love you." He pulls back, tasting my lips once more. "I'm going to make you sick of hearing it."

"Not possible." I giggle against his lips. "What about breakfast?"

"What do you mean? I'm about to have it..."

A flush spreads across my cheeks in the way only he can cause.

The sound of soft voices floats down the hall, but he doesn't even pause in his strides. I hear a snicker and a stifled groan before the door to our bedroom is closed behind us. My body falls into the plush mattress and silken sheets as he kneels before me.

His eyes lock on to mine. "I love you, Rosa."

His hand moves over my legs, causing my body to shudder with pleasure. "I love you too, Camillo."

"Good. Now let me show you how much."

A thrill of need shivers through my body, and I can't help the laugh that leaves me.

This man wants *me*. Loves *me*. I never believed I'd get so lucky, but Camillo has turned my whole world upside down.

And I can't think of a better way to live my life than tied to this dark angel of a man.

***

Camillo's just taken Ethan up to bed while I finish up the dishes. As soon as I'm done in the kitchen, I head up to them, loving the bedtime routine that's always so special now. It's probably one of my favorite times of the day, more so now that Camillo's always part of it too.

As I reach Ethan's bedroom, I pause by the door. Ethan's already fast asleep, and I watch Camillo as he tucks the comforter around his small body, speaking to him in a low voice.

"I know you're asleep, buddy, but I've been thinking about a really special story that I want to tell you."

My brows knit into a frown. Aren't they supposed to be reading *Treasure Island* at the moment? But I listen as Camillo starts the story...

"Once upon a time, there was a big grizzly bear and a cute gentle koala.

The grizzly bear thought someone as sweet and gorgeous as the koala could never love someone as scary and brutal as him. But then she surprised him—by showing him that she did love him.

And what's more, she had a baby koala secretly tucked into her koala pouch, surprising the grizzly bear in the best possible way when she brought her little boy out and introduced them.

And they showed the grizzly bear how to love, and it was a frightening feeling for him, but it was also the best feeling in the whole wide world.

The grizzly bear fell madly in love with not just her but also with the baby koala called Ethan.

And they gave the grizzly bear the one thing he'd wanted more than anything else in his entire life—his own family.

And you know, I might not have seen the ending of this story yet, but I just know that they're going to live happily ever after..."

I watch as he smooths back Ethan's fair hair from his forehead with a tender touch, and tears pour down my cheeks as I hear this. How did I find a man as wonderful as Camillo?

And I want this moment to last forever, thinking that things can't possibly get any better...

EPILOGUE

ROSA

I clutch my stomach as tears gather in the corners of my eyes. Cate and Juliana's laughter joins mine as we lounge in the backyard watching the kids go wild, trying and failing to climb onto the floaties in the pool.

Danio and Debi are both back from Italy and have joined us out here, as has Alessio. Alessio is currently trying to tame the beast, but much like the kids, having no luck. So far, the floatie has remained the champion.

"Where's my phone when I need it?" Juliana snickers, searching her lounger. "Marco needs to see this."

"You'd think they'd try a different tactic," Cate says before sipping on her lemonade.

"You'd think a grown man would do better." Debi laughs as she watches Alessio, clutching her stomach.

Juliana eyes me. "So…"

"So?" I parrot the tone, knowing exactly what they'll ask me.

Despite the unease I felt with them to start, they've been nothing but welcoming, going so far as to even welcome Kori and Kristopher to a few play dates. The utter joy that swells every time I think about having a family like this is surreal.

And that's what they want to know about now. They're asking about a certain tattooed man who's swept me off my feet.

Things with Camillo and I are...*perfect*. Better than I ever thought I'd have in life. It's not the sort of life I'd imagined, but it's exactly what I need—and what Ethan needs.

"Do you know what Camillo's up to?" I ask. We came out here with our drinks when he kicked us out of the kitchen.

"No." Juliana shakes her head. "Just that it's a surprise and not to come in until he says so." She shares a look with Cate and Debi.

"Do you all know something?"

"What?" Debi says with an air of innocence.

"No," Juliana adds with too much emphasis as she goes back to watching Alessio and Danio playing with the kids in the pool.

"You totally do know something..."

But they busy themselves with their drinks and phones. I take a long sip of my iced tea before pursing my lips.

"Rosa?" Over an hour later, some time after the kids and guys have left the pool and started a game of baseball, I hear my name called. Turning to see Camillo, I bite my lip to keep from laughing. Camillo's black T-shirt is covered in white powder, and a streak of it is marring his hair and cheek. The apron around his waist is also covered with splotches of colors.

Juliana and Cate are not so polite. Their laughter fills the yard, and Camillo ducks his head a little, scowling as his cheeks stain with color.

"What happened to your shirt?" I ask.

"What?" His head snaps up. "Oh this? Um, nothing. Will you, uh, come to the kitchen?"

I slide from the lounger, adjusting my cover up as I go. While I might have made big strides in conquering the damage done with my eating habits, there's still a lot of work to do—it's an ongoing journey and one which Camillo is helping me with every step of the way.

Camillo's gaze eats me up, and I catch his tongue swipe over his bottom lip. I flush, knowing exactly where his mind is going. Like most mornings, Camillo started the day with what he calls his favorite meal. The wicked things this man can do with this tongue never cease to amaze me. And the fact that he demands it be done with me on top of him sends my body shivering.

Lacing my fingers with his, he guides me toward the kitchen. The smell of freshly baked lemon cake wafts around me, making my mouth water.

The ugly voices in the back of my head tell me I shouldn't want it, but I push them away. One cupcake isn't going to kill me. Anyway, Camillo will certainly make me work off any negative effects later.

I smile at him, squeezing his hand.

Then, as we turn the corner into the kitchen, my jaw drops.

And I stop in my tracks as I take in the sight before me.

The door to the fridge is wide open. The counters are covered in white powder—flour, or sugar, or both. Batter drips from the edge of the island onto the floor. Bowls, whisks, and God knows what else are piled high in the sink. It looks like a bomb went off.

"*Jesus...*" I mutter. "What happened in here?"

Camillo tugs my hand again and guides me further into the kitchen. I don't miss the red on the edges of his ears as he does so.

He inhales deeply, shifting from foot to foot before turning to face me. "I can see now that this, uh, probably wasn't the best idea. I'll clean it up, Rosa. I promise."

I can only nod, too shocked to do anything more.

He steps to the side, revealing cupcakes arranged on a tray. The frosting is a bit messy and sliding off some places, but they smell heavenly.

"*You made me cupcakes?*"

"They're your favorite."

I step closer, reaching out to take one.

My hand freezes midair as I catch the writing over the top of them.

My brain forgets to work.

My lungs forget they need oxygen.

And my whole world tilts on its axis and almost topples right over.

Because there are twenty-seven cupcakes.

And twenty-six of them have a letter iced on them.

While the very last cupcake is iced with a question mark...

And they spell out the most beautiful sentence I've ever seen.

They say: *I love you, Rosa. Will you marry me?*

"W-what?" Surely, I read that wrong. It can't be...?

Tears blur my vision as I turn back toward Camillo when he doesn't say anything.

But the space where he stood is empty.

Instead, he's kneeling on the ground, a ring in his hands.

I gasp, covering my mouth.

His eyes spear me with a look that warms my entire body. It's the same look he gives me when he doesn't think I'm looking. One full of raw emotion and love. Like I'm the only thing he'll ever want in life. Like I'm his saving grace.

When in reality, he's mine.

"You're serious?" I choke out.

He nods. "Like a fucking heart attack, baby." Another deep inhale from him. "And I could have done a million more romantic things, but none of them felt more like me and you. You've done more for me than you'll ever know. And I might not be perfect, but I'll die trying before ever letting you go. So, will you do it, Rosa? Will you marry me?"

I can't speak for a few moments.

Is this really happening?

"Oh my God. Yes, yes, *yes*," I say with a watery laugh. "But only if you promise not to bake ever again without supervision."

His deep chuckle fills the room. "Deal." His hand trembles just slightly as he stands and slides the ring onto my finger. He leans closer, his lips brushing the shell of my ear.

I look down, my gaze wide at the glossy platinum band and the glittering pear-shaped diamond which is positioned between several smaller round diamonds. It's utterly breathtaking. I swallow back a sob. No one has ever gone to such lengths for me.

"I'm so happy," I murmur. Words I never thought I'd say to a man like Camillo. For his hardened ways and brutish exterior, he's the only man who's ever looked at me the way he does. Who's shown me kindness and love. I thought I was way too broken to give love to a man. But he's a man I can see myself falling in love with again and again for eternity.

His lips press to my forehead. "There's more."

"*More?*"

He nods, smiling like a kid on Christmas Day. It's a smile that takes my breath away.

His chin jerks behind me, and as I spin around, I nearly lose my footing, but his arms keep me steady and upright. "Careful, baby, there's flour all over the floor."

My gaze lands on a second tray of cupcakes. My brow puckers as I come closer.

And I can't say a single word for several long seconds. "You're...serious?"

"Yes. If I'm going to have you, I want all of you and all of your life. And I want it to be official." His arms wrap around my body, pulling me into his flour-covered clothes. "But only if you approve?"

I nod, giving him a grin. "But does this mean that the second oven is as much of a mess as the top oven?" I giggle as tears shine in my eyes.

A movement behind Camillo catches my eye, and I see Cate and Juliana peering inside, followed by a flash of Debi's head.

"Probably." Camillo laughs as he gives an apologetic shrug. And then, he calls out to the girls. "You can come in now!"

Squeals fill the room as Juliana, Cate, and Debi file in.

"Let me see!" Debi gasps as she rushes toward the cupcakes.

Juliana claps her hands together with glee. "I can't believe it actually worked."

Cate holds up her phone. "I filmed the whole thing so we can play it at the wedding!"

"Welcome to the family!" Juliana cries.

"Thank you," I giggle.

"You're all so nosy," Camillo mutters, rolling his eyes at the girls and grinning at the same time.

The girls pull me into their embrace, hugging me and lifting my hand for their inspection, each giving an approving look or a sigh of appreciation. Their warmness and clear joy for me make me melt.

"Alright, alright, enough. Out, out." Camillo shoos them away with a snap of the towel on his shoulder. "I'd like some alone time with her now. You can pester her later."

"What about dinner?" Debi asks.

"Debi, you might be my sister, but if you don't fucking leave, I'm not responsible for the therapy you're going to demand."

The deep timbre of Camillo's voice sends a thrill racing down my spine. I give Debi an apologetic smile before I'm tugged into Camillo's arms once more, and I don't even take a breath before his lips crash into mine.

He holds me to him and kisses me like he's a dying man and I'm his last meal. Butterflies erupt in my stomach, and my legs turn to jelly.

"You're mine," he whispers against my lips. "For fucking ever, and then some, Rosa."

"Yours." I nod in agreement, still a little drunk on his kiss. "But you're mine too."

"Only yours, baby." His lips trace over mine, parting them with expert ease.

My fingers fist his shirt, and I tug him closer.

"How long do you think we have until the kids want to come in and demand dinner?" he rumbles.

"Probably twenty minutes?"

"Perfect." Without warning, he lifts me up over his shoulder. It never ceases to surprise me how effortlessly he carries me. A sharp slap to my ass makes me gasp, and I can't help the soft, needy sound that leaves me.

"Wait," I laugh. "What about Ethan?"

I swear I hear him making a pros and cons list in his mind before he drops me back to the ground. "After?"

"After, we're cleaning the kitchen," I remind him.

The hungry look in his eyes makes me shiver. His pupils are blown wide, his eyes nearly black. A wicked, dangerous smile tugs at his lips. He stalks forward until I'm backing into the edge of the counter. "You're torturing me, baby."

"I think you can manage."

He presses in further, his nose skimming along my throat, making my eyes roll back in my head.

I squeeze my thighs together. Every single one of my nerves is on fire for him—and he knows it.

He sucks at my sensitive skin. And I can't help the soft sound that leaves my lips.

His fingers play with the sash of my cover up. "I think you want this just as badly as I do, baby..."

I nod, tilting my head back to give him more access.

He pulls back to gently lift me onto the counter. And he exposes my bathing suit to him.

"Fuck me, Rosa." He breathes against my skin as his forehead rests on my shoulder. "When did you buy this?"

"Last week..."

"And you've had it this whole time?"

I nod. It's the right balance between sexy and classy. High-waisted bottoms that cut high on my hips and a halter top that cups my breasts while showing just the right about of cleavage.

It's not something I'd usually buy, but after a lot of persuading, Kori, Juliana, Cate, and Debi managed to convince me. Of course, I'd spent all this afternoon with it covered up—I'm a work in progress—but I'm glad that Camillo is seeing it now.

"Damn. We never would have left the bedroom if I knew you were going to be wearing this today." His hot breath sends a shiver down my spine, straight to my core. "Fuck, baby, how am I supposed to resist you when you're dressed like this and look so damn delicious?"

"There's always dessert after dinner," I tease, but I'm just as wound up as he is. Fingers roaming over the hard planes of his shoulder and back, they slip under the fabric to feel his heated skin.

"Fuck that." His finger drags down the center of me and between my legs, my hips rolling in response.

"Hope everyone is decent!"

Camillo groans. "I swear to fucking God someone better be dying," he mutters in reply to Marco's voice.

I giggle, earning a low rumble from him as I brush my body against his, stretching my way down to the ground once more. "Be nice. He's your brother."

"Brother? I don't have a brother. That man is dead to me if he keeps on cock-blocking me."

"Someone wants a drink!" he announces from the mudroom before I hear the soft click of the door and Marco lets Ethan into the kitchen.

Camillo grumbles once more—something about payback. I swat at his chest, laughing as I spot the top of Ethan's head.

"Wow... Momma is gonna be mad."

Camillo gives me a sideways glance. "Is she now?"

Ethan's eyes are as wide as saucers. "Uncle Millo, you made a mess. A really *big* mess."

"I did, yeah." Camillo rubs the back of his neck before moving to hoist Ethan into his arms. His small, squealing giggle fills the air, and I melt even more for this man. "You're thirsty?"

Ethan nods. Seeing Camillo with my son, seeing them interact, never ceases to amaze me. I don't know what I did to deserve this man before me.

I never thought I'd ever end up being surrounded by people I care about but who also care about me. I've never felt like this in my life. *Wanted. Cared for. Loved.*

Camillo hands Ethan a juice box from the fridge. "Alrighty, Ethan. I also have a surprise for you, okay?"

"Me, Uncle Millo?"

Camillo carries him toward the second tray of cupcakes which are red velvet—Ethan's favorite flavor.

I watch as Ethan's brows furrow. He tries to sound out a few words before he declares his name loudly.

Then, Camillo softly reads out the writing he iced on the second tray of his cupcakes.

There are thirty-four cupcakes this time.

And they also end with a question mark.

And they say: *I love you, Ethan. Will you let me be your dad?*

Ethan's face bunches again. "R-really?"

"Really, buddy. But only if you want that, of course. You and your mom, you're my family now."

I try to keep the tears from blurring my vision as Ethan nuzzles his head into Camillo's neck and nods. I'm not sure he understands the full extent of what being adopted will mean. But he will one day. And what I do know is that my son loves this man as wholly and unconditionally as he loves me.

His arms clinging for dear life around Camillo's neck squeezes my heart like the best hug ever. "Does that mean I can...call you Dad now?"

"You can call me whatever you want—Dad, Uncle Millo, or even Santa Claus. I don't care what you call me as long as you and your mom are here with me."

I can't hear Ethan's exact response, but I can tell the gist of it from the look of sheer elation on Camillo's face.

This. Right here. *This is what I've always wanted.*

Thank you so much for reading. See here for a free **BONUS EPILOGUE** for details of Rosa and Camillo's wedding, steamy honeymoon, and what happens next with Ethan: https://dl.bookfunnel.com/2gzmhsfqea

Continue reading for a **SNEAK PEEK** of another book in Isa Oliver's mafia world...

STANDALONES

.

.

Printed in Great Britain
by Amazon

55766158R00231